Praise for *Lord of Secrets*

'I loved it! It surprised me many times . . . It was a perfect
mix of traditional and new. A fascinating take, really'
Charlie N. Holmberg, author of *The Paper Magician*

'Rich and satisfying . . . Teintze has concocted a fascinating world,
with clever twists and loops to her plotting as well as a range
of believable (and deeply likeable) characters'
SFX

'*Lord of Secrets* is a fast-paced necromantic adventure. The characters
are sharp, the dialogue is funny – and wow, Teintze can really write
a monster! . . . I was alarmed and delighted at every turn'
Emily Tesh, author of *Silver in the Wood*

'A delightful necromantic romp . . . All I want is the next book, NOW'
K. A. Doore, author of *The Perfect Assassin*

'Deftly plotted and great fun'
Guardian

'A thoroughly refreshing and light-hearted romp of a novel . . .
If you want an exuberant and upbeat fantasy, then
this is definitely recommended'
Birmingham SF Group

'In a word: great! . . . A dazzling debut!'
Life Has a Funny Way

'After reading this, I felt refreshed and almost like
a "faith restored" feeling for fantasy'
Moon Kestrel

'A clever, interesting fantasy with complex characters
and I would recommend this as a good read'
Storgy

LORD
OF
SECRETS

BREANNA TEINTZE

Jo Fletcher
BOOKS

First published in Great Britain in 2019
This edition published in 2020 by

Jo Fletcher Books
an imprint of Quercus Editions Ltd
Carmelite House
50 Victoria Embankment
London EC4Y 0DZ

An Hachette UK company

A CIP catalogue record for this book is available
from the British Library

PB ISBN 978 1 78747 625 7
EB ISBN 978 1 78747 623 3

10 9 8 7 6 5 4 3 2 1

Typeset by Jouve (UK), Milton Keynes

Printed and bound in Great Britain by Clays Ltd, Elcograf S.p.A.

Papers used by Quercus are from well-managed forests
and other responsible sources.

For Phillip:
This is all your fault.

ONE

Rather inconveniently, I happened to be invisible that day. I hate invisibility. All the optical conjuration spells give me a headache and a sore throat – I think it's because you have to swallow the runes – but invisibility is the worst.

Of course, there are reasons to put up with a sore throat. If nobody can see you, they can't catch you and hang you. The miserable thing about invisibility, though, is the spell's action. It manipulates light to confuse the eye of the observer, but it also alters the vision of the person inside the spell in nauseating ways. By the time I found the barn, I had been nursing a migraine for three days and wanted nothing but to pass out on a haystack until the spell wore off. Well, and a cup of hot water and honey, but that wasn't going to happen. A leaky sod barn on the cold moors outside Fenwydd that did *not* contain twenty shitting goats was already a piece of luck. You can't have everything.

I probably would have noticed the woman sooner if I hadn't been invisible and trying not to look at anything. She certainly would have seen me when she came sprinting into the barn and dove into my haystack. And my lap.

'What the hells –' She twisted on top of me, digging a sharp elbow into my gut.

'Ow,' I said.

Even in the dim light of the barn, I saw her eyes fly wide a split-second before she inhaled. I grabbed her shoulder and clapped my other hand over her mouth. 'Please don't scream.'

She punched at the air in my general direction until she connected with my elbow.

'Ow, dammit!' I let her go, cradling my numbed hand.

She scrambled away from me, but didn't run for the door. 'Where are you?'

'Sitting on a haystack, hoping you didn't just break my arm,' I said. 'Where does it seem like I am?'

'Why can't I see you?'

'I'm a ghost,' I suggested. 'Wooooo. Go away.'

She squinted at the haystack. 'Is it magic?'

Gods and little saints. 'No. Invisible people are an entirely natural phenomenon.' I took a deep breath and endeavoured to peer past the migraine enough to examine her. 'Are we going to have a problem?'

She must have been somewhere in her mid-twenties, but for someone with a wicked left hook, the woman wasn't very big, disappearing inside a homespun shirt and trousers made for someone much larger. She had dark brown eyes with an odd circle of green around the pupil, light hair and a spray of freckles across her nose and jaw like a constellation. And her feet were bare, which made me pause. Even farm servants usually had moccasins. All in all, I didn't think her reason for being in the barn was any more legitimate than mine.

'You *are* a wizard, then,' she said.

An alarm rang in my head. 'Yes. No.' I pressed the heels of my hands to my throbbing eye sockets. 'I'm not anything. Why are you here?'

'Don't hurt me,' she said. 'I just – I need a place to sleep.'

I winced. 'So sleep. Whatever you want. Of course I'm not going to hurt you. Just be quiet.'

I saw her searching eyes find my outline, probably from the motes of hay dust stuck on me. I tried to decide whether I dared lie down again. Even if she ran off and told someone I was here, what were the odds they'd believe that an invisible wizard was sleeping off a spell in their barn? The Guild won't even officially admit invisibility *exists*.

Then again, the woman hadn't run away, which was a bad sign by itself. Most normal folk view magic with distrust at best, and with active superstition at worst. I had too many people hunting me to waste a couple of hours dealing with a curious interloper who, alas, would certainly remember me. It was time to leave, before she could learn what I looked like.

I got to my feet, but I'd been down long enough that my bad knee had locked up. A pop of brilliant, multicoloured pain burst over me and I had to wait and breathe until it passed. I must have groaned.

'Are you . . . sick?' She stretched out a hand, creeping closer.

I wasn't going to stand around and be *felt* for. 'You can have the barn. I'm leaving.' I tried, unsuccessfully, to push past her.

'No! You have to stay here!' She clawed at the air and caught my sleeve. 'Just wait. They could still be out there.'

I halted. 'Look, my head really hurts. Who could still be out there, and why should I care?'

She hesitated, a shade too long. 'The men chasing me.'

'In case that isn't a lie, I promise not to tell them you're here.' I wrenched my arm away from her. 'Let go.'

'But they'll see you.'

It took me a second to get the implication past the roaring pain in my skull. I looked down and saw my own trouser-clad knees shading into existence. At exactly the wrong time, the spell was finishing. Shit.

The woman stared at me. Or past me, actually. A wash of cold air across the back of my neck made me turn around. The spear pointing at my belly made me raise both hands.

A small door at the side of the barn was open. A priest in a dirty, cream-coloured robe and three other men stood just inside; one had a crossbow trained on the woman. Another was pointing the spear at me, goggling at my robe and, presumably, the parts of me that were still invisible.

'Don't move! You're under arrest!' The priest's shrill voice cut through the air – and my head – like a steel spike. He was looking from the woman to my mostly-revealed left wrist, where my forged licence sigil was tattooed. 'Careful! He's a wizard – we'll have to gag him.'

I flinched. 'Keep your voice down. I haven't done anything illegal. You can inspect my licence if you want.' I waggled my wrist. My sigil had got me out of similar situations in the past. It was expensive, and realistic.

'Tie his hands,' the priest said. 'We'll let his own people sort him out.' But none of his helpers moved, watching me uncertainly. Angering the Mages' Guild isn't done lightly.

'The Guild has feelings about outsiders arresting its members.' I forced my voice into bored, threatening tones. 'What do you suppose they're going to say about you poaching on their prerogatives?'

He smiled thinly. 'What do you suppose the Guild will say to you consorting with a blasphemer? You'd obviously arranged to meet here with your criminal associate.'

Dealing with a blasphemy shakedown was another bother I didn't need. I didn't know much about the laws in this part of Varre, but blasphemy was sometimes punishable with death, and rarely a nice, quick death, either. I glanced at the woman, whose carefully flat expression did not quite hide the fine edge of terror in the lines of her body.

'All we've established is that I am standing in a barn that all of you are also standing in,' I said. 'If you arrest me, I'll demand a representative from the closest Guildhouse. I will be angry. The Guild officer will be angry. You will be forced to explain how a low-level priest thought it would be a good idea to importune a wizard–'

'Turn out your pockets.' The priest rounded on the woman. 'Thief! Do as you're told!'

'—with trumped-up charges that Temples doesn't have jurisdiction over anyway.' The priest was ignoring me, grabbing at the woman.

'I'm not a thief,' she growled. 'Don't touch me!'

He clutched her arm. 'Temples has jurisdiction over anyone caught violating sacred property. I know you have it. Nobody else could have taken it.' The priest thrust his hand into the depths of the giant, shapeless garment she wore, and pulled out a pair of small gold icons, no bigger than my thumb. 'There!'

She twisted in his grasp. 'That's not mine! You planted that!'

He smiled. 'No, you were bringing it to your accomplice. He just hasn't had time to hide it yet.' He gestured to the others. 'Gag this man. And tie his hands.'

This time they obeyed.

We were soaked through by the time they marched us through the rain back to Fenwydd, which I had only seen briefly three days earlier. This visit confirmed my earlier impressions of it as a farm town which gave itself airs. The houses crammed inside the city wall were all stacked on top of each other, mismatched. Timber cottages squatted next to brick neighbours whose upper storeys overhung the street and dumped random streams of freezing water on to passersby. The only important thing about it was a squalid little castle – a fort, really, with walls that were half earthworks – which looked just large enough to contain a decent dungeon.

The woman had been talking constantly while we walked, maintaining her innocence without convincing anyone. As our captors turned us down a narrow lane that led towards the castle, she fell silent.

We passed into a courtyard with claustrophobic stone walls and slippery brown cobblestones. Two soldiers lounged at a booth near the entrance, straightening as we appeared. A pair of stocks loomed beside a stained wooden block the size of a table, the axe grooves hacked into the block testifying to its purpose.

My stomach turned over. Maybe this *was* a duchy where they beheaded you for blasphemy.

'Open the gate.' The priest gestured at an ugly wooden door. I don't know that I would have dignified it by calling it a gate. Still, it was thick, and a problem. I had been hoping for an ecclesiastical prison, where the doors are usually very old and decorative.

The men who had helped capture us left now, after being admonished to deliver their official testimony about the capture to the militia captain. The thrice-cursed priest did not leave, supervising as the soldiers hustled the woman and me inside. They brought us to a low, dank room lit by a couple of high, narrow windows. A thick layer of rushes covered the floor, an unsuccessful attempt to keep down the stink of vomit and old blood. A set of manacles dangled from rings in the ceiling, and an unpleasant collection of rusty iron instruments littered a table nearby.

They clapped the woman into the manacles, backed me into a corner and threw my leather satchel on the table. Only then did they remove the twist of cloth tied around my mouth.

'Gods, that gag was none too clean.' I spat on the floor and looked at the priest. 'Well? Where's the Guild representative? What's this all about?'

'You and your accomplice are charged with blasphemy and unsanctioned incantations. Because blasphemy is the more serious matter, you'll answer to Temples before the Guild is alerted to your crimes.' He folded his arms. I suppose he was trying to look menacing.

'She isn't my accomplice,' I said. 'I don't pick accomplices out of mud puddles.'

'Even if she isn't your accomplice, you're still a thief,' he said. 'She stole from the temple, and then you stole her. If you stop wasting my time, you might suffer less before this is over.'

Stole her? I needed time to think. 'What precisely am I supposed to have done? Which unsanctioned incantations, I mean?'

'I don't truck with wizards' impious attempts to manipulate nature,' he said, coldly. 'The incantations are a matter for the Guild to determine. My concern is rectifying your violation of the sanctuary of Jaern.' He dug in his pocket for the tiny gold icons. 'These were stolen from that temple library.' He reached into my satchel and came out with a book. 'And this is a restricted codex, taken from the temple of Neyar three days ago. Blasphemous intrusions, the both of them.' He fingered the seal embossed on the front, and then glanced inside and frowned. 'You stole an *accounts* book?'

It was actually the food purchase records for a group of Guild prisoners, forced labourers at the stone quarry in Denelle, fifty miles to the east. It had been a false lead.

'They owe me money,' I said.

He handed the book and icons to one of the soldiers. 'Regardless, clearly a criminal act. And demonstrating an unhealthy interest in meddling with books.'

I shrugged. 'In that case, I see nothing for it but to decapitate us immediately. There can't be any other punishment for book-meddling.'

'Agreeing with me won't buy you leniency.' The priest, who had evidently never been exposed to sarcasm in his life, waved the soldiers towards the door. 'She was obviously bringing the icons back to you.'

'Obviously.' I slid the heel of one foot through the litter on the floor. Under the rushes was a brownish-black, crusty stain that I didn't want to identify at that moment. The rushes didn't stay parted long enough for my purpose. Besides, even this dolt would probably notice by the time I got six runes traced on the floor.

'This isn't right,' the woman said. 'You're not supposed to –'

'Shut up.' He slapped her, hard enough to turn her head. 'Did I tell you to speak? Don't toy with me, tart.'

'Ugh,' I said. 'Don't make us imagine someone *toying* with you.'

7

I didn't see him move. The fist that he sank in my gut took my breath away, and for a moment I couldn't see. When my vision came back, his face was inches from mine.

'Leave,' he said, without taking his eyes off me. Both the soldiers who had accompanied us into the room departed, the door clanging shut behind them.

He wandered over to the instruments and selected one, a slender knife with teeth and a hooked tip. 'This is a surgical knife.' He brought it to me and pressed the serrations against my cheek. 'It'll go through bone. It takes a long time, but . . . eventually . . .'

A pulse of cold, instinctive fear flooded my veins. I could deal with pain – practising magic teaches you that quickly enough – but I recognised the dreamy contemplation in his voice. He wasn't just out to get answers. He intended to *enjoy* hurting me. If I didn't end this conversation soon, he'd carve me and the woman up regardless of what we said.

'Now.' Saliva clung to the priest's teeth. 'You and I are going to understand each other.'

Something boiled over inside my skull, flowing down to the tips of my fingers. I scratched a curving symbol into the dirt on the wall behind me. 'You're spitting,' I said.

He frowned. You could almost hear the creaking as he tried to think. 'I—'

'You're going to hurt me if I don't answer questions,' I said. 'Understood. So ask something.'

He drew the serrations sideways. The cut was small, but it burned. 'I know you want to steal something from my god. It's the codices, isn't it? Like the one you stole from Neyar-temple?' A drop of blood rolled down my jaw. His eyes followed it lovingly. 'You won't get them, but I do want to know who told you they were there.'

Codices. The word was significant enough that it momentarily distracted me from the knife. Jaern-temples were usually just places of worship, but some of them had libraries. Because priests of Jaern take secrecy seriously, the rich and important pay the librarians to store things that they want kept secure and private: royal financial accounts, say, or torturer's interrogation notes. Or locations and inmate lists for the Guild's secret prisons.

'I don't know what codices you're talking about.' I forced myself to concentrate on the pattern growing behind me. 'I thought this was about icons.'

He made a second cut, flicking my earlobe with the blade. It surprised me, driving a gasp from between my lips. But it gave me time to scratch another symbol.

'Stop it!' The woman's voice was low, fierce. 'This is illegal. You said the Guild was supposed to deal with him. This is—'

'I'm not going to be lectured by a temple-robbing little witch,' he hissed. 'This isn't Guild business. He's carrying a book from Neyar-*temple*. He's stealing secrets. So—' He put the tip of the blade just below my eyebrow. 'Who told you? I can take your eye. Or one of hers, if you don't find that convincing.' His gaze, glassy with desire, wandered towards her.

Most libraries were nearly impossible to break into without knowing the correct countersigns. If this woman had gotten inside the library *and* managed to escape afterwards, she had abruptly become more interesting. I needed her, and she would presumably be less able to circumvent complicated wards if she was missing an eye.

'No, stop!' I had to keep his attention on me. 'I'll tell you,' I said. 'Leave her alone.'

He turned back to me, grinning at the urgency that had leaked into my voice. 'I'm waiting.'

Another flick of the knife, this time against my eyebrow. Another drop of blood.

'And I'm cooperating.' I fought the desire to twist away. I needed to scratch one more character on the wall behind me. 'I just want a representative from the Guildhouse here, first. The law entitles me to that. Magic is their jurisdiction, not yours.'

'Jurisdiction?' The priest's nostrils twitched, and he smiled. 'Over a man using their precious incantations to rob the gods? Do you really think the Guild will care what happens to you, as long as you end up dead?'

'No, I know they won't.' I wasn't going to be able to distract him another way. What he wanted was blood and fear. I'd have to give it to him. I swallowed and allowed my voice to tremble. 'Please. Don't hurt me. I'll do what you want.'

'I know you will.' He brought the blade to rest against my chin and licked his lips. 'I suppose you think you're brave? Most of them do.'

'No.' As I spoke, my finger traced the last symbol. 'Just very good at writing things down without looking at them.'

He blinked, startled. He was, I suppose, expecting something else. Pleading, maybe. Instead, I pronounced the spell.

The symbols under my hand lit with red fire and rose into the air, the light coming together in the fluttering form of a bat. It flew straight to the priest's neck and latched on. He twisted, slapping at it, his fingers passing through its body. The priest twitched for a moment and then fell, first to his knees and then prone on the floor.

The woman stared at me. 'What did you do?'

'Hush.' I moved to the table, scanning the mess of tools on it as quickly as I could.

'Is he dead?'

'No, dazed. Now be quiet – my head still hurts and I'm trying to be efficient.' I located another filthy blade. It took a bit of manoeuvring, but I managed to saw the cord around my wrists over the blade until it parted. I shook out my tingling hands. My mouth tasted sick and metallic with the remnants of the incantation I had thrown at the priest. The toxicity was going to hit hard. I didn't have much time.

'How did you do it?' She was whispering. 'I thought wizards had to have special paint to cast spells.'

'You can see that I didn't.' I pulled my sleeves down over my wrists, grabbed my satchel and slung it across my shoulder. 'Paint helps, but all you need is something that will ensure that the runes stay the right shape long enough to pronounce them.' I bent over the priest. 'A more detailed answer will take weeks, and I doubt very much if you'd understand even then.'

She glared at me. 'Prick. You think nobody else knows anything about magic?'

'At the moment it seems more relevant whether somebody knows where the key is.' I pawed through the priest's dirty vestments. 'He has to have one, right? Or the guards wouldn't have left him alone with us?'

She opened her eyes wide, mocking. 'Are you asking me whether I saw where he put it? Even though I'm too stupid to understand paint? It's on a cord around his neck, sirrah.'

I found the key ring, yanked it free and straightened. 'Listen, I need to know. Did you get into Jaern-temple, or did the priest really plant the icon on you? Lord Toy-With-Me over there is going to wake up soon, so I suggest you answer quickly.'

Her tongue passed over her lower lip. 'What if I did?'

'I am interested. I will bargain.' I held up the keys. 'I'm going to let you out. In return, you're going to get me into that temple long enough for me to get at the books. Agreed?'

'Why?' She did not appear to understand how short our time was. 'I've got no reason to help you. I don't even know your name. What's in the books?'

'Nothing that would be useful to you. A list.' I glanced towards the priest. If this went on much longer, I'd have to find a way to tie him up. 'You do realise that they're going to cut your head off if I don't let you go?'

'And you evidently can't get into the temple without me.' She raised an eyebrow. 'As far as I can see, I have something you need. A list of what?'

I moved to the door. One of the keys on the ring unlocked it, but I had no way of knowing what was on the other side. Had the guards gone back to the shack in the courtyard, or were they down the hall in some other cell?

'Wizard,' she said.

'My name is not "wizard".' I opened the door a crack, listening. 'It's Gray. Corcoran Gray. Are you delaying on purpose, or . . . ?'

'Whatever you call yourself.' She sounded irritatingly calm for someone who was haggling for her life. 'If you want my help, you'll tell me what you're really after. I don't think you have a choice about this.'

I could hear nothing in the hallway, not that I would unless I got her to stop babbling. My knee was starting to send warning twinges up my thigh. If I waited much longer, it would start to stiffen up, and then I'd be magic-sick *and* slow. I had to resolve this, now. I forced myself to think through everything I knew about her, systematically. There had to be something I could use for leverage.

'You're not a temple acolyte,' I said, slowly, 'or you'd at least have sandals, yet you know the temple and the countersigns well enough to circumvent the wards. And the priest was able to track you, in the rain, without dogs.'

'So?' She was once again doing an almost-convincing impression of someone who wasn't afraid.

'So a Temples slave would know all of those things.' I scanned her body. No earrings. No nose ring. The navel, maybe? 'That's why they're forced to wear trackers. A piece of jewellery, usually. Magically applied, and difficult to remove unless you know what you're doing.' I paused, met her eyes. 'I know what I'm doing.'

I was offering freedom, of a sort. We were in an urban part of the provinces, not the wild border country where slavers were allowed to hunt anyone who wandered. If she stayed in towns, she might be able to live a decent life, even without the expensive official papers that would have ensured her legal status as a freewoman.

Her jaw tightened. 'You're saying you can take it off? Make it so they can't find me again?'

'Yes. I unlock you, you get me into the temple and then I unbind your tracker. In that order, to keep everyone honest.' I held up the key. 'Do we have a bargain, or not?'

She swung her wrists towards me. 'Yes. Just hurry, Corcoran.'

'Finally.' I grabbed her chain and began trying one key after another. 'Call me "Gray", not the other. And you're supposed to tell me what your name is after I tell you mine. That's the way it's done in polite society.'

The manacles opened for the third key. She drew her wrists out. 'Do you have a plan to get us out of here?'

I dug through my satchel. 'How about an alias? I would be content with an alias. It gets inconvenient just calling someone "you".'

'Brix. My name is Brix.' A wrinkle appeared between her eyebrows. 'You're a very strange person.'

'It's part of my charm.' I found a scrap of parchment, a mostly-empty wineskin and a pencil. 'How would you like to be invisible?'

TWO

The prison was only a hallway with a half-dozen cells, empty except for one snoring drunk. Brix had grasped a handful of my sleeve as soon as I finished the spell and led me and my newly-revived headache towards the courtyard. The two guards were once again at their post, shielded from the afternoon rain by the thatched roof of their booth.

'Ugly little snit,' one was saying, as we approached. 'I don't know why Lord Fenwydd puts up with him.'

'Because Halling has my lord convinced he has a bridle on the gods.' The guard opened a pouch and took out a pinch of *shan* leaves before offering it to his friend, who also took a pinch. They both chewed solemnly.

'I suppose we should look in on him.'

The second shook his head. 'Gods, no. He won't be even halfway finished yet, even if the prisoners are talking. It'll be bad enough cleaning up later.'

The pressure of Brix's grip made me move forwards, following her through the shadow along one side of the wall. We exited the courtyard and found ourselves confronted by a broad, muddy square. It must have been market day, with carts of vegetables hulking amid a crowd of people, goats and a pair of women selling pastries. Luckily the soldier guarding the doorway we had just emerged from was

14

occupied in talking to a girl with a baby on her hip, and we got past him without any trouble.

I spied a nook behind a pastry stand, some twenty feet away, that would offer shelter from prying eyes. Brix let go of me and I grasped at the air for a minute until I caught her clothes. The startled squeak she gave made the soldier look up from his conversation, confused. Time to go.

I held on and hustled her towards the pastry stand as quickly as I could. When we reached it, I crouched between the stand and the city wall and yanked her down beside me. The owner of the stand was hawking her wares closer to the street, in a raucous sing-song that would have drowned out a trumpeter.

'Look for an inconspicuous path,' I said. 'Our footprints will show if the mud is too deep.'

'What?' Brix's hand found mine, trying to pry my fingers from the cloth I had grabbed. 'Let go. I find it hard to concentrate when a man has a handful of the seat of my trousers.'

I let go and jerked my hand back to myself, glad she couldn't see me blush. How had I managed *that*? All I could find to mumble was: 'Sorry.'

'No matter,' Brix said. 'You didn't aim for it. Will the spell last until nightfall, you think? I don't see very many places we can move without leaving tracks in the mud. I suppose we could keep along the wall.'

Keeping along the wall sounded good to me, but I still didn't know how I was going to survive until I could get outside it. The runes I had washed off the parchment were sloshing around in my stomach, mixed with wine and bile. I hiccupped, and grimaced at the acrid taste in my mouth. The magic was finishing, too quickly. Invisibility has an unpredictable duration, but it shouldn't have been *this* unpredictable. It had been a mistake, using the spell again before I had recovered from the last time.

'I don't think we should wait,' I said. 'The spell is degrading. Breaking up, I mean.'

'Where are you?' Brix's fingers stabbed me in the knee. They stopped there, grasping the hard outlines of the copper-and-leather brace I wear on my left leg. It fits under my trousers, I don't limp unless I'm very tired and usually people don't notice it. 'What in the world . . . ?'

No, I wasn't going to answer questions about that. I grabbed her hand and carried it away from the brace. 'Look, could we get on with it? Now you have my hand, and I have your hand, and neither of us needs to go fondling the other.'

Which wasn't quite fair, but it did shut her up.

She changed her grip, sliding her hand up until it was wrapped around my sleeve cuff; I gripped her wrist in turn. We got to our feet. I let her drag me along the wall at a trot. My headache was worsening, though not as quickly as I would have expected. More troubling was the snake of light that kept pulsing across my field of vision. I must not have written my shielding runes perfectly.

Brix led me away from the main road into the alley behind an inn. A short distance away stood the inn's stable, filled with yokels shouting to each other. Each noise seemed to hook into the back of my eyes.

I halted, only to have Brix pull on my wrist again.

'Don't let go of me,' she said. 'I'll never find you again.'

I wasn't about to let go of her; I could barely see. I dug my heels in. 'I need to stop.'

'We can't.' She tugged. 'We have to find a safe place, or they'll find us again. You have to keep going.'

'But–' I bent at the waist and threw up.

'Hells!' Brix didn't let go of me, though I think she jumped backwards. 'What's the matter with you?'

'I'm bloody invisible,' I snapped. 'It hurts. I want to sit down.'

BREANNA TEINTZE

Behind us, a cacophony of distant bells erupted. Light exploded through my head. I gasped and stumbled, just managing to miss putting a knee in the puke puddle. 'Listen—' My tongue felt thick. I couldn't make it say what I wanted it to. When I tried, a weird groan came out.

'Those are the prison bells. They know we're gone.' She yanked, trying to heft me back up on to my feet. 'We've got to go. Now!'

'Right.' It took all my concentration to get the word out. I let her put my arm around her shoulders and staggered along beside her. We went through a maze of tiny lanes, finally coming to another inn, this one not prosperous enough to possess a stable. One horse and three donkeys were tied to a railing in front of the three-storey house. We made our way past the donkeys and paused behind the row of buildings.

I peered down the alley, trying to think past the jagged pain rolling around in my head. 'What are we doing?'

'You said you needed to stop, I'm finding you a place to stop.' She dragged me forwards. 'If you don't like this, we have to find somewhere else. A barn or—'

'Not another barn,' I said.

'Well, we'd better choose soon.' Brix held up my hand, and I could see the ghostly outline of her fingers wrapped around my forearm. 'We're getting visible again.'

'Something is wrong with the damn spell.' I shook myself loose of her, irritated. 'Aren't you uncomfortable? You should at least have a headache from the runes I made you swallow.'

'I do have a headache,' she said.

A bad smell coursed over me. I was out of time; in another moment I wouldn't be able to walk. I went down the alley as quickly as I could.

Brix followed. 'What's happening? What's wrong?'

I found a notch where the walls of two brick buildings met each other and curled myself into it, sinking to my knees on the dirty cobbles, overwhelmed by the stench I knew was only inside my head. I wanted to say something, warn her what to expect, but my jaw was already tightening. I lost what was left of my vision.

The rest of it I don't remember.

Hours later I came back to myself, blinking in the light of a red sunset. My head still throbbed, but the pain was bearable now. I must have slept. I'm always exhausted after a seizure.

I had been propped up to sit against the wall. Brix sat next to me, her knees drawn up to her chest. When I lifted my head, she turned towards me. 'Awake?'

'Barely.' I tried to decide how bad the seizure had been. It had been months since I'd had one, and I had been hoping I had discovered the right combination of shielding magic to prevent them.

'What happened?' Her voice was quiet. 'I thought you were dog meat.'

'It's nothing.' I rubbed my eyes. 'A seizure, a kind of reaction to the spell. Invisibility is more toxic than most incantations. I shouldn't have tried it twice in such a short amount of time, but I don't know what other choice we had.'

She studied me, a small frown between her eyebrows. 'I don't want you to die before you get my tracker off.'

'I said I'd take it off, and I don't intend to die and renege.' I glanced up at the sky, where the sunset was already fading. 'Speaking of, how long have we been here? Halling will eventually remember he can use the tracker and divine for you. We should get moving.'

Her arms moved instinctively, clasping over her belly. 'Why don't you just take it off me now, if you're so worried?'

'Because that wasn't the agreement.' I paused. 'Look, I *need* to get into the temple. You promised me you could do that. If you were lying, just tell me now and we'll go our separate ways.'

'I wasn't lying,' she said, between her teeth. 'My contract used to be held by Jaern-temple in Karrad. The priest there was old. He mumbled the patterns to himself when he unlocked things every day so nobody would realise he was half-blind. It took me a long time, but I memorised what he did. Then he died, they shipped me here and I thought I'd have to start all over. But I didn't. This temple is built on the same pattern as the one in Karrad, it's just a little smaller. And the liturgy is identical – same wards, same countersigns.'

'Are you telling me that as long as you know the countersigns, you can just walk into Jaern-temple – *any* Jaern-temple – whenever you want?' She nodded. I let out a low whistle. 'So you took more from them than just a few icons. No wonder Halling came after you.' I frowned. 'But if you worked for his temple and you're wearing that tracker, why did he act like he didn't know you back in the barn?'

'I only got here three days ago. He's barely seen me. At first, I said I was sick, hid in the slaves' quarters, but I knew eventually I had to . . .' She stared down at the cobblestones, expressionless. 'You saw what kind of a man Halling is. What he likes to do to people.' Her hands tightened in the fabric of her shirt, twisting, white-knuckled. 'The tracker is just a copper ring. It doesn't look that strong. I thought if I stole a couple of icons, I could bribe a blacksmith to take it off, have a chance to get away. His tinsnips broke on it. You can *really* take it off?'

'Of course tinsnips broke,' I said. 'It's held on with a spell, not with the metal itself. I have to do another spell to remove it.' I paused. Her desperation made sense, but there was something happening behind her eyes that I couldn't interpret, a deeper layer of fear and calculation. 'I'll teach you the incantation, if you like,' I hazarded.

'What? *No.*' She shot me a startled glance, as though I had offered to strip naked and dance. 'Just see that you keep your end of the bargain, and I'll keep mine.' She stood and smoothed her shirt with trembling fingers. 'Last time it took them six hours to find me. That gives us a little time. Let's go.'

We left the alley as the twilight shaded into night, and I followed her through a series of narrow streets that swirled with mist and the smell of cooking. Lamps glowed inside buildings and we occasionally passed a brazier in front of a business or a larger house. Otherwise, it was so dark that even if we had passed a guard patrol, they probably wouldn't have seen us.

At the end of the fifth alley, she pointed. 'Here.'

The temple towered over the street, less grand than the painted, pillared buildings I'd seen in the past, dedicated to Mother Ranara or the Lord of the Afterlands. This was just a large cube of grey stone without even a statue outside to show which deity it belonged to, only its sprawling size hinting at the mysteries that supposedly dwelled inside. Above the entrance a hanging lamp bathed the front of the building in a scarlet glow. The only attempt at decoration was the pewter studs winking on the pale oak door, displaying the outline of Jaern's symbol, a half-shut eye.

It felt wrong to approach the place so boldly, although I knew there wasn't another way in. Being dedicated to the Lord of Secrets, Jaern-temples famously have one entrance, no windows and impenetrable security. I still didn't like it. 'I could do without the lamplight,' I muttered.

'Either you want to get inside, or you don't.' She grabbed my wrist. 'Come on, stay close to me.' She led me forwards, halting just outside the circle of light as though gathering herself, studying the lamp and the studs on the door. Her grip tightened, and she lunged forwards.

We stood in the pool of scarlet. I looked up. Looping, malicious lines of runic script glowed in a spiral on the underside of the lamp basin. I recognised the spell, a nasty one. The wards were ready to immolate us.

'Brix,' I said, alarmed.

She ignored me, counting under her breath. Her fingers moved, almost too quickly to see, touching the studs on the door in sequence.

The latch clicked, she pushed the door open and dragged me inside. She shut the door behind us and leaned against it, letting out a long, shuddering breath. The whole thing had taken under twenty seconds.

We stood in the dark. Directly ahead, a dim light gleamed. We stepped towards it, to find ourselves in a wide, circular room with a black floor. In the centre stood a dark chunk of granite topped by a silver figurine and two huge silver candlesticks, which shed surprisingly little light. Bundles of smaller, ritual candles lay in heaps at its base. Patterns crawled over the altar, sinuous lines of runes carved into the stone and inlaid with pewter.

'Don't touch anything in the sanctuary.' She led me through the shadows to the altar and grabbed a small candle, dipping its wick into the flame of the larger one before touching it to the lips of the idol – a grotesque, eyeless baby that I took to be a representation of The Empty One, the ghost that, according to Jaernic doctrine, whispered the six foundation runes of magic to the god Jaern at the beginning of time.

'That,' I said, pointing at the idol, 'is the ugliest version of The Empty One that I've ever seen.'

'I know. Halling *kisses* it during prayers.' Brix glanced at it again and shuddered before crossing the floor to a small side door. The room beyond was stuffed with bales of incense, stacks of candles and a cupboard that held a collection of flasks, their green contents gleaming. My eyebrows went up. I had always known that the visions seen in Jaern-temple were probably not divine, but I hadn't suspected the priests were using yavad.

'Can I touch these?' I said.

She glanced at the cupboard, nose wrinkled. 'If you want.'

Yavad was an acquired taste, but it was also expensive, and you never knew when it would come in handy for trade. I grabbed three flasks and put them in my bag. 'Where's the library?'

'It's through here.' Brix pointed towards a door that was so small and inconvenient that it could have been mistaken for a closet. 'The slaves' door is safer than the official entrance from the sanctuary.'

I hesitated. 'You first.'

She rolled her eyes. 'Gods. If I was going to get you stuck, I'd have let you burn outside.' She pushed the door open, crouched and stepped through. I followed.

A set of double doors took up the entire wall opposite us. Three shelves, as tall as I was, lined the rest of the tiny chamber, crammed full of scrolls, folios and gigantic tomes that were as thick as my arm. In the middle of the room was a square table dominated by a gold-covered bust of Jaern and an empty bronze candelabra, surrounded by dozens of smaller icons of various saints.

A familiar mixture of hope and anxiety churned in my belly. If I was lucky, somewhere in that heap of words was the name and location I was looking for: Acarius Gray, my grandfather. In the last six months I hadn't been lucky, not once.

'Watch the prayers,' Brix said. 'They'll only wake up if someone crosses the sanctuary without letting the Empty One taste fire, but it's still bad luck to touch them.'

I glanced down. A series of characters was painted in red around the edges of the tile floor. It was a spell, not a prayer, but this wasn't the moment to argue about the differences between Temples and Guild magic. The runes were indeed inert, so I stepped over them and strode towards the nearest stack of likely-looking books. 'Can you bring the candle closer?'

She picked her way over the runes and deposited the candle into the holder on the icon table. What the light revealed was less than encouraging. If I had to go through every volume, it could take the rest of the night. I scanned the shelves. The scrolls were likely to contain theological arguments and not much else. I trailed my fingertips along the thick spines of the codices. The first one I opened turned out to be a bound collection of tax rolls from ten years ago. Useless. I shoved it back on to the shelf and glanced sideways at Brix. 'Well?'

She hadn't moved. 'Will this take long?'

'I have no idea. I'm not going to take your ring off in here, if that's what you mean. It takes too long – wouldn't be safe until we're someplace more secure.' The next book was a treatise written in crabbed, painstaking script about the Tirnaal, a reclusive group of tattooed, half-civilised folk who are only interesting because of the fact that they are almost immune to magical toxicity. The author theorised that their immunity was a result of sharing bloodlines with djinn, but since djinn don't actually exist this was not a promising start. The one after that was a stack of sacred poetry about mysteries and bees. The final volume on the first shelf was an inquisitor's guide, with instructions for finding, incapacitating and executing necromancers and their 'magical progeny', which seemed to reference various forms of undead. The execution portion was particularly detailed. I swallowed and shut it hurriedly.

Brix wandered to the icon table and began sorting through the statues, looking, no doubt, for something that wouldn't be too heavy to carry. I dug, with growing frustration, through piles of slender folios, all of them genealogies detailing the families of royal bastards. The only thing that I could see that might be remotely relevant was a judge's diary. I was scanning it for Acarius' name when the sound of a key grated in the lock.

My head came up. The handle on the door that led to the main sanctuary was rattling. I stuffed the book into my bag, Brix grabbed the candle and we scrambled for the slaves' door.

In the storeroom she blew the candle out and we stood, listening. A murmur of voices began in the library: two men, arguing. I groped for the door to the sanctuary and pushed it open a crack.

The candle on the altar still made a lonely pool of illumination in the middle of the dark room. The big double doors to the library were open, though, spilling the sound of bickering and wavering lamplight across the floor.

'I don't understand it, my lord.' The high, frantic voice of Halling the priest came, panting, over a noise that sounded like someone dumping things off shelves. 'The divining said she was *here*. I'm sure it was correct, I–'

'Do you think she's hiding behind the scrolls?' The angry baritone of the other carried across the room. 'All you were supposed to do was hold him, keep him off the Guild books. That's the only reason you were involved. *I* would have dealt with him. But you had to punish the woman and play with your knives, and now you've lost both of them! Is this what I pay you for? Do you know how expensive this has been?'

We had to go, quickly, before they came back out of the library. I eased my way out into the sanctuary, heart hammering against my breastbone. I turned back to signal to Brix, but she had already slipped out beside me. She pressed her finger to her lips and disappeared into the shadows along the wall.

I crept along after her – or at least, after where I thought she was. This far from the altar candles I couldn't see her, and I couldn't risk even a whisper to try to locate her.

'Don't.' Halling was begging now, panic stark in his voice. 'I can look again, I'll find them!'

The baritone began to chant. The hair rose on my arms. Did I know that voice?

'Please!' Halling screamed. 'My lord, don't–'

His voice cut off with a quiet gurgle.

I pressed against the outer wall of the sanctuary, craning my neck to see who had cast. I thought I recognised him, but gods, I hoped I was wrong.

A big man in a black robe stood in the wreck of the library, his back to me. He was looking down at what was left of Halling. The priest was crumpled on the floor, neck bent at an unnatural angle, mouth open in a look of pitiful surprise. A candle still guttered in one of his hands.

The big man bent, grabbed Halling's collar and slowly began to drag him into the sanctuary. I kept moving. I could make out the shape of the front door now, only a few steps away. Brix was nowhere to be seen. I hoped she had already exited. I reached for the latch, then paused. Had it made a sound when we came in, or not?

No time. I gritted my teeth and turned it.

Click.

The big man dropped the body immediately and spun on his heel, chanting again. I threw myself to the floor as a burst of purple lightning slammed into the wall above my head.

I got on to my hands and knees. The flash had dazzled me. Which way was the door?

'Well.' The big man's chuckle echoed through the chamber.

My vision adjusted just in time to see him stride towards me, the lavender residue of the spell still gleaming under his fingernails. 'I wouldn't have thought you'd be the devout type.' His teeth flashed in the scanty yellow light. 'Hello, Gray.'

THREE

I knew his voice even without seeing his face: Keir Esras, Guild Examiner General, looming not four feet from me. There were approximately seven thousand people I would rather have met at that moment.

'What,' he said, 'are the odds you'll come quietly?'

'Not excellent.' I got up. 'I didn't go quietly last time, if you recall.'

'Stop there.' Keir raised his hand. The purple light crackling over it threw the crooked bridge of his nose into shadowed relief. 'Or you'll learn what lightning tastes like. Be wise. All I want is a little cooperation. We know Acarius sent the information to you.'

I stopped. 'Where is he? Where have you bastards taken him?' I knew Keir was probably lying, trying to throw me off balance. It still hurt to hear the old man's name, more than I had thought possible.

'Somewhere you'll never find him. He might as well not exist.' Keir smiled. 'It looks like we have good odds for your cooperation, after all.'

'How's the nose?' I said. I had broken it with a spell the last time he'd tried to arrest me, three months and six towns ago. Now that I looked, I thought there was still a little bruising around his eyes.

The smile dropped off his face. 'Start talking, now.'

I chewed my lip. His handful of purple sparks was the problem. I didn't have any spells scribed. He had to know that I had just seen him commit murder. He had to kill me, whether I cooperated or not.

I lunged at him. My arms locked around his waist, my momentum carrying us both to the floor. He landed with a startled grunt that drove the air from his lungs, swinging his hand towards me.

Purple light sizzled past my face, heating the air near my right ear so much that I smelled burned hair. I scrambled to pin his arms down, to direct the spell. Lightning has such an affinity for human blood that it's been known to turn on its caster, but I wasn't bleeding, so he'd have to take aim. If he couldn't turn the magic towards me –

Keir's knee thudded into my stomach and sent me sprawling backwards. I tried to sit up to gain better leverage, only to be met with another blow from his knee. He rolled. I hit the stone floor with a grunt.

And he was on top of me. Gods, he was heavy.

'Now stop, or I'll just kill you now.' Keir's voice rasped, harsh. He had a hand on my throat, squeezing just enough to make it hard to breathe. The other hand hovered above my face, the lavender of the lightning spell throbbing, outlining the veins in his wrist. I had lost.

'Lightning is illegal,' I croaked.

He snorted. 'Don't pretend like you care about the Royal Charter. You and I both want it abolished. The king is an illiterate fool who doesn't deserve his throne, the state of magical research is a disgrace and yet you're *still* filth, Gray, piddling about with illegal spells for no higher reason than making a bit of coin, like a tinker.' He glanced down at my satchel. 'Now reach in the bag, take out any piece of road trash you've got runes scribed on and put it on the ground. Slowly.'

Stuck-up Guild bastard. I was no road conjurer, tramping from village to village mending pots and curing sick goats. Acarius had seen to my education better than that.

I put my hand in the satchel. There was nothing helpful inside, magically speaking. I'd used up my parchment escaping from the jail. Even if I'd had runes scribed, I couldn't pronounce anything with Keir's hand on my throat, ready to silence me forever.

I'd be in a Guildhouse by dawn, gagged and mindblown. I had failed.

My fingers touched smooth glass. One of the flasks of yavad. I swung it upwards and smashed it into the side of his head.

He gave a muffled cry. His lightning spell crawled up over his neck; it mingled with the blood running down his beard from where the breaking flask had cut him and instantly enveloped his head. His lips moved, swearing at me as his fingers tightened on my throat.

My heartbeat pounded inside my skull. I chopped at his wrist with one hand, but he didn't move. Panic pulsed through me, yammering, blind.

Then he let me go, arching backwards, hands flailing.

Brix stood over us. She raised a fist-sized icon of Saint Simanus – patron of executioners – and hit Keir again. He flopped sideways, unconscious.

I gulped air. She grabbed me by my belt and hauled me to my feet. She wasted only a few seconds checking me over before her hand locked around my wrist.

We ran.

The city gate, of course, was shut.

We only paused long enough to pant for a few seconds behind a cart, parked not three houses over from the little hut beside the gate where the gatekeeper was chatting with two soldiers. My guts dropped into my boots. Brix, however, seemed unfazed. She led me through the darkness to the wall. We followed it until I heard the gurgle of liquid.

A grate extended from the stones and disappeared into the small stream that, confined to a masonry channel, flowed under the wall and into the city. Brix waded into the freezing water and dragged me after her. I followed as closely as I dared, worried that I'd lose her in the dark. She led me to where a section of the grate was broken away under the wall, ducked and slipped out like a fish. For me it was a closer squeeze, working one shoulder through at a time.

And then we were free, beyond the wall in a wide pond, soaked through and wading for the shore. This must have been how she'd left the town the first time, running with Halling behind her.

We made for the road.

For a long time, there was nothing but the slippery feel of field grass under my wet boots and the steady, wretched wish that the wind would go away. When we finally got to the high road, it was worse, with no trees close enough to shield us from the biting breeze. Brix huddled into herself, her mouth set in a dogged, miserable line. I don't know how many miles we went under the stars, but when the sun rose I couldn't see Fenwydd anymore. Pink dawn light fringed the horizon and touched the tips of the barley in the fields around us with rosy fingers. It would have been pretty, if I hadn't still been wet from the hips down.

Brix, ahead of me, stubbed her toe. 'Damnation!' We both halted. She shook out her foot, scowling. 'Look, are you going to remove my tracker? Otherwise, I don't see why you need to keep going in the same direction as me.'

'That *was* the agreement.' I flexed my bad knee, trying to keep the discomfort in it from sharpening to an ache. It was already distracting. There was a stand of chokecherry bushes along the ditch. I pointed towards them, although I wasn't relishing the thought of slipping around in the weeds. 'We should do this off the road. I'll have to see the thing.'

We scrambled down behind the bushes. Brix hesitated, then lifted the hem of her shirt, just enough that I could see a thin strip of her belly and a copper ring gleaming in her navel. It looked solid, but I knew it wasn't.

'Hurry,' she said.

I squatted in the long grass in front of her, easing my bad knee down as carefully as I could, and squinted at the tiny runes engraved on the copper. It was a simple incantation, just a static sequence to keep the two halves of the ring in place and then a beacon sigil. I dug through my satchel for a brush and a small jar of red alchemical paint. I glanced upwards. 'I've got to write the runes on your stomach, so don't knee me in the teeth, all right?'

She set her jaw. 'Just get going.'

I hunched my shoulders, took a deep breath, and cleared my mind. She did well holding still under the ticklish precision of it as I painted the characters for a breaker spell in a circle around her navel, one that mirrored the lock on the ring. When I pronounced it, the runes lit briefly and the copper ring snapped in half.

A twinge of pain crossed through my body, but the satisfaction came, too. Finishing a well-formed spell, one that does what you want it to, elegantly and fast – there's no other feeling like it. I smiled.

Brix tugged the ring free and stared down at the bits of metal in her hand. 'I've worn this since I was thirteen.'

'Yes, well, dump it somewhere. It's too distinctive.' I rose, wincing. 'And you'll want to wipe the circle off of your skin. Runes put out a lot of energy; leave them there and they'll eat at you. You'll get sores.'

'Ugh.' Brix shuddered and scrubbed at the paint with her sleeve. 'Why write it on skin, then? You used parchment earlier. Why not carry your spells in a book?'

'Pages of a book touch each other. The spells interact, start fires. You can write an incantation spiral on a single piece of parchment, but you have to use it very quickly. It's just thin leather – skin, like your skin. Given enough time, the runes eat through it.' I stuffed my tools back in my satchel.

'You're not a Guild member, are you?' She crossed her arms. 'You lied to me.'

'We met in a *barn*.' I started moving again. If I concentrated, I could keep my limp minimised. At least I hoped I could; if not my knee would be used up soon, and I'd be stuck until I could get the swelling down. 'I don't know what you expected.'

'That man at the temple, the one I hit.' She was walking, too, still holding her arms clasped around herself. 'What did he want with you?'

'I'm leaving at the crossroads,' I said, 'so it doesn't matter.'

'And I saved your life, so it seems like that should have bought me something.'

I twitched my shoulders, annoyed. Nobody asked her to save my life. 'You wanted your tracker off, now it's off. At least, I can't imagine another reason why you would think braining Keir was a better option than running away.'

'I didn't—' Worry hummed in her voice. 'I *wasn't* thinking, if you want to know, I was angry, stupid, I was—' She blinked, trembling with something that I was startled to recognise as a deep, quiet rage. 'I hate them. I hate how they hurt people. And I didn't start thinking again until it was too late, and now I've messed everything up and I don't know what I'm going to do.' Her eyes fixed on me. 'This is your fault, so *start talking*. I need to know if they're going to hunt me because of you. This isn't a game for me, wizard. I can't just cast a spell and run away.'

I exhaled. 'His full name is Keir Esras, he's the Examiner General to the Royal Mages' Guild and he's supposed to hunt dangerous wizards, not escaped slaves. You'll be fine. I don't think he even saw you.'

She eyed me. 'Why was he after you?'

'Clearly because I'm a dangerous wizard,' I said.

'*All* wizards are dangerous,' she said, bitterly.

I sighed. 'Look, the Guild regulates magic because although it's handy to have a supply of wizards, gods forbid you let people who can throw lightning wander around without supervision. They might get above themselves and question the authority of Temples, covet the throne – you see how the war would go? So the king grants them a charter as an alternative, which allows them to study the narrow bit of magical knowledge that the throne and Temples agree is safe. In return for survival, the Guild fights for the throne when necessary and hunts down anyone who practises outside the Charter.' I shrugged. 'Like me.'

'But that's not why they're hunting you,' she said, 'or at least it isn't the only reason. You and Keir both mentioned someone called Acarius.'

'Leave it.' I put my head down and tried to walk faster. I wasn't going to talk about that. Keir had arrested Acarius six months ago, and every day that passed meant more risk that the Guild was torturing him, more chance that I'd never find my grandfather alive. Wherever they were holding him had to be heavily warded against divination. I had half killed myself with scrying and hadn't got even a hint of his location – just whispers of emotion, waves of fear and pain. I'd searched jails, bribed officials and had been sneaking into libraries and records rooms for weeks with no luck. The judge's diary in my satchel was the first thing that had even looked like a lead. Gods knew I didn't need any reminders of how thoroughly I was letting Acarius down.

'No,' she said. 'You're still lying.'

'Saints, leave me alone!' I snapped. 'I don't bother you with a lot of questions about why you were running away, do I? Fuss at you about whether you're endangering me? Can we just *walk*?'

She went silent for the next few miles. I breathed in the scent of the grain fields, with just a musty hint of the river that snaked along to our right. The sun on my shoulders and the free road stretching in front of me felt good, and I could almost distract myself from the pain in my knee with the rhythm of my own steps. But my mind wouldn't stop churning. The Guild wasn't holding Acarius in a normal prison, with the road conjurers and black-market witches that they picked up in their enforcement sweeps. Keir's gloating had been too convincing for that to have been a lie. They had hidden my grandfather, somewhere secure. Somewhere private, where they could force his immense magical knowledge out of him, question him.

Hurt him.

I blinked, but my eyes still burned, gritty with fatigue and guilt. There was no point in circling back through the same thoughts that had tormented me for six months. I had to find a place to stop for a few hours, give myself time to examine the book closely and try to piece together whatever clues it might hold. I needed sleep, and food.

It took us until noon to reach a place where four roads met, by which time my knee was a white-hot ball of pain and I was dozing on my feet. Brix halted in the middle of the cross, biting her lip uncertainly.

I jerked a thumb towards the path that broke to our right, leading down towards the river and, filtering up through the willow trees along the water, the smoke of what was probably a town. 'I'm going that way. It's probably best if you pick a different direction.' I waited, but she didn't say anything. I'm not sure what I was expecting, considering that she had only known me for nine hours or so. *Good luck*, maybe, or *sorry for getting you arrested*. I shrugged and started down the path. 'Safe travels, then. It's been . . . interesting.'

'What would be so bad about staying together, just for a little while?' she said. 'Do I *have* to pick a different direction?'

I paused and looked over my shoulder. 'I don't know why you wouldn't. I'm a dangerous wizard, remember?'

'I just—' Brix hadn't moved, her hands balled into fists, watching me. 'Are you going to tell Temples where I am?' Her voice was low, intense. 'I can't go back there. You don't understand how they hurt you. You don't know what they can make you do.'

I touched the barely-scabbed cut that Halling had left on my chin. Being tied to a temple would be difficult enough, but Brix would also have had to go about her work knowing that Halling was always lurking behind her in the dark, watching, fondling his knives.

You don't know what they can make you do. I had to swallow, hard.

'No,' I said. 'I'm not going to tell them. It's none of my business where you go. If you wait until I'm gone before you leave, I won't even *know* where you go.'

Her ears and the tip of her nose went pink. 'Thank you.'

'It's nothing.' Temples wanted her, but the Guild wanted me. Even if I'd had the sort of ethics that found it acceptable to send someone back into slavery, it didn't make sense to attract the attention of either organisation. Besides, by choosing my direction first, I had the advantage of stopping in the closest town. She'd have to walk further, in her bare feet. The only thing I dislike more than feeling indebted to someone is being thanked when I'm not being altruistic. 'Right,' I said, suddenly anxious to be gone. 'Well, goodbye.'

'Good luck, Gray.' She gave me a tiny smile, but I didn't altogether like the shrewd calculation in her eyes. She knew where I was going. Maybe she wasn't being altruistic, either.

I left her standing there and moved quickly down towards the willows. Now that it was over, and I'd never see her again, I wanted to be away from her. Even after I'd passed into the trees, it still felt like she was watching me.

FOUR

The village squatted along the banks of the river, all smoke and peeling wattle-and-daub. I wasn't expecting much in the way of an inn, but Pavel the tavern-keeper still managed to disappoint me. I had in mind to barter for a meal and a night's rest. Most tradesmen that I've met have something they want enchanted – say, hens that aren't laying. Simple enough to write a rune spiral for a witchlight to glow on the coop roof and solve that problem. As it happened, however, Pavel thought magic was unnatural and wizards were deviants. It wasn't until I offered him one of the two remaining vials of yavad that he stopped picking at a gravy stain on his apron and perked up.

'You can have a bed, until tomorrow morning.' He gestured to where a few straw-tick mattresses were rolled up against the wall. It was less than ideal, but at least I could rest for a few hours before the evening crowd began to gather. I chose the cleanest-looking mattress and the most inconspicuous corner. I tucked my satchel under my head, one hand gripping the book through the leather, and managed to sleep until Pavel and his wife began clattering around, preparing the evening meal and arguing.

I sat up, bleary and sore, feeling every spot where Keir had landed a blow the night before. I rubbed my eyes, carefully extended my left knee in front of me so it wouldn't lock up and took the book from my satchel.

Back in the temple I had assumed that it was a judge's diary for Guild tribunals. And indeed, the first year or so of cases were nothing out of the ordinary: a Guild member censured for selling divination without charging official prices, convictions for a few petty spell-forgers and a court-ordered silencing for a village sorceress who had been providing prophylactic incantations. The last one made me wince – silencing meant they'd removed her tongue.

But the handwriting of the scribe changed after about twenty pages. Some ten months ago the tribunal had taken an interest in necromancy cases. Death magic is both unsavoury and uncommon, yet someone had managed to dredge up every necromancer or suspected necromancer between Varre and Llana, extract detailed information about their practice and then execute them. Overall, some twenty wizards had met their end. I was unsurprised to see Keir Esras' signature as sentencing judge, but finding Halling on the list of witnesses gave me pause. What would a Jaernic priest know about necromancy, and why did Keir care? What was he planning?

Don't pretend you care about the Charter. You and I both want it abolished. Now that I wasn't trying to keep myself from being strangled, Keir's comment during the fight struck me as odd. There had been pushes in the past to revise the Charter. It was possible that Keir belonged to some splinter group that wanted more freedom, I supposed. But then, he had said 'abolish', not 'revise'. Everyone knew that there were factions within the Guild in the same sense that everyone knew there were factions at court, but this was the first time I had seriously wondered whether one of those factions was going to attempt a coup.

I turned the page.

Acarius Gray, guilty. Before the Examiner General, secret tribunal, Greater Fenwydd Guildhouse. Third session. Involuntary testimony.

It took a while to get my eyes to leave the words. Beneath them, labelled *soul-catcher*, was a pencil sketch of something that looked like a small glass flask or vial, the kind of thing you'd keep perfume in. A list of specifications was scratched across the facing page, ranging from those I understood (*leaded glass*) to those I didn't (*rennen*), and a note: *In the opinion of the court, the subject is still not being entirely forthcoming. Found attempting unsanctioned communication incantation with candle grease. Recommend removal to a more secure location with suitable interrogation facilities.* It ended with an inscription that simply said *subject transferred north* and Keir's cramped, untidy signature.

North. Half the damn country was north of Fenwydd.

Involuntary testimony.

I shut the book and took deep breaths to keep from throwing it across the room.

Eventually, the meaty scent of whatever it was that was boiling on the hob made its way to my nose and my stomach cramped with hunger. I glanced up to find that the room had filled around me, a mixture of locals in from the fields and a raucous group of what looked like merchants off the road. Everybody seemed to be enjoying themselves more than I would have imagined possible in a place where the beer smelled like watery piss. I raised a hand as Pavel passed me, harried, carrying a tray of food.

'Can I have something to eat?' I said. 'It was included in the price of the bed, right?'

'Aye, in a minute.' He went charging across the room to where the merchants were drinking. I stretched my stiff neck from side to side, trying not to think too hard about what 'something to eat' would probably entail. Baked cabbage, maybe. I tried to return to my book.

But the merchants who were delaying my dinner burst into noisy laughter, and I glanced up, annoyed. A small, familiar form was trying to pass their table, arms crossed protectively over her chest.

'No.' Brix's voice carried across the room, with a hint of fear underneath the anger. 'Let me by.'

One of the merchants, a sweaty fellow with a paunch, patted his knee. 'Oh, come on now, lovely. The ale tonight is the best I've ever had in this place, and we had a profitable day in town. Let me buy you a drink.'

'I'm not interested,' she said. 'I just want—'

'Now, then.' The merchant's oily confidence faltered. 'Wouldn't be the first drink you've had on a man's lap, I'll wager.' He made a swipe for her.

'I said no!' She jumped backwards. Pavel, who was putting the fourth round of drinks on the merchants' table, ignored her. Brix stared at him for a moment, then looked around the room, searching for something – an ally, maybe. The locals were all carefully absorbed in their own conversation. They weren't going to interfere with a group of open-handed merchants, not for a stranger.

'Little snob,' growled the merchant, starting to rise. 'I'll teach you—'

'Pavel,' I said, loudly. 'How about that food? Do I have to get it myself?' I waved at Brix. 'Hello, friend. Took you long enough to get here.'

Relief flashed across her face. She crossed the room and plopped down beside me as Pavel bustled his way over to the kettle on the fire.

'Can I just sit with you until . . .' Her eyes were on the merchants, who had subsided into grumbling and occasional bursts of intoxicated giggles.

'If you like. I wasn't using that piece of floor.' I closed the diary and stuck it in my satchel. 'Interesting secret destination you ended up choosing.'

'I'm not following you, I promise,' she said. 'I found out that this is the only village for miles, and I need to find someone who'll let me ride in their cart tomorrow. I didn't think you'd still be here.' She looked down at her hand, picking at her fingernails.

'How are you planning on paying Pavel?' I said. If she still had the icons, she'd snatched from the temple she could trade one, but that would be dangerous. Not only would it leave a trail for anyone taking the trouble to try to track us out of Fenwydd, but they were more valuable than anything in the village. Offering one might give Pavel ideas. After all, why be content with one icon when you can simply rob someone and have all of their icons?

She gave me a tight little smile. 'I'll be all right. There's usually some work someone wants done. I can barter.'

Pavel stomped up to us then and held out a half-filled bowl with a spoon stuck in it. Brix ignored the food, humming faintly to herself, a tune I didn't know. It didn't keep her stomach from growling, emphatically.

I sighed. 'Two dinners, Pavel. There are two of us. Do try to keep up.'

His face clouded. 'You bargained for one.'

'A dinner for me,' I said, 'and a dinner for her. It's my yavad that you've been spiking everyone's ale with, isn't it? Lowers the inhibitions so nicely, puts people in a mood to spend money, to not notice if the ale is watered . . .' I smiled. 'Funny how some people don't like it. It's probably just as well that I'm a discreet man.'

He went red, but turned and went back to the kitchen. When he returned, he brought a tray with a loaf of doughy bread, some strong brown cheese and a couple of bowls of what he alleged was lamb stew. I wouldn't have ever thought I'd wish for baked cabbage, but apparently there's a first time for everything.

Brix put the tray on the floor between us and grabbed a bowl while I took a piece of bread and cheese. She paused for a second before taking a bite, muttering a rhyme under her breath. The prayer tugged at a very old memory in the back of my head, where I keep the scraps I have of my mother's voice.

'A blessing of Ranara,' I said, without really meaning to. 'You pray to the Mother of the Moon?'

'Yes.' She took a bite. 'Why? Who do you pray to?'

I shouldn't have asked. I don't really pray to anything, not even the little lucky saints. But saying that makes people uncomfortable, so I took a bite of bread and pretended like I hadn't heard the question. The vice-toothed ache in my knee was getting harder to ignore. I straightened and bent it gingerly and pinched at the kneecap, wishing I could take the brace off and stretch.

'If you tell me why your knee pains you, I might be able to help,' Brix said. 'Pay you back a little for all this. I'm no Healer, but—'

'No.' I should have had the sense to leave my damn knee alone. 'You can't help.'

'Why not? Is it something to do with magic? A spell-caused injury?'

A bitter laugh pushed past my lips before I could catch it. 'Nothing so exotic, alas. It's garden-variety lameness, not worth talking about. It'll be better in the morning.'

'I knew an old man who had good success with rubbing lard on his joints.' She hitched herself a little closer to me. 'And a girl with palsy—'

'A tanner broke my leg with an axe handle when I was eight years old and it didn't heal correctly.' It was work to keep my tone flat, but it was worth it. Otherwise I would be shouting at her and making everybody notice us. 'You can't help. Nothing will. It will be better in the morning. And I'm not going to talk about it again.'

She went silent and finished her dinner. I leaned back against the wall and counted the wee clay house-gods Pavel had lined up above the fireplace. (*Two mothers, a cattle-blessing, six wealth-saints, one with a sheaf of barley.*) I did equations in my head. (*Runes for repairing stone walls, runes for breaking them, runes for water-based divining.*) Recited a list of principal rivers. (*The Varr, the Nelta, the Rovidden . . .*)

After a while it worked. The tanner and the old village and the pain and the past all stayed where I wanted them, and my knee was only an ache.

'Where should I sleep?' Brix said, the closest to subdued that she had been yet.

I hadn't thought of that, but of course she couldn't wade back through the drunks to get her own mattress. 'In the bed, where else?'

'I–' She flushed. 'I know I'm here more or less by your courtesy, but–'

Gods. I pinched the bridge of my nose. 'Look, you won't wake up to me pawing at you. If I wanted a girl, I could get one without poking around in barns.' Theoretically. Aphrodisiac spells aren't that difficult. 'It's probably best that we sleep in shifts anyway. Take the first one, I've got work to do.'

She smiled. 'Thanks, Gray.'

I was getting tired of being thanked all the time. I looked at the toe of my boot. 'Go to bed.'

The locals had taken themselves home and the merchants had passed out on the floor when I took my book out again and crept closer to the hearth to try to study it. I put another couple of sticks of wood on the fire and stirred it up, hoping for better light.

I rifled backwards in the pages and reread the account of Acarius' interrogation. I was missing something, I knew I was. My eyes slid over the words that I had already nearly memorised, fretful. *Guilty . . . involuntary testimony . . . found attempting unsanctioned communication incantation with candle grease –*

I stopped.

Corcoran, you idiot.

Acarius wouldn't have attempted such a thing lightly. Communication spells were incredibly taxing, almost impossible for a single caster to maintain without a focus or a helper. Some were slightly more flexible and could be left inert, only radiating poison once they were activated. The main difficulty with inert communication, of course, was that the person you were speaking to had to be relaxed and receptive, or, failing that, know you were trying to contact them and *get* relaxed and receptive.

Everyone was asleep now. Brix's even breathing and the sodden snores of the merchants testified to that. I slipped off my bag and dug through it until I found a grease pencil, the last flask of yavad and the little tin cup I use for measuring reagents. Taken in the correct dose, yavad drops inhibitions and turns pain into something misty and faraway. I scrawled a tight bundle of runes on both of my wrists and then measured a half dose of yavad. The thick green liquid clung to the vial before rolling sluggishly into the cup.

I took a deep breath, pronounced the runes and then swallowed the yavad as quickly as I could. A cough clawed its way up my throat, and I had to bury my face in the crook of my elbow to smother it. The liquor burned its way down into my gut.

'Come on,' I murmured, willing my muscles to loosen, reaching out for my grandfather with my mind. 'Come on.'

I looked up. The room was gone. I appeared to be sitting on black, empty space. I had either managed to tap into Acarius' communication spell, or the yavad was potent and I was very stoned, indeed.

'Cricket.'

Acarius' voice, floating out of the nothing. His form followed, sitting cross-legged on the darkness a few feet from me.

Dizzying relief broke over me, but I couldn't get distracted. 'This seems like the wrong time for nicknames,' I said. 'Talk quickly, Acarius, before I sober up.'

'I take it you're fooling around with yavad, then.' Acarius smiled, the wrinkles around his green eyes deepening. 'Well, no matter, if it finally relaxed you enough to let me through. I can't keep incorporeal projection up for long by myself.'

He was a very accurate incorporeal projection, from the close-cropped white hair to the homemade spectacles and tidy goatee. Gods, I have missed him.

'Scribe it with candle grease again?' I said.

'No.' He rearranged his ankles. 'My interrogator dropped his pencil as he left me, the first mistake they've made.' Worry passed across his eyes. 'It might not even *be* a mistake. They might be listening. But I had to take the chance, scribe the spell. I had to talk to you. Pay attention now, boy. I haven't got much time.'

'Where are you?' I leaned forwards. 'I'll come and get you.'

'*No!*' Acarius' face twisted with alarm. 'You can't risk yourself like that. There's something else I need you to do. You know the research I was doing when you left home? You remember the topic?'

I frowned. Acarius' interests changed so rapidly that it was difficult to remember which tangent he had been on that month. And when I had returned to the cabin, there had been nothing except churned earth and scorched wood. Even the books had been scorched. The books . . .

'Yes,' I said slowly. He had been reading about the god Jaern. I got the impression that he didn't want me to say as much out loud, though.

'Good lad.' He looked relieved. 'And the year you were fourteen I took you to the coast. You remember the city?'

'Yes.' It had been the city of Ri Dana, but I didn't like having to play this game. What could be so important that the Guild would risk letting him contact me just so they could spy on the conversation?

'Go there. Find a man named Lorican. Mention my name to him. He can take you where you need to go, to the temple of' – Acarius paused, and looked over his shoulder into the blank dark – 'of that deity,' he said, carefully. 'There's an artefact there, a child, of sorts. You'll know it when you see it. Take it and hide it, at our place. You know where I mean.'

I did, but this was hideously frustrating. 'Where are you?' I repeated.

'I don't *know* where I am, Cricket. The Guild made sure of that.' He was hoarse; abruptly he looked old and pained. And he was lying. I knew it, as surely as I knew the throb of my own heartbeat. 'Find Lorican, hide the artefact. Do you understand?'

'No,' I said, stubborn. 'I don't understand why you can't tell me where they're keeping you. What is this thing, that it's so important? I'm not going to leave you there for Keir Esras to torment. He's had twenty wizards hanged this year, Acarius. I won't—'

'Don't argue with me,' he snapped. 'They're already hunting you, and I won't have you run straight into their net.' Acarius flickered. There's no other word for it – his body winked like a candle flame in a wind. 'Corcoran, Keir is acting without the knowledge of anyone sane in the Guild. He's planning a revolt against the king, and worse. They've got all my journals, all my papers. The artefact is a necromantic tool, an instrument that can be used to create an unkillable army. Esras can't be allowed to possess it. *People will die*. You've got to do this for me. I can't keep them out of my mind forever.'

'No, no, no. Don't do this. Not this time. I don't give a damn about the king.' I reached for him. I couldn't help myself. 'Grandfather, please. Tell me how to find you.'

Acarius smiled, even as he began to fade. 'Take care of yourself, Cricket.' His lower body disappeared – we were losing the incorporeal link – and he was still trying to protect me from the truth, as though I was a stripling with a newly-changed voice. As though his obsession with secrets wasn't what had started all the trouble in the first place.

'*Please!*' My fingertips barely brushed his.

A pulse of blackness slammed through my body.

He was gone.

FIVE

'Gray,' Brix said. 'Hey, look at me.'

But it took her shaking my shoulder again before I could get my eyes to focus on anything but the low-burned coals of the fire. I must have been sitting there in the dark for hours. She squatted beside me on the hearth, frowning at me and at the yavad-stained cup that was still in my hand. 'I wouldn't have taken you for someone who needed that stuff,' she said.

'You don't know anything about me.' I stuffed the cup back in my bag, more ashamed than I should have been, especially since I felt entirely too sober. 'What made you feel the need to stick your nose in my affairs? Did I ask you to come over here?'

She rocked back on her heels, sudden caution on her face. 'You made a noise, like you were hurt. I know a little about helping sick folk, I just thought—'

'Do me a favour and don't waste your attempts at thinking on me.' Why did she have to wake up? See me like this, *hear* me? I gathered up my things, shaky. 'Leave me the hells alone.'

I went back to the bed, stretched out and rolled so that my back was to her, my arms around my bag. I was still trembling. I clutched the satchel harder to stop it, staring into the dark. The weight of the task that Acarius had dropped on me sat in my stomach like lead.

Go to Ri Dana, Cricket. Find Lorican, Cricket. Lose the only family you've got and be happy about it, Cricket.

Why would he think I could do any of that? Ri Dana was eighty miles away. It would mean finding a livery stable and hiring a horse or paying an ox-driver to let me ride along with the cargo in his cart, both options I could ill-afford. Even after I got to the city, and even assuming that I could find this Lorican person, I'd still have to get myself into another ward-encrusted Jaern-temple and steal what was evidently a holy object of some kind – all while the Guild was trying to break one of the finest magical minds to ever live.

It was all so pointless. Say I *did* find the artefact my grandfather wanted me to protect and I didn't kill myself in the process. A good hiding spot for such a deadly thing didn't exist. Even Acarius couldn't think of anything better than using our place, the hidden caches at the little cabin where he had raised me. The cabin hadn't kept Acarius *himself* safe, so how could it protect anything else? If I was supposed to prevent a wizards' revolt or stop a war or whatever gods-damned thing Acarius was certain was coming, I'd have to destroy the thing, and any advantage it could have given me in dealing with the Guild.

My jaw ached, and I forced myself to unclench my teeth. I wasn't going to lose him. Not like this. There had to be another way.

People will die.

Acarius had no right to do this, to make me choose. I closed my eyes, but for a long time I didn't sleep.

When I woke up it was barely dawn, and part of the solution was sitting in my mind, ready for me. I already knew someone who could get me into a Jaern-temple – *any* Jaern-temple. And, like an idiot, I had insulted her last night.

I slung my bag over my shoulder and rolled up my mattress hurriedly. The only people in the common room were the hungover merchants, one of whom was being drastically, colourfully sick out the window. I had to find Brix before the sun got any higher and she disappeared down the road.

I burst out of the building into the dooryard, only to bounce off her as she was coming from the direction of the chicken yard with a basket of eggs.

'Holy Neyar!' She stumbled sideways. 'Watch it!'

'Sorry.' I grabbed her elbow to steady her. 'Sorry, I didn't see you, I thought you had left. I was thinking—' I stopped. She was scowling at the ground. 'I need to talk to you,' I said.

'I'm busy. I'm supposed to take these eggs inside, then I've got to milk the goats and do some other chores before they'll give me breakfast and then I have to find a way to get up the coast.' She pointedly removed her elbow from my grip. 'So I don't have time to talk to you, wizard.' She stalked inside.

I followed. 'You're going up the coast? North?'

Brix didn't answer, depositing the eggs on the bar.

'I admit I was an arse last night,' I said. 'I apologise. Look, I just want to talk. I have a business proposal for you. You're here long enough to eat, anyway, aren't you? Hear me out while you eat.' She ignored me and moved back towards the door. 'I'll help pay for breakfast,' I said.

She paused, with her hand on the latch of the door. '*You* milk the goats,' she said.

I did, poorly. When we'd traded the milk and the turnips she'd pulled out of the garden for bowls of barley and onion porridge, we retired to one of the tables.

I leaned forwards on my elbows. 'I was thinking—'

She took a bite of her porridge. 'What, again?'

Uncalled-for, that. 'I want you to teach me the countersigns to get into a Jaern-temple,' I said. 'We can work out some kind of trade.'

'I can't,' she said. 'I mean, even if I had time, I couldn't teach you without being at a temple, to show you where to touch the doors and things. Besides, you have to use different countersigns on different days. It took me three years to learn all the patterns.'

'Then come with me,' I said, recklessly. 'I'm going up to Ri Dana.'

She stopped chewing, startled. 'What?'

'You said you were going up the coast anyway.' I stabbed at the porridge with my spoon, anxious to be done with this and out from under her scrutiny. 'Go with me, get me in the temple there. We can hire a cart. I'll promise not to speak to you the whole way there, if you like.'

'I've got to meet up with someone,' she said. 'Why do you want to get into another temple, anyway? More books?'

'You'll notice how carefully I'm not asking you your business in the north.' I took a bite and frowned at my bowl. The porridge could have done with more salt and fewer onions. 'I don't ask you, you don't ask me, you go your way as soon as I'm finished at the temple. It works out.'

'And I need money.'

'I'll pay you.' I glanced at Pavel, who was giving the merchants their breakfast. They were all more subdued this morning, nursing sore heads. I lowered my voice so they couldn't overhear me. 'I think you took that icon of the executioner's saint, yes? But it's going to be difficult to spend or sell until you get to a larger town. I can pay you in coin.'

'How much?' Her eyes flicked up, abruptly urgent. The green circles around her pupils caught the morning sun and shone like old jade. 'On top of paying to get us to Ri Dana, I mean. How much will you give me?'

I thought about the measly pile of copper and silver at the bottom of my bag. It was everything I had been able to scrape together from Acarius' money box after the arrest, back when I had hoped the whole business could be solved with a bribe. Even without subtracting what it would cost to pay a carter, it hardly qualified as a fortune. 'How much would it take?' I said.

She scraped the last bit of porridge in her bowl into a tidy spoonful and swallowed it before answering. The merchants drifted outside, one of them still looking a little sick, the sound of their grumbling following them into the stable-yard. I sat and ate and tried not to twitch with impatience. It seemed like a lot of thought to spend on a decision that, after all, only meant taking a journey and opening a door.

'Forty,' she said, hesitantly. 'In silver. Could you do that?'

My heart sank. That was enough to buy a couple of cows, or passage on a ship. I had all of eight silver coins.

'Done.' I heard the lie slip out, almost without my volition, and had to bite down on my tongue to keep from taking it back. I'd pay her whatever I could, after she helped me retrieve the artefact. It would have to be enough, even if it meant she had to wait a little longer to buy her cows or their equivalent. Acarius' life was at stake, not to mention the lives that this artefact of his could supposedly end.

'Done? Just like that?' Brix looked at me with mingled surprise and chagrin. 'You're carrying that kind of money around and you milk goats to buy your breakfast?'

I shrugged. 'I like goats, and I don't like Pavel. Why should he get stamped coin?'

The corner of her mouth quirked upwards. 'Then I suppose we have a deal.'

'Good.' I let my breath hiss out between my teeth and became aware, vaguely, that the room was too quiet. The merchants outside had been swearing at each other and dealing with their packhorses while Brix and I were talking, but now the jingle of harness had stopped and the constant chatter of conversation had suddenly dropped to a low mutter.

'And you *were* an arse last night, by the way,' Brix said.

'I *think* I already apologised for that.' I stood, listening. The voices outside continued, muted but urgent.

Abruptly all my senses were on edge. Something was happening.
'What is it?' Brix said.

I put my finger to my lips and eased my way towards the window, trying to see out without showing myself. In the stable-yard stood two of the merchants, holding conversation with two people in robes – a woman and a man, both in the light blue of new-fledged Guild apprentice wizards. The apprentices were showing the merchant something on a piece of parchment.

And now the merchants were nodding and pointing at the tavern.

'Guildies. We need to go, right now.' I turned on my heel, fully expecting Brix to argue, but she sprinted for the side door. I followed, lagging further behind her with every painful stride, my knee grinding and clicking.

We made it past the goat pens and ran towards the thin strip of willows that stood between the village and the road. Brix outstripped me easily, disappearing into the stand of bracken. I halted as soon as I was out of sight of the tavern, grabbed a grease pencil from my satchel and scrawled runes down my forearms. Apprentices travelled in threes, by Guild regulation. There had only been two of them in the tavern stable-yard. If they were smart, they would have tried to leave the third somewhere to cut off our retreat, and with nothing scribed I was unarmed.

I wrote feverishly, waiting for the flurry of noise from the direction of the village that would mean they were turning out to look for us. I had only four characters left to scribe when Brix screamed.

Branches whipped across my face as I bolted towards the sound. I knew terror when I heard it, knew what it was like to catch a spell between your teeth. The other apprentice must have been waiting on the road.

She was close, close enough that even over the roar of my heartbeat I could hear her frightened cries and a man's angry mutters. He had caught her, and if he killed her my one chance to get into the temple in Ri Dana would be dead. I ran towards the sound, crashing through the underbrush and slipping in the loamy soil as I scrambled up the slope towards the road. I burst out of the trees in time to see the man twist her to the ground with one arm.

Without waiting to think, I stooped and grabbed the only thing I could find, a single round stone. I threw it, as hard as I could.

Which must not have been very hard, because when it thudded between his shoulders he didn't fall. His head jerked around.

Not a wizard. Pavel, the innkeeper.

'What in the hells do you think you're doing?' I hated the quaver in my voice, but it was the mark of sanity. This was a bad situation. I had no sort of weapon – not a completed spell, nor even another rock, and sprinting uphill had dangerously loosened my brace.

'There you are.' He sneered at me. 'Think a bit of yavad buys you the right to order me around in my own place? I knew you was nothing but a dirty fake. The merchant was too blind drunk last night to remember you, sent those proper wizards in to see me. I knew who they was looking for well enough, even before they showed me the paper.' His hand tightened on Brix's arm, and she made a soft, pained sound, her feet scrabbling at the dirt, twisting against his grip without doing any good. 'I'm not sharing the bounty with anyone. While my wife is keeping those wizards drunk and chasing their own tails, I'll haul you back to the Guildhouse in Fenwydd. I'll have that money.'

I needed to knock him down, and keep him down long enough to let Brix get away. I had to keep him focused on me.

'Then you'll have to come take me,' I said, pleasantly. 'Because the bounty isn't on her, pigface.'

'I reckon she'd bring a price, too, if a man knew who to ask.' He let go of her, though, and advanced towards me. 'If you was a proper wizard, you'd have ensorcelled me by now. You're not a wizard. You're not anything.'

The man was a walking heap of ugly. I hit him.

My knuckles skidded across his teeth. He grunted, and batted my hand away.

'Shit,' I said, and his fist slammed into my mouth.

The first blow didn't drop me, but it made me wobble enough that I accidentally avoided the second one. My knee filled with hot, liquid pain, and I wrenched my weight off of it. How was I going to get through this without falling?

I lowered my head and ran at him, hoping to bowl him over backwards. He hooked a left into my stomach and the air left my body with a pathetic wheezing sound, doubling me over. Before I could straighten, his fist caught me in the face again, and I couldn't see.

If I went down, he'd kill me. I pulled myself upright, listening frantically to figure out where he was.

A rush of steps. I swung my fist towards the sound and connected with something. Pavel swore. I peered at him through just-returning vision and saw that I'd bloodied his nose. His foot snared my ankle and I stumbled backwards.

Something – it felt like it was at least the size of an ox hoof – crashed into my face. I heard myself grunt and concentrated on not shouting as I hit the dirt. Brix was screaming again, this time at me. I could hardly make out the words.

'Get on your feet!' she shouted.

As I struggled back up, over the seething agony in my knee, I found it rather annoying. She needed to stop making noise and get the hells away while she could.

I dragged my swollen eyes open in time to see Pavel draw his arm back one more time. The thin, blue dawn light made his teeth look even more stained as he grinned at me. 'You should have stayed down.'

'Tiny-pricked son of a goat,' I croaked. At least it wiped the smile off his face. I wished I could see Brix – I hoped she had taken the opportunity to run.

Crunch.

Warm blood gushed down my face, and I couldn't breathe through my nose. I went back to my knees, and this time I couldn't get up. I could see, though. I sat there, panting, waiting for him to kick me. I had one chance left.

'A lot of trouble,' he spat, 'for a little whore.'

He swung his foot at me hard enough that, had he connected, he would have caved in my ribcage. As it was, I caught his ankle and threw myself sideways, using his own momentum against him. With a yelp of surprise, he went down.

I may know nothing about fighting, but I'm good with leverage.

Scrambling forwards, I got a hand on his ear and twisted. 'Little whore?' I said. I lifted myself on my knees and brought my elbow, with all my weight behind it, into his chest. He cried out and curled into himself, wheezing.

'That's enough!' Someone grabbed my hair and yanked me away from him. I couldn't halt my backward progress and found myself sitting in the dirt, staring up at Brix. She stuck her hands under my armpits and dragged me up on my feet. 'Let's just go,' she said. 'They could have got tired of waiting, and then they'll be here any second. Don't waste any more time on him.'

Panting, I forced my sore fingers to bend enough to find the pencil in my bag and finished scribing the spell on my left arm. She was right that we had to move, but I had to deal with Pavel. Before long he'd get his wind back and get up. He'd tell the Guildies which direction we went, set them on our trail like hounds.

'*Gray,*' Brix said, urgent. 'They won't stop hunting us if you kill him.'

I walked back to Pavel. I wasn't going to kill him. I bent, put my hand over his mouth and pronounced the spell. Blue light flowed from my fingertips and into his open, gasping mouth. A ruewrack spell tastes like honey, and the sensation is so cold and so startling that most people swallow the magic before they think about it.

Pavel swallowed. I watched as his eyes went wide, pupils blown out to the edge of the irises, and he scrambled away from me, backwards, like a crab.

'Stay back!' His words scratched from his throat, screechy, frightened. 'Don't touch me!' He rolled on to his hands and knees and to his feet. He scrambled back down the hill and into the trees, talking to himself, chased by the hallucinations I'd dumped into his mind.

'There.' I winced as the toxicity blossomed in the middle of my skull and shaded my eyes with one hand as I limped back to Brix. 'It won't kill him, but with any luck he won't talk sense for the next eight or ten hours. We can get the hells away from here, hopefully before the Guildies catch on to what's happened and think to come after us.' I stopped, nausea surging.

'You look awful.' She was massaging her bruised arm. There was also a red mark on her cheek, now that I got closer to her. 'I've never heard of a wizard getting so sick so often.'

'That's because most Guild wizards don't practise like I do,' I said, with my head between my knees. 'They either do much less toxic spells and then spend more time recovering, or they dump the toxicity they acquire into other people. They cheat. I don't.'

'Other people?' There was a strange note in her voice.

'Slaves, mostly.' I clenched my teeth and tried to breathe deeply enough to keep my breakfast where it belonged. 'There are people who can absorb magic toxicity without being hurt. Tirnaal, a folk that mostly come from Genereth, in the south. Guild wizards mark them with runic tattoos for various ostentatious spells – bindfoot, speakfar, that kind of thing. Supposedly they've even got unique bodies, can be trapped in bottles, like bard's-tale djinn. I don't know that it works the way the Guild says it does, though. You don't see many Tirnaal – they never become wizards themselves, and–' I paused, closed my eyes. 'And I think I'm about to puke, so this seems like a very stupid moment for this discussion.'

'You could have run away. You didn't have to help me.' She almost sounded accusing. 'Why did you?'

The nausea began to subside a little. I swallowed, straightened and began to walk north as rapidly as I could. Which was not, of course, all that rapid.

'Answer me,' she said, keeping pace with me.

'Gods, it's not a big mystery.' My mouth was bitter with the aftertaste of magic. I didn't much like the flavour of this conversation, either. 'I *can't* run. I can't even jog most of the time, certainly not after walking so much yesterday. So if I was stuck going slow, Pavel had to be dealt with.' I glanced at her. 'Also, you're supposed to get me into a temple, remember?'

'Well,' she said. 'Thank—'

'Stop thanking me for everything,' I snapped. 'It wasn't a present. I don't give presents. This balanced our accounts. That's all.'

And that *was* all. I couldn't start caring what Brix or anybody thought of me. Not when I had so little time. What mattered was getting to Ri Dana and finding Acarius' artefact. What mattered was finding *Acarius*, before the Guild snuffed him out like a candle. I had to free him. I had to repair the rift between us.

Acarius was my family, and this was my last chance.

SIX

We walked north for three days, scrambling off the road whenever we heard hoofbeats, fearful of Guild pursuit. It was Brix who finally caught a cart, a couple taking a load of wool up to Ten Rivers, the next big market town. Brix explained my ruined face with a whispered story about running away from a purchased marriage, and how her arranged bridegroom had tried to kill me – her *brother*, if you please. The couple agreed to help us, although they clearly believed I was, in fact, a rival bridegroom. I paid out one of my silver coins and spent the next few days reflecting on how uncomfortable it was to pretend to be a brother while two deeply interested men asked you sympathetic questions.

At Ten Rivers, Brix told the next carter that I was her cousin, fallen afoul of moneylenders. We rode with knobby bags of yellow onions up the road to Vasanth, where I spoke up for myself for once and decided to be a cobbler who had got into a barfight.

There was time to talk as we bounced over the roadstones, but we didn't. Brix seemed content to dangle her feet off the back of the cart during the day and hum low songs to herself at night, never tunes that I recognised. She made noises in her sleep, too, fitful, unhappy little sounds that reminded me of my own dreams.

The country around us changed as we patchworked our way up to the coast, from grain fields to hills, and then to a high, rocky scrub land. Brix kept exclaiming about the different landscapes. I've never cared for the look of the scrub land. It's dry, and the dirt is the wrong colour, pale and chalky and full of strange, gritty seashells. When I said so, she called me stupid. Our relationship, apparently, was getting better.

After about a week we began to smell salt on the air, and then one morning, sharp pinnacles rose on the horizon and we saw Ri Dana.

'It's pretty,' Brix said.

This time I agreed. Almost anything can be pretty from the right distance. From far away, Ri Dana's slender towers and rounded walls looked like elegant black filigree, as though someone had dropped a wrought-iron crown in front of the white cliffs. I had been all of fourteen last time I had been inside the city, but as I recalled it wasn't so pretty up close.

Our cart arrived at the wall as evening fell, and Brix and I jumped down before it took its load of apples to be inspected by the duke's revenue officer. We stood in a string of travellers waiting to pass through the nearest of the city's seven gates. The line inched along. As we drew closer to the wall, I could hear the bored voices of the pair of militia-men who stood at the gate questioning those entering.

Where are you travelling from? And your business here? Did you see anyone unusual on the road? A man and a woman; the man in a robe, the woman wearing a shirt and trousers stolen from a Temples vestment room. Wanted for the murder of a priest.

'Step out of the line,' Brix whispered, at my elbow. 'Quick, while they're talking to that woman. Don't draw attention.' She turned sideways to walk into the twilight. I followed her.

When we had moved far enough along the curve of the wall to be out of sight of the gate, I stripped off my robe and stood there in just my shirt, trousers and tunic.

'Maybe at one of the other gates,' I said. 'There are six more.'

'You're not thinking of still going into that place?' Brix was looking miserably at her own clothes – which clearly *were* modified Temples vestments, now that I'd had my attention drawn to them.

'I don't have a choice,' I said.

'That's mad. You're mad.' She stared at me. 'They think we killed Halling. They're not going to listen to your version of the story. If they catch you, they'll hang you. What kind of book do you think is worth your life?'

'But it's *his* life,' I blurted, and instantly regretted it.

She froze. 'What?'

My damned hands were shaking again. I wadded my robe into a ball and squeezed it to still them. I had to risk the truth. 'The Guild arrested my grandfather six months ago. For nonstandard incantations and necromancy and every other charge they could think of. I can't find him. I can't help him. But there's an artefact in the temple of Jaern here that he told me to get, and the Guild wants it. If I can find it before they do – if I have something to bargain with–' I paused, but the words were already out. It was the first time I had articulated, even to myself, the temptation that had been throbbing like a splinter in the back of my mind since I'd left the inn.

Brix's eyebrows twitched together. 'He told you to get it to ransom him?'

People will die.

I shook my head, as though that would clear the memory of the bloodstained cabin and Keir's smug grin the first time I had seen him, sitting in a Guildhouse office. Fool that I was, I had tried to offer him a bribe. Keir had tried to stuff a shacklebright spell down my throat.

'They're hurting him,' I said. 'I can't just–' I swallowed, frustration burning in my throat. This was pointless. There was nothing to tell Brix that would keep her with me. Nobody ever stayed with me.

Her hand wrapped over the back of one of mine. 'Think. Let's just ... think for a minute. Maybe there's a way to do this that isn't completely crazy.'

I looked up quickly, startled. 'You're going to help me?'

She fingered the fabric that I held. 'It would be safer if we change how we look. I could borrow your robe, at least long enough to get into the city. We could go in separately.' She rolled her eyes. 'Listen to me, talking like this makes sense.' She took the robe from me and swung it around her own shoulders. It covered her clothes completely, sleeves skimming her knuckles and hem brushing the ground. Instantly, she was a respectable wizard. 'How did they know to look for us in the first place?'

'Keir Esras,' I said. 'Has to be. Keir's the only one who has a reason to pin Halling's death on us, and he's been hounding me since they took Acarius. He probably sent pigeons to all the nearest major Guild-houses. I suppose it was only a matter of time before he decided to ask for help from the militia.' I glanced at her. I didn't want to question this piece of luck, but I couldn't help it. 'Brix, why are you doing this?'

She picked at the uneven thread of a place where I'd darned the sleeve of my robe. 'I know what it's like, not being able to help some-one that you care about.'

'Who—' I began, and then stopped, as a wash of pink travelled across her face. Uneasily, I wondered whether she needed the money for something more important than a ship's passage. 'Thank you.'

She grinned. 'It isn't a present. I don't give people presents.'

'I'll repay you.' I was making the promise to myself as much as I was to her. I had to get Acarius safe. Then I'd figure out a way to clear this debt, even if it killed me.

'That's a given, wizard,' Brix said, quietly. 'But if we're going to work together, you're going to have to learn to take my help.' She made a little shooing motion with her hands. 'Now, move. Show me which way to go.'

Well, at least that was settled. 'Let me scribe a couple of spells, first,' I said.

We entered through the fourth gate, which was manned by a single resentful militia-man who seemed to have a bad back and a determination not to work any harder than he had to. He smiled respectfully at wizard-Brix as she crossed under the gate, but was scowling and muttering a saint-chant when I approached a minute or so later.

'Filthy spelldogs,' he said, looking in the direction she'd taken. 'I hate 'em, trailing poison everywhere they go, dragging djinn-bloods into the city. The wizards' slaves can spoil your luck, you know, just by touching you.'

'Damn wizards,' I said, and hurried after Brix. White cobblestones edged with black walls opened before us, blue-plastered buildings crammed along streets that spread from the gate like the spokes of a half-wheel. Above us to the west, the inner wall surrounded the high ground of the city and the roots of the blackstone towers that dominated the skyline. I joined Brix as, around us, people rushed to get home before night fell and it became dangerous to be abroad.

'What a narrow-minded pig,' she muttered, as we moved away from the gate.

I shrugged. 'Wizards more or less deserve it.'

'Maybe, but Tirnaal aren't bad luck. They don't have djinn blood.' She crossed her arms. '*Nobody* has djinn blood. Djinn aren't real.'

'You're an expert on the Tirnaal?' I had been trying to get Ri Dana's geography straight in my mind, and being yanked into conversation again was disorientating. 'I was an idiot, then, explaining them to you after the mess with Pavel. I've never even seen a Tirnaal slave – wouldn't know where to find one outside of Genereth. You should have told me to shut up.'

'I met a couple of them working for Temples.' Her cheeks flared crimson. 'And they're not all slaves, you know, there's plenty living free in the provinces – they just don't flaunt their ink in front of everyone. There's probably some in this godsforsaken city, passing back and forth in front of the pig at the gate every day. They don't look different than anybody else. All they would have to do is keep their heads down and avoid the notice of wizards.' She cocked an eyebrow at me. 'A bit like *you* do.'

'Well, I hope it works better for them than it does for me.' The scent of a hundred boiling dinners wafted past me, mingled with dust and spices, blood and sweat. A puff of another odour made both of us halt.

Brix wrinkled her nose. 'What is that stink?'

'Clifftown.' I remembered that much – anyone who's seen Ri Dana's slum does not forget it. I pointed to the east, where ramshackle dwellings were carved into the crumbling limestone cliffs that plunged towards the sea. 'You can smell it at low tide. Luckily I don't think we have to go that way.'

I struck off down a narrow by-street. Phosphorescent witchfire lichen started to glimmer to life in the gutters as we moved past, ghostly plumes of pale green and blue that curled upwards into the dark to light the main thoroughfares. The best witchfire had been seeded long ago, when Ri Dana was still a jewel of the old Daine empire, sending treasure across the sea to the Silver Court and its king. In those days, the governor had demanded lichen-light woven in the shapes of fruit trees, rose bowers and, occasionally, a beautiful man or woman. Now the Daine lords had been gone for three generations, and the elaborate patterns they favoured had mostly been replaced by simple, easily-replicated stripes and cross-hatches. Thus all empires end, I suppose.

'You do know where we're going, don't you?' Brix said, as the sinuous green light curled around her ankles. She was somehow managing to watch both me and the lichen as we moved. It made it difficult to look like I knew what the hells I was doing.

'I haven't been here since I was fourteen,' I said. 'I'm remembering as fast as I can.' All I could recall from the trip with Acarius was that we'd met one of his friends – Lorican, presumably – in a pub, and the pub had a sign that looked like a dancing woman.

I knew Ri Dana was divided into three districts: the Spires, the Cobbles and Clifftown. The Spires was for Daine-descended lords and ladies, owners of the successful wool export ships, or merchants in silk and cinnamon. They did not, of course, associate with those from the whiterock shanties of Clifftown. But anyone could visit the Cobbles' ale-houses and pleasure halls, from nobles seeking vice to cliff-dwellers selling it. It made sense as a starting point – I hoped.

By the time we got to the cluster of inns and less reputable establishments on Jinsleet Street, at the heart of the Cobbles, the spells on my arms were itching and I was starting to lose optimism. Rows of shuttered buildings hulked around us, none of them familiar. There were six taverns, but only one with a sign that had a dancing woman painted on it.

When we entered, the low-ceilinged taproom was packed full and thick with smoke, liquor and a fume of old sweat. Everyone goggled at us as we entered. As if that wasn't enough, three youths in the blue robes of Guild apprentices huddled over their drinks at a back table. We had to cross the room to get to the bar. Wondering whether the Guildhouse here had my description was bad enough, but the apprentices were unlikely to miss Brix, wearing my wizard's robe, looking like an out-of-town colleague. What if they decided to try to chat with her?

Nothing for it but to bull forwards. I slapped my hand down on the bar to get the tavern-keeper's attention, and immediately realised my mistake. I yanked it back and grimaced at my palm, trying to figure out what sticky mess I'd touched. Beer? Mashed fruit? It didn't smell quite bad enough to be vomit.

'Aye?' The barman turned from where he had been filling two pottery mugs from a keg against the wall. He was in his late forties or early fifties, whipcord-thin, with dark hair braided into a long pigtail down his back. All in all, he was not my idea of a barman. Barmen should be portly and comforting. 'You want something?'

I *wanted* to ask him what the goo was that I'd found on the bar. Instead I scrubbed my palm on my trousers and tried to look non-threatening. 'My colleague and I would like dinner,' I said. 'And information. We're looking for a man named Lorican – used to run this tavern years ago. Have you heard of him?'

'Colleague, is it?' The barman's dark eyes studied Brix's robe briefly, impassive. 'We have bread and cheese for two pence or lamb and barley for five.'

Looking non-threatening was beginning to seem like a mistake. 'Don't you think that's a bit high, for a tavern dinner?'

'I've already been serving that useless pack of apprentices all evening,' he said. 'If you Guildies are going to keep parking members here to eat and drink and drive away my usual patrons, then that's the price for a dinner.'

Brix elbowed me. 'It's fine. We'll take the bread and cheese, and a couple of cups of stout.' She flashed the barman a smile. 'We're sorry our Guildmates have been trouble. We're happy to pay a little extra to make up for it. I'm sure it's hard to remember things like names if you're run off your feet serving difficult customers.'

He didn't smile back. 'What's this Lorican done, that the Guild is paying for news of him?'

'Nothing,' I said. 'I just want to talk to him.'

'Aye,' he said, doubtfully, and went through a doorway some ten feet away to what was presumably the kitchen.

'You can give him a silver coin if you have to,' Brix said.

'Sure.' I dug through my bag for a couple of coppers, avoiding her eyes.

'Here.' The barman returned and held out our food, which apparently did not come with the dignity of plates – two thick slabs of bread with equally thick hunks of pale cheese balanced precariously on top. I put two coppers on the bar.

Brix's face had gone dangerously empty. She grabbed the food and headed for a table in one corner. The conversation in the rest of the room had picked up again, making what would have been a comforting backdrop if it hadn't been for the table of Guildie apprentices, who were stealing glances at Brix and her robe, whispering among themselves. As if that wasn't bad enough, the runes on my arms were passing from itching to pain.

'Your stout,' the barman said. 'That'll be three more pence.'

'I don't want it,' I said. 'That was a mistake.'

He smiled, unamused. 'Look, my lad, I don't want your bribe, but I've already drawn your drinks.' He pushed two pottery mugs at me. 'I can't put them back into the keg, and I don't fancy drinking them myself. As far as I'm concerned, you ordered it, and you'll pay for it or I'll know the reason why.'

I fished out my last coppers and dropped them in his hand before grabbing the beer and going after Brix. The mugs were over-full – you had to give the barman credit for giving honest portions – and liquid slopped on to my hands. I put the cups down, sat and licked the spilled beer off my finger. I couldn't look directly at her.

'Gods, I'm a soft-hearted fool.' Brix's hands were moving in quick, angry fidgets, crumbling her bread. 'You told me that story outside, and I actually bought it. I actually believed you were trying to save somebody's life.'

'I wasn't lying,' I said. 'Not about that.'

'I came all the way here with you and all along you were–' She snorted, her jaw working. 'You don't have any money at all, do you? I can't believe I was so stupid.'

'Just *listen* to me. I don't have the money right now, but I'm not going back on our agreement. I'm not—' I stopped and frowned at my finger. Something in the beer had made my tongue go numb.

'No, you don't get to tell me to listen.' It was a violent whisper, jagged with pain. 'You don't deserve that from me.'

I swallowed my retort. There was no time to explain or apologise. 'So punish me later. At the moment, we're in trouble.'

Her face went blank. 'Why?'

'The beer's tainted.' I pushed one mug towards her, keeping my voice as low as I could. 'Probably a drug or a poison of some kind. Don't drink it.'

She touched her little finger to the surface of the beer, tasted it carefully and made a face. 'Someone trying to collect the bounty? Maybe they're trying to knock you out, so you can't cast a spell.'

'Could be. We have to get out of here, though gods know how we're going to do it without making anybody suspicious.' I took a deep breath. 'I've got spells scribed, so we'll try to walk out. If something happens, I'll make a nuisance of myself and you run away, as fast as you can. Understand?'

She stared at me for a second, then stood up, leaned across the table and gave me a hard, ringing slap across the mouth.

The patrons' raucous talk stilled. Every eye in the place was on her.

'I've had enough of this, you little cheat,' she said, in a voice loud enough to carry across the room. 'You bring me here with false promises and then you expect me to be understanding when you get caught? What else have you lied about?' Brix's cold eyes held mine for a moment longer. 'I'm leaving, and I don't want to see you again.'

'Wait,' I said, my mouth still tingling from the blow. 'Let me—'

'No. Leave me alone, prick.' Brix spun on her heel and made for the door. A scattering of chuckles followed her as she exited.

'Shouldn't have kept a doxy, ye wicked boy,' called one old man in a corner, and the room erupted in laughter.

Hot blood rushed up the back of my neck. I sat there with my untouched beer in front of me, as red as if I really was a philandering partner. I made myself count to three hundred. I would have counted to five hundred, but the Guildies got up and went to the bar to pay their tab. If Brix was waiting outside, I didn't want them to catch her unawares. I made my way out, ignoring the amused glances of the patrons.

Once outside the tavern, I crossed the street and halted, shivering in the dark between two houses, breathing hard and searching for human shapes against the cobblestones.

Brix wasn't there.

'Shit,' I whispered. 'Good work, Corcoran. You've driven her away for good, now, and it serves you right. Idiot.' Waves of sticky, familiar shame rolled over me. Why had I allowed myself to hope she'd wait for me? I wasn't usually this foolish.

Someone cleared their throat. I froze.

'It was an act, wizard,' Brix said, 'to get us out of the pub without making them suspicious. But it did serve you right.' It took me a moment to find her silhouette, standing just outside the pale light of the lichen to my left. 'What are we doing now?'

We? Whatever happened to *leave me alone, prick*?

'*I'm* waiting to see if the Guildies follow me out,' I said. 'If they don't, I still need to find Lorican. *You'll* do what you think is best.' I studied the row of buildings on either side of the tavern. If I could get behind it, I could try to use a divination spell to see if Lorican was anywhere in the building. 'There's got to be an alleyway, doesn't there?'

'Are you contemplating breaking into the same place we just got out of?'

'What do you care?' I said. 'I'm a liar, remember? Or are you saying you're still willing to get me into the temple?'

'You still owe me something, if you've forgotten,' she said. 'Forty silver coins. I'm stuck in this city that I know nothing about because of you, and I'm not going to let you die or run off until I've been paid. I reckon that the surest way for you to have the money to pay me is to get you into the temple so you can steal something, in addition to whatever it is that you want. Am I right?'

'Yes.' I caught myself before I could flinch. I had no idea whether there would be valuables to steal. The important part was getting into the temple, getting the artefact for Acarius and finding a way to rescue him. Clearing my debt had to remain secondary, no matter how much I wanted Brix and her shrewd eyes and her left hook out of my life.

I started walking, and after a moment she followed, catching my wrist as we made our way through the dark. It didn't take us long to find a gap in the brick walls. The alley hadn't been seeded with lichen, however, leaving nothing but starlight to see by. I stopped, blind and overwhelmed by the eye-watering stench. Apparently, the alley had been used as a privy by every drunk the tavern had ever hosted.

'I don't suppose you have a plan?' Brix said. 'Do you *ever* know what you're going to do next?'

In the dark heart of the alley in front of me, a blue flame spurted to life.

'We're going to get into a fight,' I said. 'Duck.'

SEVEN

They were apprentices, just kids, and ignorant. I knew that much from their robes, the way they stood three abreast and also from their stupid choice of first spell. In a wizards' duel, speed wins. These clods chose to cast simple illumination, a tongue of floating blue fire that would hover where they told it to. Of course they meant to send it towards us, but in the split second it took me to push my sleeves up, it lit *them* up beautifully.

I lifted on to my toes and pronounced the runes written on my left arm. They activated with a sizzling sound against my skin – pain, certainly, but the kind of pain I live for. Gouts of emerald fire burst from my fingertips.

'Might want to run away, children,' I said, and sent a bolt of green at the middle wizard. It hit and enveloped her, cutting off her incantation mid-syllable. She hit her knees and began heaving up her guts, splattering everything she'd eaten in the last ten hours or so on the pavement. Nausea spells have so much utility.

I couldn't keep myself from smiling. Even though magic hurts, there's something about it like poetry, or music. A week without spells of any sort on the road had left me lonely for it.

'You're under arrest!' It was the one on the right, trying to shout threateningly. And gods, his voice was cracking under the stress. How old could he possibly be? Seventeen? Eighteen?

He put his hands together and a beam of violet pulsed from between them. I dropped to the ground and waited, the hair on my body prickling as the spell missed me. That's the downside to a paralysis spell: you have to aim it. A confusing choice, if they wanted to arrest me. Paralysis can stop a subject's breathing – it's a spell for killing.

The second string of runes, the one on the inside of my arm, left my mouth as rapidly as I could get them out. Either the Guildies wanted to murder me and Brix, or they were so naïve they didn't know that what they were doing *could* murder us. I didn't want to kill them, but I wasn't going to die for them, either. Slipknives it was, then.

The weight of the spell settled on me, and I grunted. The shielding runes were holding, though, better than I had thought they would. I got my feet under me and rose to a crouch, one hand pressed to the slick damp of the cobblestones.

The light that left my hand was white, writhing along the pavement like a snake. It took the form of a set of spinning blades, chopping their way towards the apprentices. I held my hands out, focusing on controlling the incantation's direction. A cramp started at the base of my neck, tightening into a shrieking muscle spasm that jerked my shoulders backwards.

Concentrate. I kept my eyes fixed on my opponents and pushed the slipknives towards the one on the right, the one who had tried to paralyse me.

He danced to avoid it, failed and yelped. The sound came to me muted, as though I was submerged. Bright blood flew in little arcs from his legs and feet. He slipped and stumbled backwards.

I let the spell end and breathed again. Maybe now they'd have the sense to run.

The bleeding one and the puking one both looked like they were having second thoughts. The third kid must have been the one running the illumination orb, and it seemed to take his full attention.

There wouldn't be any additional casting from him, not unless he let the alley go dark.

'Come on!' I shouted. 'Run away! Don't – be – stupid!' My right arm was already tingling, as though the runes wanted to be called up . . . alas, I knew it was just the noxious effect of the paint. I'd have sores the next day.

The bleeding one, apparently a resourceful chap, dipped his finger in his own blood and began writing on the pavement. I glanced behind me to see Brix lying on the pavement, unmoving, eyes wide and glassy. The paralysis spell I had dodged must have struck her.

I didn't have time to feel the panic that sliced through me. The spell paralysed limbs first, then moved inwards towards the organs. Soon it would be tightening around her lungs. I only had a few minutes to end it.

Written on my right arm was my own invention, a combination of fire and illusion. It would hurt, both them and me, but I had no choice. I strode towards them, pronouncing it as I went.

The bleeding one managed to get his spell off, a simple ball of red force that flew at me like a hammer. It caught me in the chest and knocked the breath out of me. They started running towards me just as I got my wind back and spat out the last six syllables.

My arms flew wide. From between them blasted a sheet of flame. The hair on my forearms singed off.

As the fire licked at the apprentices, I heard them screaming and I knew it had worked. To them, the illusion would make it look like I had been consumed with my own spell. I stood, frozen, arms stretched out. All of my mind was bent on controlling the magic, on building the tower of fire and death, on frightening their wits away. Their robes burned and they ran, slapping at the flames, cursing by the name of every god in the pantheon.

A bead of sweat rolled down my spine. It was hot; not all of the fire was trickery.

I waited, holding the wall of fire between me and them, even though I could feel the shielding runes starting to degrade. If they looked back, I had to keep the illusion strong. I reached out with the spell for their minds. One of them *would* look back. Someone always did.

It was the one who had been running the illumination spell, just before they turned the corner to get out of the alley. The orange glow from the flames outlined his face as I gave the spell one final push.

Boom.

He stumbled to his knees, then clawed his way to his feet and sprinted away from the explosion that had rocked the alley . . . in his mind, anyway.

I held the illusion for a count of thirty after the last one had disappeared from my view. Then I let it drop and ran to Brix.

She hadn't moved, but was still breathing, barely. I kneeled beside her and sorted through my satchel with trembling fingers.

'I'm sorry.' My voice was ragged in my ears. I could hardly see. Where were my paints?

I finally found the case of vials and had to scribble the same stupid illumination spell that the apprentices had used on to the pavement next to her head. Once I had light, I opened her robe, searching frantically for enough skin to work with. I tried to preserve her modesty, but I had to write the runes where they would do some good. I unlaced the collar of her shirt and then stopped, startled.

Dark blue tattoos spread under her collarbones and out towards her shoulders. They were runes, rows upon rows of them, and nobody should have been able to carry that many spells without the toxicity burning through to their bones.

'You're Tirnaal,' I said. Her eyes were fixed on the spot behind me. She couldn't look at me, had lost even that much control. 'I'm sorry,' I said, again, hurriedly pulling her shirt up to cover the runes. 'It's going to be all right.'

I uncorked the vial of green paint and started scribing across her shoulders, above the delicate edges of her collarbone.

There's no way to deactivate a specific spell, but you can ruin the ley – the ability for spells to take hold – in a small area, for a limited amount of time. If I did that, the paralysis would break. With the wizard who had cast it gone, Brix wouldn't have to worry about the spell coming back. Of course, wrecking the ley would deactivate *all* the magic in the alleyway, including the protective sigils on me. Still, I didn't see what choice I had.

The ley-breaker required thirty-six characters. I had written thirty when the knife pricked the soft skin beneath the right side of my jaw.

'Don't move,' said a man's voice, 'or I'll kill you.'

'Let me finish,' I said. 'Then you can kill me.'

A soft laugh, and a hand took hold of my left ear. 'I saw what you did to those apprentices just now, wizard. You think I'm going to let you write what you want? Get your hands up, where I can see them.'

I lifted my hands out away from my body, wet paintbrush still between my fingers. I couldn't see Brix's chest moving anymore. 'Please,' I said. My chest heaved as though I was trying to breathe for both of us. 'Please. She's dying.'

Silence. I've never heard one so long. Finally, the hand released my ear and took a grip on my collar. 'Finish, then. But watch what you say – my knife is quicker than your tongue.'

I finished the string of runes and pronounced them. They flared with blinding light. The ley-breaker was taking hold, and it was much stronger than it should have been. Something about her was . . . what, amplifying the magic? Making it go faster?

My protective sigils went dark and then crumbled, going cold against my skin one by one. A wave of torment crushed me into the ground as the toxicity from all of the spells I had used in the fight roiled through my gut, poison pulsing up my spine.

A stench worse than sewage surged through me. It was in my mouth, crawling down my throat, stretching to the very edges of my being.

No.

I think I said no.

I know I didn't moan until after I saw Brix sit up and gasp for air. I didn't start to seize until I had fallen forwards into her arms.

Most of the time – when the gods are feeling merciful, I suppose – I don't remember what happens during a seizure. But occasionally I'm aware enough to see myself, as though I am a hovering outsider, watching the thrashing mess on the floor, the cost of all my magical cleverness brought home to me.

Brix held my arching body as best as she could, and screamed abuse at the man who had been standing behind me. He just stood there, knife in hand, watching. I couldn't make out exactly what Brix was saying, couldn't get past the buzz in my ears.

Eventually the gabble coming from their mouths resolved itself into speech.

'I'll kill you.' Brix spat the words. 'Fix whatever you did to him, or I'll kill you. Who in the hells are you, anyway?'

'I didn't do anything,' he said.

I tried to tell her it was all right, to tell her what the solution was, but my lips, heavy and far away from me, didn't move. All that came out was a thick sound.

Her breath puffed across my face – she must have been just inches from me. 'Corcoran? Can you hear me?'

'Lor . . .' My lips went numb again.

'What did you do?' she shouted, presumably at him. 'If he dies—'

Oh, Neyar's pups. This was getting out of hand. I grabbed frantically for consciousness, for the will to make my mouth do what I wanted it to.

'Not – daying–' That wasn't right. I heaved myself away from Brix and sat up under my own power. 'Dying. Not.' I concentrated. 'Lorican,' I said. It took what seemed like another couple of minutes to get my neck to turn my head so I could see him. Or, at least, the smudge on the darkness that I thought was him. Damn ley-breaker had wrecked my illumination spell, too. Or there was something wrong with my vision ... or both. 'Corcoran – Gray. Acarius ... grandson. Pleased ...' *Just a few more words.* This was like chewing mud. *Come on.* 'Meet you.'

'Gods,' whispered Lorican.

Nobody sounds that gutted when they *don't* believe something. I had him. I let my eyes shut.

'No. Don't.' Brix was close to me again. Cold fingertips were on my temples, pushing my hair back. 'No, Gray, you're going to stay awake.'

She cupped her hands under my chin. Gods, that felt good. I had to sleep, though. If I could sleep, I wouldn't have to feel the poison as it worked its way through me.

'Sorry,' I mumbled.

EIGHT

At some point they got me back inside the tavern through a kitchen door. All I really remember is getting hit with the stench of stale beer and puking on Lorican's shoes, which I found satisfying. It was his fault, after all, that I'd been in that alley in the first place.

We wound up in a little white-walled room off the kitchen, where Lorican said he slept. The closest thing to a bed that he could provide was a cot near the fire. I stretched out, grateful to be horizontal. Brix sat in a chair across the hearth from me, bolt upright, arms crossed.

'Right.' I heard Lorican's voice, vaguely, as though someone had packed my ears with wool. 'I'll close the pub, and then we can talk.'

I waited until his footsteps had faded, then got up on to one elbow and peered at Brix. 'Are you all right? Breathing back to normal?'

'Yes.' Something strange rippled through her voice, like a vein of gold through quartz. 'You saved me – again.'

'Sorry.' I had already said that, but it felt like I should repeat it. She didn't *seem* all right.

'It would be easier if you weren't, Gray,' she murmured. 'I've never met a good man before. I'm not sure what to do with you.'

'Hells, I am not a good man.' I let my elbow slip out from under me and closed my eyes.

75

When I woke up, it was daylight. Brix wasn't there. Instead Lorican sat across from me, eating a bowl of something that smelled like fish stew. When I stirred, he straightened.

'Awake?' he said.

'No, talking in my sleep, with my eyes open.' The sarcasm was impolitic, I admit. But I was tired, and I hate it when people ask stupid questions.

Lorican leaned back in his chair. I got the impression I was being studied, and that it wasn't turning out very well for me. 'That thing on your wrist,' he said. 'I didn't think they could be faked.'

I ran my thumb across the silver sigil and felt my pulse throb beneath it. It was yet another thing that Acarius and I had disagreed about. It made it easier to find work, safer. Acarius still hadn't wanted me to get it, had insisted that it would only make the charges worse if the Guild got hold of me.

'They can't, really,' I said. 'A Guild wizard could tell the difference between this and a real one, given enough time. I just don't give them time.'

'Aye, I saw that.' He ran his knuckles across the scrubby beard on his chin. 'You fight like Acarius. I should have guessed you were related to him, but the tattoo threw me. Dangerous, that magic of yours.' He picked up a stick from the bucket of kindling beside the fireplace and used it to push the unlaced cuff of my sleeve upwards. My forearm was a mess, smeared with dried blood and the remnants of alchemical paint. 'Hurts, I would think.'

I batted the stick away. 'Sometimes.' I wasn't going to get any more sleep; my nerves were too jumpy. I sat up and held still for a few seconds, waiting for the dizziness. It didn't come. So the shielding runes had taken a majority of the poison, before I had deactivated them. Interesting. I hadn't done anything different when I had scribed them, so the simplest explanation for their extra effectiveness was ... Brix. Just like she had made the ley-breaker stronger. I really needed to talk to her. 'Where's the woman who was with me?'

'I don't think we're done talking,' Lorican said.

I didn't like this. Acarius thought Lorican was reliable, but the old man was in prison, and *someone* had helped Keir capture him. Of course, if Lorican had been wanting to hand me over to the Guild, it didn't make much sense for him to have taken the knife away from my neck. But then again, I had an idea that Keir and the Guild proper weren't always working in unison. The Examiner General and his group of conspirators probably weren't all that interested in taking me to trial, if their goal really was to get out from under the Charter and seize power. It was always possible that Lorican was just supposed to keep me in one place until I could be neutralized.

I got to my feet. 'And I don't think I care for people who poison my beer.'

He grinned. 'You're the one with a spelldog mark on your wrist, showing up in my pub panicking about a five-pence bill and asking questions. You smelled wrong. I had to have time to find out who you were.' He stretched long legs out in front of him, crossing booted ankles. The boots had cutwork tops. 'It was trinity syrup, by the way,' he said. 'It wouldn't have killed you, just put you to sleep long enough for me to ask around. And then you gave me a busy night for my trouble anyway, so I think we're even.'

I shook out my shoulders, irritation flickering in my muscles. 'Can we stop this? I'm not a Guild spy. The only reason I'm here is that Acarius said you could help me get to the temple of Jaern. If you won't, then I'll leave. It's as simple as that.'

Lorican hadn't moved. 'They looked for Acarius' friends for weeks after they caught him, you know.'

It took a moment for it to sink in. 'Are you implying that I would work for the Guild rats against my own grandfather?'

'Men have betrayed their own blood before,' he said. 'Besides, you wouldn't be working against him, necessarily. Maybe they offered you a deal, promised to let him go if you give them something they want.' He shrugged. 'Desperate people believe thin lies.'

This wasn't how I had pictured this conversation going. My lead was slipping through my fingers. If Lorican let me down, it was done. Ended. Acarius would die. I hadn't even really *asked* him for help yet, and he already seemed poised to refuse.

'I . . . am desperate.' I stared at the fire, my fear slowly draining away into something darker. 'I could disable you, I suppose.' The words came out flat, quiet. 'Paralysis. Not a demanding spell, as you saw; that boy could manage it. I wouldn't have much time, but I work fast. With the proper runes scribed across your forehead, I don't suppose your memories would be too difficult to crack.' The flames twisted like dancers, caressing the log they were destroying. I kept my eyes on them, kept my mind on the problem. 'But that would likely leave you mindblown. I can't decide whether that's something I could stomach.'

But I knew, as I said it, that I couldn't. A mindblown person isn't a person at all. They're just empty flesh, with no wit or memories to animate them. It would have meant taking a life, as surely as if I'd cut his throat.

'Easy now, brat.' He stood and put his bowl on the mantelpiece. There was a tone in his voice I couldn't identify, a kind of gentleness that didn't belong. 'Acarius saved my life. I owe him a blood debt, and that's something I take seriously. You won't get to the temple without my help. The Erranter that live around it don't like outsiders.'

'You're Erranter?' I said, frowning. He certainly had the look of one of the Walking People, with elaborate braids and a broad, flat nose. But it didn't make sense that he was so settled. Erranter typically worshipped the sun-goddess Linna, Lady of Change, and they believed personal property was mostly a snare for the sinful. I had never heard of one impious enough to own a tavern. 'How in the hells did you meet Acarius?'

'As far as the city militia are concerned, I'm Erranter enough to shake down twice a month,' he said, dryly. 'Acarius and I met a long time ago, travelling. I had bad luck, he gave me my life back, and that's all you need to know. The point is, I'll help you. I just had to be sure of you.'

I let my breath out, disorientated by the sudden wave of relief that burst over me. 'Brat. Why can't anyone ever call me by my name?'

Lorican made an odd sound, something between a cough and a sneeze. 'Gods. Didn't realise it was a touchy subject.'

Was the bastard *laughing* at me? I flushed. 'It isn't. If we're done here, I want to talk to Brix – where is she?'

He hooked one thumb at a door across the room from us. 'The kitchen, washing her hair or some such. Said she got muck in it, during that tussle in the alley. By the way, you're Acarius' grandson, but who is she?' He raised an eyebrow. 'Certainly not your *colleague*. She's no wizard, Guild or otherwise.'

'A friend,' I said. It was the only thing I could think of that was vague enough. 'She has special knowledge. She's helping me.'

He crossed his arms. 'You'll want to be sure of your friends. The Guildhouse in Ri Dana seats thirty-five wizards. Those boys you let live will have told their masters some story, even if they think you're dead. If the Guild is looking for you the way they were looking for Acarius–'

'They won't find me,' I said.

'Why did you let them go?' He cocked his head sideways, curious. 'Three rats attack you in an alley, you're clearly their match, so why not finish them? Because it seems to me that guarantees they *will* find you.'

Because they had been so afraid. Because *I* had been so afraid. Because I didn't want to be that sort of person. But showing feelings was always a mistake. It just meant displaying a bruise that the other person could push on.

'Because they were just kids,' I said, 'and stupid kids at that, and because the story they will report is that a rogue wizard blew himself up behind your alley. That illusion I did was a good one – you saw it yourself. It's unlikely that they'll come searching for my body, I think.'

'Aye,' Lorican said. 'So you say. But every fool knows that wizards lie.'

I forced my jaw to relax. 'Then what's the point of asking me questions?'

He smiled. 'No point at all. Although I would like to know more about what Acarius thought I could do for you. Why do you want to go to the old temple?'

'He seemed to think you could help me get an artefact of the god Jaern,' I said. 'I imagine you'd find such a thing in a temple, although if you happen to know a good shop –'

'I was afraid of that.' Even the hostile smile faded now. 'After the trouble last year Acarius said nobody would need to go there ever again.' He crossed his arms. 'What changed?'

'Last year?' I said. 'What happened last year?'

Lorican's eyes narrowed. 'Didn't he tell you?'

'I –' I bit down on the inside of my cheek, focused on the sensation of pressure and the taste of blood, stuffed all the grief and guilt and anger into a box in the centre of me until I could get the words out steadily. 'I wasn't home for most of last year.'

Lorican waited, with the patient, bland expression of a man who knows a liar when he sees one. I had no idea what to say next. If I pressed him for details, he'd expect me to explain why Acarius and I hadn't been speaking, and I couldn't bring myself to do that. I was a fool and a coward, but I couldn't expose myself that way in front of someone I'd only just met. I'd have to find some other way to get the information.

Eventually, Lorican stirred himself. 'Well. There's stew in the kitchen. Don't take too long with your girl. If we're to go to the Deeptown temple, we've preparations to make, and I've got to see that the taproom is closed up properly.'

'She's not my girl,' I said.

'I see.' He gave me a look that he had probably given hundreds of unconvincing people while he filled their cups. 'Just be quick, brat.' He disappeared into the taproom.

I made my way into the tidy kitchen, where a pot of fish stew was indeed simmering on the hob. There wasn't much furniture beyond a table full of carrots and turnips in various stages of preparation. Brix was still in my robe, drying her hair in front of the fire, bent over at the waist.

Not my girl. I wasn't even sure she was my friend, at the moment.

I knocked on the door jamb. 'Can I come in?'

She straightened, flipping her hair backwards. 'Aren't you already in?'

I pulled the door shut behind me, but didn't advance towards her. I couldn't figure out how to begin. She watched me, thoughtful.

'What is it?' Her tone had a familiar edge in it. I had just been doing the same thing with my own voice when I was talking to Lorican, trying to sound at ease and unafraid. I wondered if I'd failed this utterly.

'Last night, when I had to write the ley-breaker.' There was probably some delicate way to say this, but I couldn't find it. 'There was – I *had* to scribe it near your throat. I promise I wasn't looking, wasn't being – I wasn't–' What was it about talking to her that made me sound so damn unconvincing? I closed my eyes briefly. 'Your ink.' The words spilled out all in a rush. 'A binding spell and speakfar, from what I saw. They're tattooed on to you, and you're not debilitated by them, so that has to mean that you're Tirnaal. Doesn't it?'

The silence changed. It almost hummed. Brix was looking at me as though she could see through to the wall behind me. 'I don't think you know what you're saying.'

'I've heard that Tirnaal carry magic, but they don't use it,' I said. 'I don't understand why. But I know that when I cast and you've been touching me, the magic behaves differently – the effects are accelerated, and stronger. I know Tirnaal don't sicken from magic, or at least that's what the rumours say. And I know that some wizards buy Tirnaal slaves and use them, somehow, to absorb the toxicity of their spells.'

'And do you know what that feels like?' She didn't raise her voice. It would have been more reassuring if she did. 'To have someone pour all their poison into you? The Guild slavers snatched us, my baby sister and me, in the street outside our house, right in the city. They did that when I was thirteen, wizard. Stolen from our mother to be tools. Not even livestock, or pets. They didn't care that what they did was illegal, didn't even think of us like we were alive, just used us so they could keep doing their spells without having to pay the consequences. It *hurts*. We lose *ourselves*. Do you know about that?'

My eyes stung. I shook my head. So that was why she needed the money, that was who she had to meet up with. A sister, stuck in a Guildhouse somewhere, drowning in poison and pain. Nausea clawed at my stomach, and for once it had nothing to do with my magic hangover.

'Brix,' I said, carefully, 'I'm not going to –'

'*What?*' She spoke between her teeth. 'Tattoo binding spells on my skin to keep me tied to a prison? Use me so you can keep practising magic without having seizures? Dump sleeping powder in my soup and sell me to Temples for *them* to use?'

'–touch you,' I said. 'Ever again. You won't have to have anything to do with my spells. I'm sorry I didn't know what was happening before. And I'll find a way to get you the money I owe if it kills me. I promise.'

She stared into the fire, blinking hard. After a moment she let out her breath, walked past me and put a carving knife on the table, next to the turnips.

'Great Farran.' I leaned on the table, my knees abruptly wobbly. 'Great dancing Farran, you were going to stab me.'

She went to the hearth and took a pottery bowl off the mantel shelf. 'Do you think you want to eat?'

I thought we had a number of things left to discuss. 'You were going to *stab* me,' I repeated.

'I don't know what I was going to do.' She sounded unsteady. 'I didn't expect–' She filled the bowl with quick, irritated motions and plopped it on the table. 'Eat, wizard.'

'Dammit, that isn't my name.' I shoved the bowl towards her. 'And you're not a servant. I can get my own stupid breakfast.'

She finally met my eyes, searching. After a long moment, the line of her shoulders relaxed a little. 'Corcoran, then,' she said.

'It's Gray,' I said, 'unless you're just insulting me on purpose, now.'

Her mouth softened. I think she would have smiled if Lorican hadn't come banging through the door at that moment as though the hells were behind him.

'Out the back,' he said. 'Now.'

The pair of Guildmasters had evidently come into the pub with a bounty sheet and threats thinly veiled as apologies. According to them, their apprentices had spotted a dangerous fugitive and unwisely confronted him. There had been a sorcerous explosion and they had members asking about it at every tavern. If the unlicensed wizard who'd caused the explosion was alive, he was a serious threat. If he had blown himself up, they insisted the *corpse* could still be a threat, leaking magical toxicity. The Guildmasters had explained, smoothly, that they were worried about Lorican's safety.

'So I told them that I was just as happy to not serve any stinking spelldogs at all,' Lorican said, hustling us down the fourth alley since leaving the tavern, 'and that if they wanted my help finding corpses that probably didn't even exist that they'd have to pay me for their apprentices' bad behaviour.' He snorted. 'They tightened right up when I mentioned money. Wizards always think they're the only skull in the room that isn't empty.'

Which probably wasn't meant as a poke at me, but still felt like one. He had us trotting down side streets and around corners too quickly. Things were out of control. 'Stop,' I said. 'Where are we going?'

'The temple of Jaern. Isn't that what you said Acarius wanted?' Lorican pulled us down a lane that I had mistaken for a crack between two buildings, half-jogging.

We were strung out in an awkward line with Brix behind me. I was having a difficult time keeping up with him on the slippery cobbles, and shivers of unease kept crawling up my body.

'Wait,' I said.

'The spelldogs aren't going to actually go away, brat,' Lorican said, without looking back at me. 'They're going to go find my landlord in the Spires and get permission, and then they'll go through the alley looking for your bones whether I say they can or not.'

I halted. 'I know, but just wait, dammit.' The claustrophobic closeness of the houses rising on either side of me was making my head spin. I put a hand on one of the flaking blue plaster walls and threw my weight on to my good knee. 'Just let me think. If the Guild knows I'm in town, and there are thirty-five of them, then sauntering into Temples in broad daylight is stupid. They were working with the priests in Fenwydd – they could be here, too.'

Lorican shifted from foot to foot as thought the cobbles were burning him. 'You said the temple of Jaern, Acarius' temple.'

I felt like there were eyes on me, with as much nervous clarity as a bird being stalked by a fox. Almost worse was the nagging sense, at the back of my mind, that I should have known what it *meant*. I had spent the last twenty minutes purposely lingering at corners, looking for pursuit. There was nobody following me but Brix, and she was focused on keeping up with Lorican and not wasting much attention on me. Feeling like you were observed without anybody actually observing you was a symptom. I should have known what it indicated.

I pressed my knuckles against one eyebrow, trying to force myself into coherence. 'So?'

'So that's not at Temples square. There isn't a normal temple of Jaern here, just the old one.' Lorican frowned. 'Didn't Acarius tell you?'

He hadn't, of course. Acarius not telling me things was a pattern. But this seemed wrong, charging blindly through the streets on the word of a man that I'd only met a few hours ago.

Out of the corner of my eye I saw Brix edge towards me. 'Gray, what's wrong?'

I glanced upwards, but there were no windows, nobody peering down at us from the roofs of the houses. Indeed, the walls leaned towards each other so steeply that the thin, pale line of sky was barely visible between their ragged eaves. I still felt like someone was staring at me. 'Nothing,' I muttered. 'Let's go.'

Lorican led us through more backstreets than I had known existed in any city. At first I thought the turns were random, meant to confuse pursuit. Then I realised we were heading steadily uphill, towards the Spires. Soon the cobbles changed from white to a dirty grey – they had probably been black at one time, expensive stone that had to be hauled from far away. The houses changed, too, growing grander – no more flaking plaster. These had extra storeys, scrollwork under the eaves and eventually, when we were close to the Spires, gilding around the doors.

The inner wall stretched above us, topped with black, carved spikes that soared upwards, capped in sparkling brass. After a long time weaving our way along it, Lorican came to a halt and motioned for me and Brix to stay where we were, crouched in the narrow space between a house and the warm black rock. He inched forwards along the building, towards the street it faced. He only stayed at the opening for a moment before ducking back.

'Hells,' he whispered, crouching beside me. He jerked his chin at the place he'd just vacated. 'Where did they come from?'

I eased myself past him to peer cautiously out at the street, which ran up to a bronze-bound gate. The gate was engraved with rose vines, their spiny thorns as thick as my thumb, and it was open, as it probably had been since the king's ancestors had broken Ri Dana's fortifications and driven the Daine out of Varre. Three Guild wizards stood, chatting easily with each other, inside the boundary that separated the rabble from the Spires.

A fourth wizard was silent, leaning a black-robed shoulder against the gate and staring out at the genteel crowd flowing in and out of the shops that lined the road. Keir Esras was apparently not one for chat.

'It's about damn time,' one of the wizards was saying. 'The king can't even read. Some regulations are necessary, everybody agrees with that, but limiting research so severely is just pure superstition. Next they'll be insisting that magic happens because we drink the blood of babies.'

'Shh.' The wizard standing next to her, a short man with an inadequate scruff of beard, shifted uncomfortably. 'It isn't that I don't agree, but we're on the street, and technically – I mean, if anybody heard you –'

'Technically.' The female wizard spat down on to the cobblestones. 'I'm tired of being afraid of technicalities. Aren't you?'

'Of course, or I'd still be at the Guildhouse with the rest of the Charter-loving sheep,' the bearded one growled. 'But until we're in a more secure position –'

'Shut up,' Keir said, without moving. 'Be observant, be quiet and wait.' He never turned his head, his attention focused on the street that led to the gate. 'They'll be here, soon enough.'

I worked my way hurriedly backwards. *That* was why I had felt watched.

'They've been divining for me,' I whispered. 'I should have known.' Acarius' voice echoed in my head, scolding me for not paying more attention during lessons. I hate divining. It's maddeningly vague, unless you know enough that you don't have to ask the questions in the first place ... and it has an effect on your subject, who, over time, can begin to feel you searching for them. How had Keir managed this kind of precision? And, gods help us, what did they mean, *a more secure position*? I couldn't imagine the Guild leadership risking its position over something as uncertain as open revolt against the king. Keir himself, though ...

'They know we're here?' Lorican's body went tense, poised to flee.

'No, divining doesn't work that way. They probably know which direction we were going – uphill, so the Spires. But if that's the only way through the wall, simple enough to wait for us.' Even so, the Guild shouldn't have been *this* close on my heels. I'd kept ahead of them for six months, so how had their divining technique suddenly got better? I watched the bartender, who was dragging the back of his hand along his forehead, wiping away sweat. How was I going to be able to tell if he was leading me into Keir's arms? 'Lorican, I can't deal with four of them, not by myself. Those are senior wizards and the gods-damned Examiner General. Is there any other way to get into the Spires?'

'We don't have to get into the Spires,' Lorican said, squeezing past Brix and me. 'There's another way down, it's just less convenient. Come on.'

Down? I had questions, but there was no time to ask them. He was moving again, Brix at his heels. I had to bring up the rear as we crept along the sweeping, salt-stained curve of dark stone, away from the sea and towards the centre of the city. None of the buildings actually touched the wall, although some came close.

After ten minutes Lorican stopped beside a squat blackstone building that had probably at one time been a Daine gatehouse or tax office. Its windows were gaping holes, and the whole thing looked like a property that a Spires landlord had simply forgot he owned. Lorican rapped four times on the barred door.

The door swung open. Beyond it yawned darkness. Lorican extended a hand. 'After you, wizard.'

'After me to where?' I said.

'Deeptown,' Lorican said. 'Where else?'

Every instinct I had was screaming at me not to step where I couldn't see. But I knew the menace behind me, and whatever was in front of me couldn't be as dangerous as Keir Esras when he thought the throne was within reach.

I took a breath, and walked into the dark.

NINE

As soon as Lorican and Brix had entered, the door shut and blackness enveloped us.

'Don't move,' whispered Lorican.

'Why not?' I said.

'You're being examined,' he said. 'If you go moving at the wrong time, someone's liable to put a dart in your eye.'

I stood stock still, listening and sniffing the dead, dusty air. 'How can anyone see me well enough to do that?'

Out of the darkness to my left something glimmered green. As I watched, it grew to a flame, lighting up the seamed features of the oldest woman I had ever seen. Her eyes were milky with cataracts, startling in her dark-skinned face. The green fire burned on the end of her extended little finger, as though it was a candle.

'Lorican,' she said, 'what do you think you're doing here? The wizards have been harassing the whole town, the militia is hunting priest-killers and you decide *now* is the moment for a visit home?'

'Paying a blood debt, Lady Mother.' Lorican sounded strained. 'Nothing else I could do. I've taken every precaution I can think of. This one needs to go to the old temple, and I've promised to take him. I couldn't bring him through the door in the Spires. It's being watched.'

She gave a short grunt of acknowledgement. 'That seems very foolish, given what happened to you last year. You're prepared to do what you have to, if your precautions aren't enough?'

There was a short silence, then Lorican spoke again. 'Yes.'

The hair rose on the backs of my arms. 'What is she asking you to promise?'

'Keep your tongue between your teeth,' Lorican hissed.

There was a rustle of fabric and a soft jingle. She was either standing or walking. The green flame huffed out. 'Take them down then, Lorican.'

A click. Someone opened a door ahead of us, letting a flickering light into the space. Lorican pushed past me, catching hold of my wrist and leading me like a blind man.

'Take hold of your girl,' he said. 'It gets a bit dodgy, here.'

I hesitated, glancing back at Brix, but her hand was already brushing my sleeve.

'It's all right,' she said, quietly, using her grip on my shirt to pull herself closer to me. 'You're not casting right now, and anyway, it has to be skin to skin for it to matter.'

A trapdoor opened on to a narrow set of stairs that led downwards. After a while the surface beneath my boots changed from wood to slick rock. Whoever was carrying the lantern walked ahead of Lorican, and I couldn't see them. Just enough light bounced off the walls around me to reveal them as progressively more ancient stonework. We passed a set of leering gargoyles and what must have once been part of a roof or wall.

'Where in the hells are we going?' I said to Lorican. When Acarius had talked about a god's artefact, I had pictured a set of ruins in the fens, or possibly a neglected building in Ri Dana itself. But this wasn't anything so straightforward. Why did the Erranter in Ri Dana have a tunnel under the city? In fact, why was there even a clan based here? Erranter were nomadic by religious imperative, embracing the holiness of change.

He didn't turn, which was probably a wise decision given the speed with which we were descending.

'Under the city,' he said. 'Deeptown and the temple of Jaern, just like you asked. I haven't seen one of the Mothers come herself to guard an entrance in . . . ever. That Guild hunt must be causing problems. You and I are going to have a talk when we stop, brat.'

The tunnel wound on, the steep slope beneath our feet eventually flattening out. The walls, which had initially been so close as to be claustrophobic, widened into a small cavern, still only lit by the bobbing lamp ahead of us.

'What did you promise her?' I said.

'Erranter don't like strangers. They barely tolerate *me*, and I'm their blood. Or I'm close enough, anyway.' Something strange hummed in his voice. 'The old temple doesn't exactly have a reputation for safety. She was asking me to promise to kill you if you turn out to be a risk for the clan.'

'And you *did*?'

'You're not going to risk them, so I won't have to kill you.' His teeth gleamed in the dark. 'Right?'

Finally, the rocks changed. We passed through an archway and stood, blinking, in the midnight kingdom of Deeptown.

It looked like nothing so much as the inside of a castle, a great hall with its windows bricked over. The walls soared away from us into blackness, both above and to each side. Here and there braziers burned like lonely stars, and by their light I saw the village.

There was no other word for it – within the dead greatness all around them, people had built small homes for themselves. Huts made from scraps of wood and chunks of old, vine-carved stone huddled around tiny cookfires. The air moved and the fires burned well, which meant there had to be numerous ventilation shafts some-where. I took deep breaths and schooled myself away from the feeling that the roof would collapse.

'Thanks, Ren, I'll take it from here,' Lorican said, when we arrived at the outskirts of the village. Our guide, a boy of fifteen or sixteen, trotted off, lantern swinging jauntily through the dark. Lorican let go of me, but kept looking back every few steps as though he was afraid I would wander off. He moved through the town, anxiety in the slant of his shoulders.

I did not release Brix's hand as we followed him, and I had no desire to wander. The people we passed were not the sort of folk you would have seen in a village on the surface, and not the sort to appre-ciate strangers poking around. As we made our way through the ragtag town, the paths – or I suppose they were really streets – changed from slick, bare stone to sand, sharp with pale, gritty gravel and tiny broken seashells. The huts and tents and campfires followed the curls of the streets, spiralling out from the middle of the cavern. Earth and salt hung heavy in the air, as well as a fruity, low-simmering odour that I eventually identified as sassafras tea.

'Why do they live down here?' Brix said.

'To survive,' Lorican said. 'This is Deeptown, the closest thing to a permanent home that Erranter will ever have. Ri Dana is one of the only places we can remain – the sea means that it's not the same as staying in one place, not an insult to the Lady of Change. Nobody owns the sea, and it's always shifting. The caves don't stay the same, either, as the water works on them. Deeptown is where we bring the old people, the sick, babies. Anybody who can't run on the road or the waves. That's why I had to promise not to let you hurt them.' He slowed and smiled at Brix. 'But you're not going to hurt them, lass.'

I did see a lot of children, dashing here and there in the dark and playing some game I didn't recognise. Now and then, high whistles burst from the adults beside the fires, and the children went quiet, scampering to stand beside their grandmothers and older siblings.

Under this uncomfortable layer of observation, we made our way to the heart of the town, where a large red pavilion stood like an empress, hung with many-coloured silk lanterns. Two armed men lounged negligently at its doorway.

'Lorican! What're you doing in Deeptown, then?' said one, grinning as we approached. 'If you're looking for trouble, I've got some you could get into.'

Lorican smiled, but it was taut and didn't quite match the guard's easy flirtation. He pulled a small waxed parchment packet from his pocket. 'I'm here to leave my offering for the goddess and the Lady Mother. Cinnamon from Genereth.'

'Going mushroom hunting?' The guard took the cinnamon and sniffed at it. 'The tavern must be doing well. Expensive offering.'

'The old temple,' Lorican said, shortly.

The smile dropped from the guard's face. 'We haven't even been letting people down the tunnel since you came back so bashed-up the last time. What in the hells is past the damn arch that's worth going back for?' The guard's eyes fell on me, hostile. 'I hope the outsiders are paying you enough if you're going to push your luck like this.'

Lorican put a hand on the guard's shoulder. 'I'll be all right, Cenn. This is something I have to do. See to my offering for me?'

Cenn didn't take his eyes off me, but he put a hand over Lorican's. 'Aye,' he said, gruffly. 'Be careful.'

Lorican motioned to me and led us past the pavilion, winding between smaller tents. The lights and noise of the village faded behind us and the dark pressed close, soft, velvety, smothering. Ahead of us, a lone silhouette stood beside a single pale flame. I kept my eyes fixed on it and tried not to think about the weight of the rock above me, and how simple it would be for someone to lose the light and wander in circles while their hunger and thirst grew, forever.

I turned my head, but Brix still had a hold on me.

'Don't let go,' I said, although she'd shown no signs of wanting to, yet.

The walls were narrowing down again. We stopped near the last brazier, where, rather ominously, a youth with a spear stood watching the mouth of a dank tunnel. Lorican went to a notch carved into the tunnel. A row of blackened, ancient lamps waited.

'Don't let anything follow you, if you come back.' It took me a moment to place the laconic voice, but it came from the boy standing by the brazier. He looked no older than the youths I had traded spells with on the surface, but at the same time there was a weary knowledge in his face that sat on him like a weight of years.

'I didn't before,' Lorican muttered. He picked up two lamps.

'Lorican,' I said, and had to clear my throat to get the fear out of my voice. 'Why is everyone acting like we're going to hunt draclings? What happened to you last time?'

He extracted lamp oil from a notch in front of him and spoke as he filled the lamps. 'Look, what do you know about Ri Dana? The history, I mean?'

I shrugged. History has never been my strongest point; Acarius felt it was generally a litany of political events, and politics is boring. 'I know it was built by the Daine during the conquest, seven hundred years ago,' I said. 'And I know it's been destroyed and rebuilt a few times.'

'Enough to be going on with.' Lorican handed Brix one full lamp and kept the other, patting at his pockets as though making sure he was carrying something. 'Ri Dana was built over a complex of caves. Apparently in olden times, they built Jaern-temples underground, made you undertake pilgrimages if you wanted to get the god's favour, that sort of thing.' He took a flint and steel from his pocket and lit the lamps. It required a couple of tries.

'So I take it we are going to an antique temple in a cave,' I said. 'Only, you're shaky enough that there must be some kind of peril involved.'

Brix knocked her elbow sharply into my ribs. Never have I been so clearly told to shut up. 'What are we looking at?' she asked Lorican.

He turned from me to her, a glint of disturbing shrewdness passing over his features. 'It's dark. There's a pilgrim's path you have to keep to. Last time I didn't pay enough attention to that – stepped off, lost my bearings, slipped and broke my wrist. I ended up lost in the dark for two hours before Acarius found me again. And even then he didn't get to me until the other things did. I was cut to bloody ribbons.'

'*What* other things?' I said, annoyed, massaging the place where Brix's elbow had probably left a bruise.

Lorican avoided my eyes. 'I don't know the fancy wizard's name for them. Maybe you can tell me when we see them. Come on.'

Brix said nothing as we followed Lorican. The passage was just broad enough to allow me to walk abreast of her. 'You shouldn't put his back up.' Brix spoke in little more than a whisper, without moving her lips much. 'You need him.'

'How was I putting his back up?' I said.

She shot me a sideways glance. 'He's taking a risk to help you, Gray, and you respond by implying he's a coward. How is he supposed to feel, when you do something as childish and petty as that?'

I halted long enough to let her get between me and Lorican. She'd be safest in the middle if there *was* any sort of creature to worry about in this stupid tunnel, but that wasn't really the reason. I didn't want her to be able to see me, not even my outline. Brix didn't know me, not really. It shouldn't have mattered what she thought about my behaviour. She had no right to make me feel like this – mean, small, careless. *Petty.*

The walls of the passage looked like those of a natural cave, shaped here and there with tools. Soon the flicker of the lamps revealed ancient, flaking paintings on the stone – men standing with a silver star, a repeating image of a crystal vial full of red liquid

95

and symbols in some language I didn't understand. I wanted to stop and look at them more closely, but Lorican didn't slow down. And then there were the glimpses of shapes at the edges of things, weird skulls on bodies with too many arms and legs.

That picture of the vial bothered me. Necromancers are the kind of folk who save blood in vials. Hells, Keir's notes in the judge's diary I'd stolen said that they claimed to catch *souls* in vials.

Which was ridiculous, of course: nobody can put their soul in a vial. Necromancers are very mortal, proved by the fact that Keir had been able to hang some twenty of them in the last year. Still, I wasn't the Examiner General, with a troop of wizards at my back. I was just someone foolish enough to follow a bartender into the dark on the word of an old man.

For that matter, I was someone foolish enough to walk into the dark without any spells scribed.

A shiver caressed me with obscene fingers, as cold as graveyard earth. I pulled my grease pencil out of my bag and began writing on my arms as we moved.

'What is it?' Brix's voice sounded loud and flat at the same time, bouncing back at us off the stone ceiling. Apparently walking in front of me didn't hinder her from watching me. 'What are you worried about?'

'Nothing,' I said, because *the unlikely possibility of lingering underground death-magic* would have sounded crazy. 'No sense in being unprepared.'

She frowned back at me. Apparently, the determined cheer in my voice wasn't better than paranoia would have been.

The light ahead of us dipped; Lorican's hand must have been shaking again. He was standing in front of a masonry arch covered in symbols. The tunnel had ended; beyond it whispered the cool, moving air of a much larger cavern.

'Well, brat,' he said. 'What do you make of this?'

I moved past him and stared at the arch. I touched one of the symbols, letting the analysis save me from the abrupt anxiety that pumped through my veins. 'They're archaic.' I swallowed, and was able to push the fear out of my voice. 'Elaborate. Decorative. But effective enough, if they were intact.'

'Wards,' Brix said, surprised. 'They look like the ones in the Fenwydd temple.'

'Right, except this one's been chipped off, so we'll be able to slip through.' The remains of the symbol under my fingers had been carved by a master. It should have been pretty, but it had an unpleasant, malicious twist to it. It was hard to read. 'It's the kind of thing you'd use to keep people away from secrets. Or from something dangerous.' I looked at Lorican. 'I'm guessing it's not anything so mundane as wyverns.'

His face was taut. 'This is almost as far as I've been, and no one from Deeptown goes even this far. Beyond the arch is the main chamber, and at its centre is the temple. In places there are phosphorescent plants that give enough light to see by, but mostly it's pitch dark. And there are things I saw when I took Acarius here that I never want to see again. Spiders and lizards made of men's bones, stinking like death and as big as panthers.'

The hair rose on my arms. 'You didn't think this was worth mentioning earlier?'

He smiled, humourlessly. 'Without the arch as proof, would you have believed me? Nobody else did, when I came back last time, covered head to toe in cuts where the creatures had clawed me. Acarius carried me out on his back. He managed to keep the worst of the creatures away from us, control them somehow. Can you do the same?'

Something cold hardened in the pit of my stomach. 'Yes.' I wasn't lying and I wasn't boasting. This was just going to be . . . complex. 'I need a bit of time, to get the runes scribed.' It would have to be offensive magic written on me, different than the spells I had just written on my arms.

In the darkness on the other side of the arch, something scraped against the rock.

'Gray,' Brix said. 'What in the hells was that?'

A sudden burst of clicks echoed around us, as though hundreds of toenails were rasping across a stone floor.

But I knew that sound, and I knew it wasn't toenails.

Damnation. I wasn't going to *have* any time. I took a step backwards.

'Stay behind me,' I said.

TEN

A puff of decay wafted past me as the creature, about the size of a goat, came into view.

I had been correct; the clicking sound hadn't come from toenails, per se. The thing's seven legs, constructed from dry femurs and jointed like a spider's, ended in a delicate, pointed filigree of human finger-bones. Whoever had built it was both creative and precise.

'What is it?' Brix wasn't shouting, but revulsion rattled in her voice.

It was a creatlach, a necromantic bone-construct, not that I had the words to waste on explanations. A splay of ribs from multiple species formed the body, fused around a knot of vertebrae that undulated atop a ball of dull orange light. It had three skulls – one seemed to be from some kind of carnivore, a big cat, maybe – but they all had empty eye sockets. So it couldn't see, which probably meant it navigated by sensing vibrations. If I spoke, it could find me.

I waved a hand at Brix, in what I hoped was a logical gesture for 'silence'. I had to make the first words I said an incantation, and it had to be the correct one. Knives wouldn't hurt this fleshless thing.

But where was the wizard? These things didn't stay animate on their own. The creatlach's creator had to be somewhere close in order to control it.

I glanced at Lorican, but he was digging through his pockets like a terrier after a rat. Unlikely he was the necromancer, then. Running a construct that size should have taken enough concentration to require him to at least look at the thing. Besides, I hadn't heard him cast, and I didn't think the story he had told me was a lie.

Maybe the thing was sentient enough to fight on its own? There's no way to make constructs *think*, exactly, but the more complex ones can carry out a set of orders even when their masters aren't near to give telepathic commands.

Brix's foot scraped against the grit on the floor of the tunnel as she moved to stand beside me.

The creatlach skittered towards her. In a split second it was almost on top of her, two of its legs raised, stroking the air. When Brix stepped backwards, the legs snapped shut around her waist, like a shackle. She screamed and tugged at the joints, but I knew it would be of no use. Bone constructs are strong – ridiculously strong.

This one was also fast. Before I could gather myself for a leap, it yanked Brix through the gate and into the darkness.

Thank the gods that she kept screaming, because she had dropped the lamp. I moved through the gate after her as quickly as I could, pausing only long enough to scoop up the lamp, and followed the noise. The scrabble of Lorican's boots on the stone told me he was running behind me.

My options didn't look promising. The only incantations I had ready on my arms were lightning and flame. Both of them had to be aimed, which meant that if I used them against the creatlach, I risked hitting Brix.

A grinding crunch echoed through the cave.

I came up on the creatlach in time to see Brix kick it again, sending the lower portion of one leg flying.

I jumped. My intent was to tackle the creature, but I wound up more or less riding on top of it. I pushed myself forwards, trying to flatten it on the ground.

It tangled in its own legs, catching mine. Brix, the creatlach and I all went down together – just as I saw the creature's nameplate: a flat piece of bone floating at the centre of the orange light, scribed with the runes that controlled it. I worked one hand towards the plate.

The thing, with whatever semblance of intelligence it possessed, had realised a second person was wrestling with it. Its skulls rotated, and the carnivorous jaws opened and snapped, inches from my face.

Brix's fist slammed down on top of the skull, but this time her blow wasn't so lucky. She gritted her teeth and hit it again, and the skull rotated away from me for a moment.

I scrambled to get an arm around a couple of the legs. How in the hells could something without muscles be so strong?

One of the legs got free and jerked towards me, joints cracking. The pointed tip left a long, hot gash down my arm.

Brix was still pinned, wriggling against the limbs that circled her waist. She wasn't screaming anymore, but her motions carried the speed of panic.

'Help.' I couldn't make the word anything but a staccato burst, while the creatlach bucked under me. 'Lorican.' I twisted my head away from the jaws, which were still snapping towards me. Thank the gods the thing didn't have an articulated neck. 'Help!'

The leg tore another cut, this one across my back. I needed to kill the creatlach before the thing stabbed me. But I couldn't let go of the legs I already had.

'Hang on.' Lorican circled me and the creatlach. A rain of something like pebbles flew around me.

The creatlach's skulls rotated again as it skittered to one side, as though it was trying to chase the pebbles. I managed to grab the nameplate from beneath the skulls, wrap my fingers around it and yank.

It came away in my hand. The creatlach held together for a moment before collapsing.

I sat, panting, in the pile of disconnected bones and looked at Brix. 'Are you all right?'

'I'm not hurt,' she said. But there was a shake in her breathing, and she kept brushing at her clothes where the monster had held her. 'How did you kill it?'

'I took its name away.' I picked through the pile until I found one of the things Lorican had thrown: a largish glass bead. I held it up. 'Vibration?'

He nodded. 'Confuses them, or at least it did last time. Why didn't you cast?'

'I was busy.' I got to my feet and turned to Brix, holding out one hand. She stared at it for a moment before grasping it and allowing me to help her to her feet.

'Thanks, Gray.' Her fingers lingered on mine for a split second.

'Don't thank me,' I muttered. She wasn't unhurt. The knuckles on the hand I'd held were scraped and bloody. I gave her back the lamp; if we got separated, she would need it more than I. 'We need to keep going. There's probably more of them, and we're making a lot of noise.'

The momentary relief on her face fled. '*More?*' Brix's voice dropped to a whisper. 'What in the hells *was* it?'

'It is – was – a creatlach.' I touched the bones with my foot, wishing there was a way to explain without speaking. 'It's . . . a pet, sort of. A tool. Necromancers make them. It's like making a doll – you can build with any bones, put together in any configuration you want and bound together with magic. But things with soft tissue are more difficult, and delicate. That's why this one didn't have any eyes.' I uncurled my fingers and looked down at the nameplate I held. It had once been something's shoulder blade. Now it was covered with tiny, carefully painted runes, spirals within spirals. 'So it tried to guess where we were based on vibration, like footsteps or speech. I was invisible to it as long as I didn't say anything or take a step. When you came up beside me, it found you.'

'Nameplate,' Lorican said, hardly audible. 'That's what you meant, *took its name away*.'

I held it up. 'It has the name of the creature and the wizard written on it. Otherwise the creator couldn't get absolute obedience, and even wizards aren't mad enough to make constructs they can't control. Pull it away from the rest of the construct and it comes apart.' The runes on the nameplate were just as archaic as the ones on the arch, but once you got through the old-fashioned flourishes and curls, it was simple enough to read:

Spindlejoint.

Like I said, whoever made it must have been a creative soul. A bit of a poet, too, apparently.

I scanned the incantation to find the name of the wizard. I half expected it to be Keir Esras. I had seen him in the city above us, and I knew he'd been hunting necromancers and studying their practice. He would have had to keep his activities secret. A position as Examiner General, where he could control any internal Guild investigation, would have been perfect. He and his ambitions towards the throne could have been the reason Acarius was here last year, and Lorican had said there was another way down to Deeptown, a door in the Spires. A lot more of this situation would make sense if the bastard turned out to be playing with death-magic himself.

But my speculation stumbled to a halt when I read the wizard's name:

Jaern.

Which made no sense at all. How had the incantation worked, if the creature was just dedicated to the god? Even if there was a mad priest of Jaern down here, he should have had to use his own name. Something was very wrong.

'But how do you know there are more?' Brix's taut voice yanked me out of my thoughts.

'No necromancer I've ever seen stopped after one.' I glanced at Lorican. 'There *are* more, aren't there? You've seen them?'

'Maybe ten,' he said, a grim set to his mouth. 'This is worse than I thought it would be, worse than it was last time. And you're right, we should keep moving.'

'I need to scribe a spell,' I said. 'Bring the lamp over here. I'll be quick.'

My hand trembled, though. It took me three tries to get the first line of runes, the ones across my belly, scribed perfectly. Lorican held the lamp, watched me work and didn't say anything. I remembered sniping at him about fear earlier, and I couldn't look up at him. It wouldn't have been practical, I suppose, for him to risk talking to mock me in return – still, it would have felt better than standing there with the taste of shame in my mouth.

We moved forwards, but slowly. We all realised that we couldn't run without advertising our presence. It was dangerous enough just walking.

I caught myself holding my breath, over and over, listening for a scratch, a click of bones, anything to tell me where the next threat would come from. I forced myself to inhale and exhale as we proceeded, agonisingly slowly. If I could concentrate on breathing, maybe I could fight the ball of mindless panic slamming in my chest.

Scrape.

We all stopped. I strained to find the sound's origin, to analyse it, get some scrap of information to tell me what I was dealing with. I had to figure out what was going on. There had to be some logical way that the necromancer was controlling the beasts. If only I could find the solution, I could *do* something.

But there was nothing more, just the dense, unbroken curtain of night outside our fragile circle of yellow light. Everything was too silent.

Inhale, exhale.

Lorican started moving again, placing his feet gingerly. Brix and I followed, both of us walking on our toes. After a while I realised that Lorican was following some sort of path carved into the rock floor, a string of pictographs. I tried to study them while also watching the darkness around us. It was a fruitless occupation, but one I couldn't pull myself away from. My body twitched with dread, as though it knew something was there, stalking us.

Inhale. My inner voice grew more stern as my heart hammered louder in my ears. *Exhale.*

The pictographs must have been intended as a kind of map for pilgrims. The symbol of the half-closed eye repeated at regular intervals, mingled with a number of other religious themes. Finally, the path terminated in a set of glossy black stairs, slick and startling against the gritty white rock that the rest of the cavern was made of.

Lorican halted at the foot of the stairs and glanced back at me. 'The temple door is just up these steps,' he whispered. 'They're slippery, so —'

He froze, eyes fixed on something the lamplight had revealed over my shoulder.

Scrape.

It was behind me.

The stink of graveyard rot was worse this time. I raised myself on to my toes and risked a half-turn, the syllables of the concussion spell already forming on my tongue.

A ring of sightless eyes stared back at me, stretching away into the dark, makeshift heads grinning atop hulking bodies. No two of them were the same. There were more spider-legged abominations, and others that were dog-shaped and crab-shaped, variation upon variation. The one that had slithered its way up to me was nothing but a string of skulls, tied together with vertebrae. It swayed back and forth like a cobra, hypnotic, listening for the two people behind me.

Fifty. The analytical part of my mind insisted on accuracy. There were at least fifty of them. My spell wouldn't do anything but delay them for a moment.

On the other hand, the spell had twenty-eight syllables, and we were close to the temple entrance. The sound of the incantation – not to mention the shock from when it hit the monsters – should draw the beasties towards me. Perhaps there was a gate or door of some sort Brix and Lorican could get behind and close, barricade. It was at least a chance.

'What's your name, ugly?' I said.

The snake stopped dancing in front of me, all of its skulls rotating so the eye sockets faced me. The topmost head chattered its jaw, almost conversationally. One of its teeth fell out and rolled across the floor, coming to rest against the toe of my boot.

I raised my hand to shoulder height and swallowed down the bile that kept rising. There was nothing else for it. The spell should buy Brix and Lorican enough time to get to safety.

Inhale.

Twenty-eight syllables.

I opened my mouth.

A cloud of beads flew into the crowd of monsters, and they exploded into a mass of writhing, creaking activity. Lorican shouted, 'Go!'

Brix grabbed my elbow, wrenched me around and dragged me with her.

And then we were scrambling up the chipped, slippery steps, fighting for every bit of footing. At the top of the stairs glowed clumps of green fungus, huge mushrooms surrounding a narrow door.

One of the creatures snapped at me from the side, so close its teeth scraped across my trousers. It looked like a surreal mixture of a cat and a lizard. I shouted the runes on my belly, and a blast of red force pulsed from my open hand. The creature made a strange noise between a whimper and a hiss as the spell smashed into its snout and threw it backwards.

The counter-force of the spell – the downside to concussion magic, alas – threw me forwards.

Brix stumbled ahead of me. I couldn't slow myself and was about to land on top of her. There was no time to think. I put my hands on either side of her waist and yanked her back up to her feet.

'Gray–' She said my name in a little gust like a sob. We were nearly to the top of the steps, where Lorican stood swinging his lamp in a wide arc and pitching handfuls of beads every few moments, keeping the creatures at bay. Brix's lamp wobbled.

'You're all right.' I forced us both up the stairs. 'Hang on to the light.'

We finally cleared the last step as claws tore at the back of my left calf, and my brace twisted. There was no time to turn and aim a spell, no time for anything but to keep running.

Lorican stood just outside the doorway, only a few steps from us. The black wall on either side of the narrow opening was smooth and shiny as glass.

'Come on!' he shouted.

The brace flopped on my shin, but we were almost there. My toes found purchase and I shoved Brix towards the doorway, pushing with my legs.

Something inside my knee ripped. Blazing, brilliant agony exploded, emptying me of everything else. I screamed.

There was no stopping the momentum I'd already bought. I fell through the doorway, sweeping Brix and Lorican along with me. We all landed inside the passage, in a heap, the lamps skidding away across the floor. I rolled sideways.

Part of the floor under my elbow moved.

Click.

I pulled away, but it was too late. Before I could even sit up, a barred gate slid smoothly into place in the doorway, between us and the creatlaches.

'We're safe,' Brix said.

But the flickers of lamplight revealed a string of white-painted sigils around the doorway. Even though I could only make out about every third word, it was enough.

'We're not safe,' I said. 'We're trapped.'

ELEVEN

Brix sprawled beside me, dishevelled and pale against the obsidian tiles under her. She got shakily to her elbows and then sat up, pushing her hair back with one hand, her eyes on the narrow doorway. 'What do you mean? They can't get in, can they?'

Slender limbs reached through the barred gate, tapping, testing the strength of the iron. A chorus of uncanny creaks told us the creatures weren't happy about losing their prey.

'Probably not.' My fingers traced the floor until I found the tiny seams. I pushed. The tile didn't sink any more than it already had. 'But I triggered the gate to close by landing on a pressure plate. It doesn't move anymore, which means the action to open the gate is elsewhere.' Outside, for instance. 'Unless we can figure out how to get those bars up again, we're stuck in here.'

'Well.' Lorican picked himself up and moved to the doorway with one of the lamps, examining the bars from a safe distance. 'At least it will give us a minute to think.'

Brix frowned at me. 'You're hurt.'

'One of the bastards tore my brace.' I stretched forwards, wincing as the tendons lengthened along the back of my leg. The straps of the brace were beyond repair, sheared through in places. I had to work quickly, before the nervous energy from the flight left me and the pain became overwhelming. 'Bring a lamp over here and I'll scribe a numbing spell.'

Brix grabbed the other lamp and swung it towards me. Another wash of pain swept over my body, the cuts on my arm and back throbbing in time to the all-encompassing fire in my knee.

I dug out my paints and began scribing on the brace. Most spells take a good bit of concentration, but I've been using that numbing agent since I was twelve years old. I could scribe it sleepwalking.

Except I couldn't. I was shaking too hard, panting. It wasn't just the pain; the residue of the terror I had managed to fight while we were in the cavern had me by the throat. I was half-blind with it.

'It's bad, isn't it?' Brix said.

'Yes.' Even my voice was shaking, dammit. 'Talk to me, Brix. About something normal. Distract me.'

She stared at me, then swallowed. 'You should know better than to expect me to talk about something normal. The closest I can get is to tell you about my sister, I suppose.'

By gripping the brush very tightly, I managed to get the first character down. 'Sister. Just one?'

'Just one.' She leaned closer and put a hand on my elbow. The stink of decay that the creatlaches had left in my nostrils faded, replaced by a hint of whatever soap she'd used back at the tavern. Something fragranced with sandalwood. 'It's just me and her. You've never told me whether you have siblings . . . or anybody.'

'Only Acarius.' I wrote a few more runes. 'Nobody else.'

'Well, you have to understand that I used to be tender-hearted.' She watched my work. With every word her voice grew calmer. Even though I knew the calm was fake, it took some of the edge off. 'My baby sister is one of those girls who knocks everyone sideways. She looks like the new moon, all golden and sharp and smarter than people think she will be. She's got a chipped tooth from this time she got in a fight with a boy over some stray kittens.' Brix touched her own front incisor with one fingertip. 'We used to steal my aunt's rabbit-skin blanket and sneak out in the winter to cover up our old brown nanny-goat. I'd sing lullabies to her, and she'd sing them to the goat.' She smiled faintly. 'Anka still has a tender heart.'

I wanted to ask where Anka was, given that Brix had been clawing her way out of a temple, but I began the curve of the rune spiral instead. I had to get it done before the pain overwhelmed me completely, had to save my concentration for the spell.

'At any rate, one time the goat got out,' Brix said. 'She followed us, with the rabbit-skin blanket on her back. And my aunt saw it and thought a bear cub had escaped from a circus or something and got into the house. She squawked like a hen.'

'Circus? Not a house in the sticks, then.' My voice sounded a little better now. The spell was almost finished.

'No,' she said, slowly. 'A house in the middle of a great city. Genereth, where my family's from. The mother-city, where the Tirnaal first became a people. Maybe I'll take you there someday, show you the red domes on the buildings, and the waterwheels and the silk-dyers' workshops. It's warm there.' She pulled a lock of my hair out of my eyes, her hand brushing against my forehead. 'If you'd travel with me that far.'

'It's a deal.' If we ever got out of this damn temple, all I had to show her was a little cabin and a stack of old books. At least the distraction had worked. I pronounced the runes I had scribed, waiting for the cold feeling of the spell to seep into my knee. The numbness took hold, but it didn't blot out the pain with its usual totality. Something was drastically wrong inside the joint.

Lorican gave up on the gate and walked back to us. 'You did more than sprain it, didn't you?'

'Maybe. I don't know.' I *did* know, but sitting around worrying about ruined joints wasn't going to do any good. Since we were stuck in a hallway, in a cave, my knee could end up being somewhat irrelevant.

The lamplight revealed writing on the black walls around us, mingled with odd, narrow pictographs. Once the paint outlining the letters had been white; now it was a ghostly grey. The language was, of course, the same difficult-to-read, archaic mess that had been on the arch and on the nameplate. But these weren't incantory runes – it was just writing, not magic. None of my education could help me interpret it.

'What is it?' Lorican looked from me to the characters I was staring at. 'What does it mean?'

'I think it must be instructions,' I said. 'But I can't read it like this. Brix.' I got out my box of paint and selected the vial of silver paint. I handed it and the brush to her.

'Instructions for what?' Lorican said.

'Pilgrims,' I said. 'A kind of a test, a way to soften up worshippers before you shake them down.' I smiled at Brix in what I hoped was an encouraging fashion. 'I need you to scribe something on me, here.' I shoved my hair back and pointed to the tender place behind my ear.

'I can't scribe magic.' Brix held the paints out to me. She did not look encouraged.

'Just watch me and copy,' I said, without taking them.

'Gray, if one little line is wrong, you could be hurt.'

'I'm *already* hurt.' I blew air out through my nose, and fought to make my tone reassuring instead of desperate. 'Look, magic is a trade, something you learn. It's just paying attention. The runes have to be written near my ear, the same as the breaker I did on you to get rid of your navel ring had to be around your stomach. I can't do it myself without a mirror. The incantation won't hurt you because you're not going to pronounce it – I am. And it won't hurt me because it's an easy spell and you're going to do fine.'

She bit her lip, but she dipped the paintbrush. I pushed my hair out of the way again and was thankful that for once she believed me when I lied to her. I hadn't worked out how to incorporate the shielding runes for translation spells yet; this *was* going to hurt me. It couldn't be helped.

By this time, it was no surprise that she was a quick study. I traced a rune in the dust on the floor, waited for her to transcribe it behind my ear and then traced the next. It only took a few minutes to get the entire spell done. I rubbed out what I'd written in the dust, steeled myself and pronounced Brix's runes.

The magic razored across my skull, so sharp that it took me a blink to realise that it had worked. The gibberish on the wall rearranged itself into words I could read. But when I tried to get up to examine it more closely, my numbed leg wouldn't cooperate.

Lorican held out a hand. 'Up you come, brat.'

I had to let him haul me up on to my feet, flinching when the muscles of my back bunched under the cut the bone-spider had given me. I was steady enough to stand by myself, though, once I put my weight on my good leg.

'Thanks.' The word sounded less gracious than I wanted it to, but at least this time I said it. If Lorican had really known what kind of threats lurked in the cavern, then agreeing to guide me down here and risk himself had required courage. I wondered what Acarius had done for him, and just how far back he and the old man went.

He shrugged. 'No trouble. What does it say?'

'Apparently we're at the beginning of a puzzle.' I brushed the dust away from the carving, but I hadn't missed anything. There wasn't going to be an easier way out. I touched the letters and recited:

'When one does not know what it is, then it is something; but when one knows what it is, then it is nothing. Prove thy worth at the middle of the web and all doors will open.'

I sighed. 'The answer is "a riddle". A riddle maze. We've got to get to the centre in order to "prove our worth". It's probably where the artefact is, but more urgently, it's probably where the lever to open the gate will be. The priests had to have a way to rescue stuck devotees. Makes no sense to let your shills die before they can pay you.'

Lorican was studying me, not the writing. 'Not a religious man, are you?'

'Not for Jaern, anyway.' I ran my fingertips across the pictograph, following its sinuous lines. I had never found the doctrine of the Lord of Secrets convincing – the idea that if you proved your worth, the god would give you secret knowledge. I had never found any of the doctrine about the gods convincing. My mother had prayed to Ranara, the Lady of Shadows, every night. It was one of the few things I could remember about her, apart from the bits that I didn't *want* to remember. Ranara hadn't kept my mother alive. Jaern wasn't going to teach anybody anything.

I cleared my throat and tapped the pictograph. 'This part says I'll go to the hell-of-ice-and-knives for my blasphemy, if that makes you feel any better. We should start the maze. Put the lamps out, before the oil is used up.' I scribed an illumination spell on the back of my hand. When I pronounced it, a tongue of blue flame bobbed above my right shoulder.

'Can't you . . . ?' Lorican pointed at the light. 'Why do we need to worry about the lamps?'

'I might not continue to be in a condition to make even a childish incantation like this one.' I met his eyes, trying to make him understand what I was saying. If the magic toxicity knocked me out, Brix and Lorican still had a chance of making it out if they had working lamps. If not, they'd be even more thoroughly trapped than they already were. 'Magic takes a lot of energy; also, miners say that lamps burn up the sweet air. Save the lamp oil.'

He nodded shortly, and put out their lamps.

There had to be more traps, of course.

The hallway led away from the gate, terminating in a 'T' shape. There was a picture on the wall where the path split in two, a mosaic of a life-sized man in glittering, semi-precious stones. His arms stretched out, pointing in both directions. Once his eyes must have held larger stones, but now they were empty, staring sockets. Over his head was a string of letters. The translation spell rearranged them for me a moment later:

The blind lost my name; the deaf found it.

I repeated it to the others, in case they recognised the riddle. They both frowned.

'What's that supposed to mean?' Lorican said.

The picture shouldn't have mattered. I should have been able to solve the maze by keeping my right hand exactly where it was – on the wall that had started to the right of the entrance. It would require traversing every corridor in the maze, but it should work.

But it didn't make sense that the instructions had promised doors – plural – would open, unless there was a way to make more of them fall. So there had to be more pressure plates, or trip wires, and a way to avoid them. It was a puzzle on more than one level. Taking a wrong turn had to have worse consequences than just getting lost. It had to mean getting stuck, having to pay some kind of penance.

'What did you come down here for, anyway?' Brix said.

'I don't know, exactly,' I said, and braced for the way they both looked at me, like I was incompetent or mad, or both. 'Acarius couldn't tell me. But it's here, probably in the sanctuary. Why do you care?'

'I thought if I knew what the treasure was, it might give us some kind of clue to this thing,' Brix said.

A child, of sorts. You'll know it when you see it. The riddle was about vision.

If only I could have shut off the pain in my knee enough to *think*, even for a moment. Acarius had believed I'd be able to get through this. Almost certainly I was just not seeing what the puzzle really was. 'Visions, visual, sight, see, look . . .' I straightened. '*Look*. It's something about the mosaic. Something we can see.'

Brix chewed her lip. 'Like what?'

'Like something out of place, maybe,' I said. 'Or a symbol.'

'Whatever Acarius was doing in here when I brought him down,' Lorican offered, 'he couldn't have got far. I was hurt, and he made me stay at the door outside. I hardly had time to sharpen my knife.'

Maybe he had come no further than this. I looked into the empty eyes of the figure on the wall and hoped that my grandfather hadn't wrecked my only clue.

Brix stepped closer to the mosaic, gesturing for me to send the light closer to her. I did, and watched as her nose wrinkled with concentration, her eyes moving. 'It's . . . the pattern,' she said. 'Some of them are shiny, like mica. Do you see it?'

I did, when she had pointed it out. If I made the light move slowly back and forth, the glittering stones in the mosaic, scattered among the flat ones, shone in the pattern of a half-closed eye. Brix looked over her shoulder at me. 'Should I try?'

'Try what?' Lorican said. 'Gray told me you know things. Are you a . . .' He looked at her, doubtful. 'Priestess?'

She grinned. 'Not quite. But I know about Jaern-temples, and this *looks* like the sort of thing they put on locked doors. If it *is* the same sort of thing, I can unlock it.' Her smile faded a little. 'If the countersigns are the same, that is.'

I didn't like the bit of doubt, but what else were we supposed to do? I swept my eyes across the mosaic, starting at one corner and scanning it systematically. Outside of the Jaernic symbol, it was just a collection of stones, arranged to look like a pretty young man. 'I can't think of a better idea,' I admitted. 'Try the countersign.'

Brix put her hands at her sides, and took the time for a couple of deep breaths. Then her hand flashed up, so quickly it was difficult to follow, and she touched the shiny stones in a rapid sequence, counting under her breath. Each one clicked as she pressed on it. When she finished she stepped back.

At first nothing happened. Then, with a high, grinding whine, the stones in the mosaic began to shift and move, flowing over the mortar like water over a streambed. Lips made of chalcedony curved into a smile. Pale quartz fingers on the right hand pointed. And the eyeless head turned, slowly, until it was in profile, facing right.

'That seems conclusive,' I muttered. 'I think we're meant to go right.'

Brix came to stand beside me and took my hand. 'Come on, then. Lean on me.' As her fingers gripped mine, the ache from the spell behind my ear dimmed, just a bit.

'No.' I twisted away from her. I *felt* weak and helpless, but I was damned if I was going to *demonstrate* my failings in front of her and Lorican. 'I can walk. I'm fine.'

'You're stupid.' She grabbed my sleeve and put my arm around her shoulders. 'You said yourself that we might not have much time before the air starts to foul, and Lorican can't help you because he's the wrong height.' With that, she started walking into the black passageway, and I had no choice but to keep up.

The passage twisted and curved, but there were no wires – no falling gates – no pits. We must have made the right choice, but it was disorientating as the hells because the walls were all the same black, shiny, polished stone. We were leaving footprints on the dusty floor, too, almost as though we were walking in snow.

The second choice came before we had walked far. We came to a larger room that branched into two passages. Instead of a mosaic this time, three obsidian statues graced the middle of the floor – a trio of female dancers. My stomach turned over as I looked at their faces.

'What's the matter with their eyes?' Lorican said.

Instead of irises and pupils, the dancers had blank white eyes, mouths open in either song or screams. I swallowed my distaste. 'They're supposed to be *yavadis* – slaves. Some of the traditionalists still use them, girls kept so full of yavad that they go blind. A way to get heavenly visions, I suppose.' Or hellish ones. I didn't like the look of those open mouths, holes in the rock. It was almost as if the statues had been a fountain once.

'There's writing on the base.' Lorican crouched beside the statues. 'Another riddle, likely – see if you can read it.'

I already knew I could read it, if I could stay on my feet long enough to get around the statues. Leaning on Brix, I limped in a circle, reading aloud as I went:

'*I am the song-killer, the city-breaker, and when I have consumed, I die.*'

Silence, while I looked at the words so I wouldn't have to look at the statues' faces. My wits felt like they were slowing with every new challenge. 'Any ideas?' I said.

Lorican wiped sweat out of his eyes with the cuff of his sleeve, in spite of the chill in the room. 'Thirst,' he said. 'The answer to the riddle is "thirst", I reckon. "When I have consumed, I die." Unless either of you has a better answer.'

'But what does it mean?' Brix's hand tightened around my forearm. 'Are we supposed to drink yavad?'

'Drinking yavad wouldn't do anything – it's a sedative, all it would do is make us tired.' And maybe take the edge off my knee, but I wasn't going to risk blunting my wits, not down here. Besides, there was a part of my mind that wanted to save the half-bottle of yavad that I had left in my pouch. If it came down to dying in the dark, I wasn't sure I wanted to be sober.

'Maybe there's a hint in the design, like last time,' Brix said.

But there wasn't, as far as I could see. The dancers weren't pointing at anything, they weren't painted, nothing was out of place.

'If there's nothing to go on,' Lorican said, 'you could divine, couldn't you? Scry for the answer?'

'It's not going to be that ludicrously simple,' I snapped. 'Divining spirals need foci – names, usually – and even if I knew the name of a maze designer who died centuries ago, I couldn't do more than divine their location, which is presumably a boneyard somewhere.' I sighed. 'Let's think. The statue is asking some kind of question. The maze is supposed to make the pilgrim prove they're worthy to learn Jaern's secrets, right? It's a temple. There's supposed to be worship happening. Maybe there's a prayer –' I glanced at Brix.

'Are you asking me to perform a miracle?' she said. 'The priests do those.'

'I don't know what I'm asking.' I pulled away from her and leaned against the wall. 'I want something to make sense.'

Lorican crossed his arms, frowning. 'When did Acarius give you this task? What exactly did he say? Maybe you're forgetting something. It's not like him to withhold information.'

'He gave it to me about two weeks ago, via unsecure intrapersonal conjuration, and it's *very* like him,' I said. 'Maybe he doesn't withhold information with you. Congratulations. All he told me was to go to Ri Dana, find you and then retrieve an artefact down here, about which he only said I'd know it when I saw it.' I glared at the statue. 'I am assuming it's not this unholy thing, but that's just because there's no way I could lift it.'

'You're angry with him,' Lorican said, surprised.

Angry wasn't a big enough word. I swallowed, and tried to wrestle back some kind of control over the situation. 'At the moment how I feel about my grandfather is irrelevant. Are we going right, or left, or back to the beginning? Does anybody have an idea how to choose?'

An uncomfortable silence descended, where Brix and Lorican both scowled at me and I scowled at the writing on the base of the yavadis statues, willing it to become coherent. I should have been able to figure it out.

'We go right,' Brix said, at last. 'If there's no reason to choose one way or the other, then someone just has to make a decision. I'll look down the passage before we go tromping into it. Send the light with me, Gray. Maybe I can see a turn, or a tripwire or something.'

'I'll go with you.' Lorican moved beside her. 'Two heads are better than one.'

'Why am I the only one who stays?' I dragged myself upright.

Lorican glanced at me. 'Because you're the only one who can't pick his feet up quickly. Quit grousing and give us the light.'

'Gods, fine.' I let myself slump back against the wall and made the ball of blue light follow them. 'Be careful. There could be another pressure plate.'

Brix looked back at me, with the glow on her hair. 'Or it could just be a regular maze, and if we're wrong we have to backtrack. Have a little hope.'

When they got to the arched doorway of the passage, she dropped into a crouch and examined the walls, then the ceiling. She slid one hand forwards along the floor, pushing through the inch of dust that coated the stone.

'I don't see anything,' she said.

'Right.' Lorican took one step, and then another into the passage. 'I don't see anything on the walls, either. If it's a trap, it's well hidden.'

That didn't mean there was nothing there. I began limping towards them. 'Wait. It doesn't have to be mechanical. Let me—' I saw it as Brix stepped into the passage, in the clean place on the floor her hand had left: a painted ward sigil, just beginning to glow. 'Wait!'

She turned, her foot scraping across the rest of the sigil.

Up from the floor exploded a gate, yanked from its slumber by the force of magic that was still as strong now as it had been centuries ago, when it was scribed. It clanged into position, filling the entire doorway between us with metal cross-hatches, glowing a dull orange.

'Help me!' I tugged downwards on the gate. 'Hurry!'

Lorican had lunged towards the doorway when the gate shrieked its way into place. Now he put the unlit lamp on the floor, curled his fingers around the metal and glanced at Brix, who took hold of the cross-hatches above her head. 'Everyone together. One, two, three.'

We yanked. Brix pulled hard enough that her feet left the ground, her entire weight on the gate. It didn't budge.

'No, dammit!' I slammed the heel of my hand against the steel.

Brix startled. 'Don't *do* that!' It was the first time I'd ever heard her raise her voice. 'It doesn't help!' She took a step back from the gate, raking both hands through her hair.

I knew what it was like to flinch when someone yelled, to watch faces and hands. I hated that when I was afraid I wanted to shout and hide and make enough noise to get people to leave. 'Sorry,' I said.

'Great Linna's fire, we're spiked,' Lorican said, quietly, studying the edges of the gate. A muscle jumped in his throat. 'I don't know that this *can* open, brat, unless you know how to get the spell to let go. There's not even a latch holding it.'

'Go a little way down the passage and see if it's a dead end,' I said. Maybe I was the one locked in, and they could go on. 'But – stay where you can see me.'

'I'll do it.' Lorican jogged a few paces down the hallway, until he could see around the corner. He turned back to me. 'It's a blank wall.'

'All right. It's going to be all right. I'll get you out.' I allowed myself to hang on to the gate, using my arms to take the weight off my knee for a bit. 'Brush away the dust on the floor, so I can see the whole sigil. Maybe I can break the ley.'

Brix squatted and swept the floor clean with the palms of her hands, heaping the dust around her feet. 'You mean you'd do whatever-it-was you did in the alley behind Lorican's tavern?'

'Knocking out the magic might make the gate fall.' The ward sigil wasn't a spiral. The runes were arranged in more of a triangle, something I'd never seen before.

'Might.' Brix's hands rested on the edges of the runes. She was frowning at me. 'Might?'

'That's—' I blinked. 'Move so you're not touching it. The magic might have been just a trigger and there could be some mechanical lock. Or the magic could be holding it. I can't read the incantation well enough to know. It's almost like it's just a . . . piece of an incantation.' What I could see of the runes didn't look promising – there was no static sequence, nothing that should have been keeping the gate in place. 'Doing the ley-breaker would at least prove it one way or the other.'

'And it would ruin the painkiller you put on your knee and wreck the light,' Brix said.

I had been trying not to think about that. 'So?'

'So you'll make yourself of no use to anybody, just on the off-chance that the gate might fall?' She leaned backwards and pointed at the runes. 'This is a prayer. You remember the one from the temple in Fenwydd?'

'That was a *spell*, just like this one,' I said, 'written with a different style of runes than Guild characters, not—'

'Stop talking,' she snapped. 'I'm explaining something to you. You don't know everything. This is half of a Jaernic *prayer*, just like the one that went around the library at the Fenwydd temple. If you'd triggered that one, it would have dropped gates too, locked you in the room with the books. The way to deactivate the prayer in Fenwydd was to let the idol in the sanctuary taste fire. So there's something that would have deactivated this prayer, too, that we missed.' She paused. 'You look like you have a question.'

'If I find the equivalent of letting an idol taste fire, will it drop this thing?' I pulled at the gate one last time, unable to help myself. It was maddening.

'No.' She rose to her feet. 'There's got to be a lever or a counter-spell for that. It's usually in the sanctuary.'

'That's it, then. You'll have to get to the sanctuary without us, open the gates and then come back to get us.' Lorican sounded like he was trying to reassure himself more than me. 'Acarius thought you could do it.'

'No.' The word burst out, scalding in my mouth. 'I'm not leaving you both here.'

Lorican's head came up. Real fear glittered in his eyes. After all, he'd only known me for a single day, and all I'd done was insult him and get him trapped.

'If you don't,' he said, 'then all of us are going to die here, Gray. If the air doesn't run out, it'll be thirst that kills us. I don't want to die like that.' He swallowed, and gave a forced laugh. 'Frankly, I always planned on dying with a knife in my guts.'

I hated this, hated *failing* like this.

'Lorican is right.' Brix reached up and touched my hand, where I was still holding on to the gate. Her fingertips were cold, and dusty, and they made a sudden, intoxicating pool of calm in the middle of my head as the poison throbbing in my blood leached away.

'Don't do that.' I jerked my hand away. My heart clattered against my breastbone in a way that didn't make sense. 'I didn't ask you to do that.'

'Just take the help, Corcoran.' She put her forehead against the steel, so she could see both of my eyes. 'Go, get it done and get back to us. I'll buy you a drink when it's over.' She smiled. It was false, but it helped, a little. 'Maybe I'll even throw in dinner.'

Lorican was lighting a lamp – just one, I noticed. The light fluttered across the walls, as uncertain as everything else around us. 'And hurry it up, brat,' he said. 'There's not a lot of oil left.'

'Right.' I took a step back. 'I won't be long. And I'll expect that drink.'

Drink. Thirst.

I halted beside the statues, with their shrieking, open mouths.

'I'm so stupid.' I didn't realise I had said it out loud until I heard Lorican make an interrogative noise. I dug through my satchel until I found the partial vial of yavad. 'Thirst. Not us, them. The yavadis. It's an alchemical puzzle. Like letting the Empty One taste fire. Stupid, stupid.' I uncorked the vial and poured half of the contents into the nearest statue's mouth.

The green liquid trickled slowly into the hole between her stone teeth and disappeared. A few seconds later, a beam of light shot out from her blank eyes, striking the rock above the left-hand passage door.

'There,' Brix said. 'Next time, don't rush. Figure it out. You had better stop mooning around and get moving.'

'I'm sorry,' I said, again.

'Shut up.' But she wasn't smiling anymore. 'Go. And gods damn you if you look back.'

I didn't. I knew, as I limped past the blank-eyed statues, that this would be one of the memories I couldn't blot out. It would go in a box in my head, along with the time I'd spent under the woodshed and the moment when I'd pushed open the door of Acarius' cabin and seen the blood on the floor. I would never be able to forget Lorican's white face and Brix's fake smile.

But I didn't look back. I could do that much for them.

The walls of the labyrinth changed and narrowed, once I was a decent distance down the passage. The black stone abruptly sprouted more pictographs, richly coloured under the layer of dust. I couldn't make much of them. They seemed to be merely repetitions of the same religious scene – a gilded figure that I assumed was Jaern resurrecting dead bodies, again and again, surrounded by feverish throngs of worshippers.

Stop it.

I hauled myself upright and forced myself to keep going. If I halted to look at the pictures, I might not be able to get moving again.

The light from the illumination spell was bothering my eyes, although, thanks to Brix, the translation spell behind my ear didn't hurt anymore. I still wished she hadn't done it. I would rather have kept my pain private.

I had to be almost to the centre. If you were going to build a temple inside a cave, with rock that you had to haul from somewhere else, how big could you possibly make it?

The passage widened abruptly. I sent the light ahead of me.

There were three arched doorways, set into a wall pocked with small alcoves. The alcoves weren't in any pattern that I recognised, although there had to be one because they were connected by lines of silver paint. In every alcove sat a grinning skull. At the top of the wall, near the ceiling, silver letters shone:

Night births me without living, day kills me without murder.

I had found an ossuary, and my third puzzle.

Gods help me.

TWELVE

It finally occurred to me that I could sit. I sank down into the dust, easing my sore knee around in front of me. I fiddled with the useless straps of my brace, taking the few intact ones out of their buckles to tie around my leg like a rough splint.

Between that and a second numbing spell, maybe I would be able to stand up without crawling over to the wall. I scribed the runes on the leg of my trousers, at the thigh, which normally would have been a stupid thing to do. I had an idea that I was damaging my knee further with every step I took. But I probably wasn't going to get out of there, anyway, so there was no use in being smart.

And then there was nothing for it but to look up at the damn ossuary again.

The little niches full of skeletal bits pocked the blue-painted wall randomly. The longer I stared, trying to find the pattern, the more confused they seemed.

All right, the riddle first. I shut my eyes; looking at all those skulls was unnerving. I kept expecting them to come towards me, which was foolish. If they had been creatlaches they would have moved already.

Come on, Cricket. Think.

Acarius. It wasn't really his voice, but the memory was comforting. What sort of questions would he make me answer? How would he dissect the riddle?

Hells, boy, it isn't that hard. Think through the words. Night and day. What exists during the night but not during the day?

Sleep? The moon? Darkness?

None of those worked. You could take naps during the day, or find darkness in a cellar. You could even see the moon during the day, sometimes. Apart from imaginary creatures, the only thing I could think of that was present at night but not in daylight was—

Stars.

My eyes snapped open. That was it. That was the pattern. The ossuary was a map of the constellations.

I crawled forwards a bit, then put all my weight on my hands and hopped to get my good leg under me. It worked, sort of. I got up to standing and tested my numb knee. There wasn't a lot of pain, but there wasn't a lot of dexterity, either.

Fine, start over. I limped to the leftmost portion of the ossuary. Even though the ceilings were ten feet high or so, the alcoves only went up about seven feet – within easy reach of a man standing on the floor. There was more than one constellation, with all of the major star pictures represented. The Lady, nearest me. The Lion. The Dancers. The King. There were more, but my eyes refused to move on.

The Dancers.

'Something's wrong with you,' I murmured.

As I recalled, the Dancers was a useful constellation precisely because it had eight stars, forming a rough diamond-shape that pointed north.

Only this representation of the Dancers had nine stars. There was an extra skull at the base of the diamond shape. I dragged myself to the niche, hollowed into the wall at about the same level as my shoulders, between two of the arched doorways.

Nothing special, this bit of bone, covered in dirt like everything else. I couldn't see any wires or runes on it.

Which, my mind insisted on repeating, *doesn't mean that there isn't anything there.*

Last time I had made a mistake, a mistake that had got Brix and Lorican trapped. The fact held me where I was, while I searched through everything Acarius had taught me. I knew so many things – too many things. So why didn't I have anything that could help me? Why didn't I know what to do?

I forced myself to take four long, slow breaths. Then I gritted my teeth, reached out and put my hand on the skull.

It moved.

I jerked backwards. The eyes of the skull lit orange, and as it rolled out of its niche, I saw the nameplate floating where the brain once was.

Shit. Shit. Shit.

But it didn't continue to come towards me. It clattered to the floor, and then rolled itself merrily down the centre passageway.

You couldn't get much more obvious than that. I settled the strap of my satchel and saw that I was trembling again. When I could get my hands steady, I limped through the middle door.

The ceiling of the passage was low. I could follow the trail the skull had left in the dust plainly enough, and it was easier watching it than it was speculating about what fiendish puzzle might be ahead.

Of course, I also had to watch the repetitive smirk on the face of that skull. Eventually the jawbone fell off. I skirted it, and kept following the weird track in the dust.

And so I saw the broken shards of skeletons before I stepped on them. The tunnel was abruptly carpeted with them, one long mausoleum.

Ahead of me was the end of the passage, yet another dark doorway into yet another room. The skull crunched through the litter on the floor, whizzing away into the darkness.

I did have to step on the bones, though.

I was expecting the sound it made – like scrubbing a tile floor – but I wasn't expecting the *feel*, like teeth grinding under the arches of my feet. I made it almost to the door before nausea rocketed through me, ripping away my concentration.

The light winked out.

I scrabbled for my satchel. The air moved around me, hinting at a bigger room than any of the others I had been through so far. In a room that size there could be anything – creatlaches, pits, poisoned spikes. I needed to scribe the illumination spell again.

I froze. The crunching sound from the rolling skull had stopped.

'Greetings,' said a deep voice in the dark. 'Shall we have a little light?'

Witchlights flared into being, one after the other, in a ring of fire with the door I stood in as the base. Each light sat in a brazier held by a statue, about four times the size of a man, rainbow-hued flames dancing between their bronze-coated palms.

The statues portrayed the nine major gods, crusted with gilding and precious stones. In front of each god was a trough that must have once been a reflecting pool. All of them faced the dais at the centre of the room, which was nothing more or less than a runic prison circle, its edges covered with sigils in red paint, layer upon layer.

The dais held the remains of seven coffins, arranged around one elaborately decorated stone sarcophagus that was so large it had steps ascending to it. All stood open.

And then there was the man.

Standing inside the circle was the palest and most perfectly symmetrical human being I had ever seen. His silver hair touched the tips of his ears, irises gleaming black. His clothes looked as antique as everything else in the temple, a faded green tunic over a black shirt and trousers, with strange, pointy-toed boots. Around his neck hung a pendant on a silver chain, a teardrop-shaped black gem.

'Greetings,' he said, again, as though I hadn't heard.

I gave him a nod, but didn't move towards him. The spell behind my ear burned, which meant he was speaking in the same old dialect as the writing on the walls of the maze. His word had been accented in some way I couldn't place – even my translation spell wasn't smoothing that out. That, combined with his clothes, gave me a bad feeling. Who goes temple-raiding wearing a costume?

'Thank the gods you've come.' And now the accent was gone. His face had changed from being as immobile as marble to open and vulnerable, like a child's. 'I thought I was never going to get out of here. It's been . . . days, I think, but it's difficult to tell the passage of time down here. What's your name?' The black eyes fixed on mine.

'What?' I blinked. 'Gray.' My name slid out without my permission, as though someone had pulled it with a string. A deep part of my mind was screaming with alarm. He was running a spell, and I had no idea which one. 'Who are you?' I said. 'How did you get here?'

'You see before you an unlucky thief.' He moved towards the open sarcophagus and sat on its steps, muscular and lithe as a cat. 'I cracked this coffin and then the runes there on the floor lit up, and now I can't get past them without passing out. If I'd thought to bring a wizard with me, maybe they could have done something.' He shrugged. 'Foolish of me, I suppose. But I don't like sharing.'

'And you got past all the traps and the bone creatures outside, without leaving tracks in the dust or any trace of your presence,' I said. 'I see. Makes perfect sense.'

He watched me, a smile spreading over his face, slowly. 'What's your explanation of me, then?'

I couldn't rid myself of the memory of the shoulder blade I'd pulled out of the creatlach that had attacked Brix. 'I think *someone* had to build Spindlejoint,' I said, and then had to face the fact of the builder's name. I wondered, briefly, whether I'd walked into some kind of spell, cracked my skull and was hallucinating while I died in a corner. 'You're not the god Jaern, though, even if you took his name.' Saying the words out loud helped, a little. 'The god isn't real. At best he's an idea. A philosophy of secret-keeping.'

'The *god* Jaern. So they still call me that. I didn't think it would last so long.' He rested his chin on one hand, the elbow on his knee, and examined me. 'You know, most people would have believed me, about being a thief. I was implying there is treasure here – they would have started bargaining for a piece of it.'

'Most people are idiots,' I said.

'True.' He didn't move. 'You're not, I take it.' He tilted his head sideways. 'But a bit reckless, aren't you? Still talking to me.'

'Why shouldn't I?' I had the spells scribed on my arms, but I was suddenly doubtful that my flame incantation would impress him much. What did I know about Jaern? What did *anybody* know about Jaern? I had only been forced to attend Temples prayers a few times in the years before I went to live with Acarius, and I couldn't remember anything about it except spending the whole time seething. The old anger and fear bubbled up my throat. 'I don't see a reason to be afraid of you,' I said.

'Well, the obvious one would be that I crawled out of that coffin.' Jaern looked at the sarcophagus with distaste. It could have held three of him. 'Which is alarming, in itself. When I last saw the sky, people believed in all sorts of unholy creatures that aren't quite dead. Of course, as you noted, even then they were idiots.' He ran a finger along the carved coffin edge. A string of the swirling runes cut into it lit under his touch. 'I'm not dead. I am old, however, and I'm curious as to how old. Who's king these days, in the daylight world?'

I made my way deeper into the room, trying frantically to think. Acarius wouldn't have sent me to face an opponent this strange without warning me. So what, then? Lorican had said that Acarius hadn't gone very deep into the maze. Did that mean that Jaern hadn't been here when Acarius was, or only that Acarius hadn't come this far?

Gods, was I actually considering this? It wasn't possible for a man to survive underground, in a prison circle, without food or water, for longer than a couple of days. Building the creatlaches would have taken months. I needed time to work out what he really was.

'You look my age,' I said.

'I know.' He stood and stalked to the edge of the runes, not two feet from me. If anything, he looked younger – and slightly taller – than me. 'You're what, twenty-five? Twenty-six? It's an attractive age. It's why I made this body.' He stretched out a pastel hand and looked at it with satisfaction. 'Better than limping around as an old man.'

'Made,' I said. The word was wrong. Necromancers don't really *make* anything, they just rearrange – and this whole place reeked with death. He hadn't *made* the body he was wearing any more than I had made mine.

But then, I was beginning to think he hadn't exactly been *born* into it, either.

His eyes flickered up. 'Good.' He sounded pleased, almost startled. 'Only twenty-six. An infant, practically, yet you caught that distinction.' He was back to examining me now, eyes narrowed. 'So you're a bit of a prodigy, too, along with being reckless. I think I like you.' He scanned me, from the top of my head to my toes and back again. 'You're right, of course,' he murmured. '*Made* isn't the best word for it. *Took*, maybe, would be more accurate. A prodigy, and you're ...' He smiled again. 'It's definitely an attractive age, even with the gimp leg. Anyway, you're a wizard. I wonder if you'll get something for me.'

I stepped backwards. The statues in the room all suddenly seemed too close. There were too many eyes. 'Listen, I'm sure a god is used to people jumping to his whims, but–'

'Don't pretend to be stupid,' he interrupted. 'You've guessed by now I'm not a god. And I'm not under any illusion that I can trick you into helping me – but I rather think you'll get what I want anyway.'

'Get what?' I snapped.

'My soul.' He swept a hand towards the statue of Neyar. 'A fitting insult, wasn't it? To put my soul in that bitch's necklace. My apprentice always had a sense of humour.' His jaw hardened as he stared at the dog-goddess. 'I don't. Every day for a year I've looked at my soul and reflected on my absent sense of humour.'

'You've been down here longer than a year,' I said.

He rolled his eyes. 'I told you to stop pretending to be stupid. How am I supposed to know exactly how many years I've been down here if you won't tell me who the king is? Judging by the very odd way you talk, it's probably been some centuries. I *woke up* a year ago, infant. An entire year with nothing to do but pace and count the hours and read and find new ways to put dry bones together, a year with nothing to *work* on.' He kicked the edge of the coffin nearest him, which I saw was filled with books, papers and rags of what could have once been clothing.

'You're running a translation spell of your own,' I said.

The corner of his mouth twitched upwards. 'Eh, some spells one wants running more or less permanently, especially if one is supposed to have divine omniscience. Language changes so quickly. Even with that pretty incantation glowing behind your ear, I doubt you could understand me if my spell wasn't active. At any rate, that's not interesting. When they locked me in here, the fifth Kaldien was on the throne of the Silver Court and Gerran Kej was the Lord Governor in the provinces. Who is it now?'

The Daine kings across the sea all took the same name upon ascending the throne. The one sitting there now was, if I wasn't mistaken, the *twenty-ninth* Kaldien. I calculated quickly, unable to escape an unwelcome jolt of pity.

'Eight hundred years,' I said. 'And there's no Lord Governor. Varre has its own king, Alastar.'

For a split second he seemed disorientated. Then he shrugged. 'So I'm nine hundred and fifty-eight years old. Will you get me my soul?'

'I came down here for an artefact,' I said.

He spread his hands out sideways. 'As you can see, the room is stuffed with them. Take your choice.'

How had Acarius put it? 'A child, of sorts,' I said.

'The *child*?' Jaern spat the words. The air in the room changed, as though someone had sucked what little heat there was out of it. 'Who told you to get *that*?' I stepped backwards, startled by the sudden menace in his face. 'Tell me.'

Instead, I turned in a slow, painful circle, desperation building inside me. Jaern's reaction made no sense if the artefact wasn't in the room, but the only things here were gigantic bronze statues. I couldn't even tip one over, let alone take one away.

One at a time. I slowed my breathing, focused on the memory of Acarius' voice, taking me through runic problems. *Be systematic.*

It wasn't Neyar, with her glowing ruby necklace and the head of a wolf – nothing about her could logically be interpreted as *child*. Not the sun-goddess Linna, reclining amid sharp brass rays, with coronas behind her head and hands. Not Farran, half-swallowed by his throne of silver-plated waves.

Ranara was closest to me. Lady of Shadows. Mother of the Moon. I'd been avoiding her. When the plague had come to our village, my mother had wrung the neck of our last chicken and put the bird in the tarnished copper hands of the village's shrine to Ranara. Three days later, she'd started coughing. A week after that, they put her in the ground.

This version of Ranara was smiling. For one hot, red second, I wanted to put my fist through her lovely face.

Instead, I made myself analyse the statue. In one hand she held a crescent-shaped brazier, and in her other she held a little gold doll to her breast as though to suckle it. *A child, of sorts.* I limped to her knee, reached up, stretching, and grabbed the doll out of her arms. It came easily, heavy in my hand.

It was a well-crafted, gold-plated version of the idol I'd seen at the Fenwydd temple, the Empty One, and it was hollow, or I wouldn't have been able to lift it. Behind me, Jaern's breath hissed out between his teeth. When I turned, he had gone quiet, watchful. He didn't seem like the sort of man who would fear much, but he'd lost some of his easy grace.

I stepped closer to the witchlight, cradling the doll with two hands. The thing was even uglier now that I could see it properly, an empty-eyed nightmare that only looked vaguely like an actual baby. Under the layers of dirt, its gold skin crawled with innumerable tiny loops of runes. And it wasn't just missing its eyes: there were sockets in its body as well, which looked like they corresponded roughly to the position of human organs. I put a fingertip in the thing's lung-hole and a spring closed softly around my knuckle.

As gently as I could, I freed my finger. I glanced at Jaern. 'What fits here? And there's a gate, back in the room with the statue of the three yavadis. Do you know how to lower it? The trigger should be in this room.'

He grinned, with something approaching relief. 'Of course I know. And no, it's not in the sanctuary.'

'Then where is it?'

He waved a dismissive hand. 'The important thing is that you've got living flesh on your bones. A creatlach is entertaining, but they are limited.' He walked to the edge of the circle of runes closest to Neyar and stood with his arms folded, his toes a fraction of an inch from the curve of the characters. 'You can see it from here, the red stone at the centre of her necklace. It should just be a matter of–'

'Is it stones?' I held up the doll. 'Two of them would have been in the eyes of the mosaic at the beginning of the maze, but I think someone already removed those. Where are the other four?' I gestured towards the closest statue, whose eyes were glittering, rune-carved sapphires. *All* the statues had precious stones for eyes. 'Stones like those, maybe.'

He glanced at it and then away, uninterested. 'I don't bargain with idiots.'

This was getting tedious. I had seen nothing else that could have been the artefact Acarius wanted, nothing unique enough to justify crawling into this hole. This madman knew how the doll worked, and he knew how to get out of the maze. He had to.

And I wasn't going to stand there and let him call me an idiot.

I took a grease pencil from my satchel, bent and wrote a quick spiral of runes on the floor. If he wouldn't tell me which of the gems in the statues were the ones I wanted, I'd find them myself.

He walked towards me. After a moment he gave a quiet chuckle. 'Gods,' he said. 'I do like you.'

'How comforting.' I stood on the spiral and pronounced the runes.

He listened, as though to someone playing a violin. The spiral lit, and my vision changed. Some of the objects in the room took on a subtle purple glow, the ones he had been thinking about. It was a mild telepathy spell – a more direct one invites resistance and is, in any case, physically debilitating – but it should have been enough to show me where the gems were.

Only it didn't. One statue after another flared with colour and then faded. The bastard was thinking about every statue in rapid sequence.

'That's only really useful if the other party doesn't know how the spell works,' he said. 'Although your version has some clever distinctions. Are you going to get me my soul?'

I broke contact with the spell. 'Someone went to a lot of trouble to put you inside what looks like a fairly impervious prison circle,' I said. 'That doesn't argue in favour of letting you out. Whatever that red gem is – because it isn't your soul – it's the key to breaking the circle. And I'm not going to get it for you.'

'Of course it's the key to breaking the circle,' he said. 'You have to have a soul to cross the barrier. A simple enough trap, but I made the mistake of trusting my apprentice.'

'You can't separate bodies and souls,' I said.

He raised a platinum-coloured eyebrow. 'Of course you can, infant. What do you think a dagger to the throat does?'

'Fine, if you want to nitpick.' I walked around the circle towards the statue of Neyar, taking care not to touch the runes on the floor. 'You can't separate a soul from a body and put it into something else. That makes no sense.'

He matched my pace from inside the circle. 'It actually makes no sense that souls are attached to bodies in the first place,' he said. 'It's very odd, if you think about it – why don't trees have souls, for instance? – but it's no more odd that you can move one around than it is that they exist in the first place.'

'If your soul isn't in your body,' I said, 'how are *you* in your body?'

'Saints, how are you in your house without becoming part of the house?' He tilted his head sideways. '*I'm* my soul. This body is something I use, but without the proper rituals, I don't join with it any more than my soul joins with the glass of the vial. This is primary stuff, Gray. Don't they teach young wizards necromancy anymore?'

I didn't like the sound of my name in his mouth. I halted at the foot of the dry reflecting pool and began searching the ground for spikes hidden among the charnel litter.

'Necromancy is forbidden by the Mages' Guild,' I said. 'Was there a Guild, when you were locked up?'

'A *guild*?' He spat the word, disgusted. 'What, like they have – had – for *brewers*?'

'My feelings on the topic exactly.' Time was running out. Brix and Lorican would be in the dark by now. I had to figure out a way to make Jaern tell me what I needed. If I got his 'soul' in hand, maybe I could think of some way to use it as leverage. 'Much as I hate to agree with them about anything, however, I have to admit to finding necromancy unpleasant. You have to get the bones and tissue to work with from somewhere. How many corpses did it take for you to build that little bone army?'

He snorted. 'Hells, it's not as though the original owners were using them. And it's not as though I was the one who killed them. I didn't even build all of them. Some of the originals were my apprentice's work, animal bones set to guard me. They had to be repurposed. There aren't any traps left around that pool, by the way. I wasted a number of creatlaches before I realised the wards ensure only someone with a heartbeat can get the stone.'

I stepped into the dry bed of the pool with my good foot, dragged my numb leg after and paused. Nothing happened. The dull emerald eyes of the goddess still stared impassively at something over my left shoulder.

'So.' I moved towards the statue, cautious. I had no time, but I still couldn't rush. Necromancers are unpredictable, always looking for new material to practise with. For all I knew, what Jaern really wanted was my sinews. 'Are you going to tell me why your apprentice put you inside a prison circle? And how you can be nine hundred-odd years old?'

'Undoubtedly he believed he had something to resent,' he said. 'Does it matter?'

'My morality seems to be less flexible than I had supposed.' I stuffed the doll into my satchel; I had reached the statue now. I took a deep breath, bent my good knee and hopped. It took two of those before I could get a grip on the goddess' lap. I used my arms and my good leg to clamber up. My dangling bad leg sent jolts of suffering through me every time it flopped at an awkward angle. The spell was failing; I wouldn't be able to move without debilitating pain very much longer.

I sat on the goddess' lap for a moment, until I could get my breathing slowed from panting. 'It does actually matter whether he resented you for something like sleeping with his wife, or for murdering a couple of villages full of people.' The bronze grated against my backside, the grit of centuries sloughing off the metal. I got on to my knees, then inched around until I was facing the goddess' belly. I grabbed the neck of her gown and pulled myself upright, balanced on my uninjured foot and studied the clean places my scrambling had made. Under the dust, the goddess was painted with runes in yellow ink. 'Oh, hells.'

'I did mention there were wards,' Jaern said, sweetly.

Time to start working on the necklace. The red stone resting at the hollow of Neyar's throat came away in my hand. It wasn't really a stone at all, but a thick glass bottle filled with red fluid. The stopper on top was made of gold, and dangling from it was a gold chain, as though it was an amulet.

I shoved it in my satchel and took out the cup I use to measure reagents. It was the only thing I had on hand that might work. I jammed the edge of the cup against the corner of one of the goddess' eyes, trying to pry the emerald out of its setting.

Something tickled my ankles, as though I was walking through long grass. I glanced down to see tendrils of magic, its yellow light shaped like tiny snakes, working its way up my legs.

'They're just attracted to your pulse.' Jaern stood as close to me as he could get without crossing the runes. 'But they can be inconvenient. I'd get down if I were you.'

'I need her damn eyes.' I wriggled the cup and finally got the edge under the gem. A moment of effort, and it popped out into my hand. It was the right size to fit into a socket of the doll. I put it into my satchel, which was getting lumpy and heavy.

'No, you don't,' Jaern said. 'You need one of her eyes, one of Ranara's, one of Linna's and one of Farran's, not to mention the two of mine you said someone took from the mosaic. Get down, now, there's a good lad. That metal contraption on your leg is confusing the serpents.'

I took the goddess' other eye, just the same. Call me mercenary, but I could think of several uses for an emerald the size of my thumbnail.

The yellow snakes bunched around my injured leg, swarming over the brace. I had to figure out how to get down without my knee dumping me on to the floor eight feet below. A drop like that wouldn't kill me, probably, but it could break my back. I swallowed and started to lower myself to my good knee, as slowly as I could.

The snakes hissed and surged up my body to my throat, writhing, squeezing. I jerked backwards.

For one sick, interminable moment I hung there in the air, arms flailing.

And then I fell.

THIRTEEN

I must have yelled; my ears still rang when I realised I hadn't hit the ground. Jaern was squatting inside the rune circle, mumbling under his breath, his arms spread out towards me. Beneath me hummed a cushion of magic, hundreds of dragonflies made of red light, hovering a foot above the cluttered floor.

As soon as he caught my eye, Jaern stopped muttering, the muscles in his neck taut. 'Careful,' he said. 'You could have broken the vial. Now come here, give it to me.' His hands curled, and he yanked the cloud of dragonflies towards himself.

I fumbled for my satchel, but by the time I got my hand on the vial, I was inside the circle. He snapped his fingers and the magic cloud underneath me disappeared. I hit the floor with a thud. With my last bit of strength, I threw the vial as far from me as I could. It skittered across the floor, coming to rest in a pile of debris.

'No!' He lunged, but it was too late. He turned on me, twitching with rage. 'Go get it!'

'We're going to bargain first.' I started to sit up when I heard him growl a spell and a ball of white light smashed into my chest.

I couldn't move.

'Bargaining is for peasants.' He spat into the palm of his hand and dipped his thumb in it. It came away a bright green, as though he had a handful of ink. 'You're just going to agree.'

'What—' My face was going numb. My heart hammered against my sternum, pumping useless energy to my frozen body. 'That wasn't paralysis, what—'

'Quite correct, it wasn't.' He smeared his thumb against my forehead, tracing a pattern I didn't recognise, and pronounced it. A needle of agony drove itself into my head, so overwhelming I couldn't even shriek. He was trying to crack my memories, to force his way into my thoughts.

'By all the false gods,' he whispered. As abruptly as it had started, he broke contact, staring at me wide-eyed, with a sudden hunger that made the breath seize in my throat. Then he blinked, as though waking himself, and used his sleeve to wipe my forehead clean. 'Who is this Keir Esras person, that you spend so much thought on him?'

Well, that was unexpected. I took several large breaths, searching through my mind to see what he had tampered with. The memories I had of Keir, obviously, but what else? Something about Acarius?

'He kidnapped my grandfather,' I said. 'And tried to kill me. Why?'

He pushed the collar of my shirt open and scribed something on my chest, below my collarbone. 'We're going to help each other.'

'What are you doing?' I couldn't keep myself from asking the question, from hoping I didn't know.

'Convincing you,' he said.

'Don't,' I said. 'Wait!'

He smiled and pronounced the spell. The ley broke.

The magic shattered, went icy against my flesh. The poison of all my spells whipped around me, mingling with the red knife of pain that shot up my leg. It clawed through my body, pumping through my veins, throbbing at the edges of my vision.

I was going to have a seizure.

'No.' The word choked me. 'No.'

His hand was on my knee, and he was chanting.

The seizure stopped.

Then, slowly, the pain began to retreat – all of it. First the toxicity, then the damage in my knee. I opened my eyes to find a jewel dangling in front of my face, swinging gently on a silver chain – the pendant from around his neck. As I stared at it, I realised it was a bottle, like the one I'd thrown away, only this held purple-black fluid. At the heart of the liquid spun a cloud of scarlet, pulsing.

'What is that?' I said. The spell Jaern had put on me had broken, too, although the witchlights still burned around us. I sat up.

He still had one hand on my knee, holding the black vial with the other. My pain was gone now, but whatever he was doing went on. Blue light glowed under his fingers and twisted up what I could see of his arm.

Something rearranged itself inside my leg. Tendons twisted, lengthened. As I watched, the bones shifted under the skin, straightened. It didn't hurt. My gorge rose, but it didn't hurt. 'What are you doing to me?'

He let go. I scrambled away from him, back outside the rune circle.

He shifted position, sitting on the stone, breathing as hard as if he'd been running. 'Proving my good faith,' he said.

I flexed my knee. This was like no numbing spell I had ever heard of. Not only was there no pain, there wasn't even any awkwardness. I stripped off the ruined brace and got to my feet.

It wasn't numb. My knee had been . . . fixed.

I didn't move towards the soul vial. I didn't understand what was going on. 'Why? Why do that?'

He shrugged and looked down at the black pendant, cradling it in his palm. 'Why not? That brace annoyed me. You look better without it.'

'But it isn't *possible*,' I said, through my teeth. 'Any healing magic can only move pain, it can't eliminate it. You need a goat or a rabbit or another person or something to absorb the damage. Where did you put it?' I scanned him. He wasn't grabbing at his knee or showing a glimmer of anything on his face except the fatigue that anyone would suffer after doing a spell of that magnitude. So he hadn't taken the pain into himself. I looked at the witchlights, which were burning as merrily as ever. 'And how is *that* still working? You did a ley-breaker. They should be out.'

'Saints.' He gave me a look of mock horror. 'For that matter, how can you still understand what I'm saying?'

I touched the place behind my ear where the translation spell had been. It was gone, nothing but a smear of paint, like the rest of my incantations.

He held up the black vial. 'This. This is where the pain went. Into this vial, into the entity inside. This is where the poison from my magic goes, if you're curious.'

Entity. A trickle of sweat, clammy, ran down the back of my neck. 'What . . .'

'It doesn't matter, but if it makes you feel better, it isn't a person.' He tilted his head sideways. 'As to the other questions, I won't be able to explain until I know the state of the magic you were instructed in. I broke the ley on *you*, not me, for one thing. It will wear off in a couple of hours.'

'This doesn't make sense.' I ran both hands through my hair. The sudden absence of pain, the weird smoothness and grace with which I could take steps, was almost as disorientating as the ache had been.

'It's simple,' he said. 'Get me out of here, and then I'll help you get what you want from these people.'

'You don't know what I want.' I walked to the soul vial and picked it up. I wondered what the red fluid was. Surely not blood, not if it was that bright after centuries in a bottle. Wine? An alchemical compound?

'I don't *care* what you want,' Jaern said, his eyes following me. 'If it's revenge, you'll find me a creative executioner. Anything less is easier.'

If the vial really contained his soul, it was the only thing on the face of the earth that would have any hold over him. I had heard enough rumours to know that bonecrafters thought a soul had to be kept together to remain viable. Therefore, to break the vial would disperse the soul and kill Jaern.

But I couldn't kill him. I needed answers from him. And I couldn't cast anything, not until the ley-breaker he'd laid on me was gone. Even if I could cast, his magic was so different to mine that I would be at a disadvantage in a duel, and he knew it.

Although it didn't seem to have occurred to him that I might know something he didn't.

'What does the doll do?' I asked, and loathed the way the question made me sound like a fart-knocking Guild rat. I could figure it out myself, if I just had *time*.

He gave an unpleasant laugh. 'You already know what it does. Get me out, Gray.'

'All I know is that my grandfather sent me to get it,' I said. 'You want me to help you, then explain.'

He chewed at one fingernail with even, white teeth. 'The doll is a host, a tool for soulwork. Without it, you're left with slapdash half-measures, fumbling in the few minutes when death loosens the strings of the soul, rushing to get the soul into any available body before it dies. These cretins you're worried about seem to know the rudiments of taking souls *out*. But that's only half the trick of immortality, which I suspect is the problem.'

'What are you saying?'

'When someone has your soul, they can take advantage of the fact that you can't die until your soul does. As you are demonstrating, they can drive a difficult bargain, get you to do and say things that you wouldn't otherwise. Torture you in ways that would kill you, if you were in your body. The pain can be exquisite. Eternal.' A flicker of deep, icy hatred passed over his face. 'I imagine that's why what's-his-name told you to get it.' His eyes caught mine, sardonic. 'Not that he, or you, or Keir will know how to use it unless I tell you. So that's the offer. Get me out, and I'll teach you to use the doll, help you rescue your kinsman. I'm *bargaining*, infant. Don't make me lower myself any further.'

It made a sick kind of sense. I knew Keir had been obsessively hunting necromancers, and, given his ambitions, it hadn't been to prevent them from flouting the Charter. I knew he was hurting Acarius; that he'd almost managed to break the toughest and most stubborn man I'd ever known. Hells, I hadn't understood until this moment how Keir had managed to capture a wizard as talented as Acarius, but if he'd taken out the old man's *soul*—

If this was true, I'd have to alter my plans, go against my grandfather's orders. I couldn't just hide the doll if it was the key to binding Acarius' soul to him.

The question was *how*. Jaern wasn't going to tell me while he was inside the circle. He evidently had all the time in the world, and my time was running out. If saving Acarius' life required making a deal with a necromancer, there was only one choice I could make.

If I could find a way to keep the soul vial in my possession *and* get Jaern out of the circle, however, I could keep him leashed. I hoped.

So I had to figure out how it worked.

'This can't be your soul,' I said again, although I was sure by now that, somehow, it was.

'My soul, some of my blood, a bit of my original heart and enough rennen to bind it.' He was bored again, toying with the black pendant he held. '*Basic* necromancy.'

'Rennen.' I held the vial up to the light.

146

'Alchemical preserver,' he said. 'I'll tell you the recipe, when you get me to the surface.'

'Poison?'

His eyes narrowed. 'Why?'

'I don't see how a non-toxic substance can preserve *and* fill the binding function in an alchemical composite.' Which was a lie, but there was no harm in letting him think I was slightly stupid. Especially given that I was about to do something tremendously stupid.

'Rennen is made of beetle guts and distilled liquor,' he said. 'It might make a man drunk, if he drank enough of it, or puke, if he was allergic to beetles. And it fills the binding function, idiot, because of the magic put on it when it's compounded, not because of its innate properties.'

Which meant that I probably wouldn't die from what I had in mind. Probably.

'A soul in a bottle.' I turned it over in my hands, expending some effort not to cringe. The bottle was weirdly warm, as though it held blood new from the vein. *Or fresh piss*, suggested the noisy part of my mind, the part that sounds like Acarius. I smiled. It helped me to keep from dry heaving.

'I thought it rather a pleasing conceit at the time,' Jaern said, dryly. 'Now I'm less fond of it. Next time I expect I'll choose a different container.'

I raised my eyebrows in what I hoped was a look of half-witted wonder. 'A different container?'

The lily-skinned weasel had the gall to roll his eyes at me again. 'There's nothing special about that one. Anything that holds liquid works. It's magic, not superstition.'

'I see.' I twisted the gold stopper open. I knew from experience that concentrating on not puking would be completely ineffective. Instead, I thought about Acarius, and what I'd say to him when I saw him again. I'd composed the speech a thousand times, always

vacillating wildly between *tell me who I am, dammit* and *I'm sorry.*
'Here's to you,' I said.

The annoyed boredom on Jaern's face fled. 'What are you doing?'

'Hells, I don't know,' I said, and put the vial to my lips.

It tasted awful, of course. Worse than awful. It was like drinking
blood tainted with lamp oil, and it burned all the way into my stomach. I had to concentrate to keep swallowing until the vial was
empty, and then it took all I had to keep from vomiting the whole
mess back up.

Acarius. Think about Acarius.

The cramping pain in my gut eased. Empty, the bottle was just a
piece of thick glass. I looked at it and swallowed a mouthful of
spittle – then two – just to be certain there were no vestiges of the
soul clinging to my teeth.

'Now.' I belched. It hurt, and tasted like lamp oil again. I stuck out
my hand, across the runes. 'Provided that doesn't kill me, I've just
become your bottle. You can touch me and get out of that circle – and
open the damn gates.'

'Little –' Jaern was staring at me. 'What have you done?'

'If you're expecting sympathy from me, the fact that I've just
swallowed a piece of your disgusting-tasting heart does not incline
me that way,' I said. 'Come on.'

He grasped my hand and stepped over the runes. Once outside the
circle he paused, as though he was waiting for something. When
whatever it was didn't happen, he smiled. 'I'm damned. It worked.'

'Yes.' I pulled away from him. 'We're on a schedule, if you don't
mind.'

He spun on his heel. Before I knew what was happening he had
me by the throat, slammed up against the legs of the statue of Lord
Farran, squirming against the spiny armour on the bronze shins.
Jaern was *strong* – stronger than any human had a right to be. I wondered if I had been severely mistaken, and he really was a god.

'Don't ever do something like that again,' Jaern said.

I fought against the urge to squirm. Anything that looked like faint-heartedness would irritate him, and this time it wouldn't be to my advantage. 'Easy, bonecrafter. Don't break your bottle. Pity to lose your soul to make a point.'

For one blind, strangling moment, I thought it wasn't going to work. He was going to kill me anyway.

Then he released me. 'And a clever bottle it is.' He slipped the black pendant on its chain over his head and tucked it into his shirt. 'You had some gems you wanted to collect, I believe.' He shoved past me and climbed the statue of Farran, like a spider going up a wall.

'You're robbing your own tomb.' I heard an odd kind of amusement in my voice, and shoved it downwards as quickly as I could. If I didn't get a grip on myself, amusement was going to become hysterics. What *had* I done?

'If it's mine, then I'm not robbing.' Jaern took a slender knife from a sheath at his waist and brushed grime from the god's face. 'Besides, gods can't steal. Almost by definition, anything we do is correct. Convenient, isn't it?' He rapped the butt of his dagger against Farran's nose. 'They're all like me, Gray. All fakes.'

He's lying. I considered the possibility and found, to my surprise, that I didn't want him to be. Ranara let my mother die, hadn't responded to any of my tormented childhood prayers, and I'd tried all the other deities before I gave up. None of them had saved me from even a single beating. The idea that there was nothing behind the statues was, strangely, less painful than the idea that they'd all found me unworthy of help.

'How did you get to be a god, then?' I said.

'Oh.' He paused for a moment. 'Well, people are always looking for something to worship.' He inserted the tip of the dagger behind the blue jewel at the centre of one of the idol's pupils. 'Might as well be me. Besides, when you get to know what you're doing with necromancy, people are always showing up asking you to bring someone back to life.'

'Which isn't how it works,' I said.

'For someone with such quaint morals you've got a remarkable grasp of reality.' The sapphire slid out into his hand. 'Of course that isn't how it works. Once you let a soul slip away, it's gone. But that didn't stop them asking. After a while, it would have been stupid to ignore the opportunity, so I started saying I was a star, fallen from heaven.' He rubbed a lock of hair between his fingertips. 'Silver. The lie seemed to make sense at the time. People ate it up. Practically begged to be deceived. It was that simple.'

He tossed the gem to me. I caught it and studied it while he climbed down. Like the first emerald I had taken from Neyar's idol, this sapphire was carved with a single runic character, one I had never seen before. All of the gems were ridiculously large, big enough to buy opulence if sold to the right jeweller. I put the sapphire beside the emeralds.

Jaern went around the room removing the left eyes of two more gods – a ruby and a diamond, respectively. When he handed me the diamond, he said: 'I take it you're not inclined to worship me. I really can teach you about magic, you know. Tell you secrets.'

'I don't worship anything,' I said.

He grinned. 'You all worship *something*. It'll be entertaining, in your case, to decipher what. It's been centuries since anyone surprised me, and you've managed it twice in the space of twenty minutes. Let's go.'

Just like that, he strode out of the place that had been his prison for the better part of a millennium, up into the darkness.

And just like that, I pocketed the gems and followed him.

FOURTEEN

I could run. Gods, I could *run*.

And it was a good thing, too, because the barmy pseudo-god whose soul was giving me heartburn started sprinting as soon as we were in the passageway. Bone chips spurted from under his toes. I followed, giddy with painless motion, with grace and freedom, pelting into the dark.

'Illumination,' I said, when the blackness closed around me. 'I'd cast, but according to you, the ley-breaker takes two hours to finish.'

In return I heard elegant, rapid-fire syllables being rattled off like a man would shout an order for venison at an inn. Light burst around me, and I recognised the constellation room. The skulls in the niches were blazing with blue fire. Jaern stood in the middle of the room, drunk with elation.

'I haven't been in here for eight hundred years,' he said. 'I could kiss you. Which way are we going? You said you had people down here.'

'Friends,' I said.

He wrinkled his nose. 'Which way?'

I pointed, and he started walking.

He cast while he moved, producing an exotic band of light that circled one of his wrists. I couldn't keep myself from making mental notes. His magic was fascinating – different, yet hung on the same structure as my own. I recognised some of the syllables, for instance, but where was his spell *scribed*? Certainly nowhere on his body that I could see, and yet by all the laws of magic, I knew it had to be written somewhere. He could have been wearing a piece of jewellery, but the light from the magic should have been centred where the sigils were, not on his naked wrist.

We travelled with what seemed like dizzying speed when contrasted with the way I had limped down the passage the first time. When we burst into the room with the yavadis statue, the first thing I saw was Brix on the other side of the bars, staring anxiously into the dark. My heart turned over.

'Gray?' she said.

'It's all right. It's going to be all right.' The words tumbled out. For reasons I didn't want to analyse, I needed to wipe the fear off her face. 'Open the gate,' I said to Jaern, and went to the cross-hatches. 'How are you both?'

'Better now that you're back alive.' Lorican rose from where he had been sitting against the wall. His eyes found Jaern and his relieved smile fled. 'Who is that?'

I glanced back at the necromancer. He was squatting beside the statue, running his fingertips along the carved base and to all appearances, enjoying himself vastly instead of doing as he was told.

'He's the god Jaern, sort of,' I said. 'I found him at the centre of the maze.'

'*What?*' Brix moved back from the gate.

Sometimes genuine telepathy would be so convenient. Talking in front of Jaern could get awkward. 'What matters is he can get the gate open. Trust me.' I had meant it to sound confident, but it wasn't. It was almost a question.

Brix exhaled. 'I do. But you're going to explain, and soon.'

Until the tension in my shoulders released, I didn't realise how certain I had been that she'd say she *didn't* trust me.

Lorican's eyes hadn't left Jaern. 'Lad,' he said, quietly. 'Whatever trouble you're in, whatever you had to promise him to make him free us, we'll get you out of it. Did you find what you need for Acarius?'

Suddenly, confronted with Lorican's kindness, I realised that it was going to be difficult explaining why I had thought it would be a good idea to imbibe someone else's soul. I wasn't entirely sure that getting me out of this situation was even possible. I flushed. 'I found it.'

Lorican gave me a small, tense smile. 'Then we can figure the rest of it out.'

'Infant,' Jaern called, from across the room. He wiped his hand on the leg of his trousers. 'Are you going to give me something to scribe with?'

What had happened to his green ink spit, or whatever it had been that he used to scribe on my forehead? I walked to him, pulling the grease pencil from my satchel as I went. Jaern took it, scribed a few quick runes and then pronounced them before kissing one of the yavadis statues full on the mouth. The runes – and the statue's lips, under his – blazed red. The gate fell back into the floor with a shriek. Lorican and Brix moved out of the dead end at a speed just shy of running.

Brix halted beside me. 'Gray—'

I stepped backwards. I wanted to know she was safe, but I knew, abruptly, that I couldn't tolerate it if she touched me. Even a hand on my sleeve would be too much. Nobody trusted me except Acarius. Why did Brix? Why did it matter so much whether she did?

'Are *you* all right?' she said.

No.

'Fine,' I said. Jaern was watching, and I wanted to get out from under his observation. Hells, for all I knew, carrying his soul around inside me let him watch me in other ways.

'Your leg seems better,' Brix said.

And how was I going to explain *that*? 'It is.' I turned to Lorican. 'Ready to leave?'

He nodded, although his attention was still on Jaern. 'Aye, it's too far underground for my liking. Let's get out of here.'

It was more or less the same at the other gate. Jaern lingered for a moment in front of the mosaic, touching the empty eye sockets with two slender, searching fingers. 'So that was what woke me,' he murmured. 'He took my *eyes*, and thought I wouldn't feel it.'

'Jaern,' I said.

The false god stirred himself and walked into the foyer without saying anything. He found a place among the pictograms to scribe an incantation to deactivate the lock, and the machinery was obedient.

As were the creatlaches. The rest of us hung back as the gate opened, but Jaern stood in the doorway, watching the bone creatures rushing towards him. He held up a hand and they all stopped.

'What were they for?' I crept forwards until I was almost beside him. The creatlaches couldn't have been *guardians*, per se, not if they were his. He would have wanted someone to find him, not have been trying to keep them away.

'Work. Something to fill the hours.' He didn't turn towards me, but that peculiar smile played at the corner of his mouth. 'To keep from going mad, mostly. Otherwise to bring me something with a beating heart, on the off-chance they ever encountered it.' He snapped his fingers.

The creatlaches fell apart. One moment they were sprightly and animated, a pack of spindly dogs watching their master; the next, they were nothing but a pile of old bones.

Something with a beating heart.

That was why the creatlach had grabbed Brix and carried her off, instead of trying to kill her. Jaern's plan had been to catch something with a beating heart, remove the heart while it was still viable and . . .

'Oh, lovely,' I muttered. 'A creatlach with a heartbeat. You wouldn't have needed me.'

He kicked a skull away from him and walked to the base of the black steps, staring out into the cavern. 'Dull, I grant you, but the best I could do at the time. Lead on.'

Brix and I had made it to the carved pilgrim's path when Lorican spoke.

'Lead on where?' The Erranter had positioned himself with the advantage of the high ground, perched halfway up the steps. He had produced a dagger from somewhere on his person. 'You're not thinking of bringing him through Deeptown? Are you telling me *he's* safe?' He pointed at Jaern with the knife.

Lorican was right, of course. The people of Deeptown were innocents and I had no right to unleash a mad necromancer on them. But I still had to get Jaern to the surface. The strap of my satchel dug into my shoulder, the doll and the gems heavy inside. I had a shrewd idea where the other two stones I needed were, given that Acarius had been the one to take them. Once I had all the pieces assembled, Jaern would show me how to use the thing, if only to retrieve his own soul. Then I would know whether I could trade the doll, or whether I needed it to help Acarius. For once, I knew where I was going next – if I could just get there.

'Isn't there any other way out?' Brix glanced from me to Lorican. 'You talked about a door in the Spires, could we use that?'

'We still have to go through the village to get to that exit,' Lorican said, 'and I'm not taking that man through a crowd of children and sick old people until someone tells me who he is.'

Before I could say anything, Jaern had stalked back up the stairs. 'I'm the Prince-Who-Speaks-to-Ghosts,' he said. 'Lord of Secrets. Heir of the Unseen. Star-Who-Bedded-the-Moon. Jaern.' He halted three steps below Lorican and spread his arms open, like a dancer. 'Or, conversely, I'm a madman who thinks I'm those things, but who isn't carrying any weapons. Search me, if you like. As a rule, I'm uninterested in villages, but even if I wasn't, one unarmed man can't usually do that much damage.'

Lorican held his ground, apparently disinclined to nose through Jaern's clothes and put himself where the necromancer could grapple for the knife.

'If anybody in Deeptown is harmed, Lorican has promised to kill me,' I said. *Break the bottle, wreck the soul.* I had the satisfaction of seeing a flash of startled rage pass across Jaern's eyes, but I was watching Lorican. I needed him to understand what I was asking him to do. He wasn't recoiling in horror, which was a good start. Lorican had to seem willing to kill me for this ploy to work.

The necromancer's upper lip curled. 'And you both respect promises, I see. How uplifting.' He set his teeth in something that was certainly not a smile. 'Then I'll make a promise of my own, not to touch anyone in this rotting village of yours. Is that good enough?'

Lorican searched my face, his fingers tight on the hilt of his dagger. For a moment I wondered whether it was really a ploy – maybe Lorican really *was* willing to kill me. He descended the steps, put the knife point to my ribs and looked at Jaern. 'Move, then.'

And, after a long, terrible moment where none of us breathed, the god . . . moved.

It was difficult to discern how much time had passed when we reached Deeptown. It must have been several hours, because the boy we had left standing sentry had been replaced by a surly fellow with a grey beard, leaning on a crooked spear. He scowled at us as we emerged from the tunnel. 'Lorican? All right, there?'

'Aye.' Lorican sounded unconvinced. 'Just leaving, thank the goddess.'

'I thought there were only three of you,' the old man said. 'Arol said –' The old man's eyes dropped to Jaern's wrist, where the magic still glowed. 'What's the matter with your hand?'

'Magic.' Jaern's long fingers caressed the air. He purred with menace. 'Useful stuff. For instance, I can use it to turn recalcitrant people inside out.'

'No.' Lorican prodded my ribs with the knife.

Jaern's eyes flicked to Lorican, practically glowing with resentment and doubt. 'You're his friend. You wouldn't hurt him.'

'I'll do what I have to.' Lorican took a handful of the back of my collar. I could smell his sweat, sour and fear-tinged, and hear the rasp of his ragged, quick breath. I watched the calculation pass through Jaern's eyes, weighing the likelihood of my death against his desire to act.

The guard thumped his spear butt against the ground. 'What's going on, here?'

Brix slipped past me, and smiled at the guard. 'Didn't they tell you why we were in the tunnel?' She fluttered a gesture back towards Jaern. 'This one, my cousin – my aunt Nedda's boy – went down mushroom hunting three days ago. Lost himself, of course. We found him without a bit of water left in his flask, up to his elbows in that glowing lichen. He's not talking sense, half-stupid with thirst and hunger. Is there something you need from us, or can we get some food and water into him? I'd be so grateful if we could.'

The guard's frown softened. 'Reckon he was lucky to have someone to go after him,' he said. 'There's many a one that never comes back from those tunnels. But I still need to take you back to the Lady Mother's pavilion before you leave. There's been trouble above, wizards on the hunt, militia insisting there's rebellion brewing, talk of a bounty–'

Jaern had listened to all this with cold, intense distaste. His fingers flickered again, and suddenly he held a gold-and-sapphire necklace.

The guard stopped mid-word, staring at the necklace. 'What's that?'

'It's yours, little father,' Jaern said. 'I'm bored. My . . . *cousin* seems to like you and I'd like to get up into the sunlight; so take it, let us go and be quiet.'

I squeezed my eyes shut and then opened them again. The necklace still seemed solid enough, except for a tell-tale shimmer just before my eyes focused on it. That shimmer meant it was an illusion – an incredibly good one. Jaern was offering the guard so much empty air.

But it wasn't just illusion; there was something else, a buzzing in my ears. The necromancer was running a second spell, doubtless one that was rendering the guard and everyone in range of Jaern's voice more suggestible. My skin prickled with aversion. Apart from the fact that I dislike being yanked down to the level of the average cabbage-brained idiot, it made me uneasy that I *still* couldn't see where Jaern had the spell scribed. It could have been under his tunic, I supposed, but when had he written it? I hadn't taken my eyes off him since we'd left the ossuary. Even if he'd had it scribed before, how in the hells could he have known he would need this particular incantation?

'Go . . . along then.' The guard took the 'necklace' and turned it over in his hands. 'It's all right.'

Lorican waited until we were a decent distance from the guard and then spoke in a rough whisper. 'That won't stop him from telling the Lady Mother about your pale friend, as soon as we're out of sight.'

I didn't stop walking. Having Jaern around people was bad, but stopping with him in a confined space like that cave was even worse. 'So let him. What's she going to do with the information? Charge us another spoonful of cinnamon?'

'Didn't you hear him?' Lorican sounded nearly frantic. 'The Guild wizards have been asking around. The king's militia thinks someone is talking treason, and they'll blame the Erranter. They *always* blame the Erranter. It's why security was so tight when I brought you down here, with the Mothers sitting at the doors themselves. They're sorceresses, Gray. What do you think the Guild would do to the Lady Mother if they decided to arrest her? What do you think would happen to all the people down here who depend on her for charms and medicine?'

'We're already leaving as quickly as we can,' I said. 'If Keir is still divining, my signature in the scrying will be moving away from Deeptown.'

'Besides,' Jaern said, 'nobody's going to tell the Lady Mother.' He slowed as we reached the edges of the murky village, taking in the buildings, bemused.

'I suppose an illusory necklace is supposed to see to that,' I said.

'The spell will see to that.' Jaern pointed to a cooking fire a short distance away, where a woman stood turning a spit. 'She's cooking a duck.' He sniffed at the air. 'Gods, that's savoury.'

I frowned. 'I didn't see you cast anything else.'

'I've a mind to have some of that duck,' Jaern said. 'Wonder how hard it would be to make her give it to me.'

'What spell?' I snapped. Lorican's grip on my collar had tightened again; I had to talk quickly, before he decided to keep his promise after all. 'And don't tell me that you need to eat, you've been in a hole for centuries.'

'Eating isn't necessary, but I deny myself no pleasure. And the spell – I gave it to him with the illusion. He won't be in a condition to talk to anyone for several hours. I kept my word.' Jaern met Lorican's eyes. 'I didn't touch the peasant, guard dog. Not a scratch. I just shut his mouth. You stood there and watched me do it. And you . . . *didn't* kill Gray, did you?' He grinned, sharp, feral, and took half a step towards the fire. 'She's looking at me. Shall we go over?'

'Stop him.' Brix's voice climbed high with urgency. 'Stop him now, he'll hurt her.'

I wrenched myself away from Lorican and grabbed Jaern's wrist, the glowing one. The magic pulsed and thrummed beneath my hand, as intoxicating as the beat of a song. His head snapped around.

'I'll get you food somewhere else,' I said. 'Leave these people alone.'

He didn't move, except for the by-now familiar amused twitch in the corner of his mouth as he contemplated my hand on him. 'Or what?'

Lorican's knife blurred. In another instant the point rested against Jaern's back at the level of his left kidney, presuming he still had kidneys.

'Or I'll kill you,' Lorican hissed. 'Maybe Gray's my friend, but you're not.'

Jaern laughed. The black eyes found me, glittering in the dim light. 'Saints, we can't have that.' He twisted gently away from me. 'Take us up under the stars, then, Gray.'

When we emerged from the abandoned house and into the streets of Ri Dana, it was dark, lichen-light patterns crawling over the inner wall and up the narrow, lovely towers within it. The salt taste on the wind was a relief after the close, musty atmosphere in Deeptown, but all I felt was exposed. Keir Esras was still somewhere in Ri Dana, and he was apparently harassing Erranter to find me.

Jaern halted as soon as we got on to the cobblestones, sniffing again. 'Fresh air.'

'With a delightful bouquet of sewage and somebody's frying mutton,' I said, shoving him forwards. 'Charming as the hells, but we're not stopping here.' I turned to Lorican. 'Look, I know you've done a lot already, but can we spend tonight, just tonight, at your tavern?' I reached in my bag and drew out an emerald, the one that didn't have a rune carved on its face. My thumb slid across the gem's facets. I had planned to give it to Brix – it was certainly worth more than forty pieces of silver, if she sold it in the right places. But we needed a safe place to spend the night, and I couldn't think of anywhere else to hide a silver-haired necromancer.

Lorican's eyes fell on the gem in my hand. 'Put it away,' he said harshly. 'I don't want pay. Some things don't work that way.'

I stuffed the emerald back in my bag and took out a pencil. The rebuke stung. I had nearly got him buried alive, so why not take money from me? Why not let me repair my mistake? It didn't make sense, this level of loyalty and friendship and touchy honour. What had Acarius done for the man? 'Sorry,' I said stiffly, while I scribed a string of runes around my left wrist. 'Didn't mean to insult you.'

Lorican gave a grunt that was more dismissal than forgiveness. He was looking up at the eaves of the buildings, where the stars were barely visible. 'It's after midnight. We have to get off the damn street, before one of the militia patrols picks us up. I don't think whatever spell you're writing will be much good against five or six guardsmen.'

I was more worried about Keir than the militia. Keir could always use the militia to hunt us, but they were at least nominally loyal to the king and I didn't think he wanted to depend on them. There was always a chance that if they arrested me someone might listen to what I had to say about Keir and his followers and their designs against the throne.

Then again, the fact that I couldn't feel Keir divining didn't mean that he wasn't employing other means to find us. I wanted to be behind locked doors, with time to sleep and think and figure out what in the hells I was going to do. I thought it would be difficult choosing whether to destroy the doll or use it to ransom Acarius, but now I had to decide whether I believed Jaern. If the necromancer was telling the truth, destroying the doll would mean condemning my grandfather to suffering much worse than death.

I shivered.

'Let's go,' I said. 'Quickly.'

Lorican led the way back to Jinsleet Street. I let Jaern go in front of me, both because I didn't want to take my eyes off him and because I wanted to walk beside Brix. After we had gone a little way, her hand found my elbow.

'I need to talk to you.' Brix shot me a sideways look. 'I need to know what happened, down there.'

'I found a necromancer and an artefact.' I skirted a puddle. 'Watch your step.'

'That wasn't really what I meant, but very well.' Her fingers tightened around my joint as she hopped over the puddle. 'Tell me about this artefact. You said it's something you're going to use to rescue your grandfather. Is it a treasure, then?'

'Not exactly. It looks like a fantastically ugly baby. I think it's an alchemical tool.' I put my hand back in my bag and grabbed the stiff limbs of the doll, pulling it up enough for her to see its bulbous head and empty eyes. 'It's like the Empty One idol back in Fenwydd, but socketed.'

'Ugly is right.' She frowned at the doll's face. 'I wonder what is meant to go in the sockets. Do you know what it does?'

'Stones carved with runes, and not really. I only have Jaern's word for it.' A prickle of caution passed over me. I tucked the doll back into the bag, my fingertips brushing the uncarved emerald. 'Why the interest?'

She let out a small, frustrated sigh. 'We nearly died to get the thing, forgive me for being curious whether it was worth it. Did you also find the stones that fit in the sockets, or was this whole thing a wild goose chase?'

'Two stones are still missing,' I muttered, 'but I know where they are, so *not* a goose chase, as long as I can figure out how the bloody thing is supposed to go together.'

'Maybe I can help you figure out how it works, if it's the same pattern as the Fenwydd idol.'

I halted. 'Why in the hells would you do that?' Her hand was still on my arm. It was almost as distracting as the way she was looking at me – frustrated, searching, surprised. Jaern and Lorican were getting too far ahead. 'Come on.' I couldn't quite force myself to pull away from her. 'We have to keep up.'

We turned down what seemed like the fiftieth dark alley. Then the stench hit me and I recognised the back of the tavern.

'Home,' Lorican said.

'Home could do with a lime treatment or six to keep the smell down.' Jaern was contemplating the alley with a disgusted sneer. 'Are we staying here?'

'Just for the night,' said Lorican.

'I don't see why I should tolerate a sewage pit even for an hour.' Jaern crossed his arms.

'Those of us without handmade bodies need to sleep, and I won't have you wandering Ri Dana by yourself.' I didn't sound particularly authoritative, even in my own head, but the words served their purpose and instantly fixed Jaern's attention on me. Now I just had to figure out how to get a spell off, without him realising what I was doing and taking action against me. Maybe if I made him angry?

'How sweet.' Jaern turned towards me. Apparently he was already angry. 'And what if I want—'

'I want you to stay here.'

Something *pulled* inside me. It was the most disconcerting thing I had ever felt, like a clay jar of bees, vibrating in the middle of my being. It wasn't *me*.

Jaern blinked, his mouth still open, stopped mid-syllable. Mingled fury and confusion blazed on his face. I struggled for concentration against the weird tug of otherness. I had to cast while he was quiet, or I wouldn't get another chance. I had to—

'Very well.' Jaern spoke the words unwillingly, looking almost as disturbed as I felt. 'Then I suggest you get me out of this stinking alley.'

Something was making him obedient in spite of himself. Something . . .

I swallowed. I didn't want to follow that line of thought to its conclusion, just then. 'Lorican.'

Lorican unlocked the door, and Jaern stalked in. As I walked past the Erranter, he stopped me with a hand on my chest.

'What *was* that?' Lorican stared towards the dark interior of the tavern. 'How did you convince him?'

'I have no idea.' I pushed past Lorican. It wasn't much of a lie. What did I know about souls? I was no priest and I didn't have any real answers. All I had was a theory and another problem.

In contrast to the alley, the tavern's kitchen smelled almost pleasant, with the ghosts of old meals hanging around the cold hearth. Jaern had halted beside the fireplace. Lorican and Brix followed me into the room and Lorican shut the door, depriving us of even the thin starlight from the alley, and he began feeling around on the mantel.

A tight knot of muscles I hadn't been aware of loosened at the base of my spine. The dark, the quiet and even the odour of past cooking were comforting. Normal. Finally, I'd have the time to think, maybe even to divine for Acarius and see if I could finally pinpoint a location.

'Damn,' Lorican said. 'The candle's in the taproom. I'll get it.'

The swinging door between the kitchen and the taproom squeaked as it opened and closed. Another scent tickled my nostrils. Acrid, chemical. It couldn't have come from the alley or the cooking pot.

No.

I swung my arm, blindly, and knocked against Brix. 'Everyone, get outside. Run, and don't look back.'

The door to the taproom banged open, green light blazing through it. The spell hit me before I could shout, a burst of pain exploding through my bones, dropping me to my knees and wrenching every muscle into a cramp.

'Too late,' Jaern said.

FIFTEEN

My knees ached where the stone floor bit into them. I couldn't see anything except green light and the blurred outline of whoever stood in the doorway.

'Corcoran Gray, you're under arrest. Don't be foolish, and we won't paralyse you.'

I didn't recognise the voice. It wasn't Lorican, and it wasn't Jaern. At least this probably meant that Jaern wasn't the one who threw the spell at me, although the choice of spell seemed awfully coincidental. This was some horrible variation on a tetany spell. The muscles in my back wrenched tighter.

Concentrating, I got my eyes to focus. A man and a woman stood just inside the doorway, wearing the elaborately embroidered robes of senior wizards. I couldn't see Lorican, but there were a limited number of possibilities. He was dead in the taproom, disabled in the taproom or in league with these Guild thugs.

My jaw would hardly open. 'Just how in the hells do you think I can be foolish in this condition?'

The wizard who had spoken, a man with a curling blond beard, smiled thinly. 'You have a spell scribed on your wrist. Who knows what you might have written under your clothes. I'm going to pull the spell back a bit in order that you and your companions may strip to the skin. Once we've seen that none of you have anything threatening scribed, you may dress, and then we will take you to the Guildhouse for trial. If you do anything that even smells like the beginning of an incantation, I will release the spell again. The tetany spell can break men's bones, you understand. I'd do it now, but it would be inconvenient to have to carry you.'

'Bastards,' Brix whispered. 'You're not supposed to hurt people like this.'

My bones had been broken before, as far as that went, but the thought of them breaking hers made my skin crawl. I couldn't master my neck muscles enough to turn towards her. 'Don't,' I said. 'There's more than one of them; they can throw another copy of the same spell if they want.'

'Indeed,' said the wizard. 'I suggest you get started.'

The spell around me relaxed, just a little. I got up to my feet, unlacing my shirt as I went. The spell still pulsed, putrid green, throbbing under my skin, ready to snap back into action at any moment. It was like moving underwater. 'There's no point in you keeping the others; the tribunal won't find anything to charge them with. The woman's useless – doesn't know a damn thing. I paid her for Temples information, and even that wasn't very helpful. And the Erranter just rents rooms.'

Brix's breath hissed behind me, but it was all I could think of. There was no other scenario in which the Guildies would let her go. I certainly couldn't let them find out she was Tirnaal. Ri Dana had a small but thriving slave market; Brix would bring a handsome price on the block – and that was assuming they didn't just drag her back and lock her up in the Guildhouse here.

'And that one?' The blond wizard pointed at Jaern. 'What excuse do you have for him? Disrobe, or we'll paralyse you all and strip you ourselves.'

Jaern had already slipped out of his antique tunic. He pulled off his shirt and dropped it into a puddle of fabric on the floor, yawning.

This was the man who had enchanted an Erranter without blinking, dammit. What was the point in having a necromancer if he wouldn't cast when I needed help?

I yanked my own shirt off, hoping that Brix would be slow with the buttons on her robe. There had to be a way out of this. There was always a way out. I pulled my feet out of my boots, one at a time. Think. *Think.*

'What in the hells did Keir tell you that I've done?' I stopped with my hands on my belt clasp, skin prickling with cold. 'Doesn't Guild law say you have to tell me the charge?' Even worse than the possibility of dying or having my mind broken, I discovered, was being faced with the idea that Brix would see me without my clothes.

'The Examiner General was very specific about you,' the blond wizard said. 'The charge is unlicensed sorcery and sedition. Someone has been spreading nonstandard practice among the Guildhouses for the last year, recruiting apprentices, whispering about uniting with Temples to overthrow the Royal Charter. We think that's you. Especially considering you travel with this woman, who matches a description Temples has been circulating as a runaway. Now stop stalling. Drop your trousers and turn around. And keep your hands where I can see them.'

I obeyed, unable not to look at Brix as I turned. She was only half-way done with the buttons. Her gaze found my leg as though looking for my absent brace, and she frowned for a second before meeting my eyes.

'They've got no reason to hurt me,' she said. 'It's all right.'

But it wasn't, and she knew it. Jaern, I assumed, could handle himself, but if I couldn't figure something out, Brix would wind up on an auction block and Lorican in the stocks or worse, and it would be my fault.

The incantation on my hands would do to knock one of them unconscious, if I could get their attention off me long enough to speak. But that would leave one of them still kicking, and they'd paralyse me in seconds. I needed another spell, and there was no way I could get one scribed.

'Those scars.' At least the blond wizard didn't sound bored anymore.

I turned back to him, relieved to get away from Brix's eyes. 'Which scars?' It wasn't an idle question; I have several sets. Usually I hate them. They're reminders of bad times, failed spells, midnight runs out of stinking villages and dead-souled towns. Right then, however, they were buying me another scrap of time.

'The round ones on your shoulder blades. What—'

'Flight,' I interrupted. 'They're from where wings attach to the skeleton, and yes, it hurts.'

'That's impossible.' The wizard's smile had faded. 'No one can fly.'

'Unlicensed sorcery has its advantages,' I said. 'Now that you've seen I don't have anything else scribed, can I please put my clothes back on?'

'It's impossible,' repeated the wizard.

I met the Guildie's eyes. 'If it was, why would the Guild have a law against it? It's not impossible, it's just expensive, dangerous and difficult.'

'You're lying.' Finally a word from the second wizard, a woman with a braid of salt-and-pepper brown hair twisted across the top of her head like a coronet.

'What would be the point of that?' I said. 'Impressing you now only gets me more torture later.' You wouldn't think it was possible to be exasperated and terrified at the same time, but I was. If I was going to get caught and mindblown, why did it have to be by these walking sacks of stupid?

Jaern was watching the exchange with some interest, completely naked except for the black amulet hanging around his neck, muscular arms crossed over his chiselled chest. The low-burning irritation in my gut blazed into outright anger. If the lazy bastard had nothing scribed on him – and I could tell there was *nothing* – how had he cast before? Was it on his clothes, somehow? Was it the amulet?

'Enough,' the blond wizard said. 'We'll get the truth about the scars when we get the rest of the information out of your mind. For now, the girl strips.'

If Brix stripped, they'd see her ink. I had to figure out how to hurt him. 'I told you,' I said, 'she doesn't know anything. There's nothing scribed on her. I'm not stupid enough to put incantations where I can't keep track of them.'

'Don't make me ask again.' The blond wizard pushed his sleeves up, revealing the runes scribed from his wrists to his elbows. One forearm was covered with the spell he was running now. On the other, though, was a sheet fire incantation, and it had not been activated. My eyes narrowed.

A risky idea, maybe. Still, if Jaern could cast using sigils written gods knew where, why couldn't I use the ones written on someone else's forearm?

I had to distract him, or I would never have the time to get the incantation finished. 'Brix,' I said, 'I'm sorry.'

'It's not your fault.' She stepped forwards. As her fingers flashed down the line of buttons on the front of the robe, the blond wizard's eyes fixed on her. She reached for the belt, the last thing holding her robe shut. I let the syllables roll past my lips.

The runes flared to life on the wizard's arm and he screamed, but it was too late. I was running the spell, not him. A wall of flame burned between us. I pushed it towards the wizards as fast as I could. Soon even a Guild idiot would realise that he could rub out the spell on his own arm and stop me, and by then I had to be close enough to touch them. I couldn't keep the spell running very long, or the tavern would catch on fire.

I shouted over my shoulder: 'Brix, Jaern, go. Find Lorican and run!'

She didn't move. 'What about you?'

Jaern uncrossed his arms, extended a hand and pronounced something. It took a moment for my mind to register what it was – paralysis, a very aggressive variation.

A patch of light blazed on the skin over the left side of his ribs. I squinted and tried to watch as best I could while keeping hold of my spell. It looked like runes scribed on the skin had come to life, but there had been nothing there. I *knew* there had been nothing there.

Jaern moved towards the paralysed wizards and rubbed out the spells on both of the blond man's arms. The flames went out and I stood there, shivering and furious.

'Hells!' I grabbed my trousers and jerked them on. 'How did you do that?'

'More to the point, I think, is deciding what we're going to do with these.' Jaern gestured towards the Guildies. 'What are they, apart from annoying?'

'No, you're going to tell me how you cast without having a spell scribed.' Again I felt that odd pull inside me, the weird buzz that blotted out other thought. Again Jaern's black eyes flashed with discomfort, just for a split second. 'And why you waited so long to help,' I added.

'It's a handmade body.' He spoke reluctantly, as though he had a sword in his back. 'When I built it, I took the skin off, scribed the most common spells on the inside and then put the skin back. My body has all kinds of useful modifications. And I waited because I wanted to see how clever you were, and how you'd deal with the situation on your own. Now, given that these two fools are standing here listening to every word we say, who are they?'

'Guild wizards,' I said.

'Keir Esras' pets?' Jaern smoothed the collar on the blond wizard's robe.

'Not quite,' I said. 'I don't think they know why he told them to hunt me. Keir was working with Temples in Fenwydd, which probably means he's the one spreading sedition inside the Guild. We'll have to question them, to—'

Jaern put his hand on the blond wizard's chest and spoke. The spell lit on the back of the god's neck before I could react, scarlet light pulsing with malevolence. The blond wizard's eyes fixed on him, panicked as a bird in a snare. Light streamed from the wizard's nostrils into the black pendant swinging around Jaern's neck. In a split second, the other wizard was glowing, too.

Blood burst from the paralysed wizards' mouths, and they slumped to the ground in two pathetic heaps.

'Stop!' I sprang towards Jaern and grabbed his arm.

He looked at me with mild surprise.

I released him, unable to look away from the people on the floor. Their skin had already taken on a sickly, yellowish cast as the circulation ceased. There was nothing left to do. 'You killed them,' I said.

'Put your head between your knees before you spew.' Jaern squatted beside the blond wizard and methodically began going through his clothes. 'Or go and find your other little friend in the taproom. Make sure he's breathing, if you want to keep him.'

I fought to steady my body. The caustic odour of magic mingled with smoke and blood in my nostrils, and did indeed make me want to retch. 'You . . .'

Jaern pulled the robe off the wizard and held it up to himself. 'Too short, but the other one is shorter.'

'You *killed* them,' I repeated. But I wasn't really talking to Jaern. This was my fault. The Guildies had been stupid, and dangerous, but they hadn't deserved to die. And I had been the one to bring the necromancer here; these deaths were mine.

'So quaint. They were going to kill *you*. What would you have done instead, since you don't have the stomach for killing?' Jaern shook the wrinkles out of the robe. 'Can you even gut a fish?'

Brix's hand was on my forearm. 'Come on, Gray. Let's check on Lorican and then get away from here.' She glared towards Jaern. 'He doesn't have to come with us.'

'She's wounding my sensibilities,' Jaern remarked. He was pulling off the dead wizard's shirt now. 'Are you going to tell her?'

Brix's eyebrows rose. 'Tell me what?'

I grabbed my satchel and stepped over the wizards' bodies and into the taproom. The odour of new death followed me, the ugly stink of bodies without spirits in them. It smelled like plague-time, like hiding in the dark and watching the survivors make pyres. It smelled like being a child again.

Where in the name of Farran was Lorican? I fished out a grease pencil, scribbled an illumination spell on my forearm and sent the ball of light to hover in the rafters. Maybe at least I could keep him from dying, if he wasn't dead already. Maybe he could give me some answers.

'Tell me *what*?' Brix had followed. 'Does this have something to do with where your knee brace went?'

Lorican was on the floor. From what I could gather from a cursory examination, he was unconscious, but breathing.

'Gray,' she said.

At least she wasn't calling me Corcoran. I sat on my heels beside Lorican, reduced to honesty. 'I don't know how to explain,' I said.

'You can talk while you work.' She bent down and put a couple of fingers on Lorican's neck. 'He's alive. Is he enchanted or something?'

'Evidently.' Lorican didn't appear to be enchanted with anything dangerous. It was probably a simple repose spell, like I'd used on the priest back in Fenwydd jail, all those miles ago.

'So fix him,' Brix said.

'He'll likely wake up in a couple of hours no matter what I do.' I took a breath. There was no sense in avoiding it any longer. Jaern would tell Brix if I didn't. 'But I can't . . .' *Figure it out, Cricket.* '. . . leave him,' I finished, even more awkwardly than I finish most things.

'Lorican?' She raised an eyebrow. 'Are you sure he'll even want to come with you?'

'I mean the bone prince in the other room picking out his new wardrobe,' I said. '*He* has to come with me. Hells, there's probably a spatial component to it. I doubt he can go very far out of my sight.'

She frowned. 'Spatial component to what? A spell?'

'It's not quite a spell.' The back of my neck was still cramping. I rubbed at it. 'Jaern did . . . something, underground, that healed my lame knee. And I may have swallowed his soul.'

Brix raised a finger. Any patience in her voice evaporated. 'You *may* have swallowed his *soul*?'

'He said it was his soul.' The cramp in my neck didn't ease. 'It could have been anything, I suppose. At least it got him to do what I told him.'

'You're saying you have two souls,' she said.

'More or less. Keep it to yourself.' I bent back over Lorican. 'Maybe I should just break the ley and wake the damn bartender up. It might make things simpler.'

She gazed at me with a kind of sickened fascination, the way some people will look at a body on a gibbet at a crossroads. 'Can you *feel* it?'

'Farran's wig!' I leaned closer to her and forced my speech down to a whisper; I was betting Jaern had modified hearing, too, and I didn't want him listening in. 'No, I can't feel it. No, I don't have the soul in the sense I have my own – I can't think with it or anything. I hope I'm just a . . . container, but I don't know that much about necromancy so I'm not sure about anything, including how to get rid of it. And I'm not any happier about the situation than you are, but if I'm going to free my grandfather, I need him.' I ran a hand down my face. 'Look, I don't think we've got that much time. Those two were radically unlucky, but they were still senior wizards. When they don't show up in the morning, their Guildfellows will divine for their sigils.'

'You mean tattoos, like yours,' Brix said.

'No. Mine is a forgery, just a pretty picture. Theirs are beacons, like the ring I took off of you in Fenwydd. The Guild *will* find them.' The words came out of my mouth at the same time that the thought completed itself in my head, and I realised what I had to do. 'You should leave now. I'll handle Lorican and the necromancer.'

'Very noble.' She loosened the laces on Lorican's shirt, as though that would wake him up. 'No.'

'I'm not being noble. I want *you* to stop being stupid.' I heard the fear in my voice and hated it, hated the weakness that made a chance to run away the best thing I could offer anyone. 'They'll catch you, and they'll sell you and you will never get back to Anka. I can't be carrying that kind of vulnerability around with me. You've got to leave.'

She stiffened as though I had struck her. 'How did you—' She pressed her lips together.

'You're Tirnaal without freedom papers, you said you have to meet up with someone and you need coin badly enough to follow an insane wizard underground. Then you finally talk about a baby sister and your eyes glow like candles, but the sister isn't with you.' I forced myself to meet her eyes. 'It wasn't difficult to work out.'

'But I still don't have the money for her freedom,' she said. 'They *sold* her, Gray, to a pig of a trader who runs a floating camp. I'm not even sure where she is. I can't—'

I grabbed my satchel and yanked out the uncarved emerald. I held it out to her, over Lorican's still form. 'Here. Take it. Sell that in the right place and you should be able to buy ten slaves. Take it and go, now, tonight.'

She didn't move. 'You *want* me to go?'

I didn't, because I was a selfish prick.

'Yes,' I said, hoarsely. 'There are two bodies to worry about, bodies that can be tracked and that will leave a divinatory trace on whoever handles them. There's me, complicating everything I touch and with a price on my head that probably just got a lot bigger. And there's that black-eyed thing that I let out of its cage, who just killed those two aforementioned people. Why *wouldn't* you leave?'

'The black-eyed thing has its uses,' Jaern said, dryly.

I snapped up to standing, the stone still in my hand. He was leaning one shoulder against the doorjamb, barefoot and dressed in mismatched robes. Somehow he'd managed to make the bloodstains disappear.

'This doesn't concern you,' I said.

'Everything concerns me, Cricket.' He sighed, and moved to the bar. 'It's not a very good tavern, is it? Nothing but dark beer.'

A wave of ice rolled over me. Only Acarius called me Cricket. How in the hells had Jaern known that? I hadn't thought he'd looked that far into my memories.

He glanced over his shoulder and whistled. Something rasped against the floor in the darkness of the kitchen – something heavy shambling towards us.

The two dead wizards – in the picked-over remnants of their clothing – lurched through the door.

'Where do you want me to put them?' Jaern said.

I thought Brix would scream. Instead she backed up until she ran into a table and chairs.

'Easy.' I didn't move away from Lorican. 'It's all right, Brix.'

The two Guildies were most definitely dead, their eyes lit from within with dull orange light, blood crusted, purple, under their nostrils.

'How can this be all right?' She would have been shouting, I think, if she'd been able to take her eyes off the things. 'How are they walking?'

'There's a necromancer standing at the bar complaining about the beer,' I said. 'Ask him.'

'Hardly complaining.' Jaern put one hand on the bar and vaulted over. 'Getting slightly bored with all this talk, however. I asked you where you wanted me to put the marulaches. I touched them, can't have more of these idiots swarming me.' He took a glass from the shelf behind the bar and filled it from a keg.

'So what, you're wanting to dispose of the bodies quickly? Make it so the Guild can't divine for us with them?' I said, trying to push past the revulsion welling in me. I glanced at Brix. 'If they were destroyed it would confuse the hell out of the scrying.'

'No!' She put a hand over her mouth. 'You can't disrespect the dead like this. It's disgusting.'

'*Disgusting*,' Jaern said, down into his cup. 'Little leaping saints, now my feelings are really going to be hurt.'

'This isn't some kind of joke,' Brix said. 'They were real people. You can't use people like that, walk them around like toys.'

'I know it isn't a damn joke,' I said, between my teeth. 'Quit lecturing me about propriety. I'm trying to think.' Nothing about this situation was right, but we still had to get out of it. Marulaches could be dangerous without orders. We couldn't just walk off and leave them here to wander the streets aimlessly. 'If you don't like the idea of marching the bodies somewhere to get rid of them, do you have any other suggestions about how to manage them?'

'We should stop this.' She crossed the floor and crouched beside me. 'You know we should. You're better than this. Wake Lorican up and then let us help you do something about Jaern. He's dangerous.'

'He *is*,' Jaern said, to his cup.

I still had the damn emerald. I could at least force her to take it, so she could get away from Jaern and the dead and me and all of it. I should have been relieved to get the debt off my conscience, but I

BREANNA TEINTZE

wasn't. *Here's an emerald. That clears the money I owe you.* Then what? *Stay with me anyway?*

I wasn't going to think about that. It wasn't going to happen. I pushed the stone into her hand.

She looked down at it. 'Gray—'

'Quiet.' I squatted back down next to Lorican, grabbed the grease pencil out of my satchel and wrote a string of characters for awakening down the Erranter's breastbone. I pronounced them before Brix could begin her question again. Awakening works to counteract simple repose spells, but has the side effect of itching like the lice of a dozen rats. Lorican gasped.

'Get up,' I said.

'Gods, my head . . .' He stirred, then sat up. He looked at the dead Guildies, and then at me and then back at the corpses. 'I'm hallucinating,' he said, slowly.

'You're not. Up.' I extended a hand to him and scratched at my collarbone with the other. 'Jaern, put those things back in the kitchen for now, I don't want to talk with them staring at me.'

The necromancer shrugged. The bodies shambled back through the swinging door.

Lorican grasped my hand and stood. He looked shaken. 'Gray, what in the hells—'

I raised a finger. 'How did the Guild know we would be here, and why didn't they kill you?'

'All I remember is opening this door,' Lorican said. 'They must have knocked me out. You say it was the Guild? Those were wizards?'

'Senior wizards,' I said. 'Angry senior wizards.'

'Why are they doing what you say? They didn't look right. I could have sworn they were—' Lorican rubbed his eyes as though to clear them and looked towards the kitchen. 'What's wrong with them?'

'They're dead,' Brix said, watching me.

'They're *what*?' Lorican's head snapped around. 'How are they walking?'

'Jaern killed them.' I was getting a headache, and the conversation was slipping out of my control. I needed Lorican to answer me. 'Then, for reasons of his own, he reanimated the corpses, I don't know how. We'll deal with them in a minute, after you answer me. How did the Guild know we'd be here?'

Lorican stiffened. 'You think I'd sell you out to the spelldogs?'

'Someone did.' And Lorican had been hiding something since I found him. I had told enough lies in my life to recognise the stink of it on him.

'Or those apprentices you let go ran back to their masters, like I said they would,' Lorican said. 'Don't be stupid, brat. I'm the last one in this room you should be worrying about.'

'Why? Because of some nebulous favour Acarius did for you at the dawn of time, and your unrelenting gratitude?' My heart banged inside my skull, sending dull jolts of pain to the roots of my teeth. The toxicity from the sheet flame spell would only get worse, and the damn itching had spread to the backs of my knees. I had to make my move soon. I still had runes scribed on my hands, and the spell would hit him hard if I was quick. Knock him out, nothing deadly. I could tie him up and stuff him in a closet along with the Guildies. By the time he got out of that, I'd be long gone with Jaern, and—

What are you doing?

My thoughts ground to a halt. What *was* I doing? Contemplating hiding bodies, pinning their murders on Lorican? Bile rose in my throat.

No. This wasn't me.

I made myself step backwards, made the anger and panic go back into their cages. If only I could convince myself we had time. Every moment made it more likely the rest of the Guildhouse would descend on the tavern.

'Start talking,' I said.

'Stop insulting me,' Lorican snapped, 'and explain what's going on. You're telling me that two people have been murdered in my back room? I didn't turn around on you, thickwits. If I was going to sell your hide, I would have done it a lot cleaner than this. It was those kids.'

'Why didn't the Guild try to take you?' *Don't shout.* I wrestled my voice down, clenched my hands into fists. I couldn't throw a spell like an arrow into the dark. Acarius had taught me better than that. I had to be sure. 'They should have tried to do more than knock you out.'

'Look.' Lorican leaned towards me, muscles flexing as though he was deciding whether or not to hit me. 'I don't know what they tried to do. Maybe they wanted to question me, maybe they wanted to hand me over to the city guard; who knows? Just because I'm not dead doesn't mean this wee game of yours hasn't done for me.' He swung an arm towards the kitchen door. 'I can't stay here, Gray. They will track those wizards to this tavern and they will arrest me. With my record—' He broke off. 'My business – my livelihood – is fair wrecked. I'd be a flaming fool to bring this down on my own head. Do you really think that the Guild would bargain with a dirty Erranter?'

The pain and fury in his voice made me wince. If he was lying, he was good at it. And there *were* other possibilities. The Lady Mother could have slipped the word to the Guild. Keir Esras could have found the other half of his wits and used it to hire a divining expert. They even might have wormed something out of Acarius' mind.

'All right.' I moved away from him. 'All right, leave it.' At the moment what mattered was staying alive, finding the last two gems I needed to complete the artefact and getting Acarius free. I could trust Lorican at least long enough to get me out of the city. After that, it would be easier to go my own way. I made the decision.

'I need to go home,' I said. 'To Acarius' cabin. Which means I need horses, or to hop on someone's wagon. Any ideas?'

Lorican grimaced. 'Saints. Fine. Let's go steal some bloody horses.'

Stealing horses proved to be simpler than I'd feared. We left the tavern, accompanied by Jaern's walking dead, and followed Lorican through the dark streets. The Erranter kept muttering through his teeth, a litany of rather exotic curses all centred on Acarius and me – I think mostly because of the marulaches, which shuffled along half-dressed, glowing a faint orange. They weren't exactly inconspicuous, but it couldn't be helped. We had to find a place to dump them.

As it happened, Lorican led us to the stables used by the Guild-house. Between a spell of mine and a suspiciously high-quality set of lockpicks that Lorican had brought, we managed to break in and remove four horses and their tack.

Jaern, who had been nothing but bored until this point, opened all the stalls, positioned the two marulaches in one corner and cast a fire spell, which he used to light the hayloft. You couldn't fault the necromancer's efficiency.

We rode away as the stable burned, panicked horses thundering through the streets behind us. The burned bodies of the senior wizards would be found inside the stable. The missing horses wouldn't be recognised as stolen for days – perhaps forever.

Logically that should have made me pleased, or at least relieved. It didn't.

Dawn silvered the sky around the edges of the black wall as we approached. The guards, busy inspecting a spice caravan that had just arrived, were too absorbed to do more than wave us out of the city. Lorican got us on the caravan road and then reined in his horse.

'Well, brat. It's your game now. Which way?'

'Thanks for coming this far.' I stuck on what I hoped was a reasonable facsimile of a grateful smile. Truth be told, I found the man more incomprehensible with every minute, and that annoyed me. Besides, the Guild had been nipping at my heels since I met him, and I wasn't sure I wanted him to know where the cabin was. 'I'll tell Acarius hello for you.'

Lorican's eyebrows shot up. 'You think I'm going somewhere?'

'I could make suggestions, if you're in doubt,' Jaern said.

I braced myself for the feeling, like mad bees welling behind my breastbone. Part of me believed it was Jaern's soul, unhappily confined inside me. 'Leave it,' I said.

This time Jaern smiled – his teeth glinted, even in the dim light – as we both felt the buzzing tug of his will fighting mine. Maybe possessing his soul made him obedient to me, but he certainly wasn't happy about it.

'At last comprehension dawns, then?' Jaern said. 'Enjoying it?'

'Shut up,' I said. He went silent. I turned back to Lorican. 'Look, anyone would agree that you've done your duty by Acarius. You don't have to come with me. Given the record of our acquaintance so far, it doesn't even seem like it would be a good idea.'

He glanced down the road. 'Thought you might need a hand getting Acarius free, since you've been doing so well up until now.'

I gave up on gratitude. 'And I thought you'd probably like the chance to go hide somewhere, since you've been looking so hard for Acarius up until now.'

'You're going to talk to me that way? Like I haven't taken risks for the old man? For you?' Lorican's face went ashy. Hurt.

My head throbbed. Some of it might be from hunger and exhaustion, or the toxic remnants from the spells I'd thrown. But most of it was due to the images I couldn't quite shut away, the pictures of the Guildies dying that flickered through my head over and over again. I had caused deaths. The line I had told myself I would never cross – I had practically leaped over it. There were too many people around me. They were too vulnerable. They made *me* too vulnerable.

'I'm not *asking* for you to take risks for me,' I said, holding on to the frayed threads of my patience. 'All debts are settled.'

'*Debts?*' Lorican stared at me. 'Of course the debts are settled, but this goes beyond that now.'

'Why in the hells should it?' My horse sidestepped under me, sensing my frustration. I was fighting the temptation to just kick the mare I rode and leave them all behind. I forced the words out. 'I don't understand why you want to help.'

'Aye, you're dense as a stack of wood,' he snapped. 'I don't know how you feel about Acarius, but I actually care about the old man more than I do my own pride. He's the closest thing I've got to family, and for six months I've been worried that he was dead. You say that we can save him, so you can either let me come with you, or you can leave and I can follow you. I'm not being left behind, no matter how big a fool you want to make of yourself.'

Pride. My gut twisted on itself. Acarius was *my* family. What right did Lorican have to care? What right did he have to imply I didn't? 'You can't–' I began.

'Gray.' Brix, who looked terribly uncomfortable perched in her saddle, brought her horse near mine. 'Slow down. Let's just take half a minute and discuss this. Lorican says he wants to help Acarius, and you need someone to help you watch the necromancer. I know about Jaern-temples. I can help you figure out how to use the Empty One.' She paused. 'And afterwards, you can divine for my sister's location, the way the Guild wizards divined for you in Ri Dana. We can both save the people we need to save.'

She was right, of course. I did need help watching Jaern, if for nothing else than to ensure he didn't do some vicious incantation while I slept. And the only insight I would have into the Empty One idol would be what I got from the necromancer, who was about as trustworthy as a viper. At least if I had Brix helping me figure out how to use the doll, I'd have a way to check what he said and make certain that he wasn't just manipulating me into some corner where he could extract his soul.

'Are we making a new deal?' I said, slowly.

Her teeth closed for a second on her lower lip. 'If that's how you have to think of it, sure.'

What in the hells was that supposed to mean? I was tired of being alone – gods, I was so tired – but that didn't make me the kind of person that anyone stayed with. Lorican was insisting both that I take his help *and* that I didn't deserve it. Jaern was still looming in the background, so angry about being silenced that I could feel it rolling off him like heat. And Brix was . . . trying to stay with me. Nothing made sense.

'Fine,' I said. 'Good. Perfect. Nobody gets to say that I didn't warn them about the possibility of getting broiled or suffocated, all right?' I glanced at Lorican, who was still scowling, and tried to address both him and Brix at once. 'If we're going to go, then we should stop talking and go.'

It was the best I could do and it wasn't good enough, but we went.

SIXTEEN

Four days east from Ri Dana, we started following the Nelta river up into the mountains and the wind stopped tasting like salt. Three days after that it grew thick with the cloying scent of beevine. That smell meant home, but it also meant trouble. I'd been dreading facing the valley again since I'd left it.

'You look like shit.' Brix halted her horse next to mine and it started cropping grass.

I glanced sideways at her. When we'd camped the previous night, Brix went to look for firewood and was gone so long that I had briefly wondered whether she had decided to take the emerald and slip away after all. She'd been quiet and preoccupied since she returned, and had spent most of the morning ignoring me. It was good to be talking again, even if it wasn't exactly complimentary.

'Well,' I said, 'I feel like hell, so I guess I put on a good front.' I sat with one leg hooked around my saddlehorn, trying unsuccessfully to get rid of the ache in my overstretched sinews. I really didn't want to look at the village in the valley below.

She studied me for a moment. 'This is a pretty place.'

I grimaced.

'Not a pretty place?' she said.

Maybe it was, if you could look at it without memories. The little nameless village was a collection of stacked-log houses at the mouth of a narrow canyon, surrounded by pastures dotted with white bee skeps. Scarlet-flowered beevine covered the canyon's walls in the spring and summer, supporting thousands of hives and the village's honey industry. When Acarius first brought me home, I used to sit on the porch of his cabin and listen to the hum and tell myself it meant I was safe. Now it would never feel safe again.

'Let's get it over with,' I said. 'I want to get up to the cabin before nightfall.'

'Cabin?' Lorican said. 'Acarius lives in a cabin?' This was the first time he'd addressed me today. He hadn't talked during the whole journey, except when it was absolutely necessary. That meant, I supposed, that he was still angry with me, touched in his honour that I'd dared to suspect him. Now he seemed to have spoken without thinking. His complexion darkened by a shade.

I still didn't know what to make of him, though the fact that the Guild hadn't reappeared for the last week was a point in his favour. I'd spent the whole trip jumpy as a rabbit, struggling to discern whether my creeping, paranoid sense of being observed was due to someone divining for me, the way Jaern kept making sly remarks, or just the fact that I hadn't slept a full night since we left Ri Dana.

'What,' I said, with some malice, 'Acarius never told you?'

'There's plenty about you that he never told me,' Lorican said, and any sense of satisfaction I had evaporated. Why had Acarius been talking about me with Lorican in the first place?

We passed through the village and into the stand of trembling poplar that lined the entrance to the canyon. The creek chuckled along the canyon floor, and just before the big, lichen-streaked rock formation, I was supposed to be able to see the lightning-blasted pine.

'So what are we doing?' Jaern said. 'I thought we'd be stopping in that village, but now we've left even that semblance of civilisation behind.'

I didn't want to talk to Jaern. The necromancer had been a constant headache for the seven days since we'd left Ri Dana, fighting every request and forcing me to make it an order. I'd confirmed, again and again, that something about carrying his soul made it so he *had* to do as I said. There was no point to his resistance, except pure spite.

There. It was the same dead tree, albeit half-swathed in stinking beevine. I slid down off my horse, moved to the tree and began stripping the beevine away.

'We are disabling the wards,' I said.

'Wards?' Brix hunched in her saddle, watching Jaern and looking faintly repulsed. 'Like the ones in the temple?'

'No, luckily,' I said. 'These aren't prayers. They're more like locks, to keep intruders away.' I yanked down the last of the vine and the sigils came to light, under my hands. A beautiful and well-crafted spiral carved into the dead wood, just as I'd left it. 'Still, I'd rather not step into the spell.'

Jaern snorted. 'I'd think not.'

'Why?' Brix looked from the necromancer to me. 'What does it do?'

I brought my paints out of my satchel and checked to see which colour had the most left. Blue, as it turned out. Blue holds its shape better and typically makes for more potent incantations, but it's also more irritating to the skin than red or green. Better to use it up scribing on a dead tree.

'It conjures a swarm of mosquitoes, as a first step,' I said. 'Most people don't keep going, once that happens.'

'And if they did, they'd find themselves sprouting hair in uncomfortable places and chased by hallucinations,' Jaern said. 'Elegant work, Cricket, if a bit simplistic.'

Cricket.

I took a deep breath and used it to keep my mind clear enough to scribe the deactivation runes. It was just an example of what had been at the top of my thoughts when he had managed to break into my memories. Jaern didn't know anything except that I had a nickname. If I didn't let him, he couldn't use it to get under my skin.

'And how are we going to get back out again, without sprouting uncomfortable hair?' Lorican said.

'They won't be active again until I reset them. I just don't like people mucking around in my business.' And I hadn't wanted any strangers up at the cabin, not even well-intentioned village folk. I scribed the last character, put my hands on either side of the spiral and spoke the incantation. It blazed faintly green, and then went dark. The ward was broken, for better or worse.

'Why didn't your grandfather take this kind of precaution?' Jaern was controlling his horse with his knees, as much at ease as if we were sitting in a parlour somewhere discussing the weather. 'Seems remarkably foolish. Did he not know he was being hunted?'

I put my paints away without answering. It *had* been foolish, and it had been my fault. Acarius hadn't had wards in place because he was expecting me to come home and he didn't want me stumbling into them. Gods knew that I never would have seen the old man's traps; he was too good for that.

The road up to the cabin had never been very well maintained, but after six months of neglect, it was wildly overgrown. Soon I gave up on riding, and led my horse while I pushed my way through the undergrowth, keeping my eyes open for the other three wards I'd placed on the path and disabling them as I found them.

Finally, as the afternoon stretched into evening, the canyon widened and the creek veered away from the road. We followed the stream until it became a pool fed by a tall, narrow cascade of white water. The horses wanted to stop and drink, but I pushed on, around the rocks that made the bed of the waterfall.

There, in a wide half-circle of grass and wildflowers, sat the cabin. It was nothing but a little four-room affair made rather haphazardly of stacked logs with the bark still on. Two steps were caved in, and an abandoned birds' nest hung skewed in the rafters of the porch roof. Beside the house was the trio of wizened, ancient apple trees that produced sour fruit every year. I loved all of it.

Nobody else was looking at the cabin, of course. They were all gawping, even Jaern, at the building *behind* the cabin.

'What,' Lorican asked, 'is that?'

'The tower,' I said.

Brix dismounted, stiff. 'Why is there a tower?' She pointed at the pinkish basalt cylinder that stretched upwards for four storeys before it abruptly became a crumbling ruin, the remnants of its battlements jutting against the sky like broken teeth.

The tower had been the reason that Acarius built the cabin in the first place, as nearly as I could tell. It was at least two centuries old, and had been constructed by some wizard of a past era. I had learned to scribe sigils by studying the old ones carved into its steps, and Acarius had his library on the lower level and his laboratory on the second floor.

'To make my life more complex.' I strode towards the cabin. 'Come on, let's get inside.'

Acarius, being Acarius, had several caches in and around the cabin. A few of them were obvious, for piddly things like the silver coins he had used to buy eggs and beer from the village or the wine he had brought up the river twice a year. Those had been left open after his arrest, searched and pillaged by the Guildies like everything else.

But that left the two secret caches, the ones I was fairly sure he didn't know that I knew about. When I was fifteen, he had forbidden me to play with yavad and hidden his vials of the stuff behind a secret panel in his bedroom. It didn't work; all it took was a few days of waiting until he was absorbed in his reading and some careful searching. Not that I really wanted the yavad, but I don't like secrets.

The front half of the house was the kitchen and a sitting room, with two bedrooms in the back. Small, and not particularly fancy. I walked into the sitting room and halted.

Everything remained as I had left it months ago, when I had arrived to find Acarius gone. Everything, down to the familiar smell of pine sap and dust. I stood there, the warm sunshine on my back, and looked at the tatty sheepskin rug, the stone fireplace, the pewter dishes on the shelf above the rough table and chairs. Worst was the stack of books along one wall, with a pair of handmade spectacles resting on top.

'Quaint,' Jaern said. He moved into the room and reached for a book.

'Don't touch that,' I snapped. 'It isn't yours.'

The bees in my chest hummed and he stopped, watching me thoughtfully. It shouldn't have hurt so much, seeing Acarius' spectacles there. For a split second, I could believe he was going to walk out of the bedroom and snap at me for forgetting to wipe my feet.

Brix came to stand beside me. She studied my face for a second before knocking her elbow against my ribs. 'I'm hungry, wizard.'

I tried to be exasperated, but the normalcy was comforting and I couldn't keep from smiling. 'My name is not—'

'I'm hungry, Corcoran,' Brix said.

I was hungry, too. The vegetable garden was now rampant with weeds, but mixed with the grass and dandelions were self-seeded peas, new potatoes and asparagus. There was also some un-rotted firewood piled on the porch, so I busied myself building a fire. Jaern refused to help dig potatoes until I ordered him to. Carrying the necromancer's soul had its negatives, but at least it kept a leash on him. When we had enough to make a decent meal, I left the others fussing with vegetables and went to the first cache.

Acarius' room was a wreck. I hadn't been able to clean when I'd been there before, and there were still blood smears, broken furniture and a scorch mark on the braided rug beside the bed. At least the smoke smell had faded.

I walked through the drifts of ruined clothes and blankets to the overturned desk. The Guild had taken everything that even looked important – all his diaries, all his papers – and had left nothing behind but an arrest warrant nailed to the front door and a giant red word scrawled across the bedroom wall in alchemical paint. I had torn the warrant down six and a half months ago, but I hadn't had time to scrub the paint off.

Lawless.

I knew that it would be difficult seeing it again, but I wasn't prepared for the blind rage that broke over me. *Lawless.* That was the sum of Keir Esras' charges against Acarius, against the man who'd taught me every scrap of morality I possessed – my grandfather, who had lived with the superstitious, illiterate folk in the village below and had never tried to frighten them. Acarius, whose magical practice insisted on consent, on honesty, on privacy. Coming from Keir the bully, the murderer who was trying to build himself a rebellion, it was intolerable.

The battered tin mirror still hung on the wall above where the desk had stood, its surface smeared with red paint. The hole in the log behind it held only a purse with a few copper coins in it and a tin medal depicting the crescent moon, the emblem of the goddess Ranara. Nothing was ever simple.

I took the money, but left the medal. It had been my mother's, and had been in this cache as long as I had been opening it. Her name was scratched on the tin in pitiful block letters, and it was the only thing I had of hers. I hadn't thought Acarius would put it back in the cache. Not after I'd thrown it at him. Not after the things I'd said.

Tell me who I am. Just tell me, what's so bad that you can't tell me? Damn this. Damn you –

It wasn't until the iron-heavy tang of blood flooded my mouth that I realised I'd been chewing on the inside of my cheek. I closed the panel, and then I had to stand there with my hand on it for a long time.

'Holy gods,' Lorican said, from behind me.

I smeared the wet tracks off my cheeks and jaw before I turned. 'I thought you were getting lunch together.'

'I had no—' He nudged the heap of torn clothes in front of him with one toe. 'I didn't know it was this bad.' His eyes left the abomination on the wall. 'You found it like this? How did they take him?'

'It's what we did – do,' I said. 'Help people who have magic problems, things that the Guild and Temples won't look into. Like one woman who came to Acarius last year. Her husband knocked her around, she ran away from him and he hired divination to find her. Nothing illegal in the divining, but it's *quite* illegal to write the hexes we placed to prevent him from finding and approaching her.' I shrugged. 'Sometimes people pay us. Sometimes they don't. This last time, six months ago – well, the villagers weren't able to be very helpful, but they said a group of people had come looking for Acarius, to ask him for help. They must have been convincing, and somehow they managed to write a trap spiral and lure him into it. Pinned him down.' My eyes drifted to the floor where Lorican was standing, where the paint smear that had been bright six months ago had mellowed to a dull orange. 'He got some spells off, I think; there was blood in multiple places.'

Lorican put his hand over his mouth. 'You're sure it wasn't his?'

I didn't answer. What was there to say? Of course I wasn't sure.

'Gray,' Brix called, from the front room. 'Aren't you hungry?'

I wasn't, not anymore. But I knew I'd have to choke the food down anyway.

When I went back into the sitting room, Brix was roasting potatoes and eating peas raw from the pods. She sat on a three-legged stool next to the fireplace, manoeuvring the potatoes out of the ashes with a long stick.

'So?' Brix said, her mouth full of peas. 'Did you find the pieces you were looking for? Is the doll ready to put together?'

'No.' I sat down on the floor next to Brix's feet, still trying to settle my emotions. Everything in this place reminded me of Acarius. Everything hurt. 'They're not in the cabin, which means they're probably in the tower.'

Lorican had followed me out of the bedroom, frowning to himself. Jaern, who was not eating, leaned against one wall and watched the room with flat black eyes.

'Well.' Brix dug around in the ashes with her stick and rolled a blackened potato towards me. 'You should eat, then, and go look in the tower before the daylight's gone. I'll come with you.'

They *all* came with me. I confess to feeling a vindictive sort of satisfaction when I led them to the wooden door of the tower, only to find it covered in carved sigils.

'Son of a whore,' Jaern said.

Lorican glanced at him, and then at me. 'What is it?'

'Wards, keyed to me.' I touched the centre of the rune spiral, where CORCORAN was carved in choppy letters, big as life. I hadn't gone into the tower the last time I was at the cabin, being more concerned with following the obvious trail of the Guildies. But maybe that was a mistake – maybe Acarius had believed I'd find all this, months ago. 'Anyone but me who goes through this door, as long as the wards are in effect, will suffer the consequences.'

'Uncomfortable hair sprouting?' Brix edged closer to the door.

'No . . .' I studied the runes. 'Leprosy.'

She jumped back. 'Well, take the ward off.'

'He can't,' Jaern said. 'Whoever wrote this didn't take any chances – he designed the rune spiral so that nobody could stick a sword in the boy's back and force him to remove it.' Reluctant admiration glittered in his voice, brittle and bright as ice. 'It's not a ward, it's a gods-damned gorgeous *hex*.'

I pushed the door open and stepped into the tower, inhaling a mixture of tallow candles, parchment and rotting straw. The narrow windows, cross-hatched with steel bars, let in just enough light to be frustrating.

I had never actually seen inside the tower cache. I had found the trapdoor that led to it accidentally one day, when Acarius had been long-winded about something – probably divination, always my worst subject. I was young enough to sprawl on my back, kicking my feet now and then when he wasn't looking at me. My heels came down on something hollow under the scattered straw that gave a modicum of insulation against the cold floor.

Acarius had paused, just for a moment, in the middle of his lesson. I managed to look as though I didn't know I had just kicked a trapdoor. When I crept back later and pushed the straw away, I found a spiral of runes in red paint that covered the entire floor. Even at ten, I had known those runes were powerful, and I left it alone.

A few inches from my feet was where the trapdoor should be. I dropped to my knees and began brushing the straw away until I got down to bare stone and wood. It didn't take long to find the door. I got it clear and then sat back on my heels, studying the sigils and considering. The sigils weren't the same as they had been when I'd seen them before. For one thing, they were scribed in green now. For another, they were keyed to my name, like the ones outside.

He had been *expecting* them to arrest him, then. The sigils on the door outside could have been done quickly, but these would have taken days. He had been expecting me to find all this.

Acarius had been studying Jaern before he was arrested. He had known something about the doll then. Had known, but hadn't done more than take a couple of gems away so that nobody could easily complete the artefact. So nobody could *use* the artefact.

I grasped the ring of the trapdoor and yanked it open. A set of wrought-iron steps wound down into utter darkness. I dug through my satchel and scribed an illumination spell on the inside of my forearm, hardly feeling the pain that slid through me when I pronounced it. The ball of soft blue light travelled down the steps. It wasn't a mere cupboard, then. I went down the steps before I could think too hard about it.

The area was about the size of a decent cellar. It contained a table and a shelf, which held a collection of carefully-sealed scroll tubes. The table was empty except for a box made of delicate, lacquered red wood.

I moved my illumination spell around the walls and floor, but I couldn't find any more runes. The box was the right size to hold two gems. I flicked the latch and opened it.

Two pieces of polished, almond-shaped obsidian with sigils carved in their centres gleamed in the dull light. If I had been choosing stones to represent Jaern's eyes, they were exactly what I would have picked.

I slipped them out of the box and considered putting them into my satchel, with the others. But it felt almost sacrilegious to be carrying runes around, knocking against my reagents and the dozens of tiny sigils engraved on the doll itself. I didn't know how the doll worked, after all. What if the runes interacted, like spells in a book?

What if Jaern got hold of the satchel? What would I have, at that point, that could restrain him?

I put one of the pieces of obsidian in the bag with the rest, and transferred the other to my pocket. I still didn't feel like I'd taken adequate precautions, but hells, I was carrying a soul-moving doll – adequate precautions didn't exist.

When I climbed the stairs, Brix was still hovering in the doorway. 'There you are.' She sounded anxious. 'Did you find it? Do you have all the pieces?'

'Yes, I think so.' I shut the trapdoor, walked out of the tower and closed the other door behind me. I glanced at Brix. There was a disturbing flatness in her face, the same sort of emptiness that I was learning meant that something was very wrong, indeed. 'What's the matter? Has Jaern been bothering you, or something?'

'I haven't touched the woman, Cricket.' Jaern hadn't moved, his eyes lingering on the wards. 'Not all of us have the same hobbies.'

'Watch your mouth,' I said.

His lips twitched. 'Why, did I mumble?'

'Nothing's the matter,' Brix said, and with a sudden, instinctive certainty I knew she was lying. It showed, in the pallor under her freckles and the tight lines of the muscles in her throat.

'Brix.' I drew closer to her, turning my back on Lorican and the necromancer. 'You can tell me.'

For a moment, I thought she was going to. She studied me, weighing her words on some scale I couldn't see. Then her eyes dropped to the satchel.

'It's nothing,' she repeated, at last. 'Really. It just . . . hit me, I suppose. It's been a lot of fear and suffering and death, and for what? An ugly metal baby and a few carved stones. I was almost hoping that the last pieces wouldn't be there after all.' She blinked, and gave me a forced smile. 'What do we do with the doll now? Do we start putting it together?'

'That's my question, too.' Lorican stood behind Jaern, his hand casually resting on the hilt of his dagger. 'How is this going to help Acarius?'

'Acarius is locked up.' I paused, unable to get the words *maybe without a soul* out of my mouth. Disquiet crackled in the air, and I couldn't find the cause. 'I think the doll is sort of a . . . key.'

Maybe it was unjust, but I knew something was wrong, and Lorican was the person I didn't understand. I had been hoping he would prove himself one way or another. Until he did, I wasn't going to talk about my plans openly – and I was going to keep the piece of obsidian separate from the rest of the Empty One. 'The next step is to analyse the doll, and it's getting dark.' I started towards the cabin. 'What do you say we discuss it in the morning?'

Two bedrooms for four people meant some scrambling. Jaern had to have Acarius' room, for the simple reason that the doorframe had magic locks carved into it, and I wanted to be able to shut him in while I slept. I expected to have to force him into the room, but he went with just a token sarcastic snort. Lorican declined to sleep indoors, and made himself a bed on the porch, where he could watch the horses and the stars. Which left Brix and I standing awkwardly in the sitting room, staring at each other.

My satchel hung, heavy, off one shoulder. I hadn't put it down yet. I needed to look at the doll and the gems calmly and figure out how they all worked together. Jaern could have been lying, of course, but the bare possibility that he wasn't – that my grandfather was trapped, soulless, suffering – had been sitting in my chest like a stone. I had to clear my mind enough to think, and find some way to get Acarius his soul back without letting Keir capture the doll. But I also had to sleep, just for a couple of hours. It really didn't matter where, as long as I kept the satchel under my pillow and scribed a spell or two before I went to sleep. Even if my weary suspicions were accurate and Lorican *was* a Guild spy, I didn't think he could get the doll away from me.

Meanwhile, Brix looked exhausted and strained, almost grieved. She needed rest, at the very least. She needed safety, too, I reckoned, and maybe someone to say something reassuring, but I was terrible in both categories. I decided to attempt gallantry. 'Take the bedroom. The mattress is lumpy but the blankets in the chest at the foot of the bed should be clean.'

'Your bedroom,' she said.

When she put it like *that*—

My ears went hot. 'I'll sleep on the hearth.'

She went into the bedroom, and I heard her moving around for a long time, presumably hunting for blankets. I banked the fire, sat down cross-legged and tried, unsuccessfully, to quiet my mind.

But she came back and seated herself exactly where I had said I'd sleep, on the warm floorboards in front of the fireplace. She didn't speak, didn't even turn to look at me, drawing her knees up to her chest and wrapping her arms around them. Eventually I let myself focus on the sinuous dance of the heat over the coals. Sometimes, watching a fire die, I can manage to let my thoughts spool out into nothing. Not that night, though. Not with her sitting that close to me.

'Your grandfather,' she said, after a while. 'You said he talked to you, but you don't know where he is. Why didn't he just *tell* you where he was?'

'Because he's a stubborn bastard,' I said.

'He's not the only one.' Brix sighed. 'It was because he didn't want you to be arrested charging in to some Guild stronghold to get him, wasn't it? I'm not trying to pry, Gray. It's just . . .' She paused. 'It seems like this is hurting you. I know my mother wouldn't have wanted me to hurt. Are you sure that your grandfather wants this for you?'

'You know your mother's voice?' The words came out before I knew they were in my mouth. 'Remember what she looked like, things like that?'

I turned my head in time to see a frown appear between her eyebrows. 'Of course.'

'I don't,' I said. 'I can remember my mother sick, coughing up bits of her lungs, and sacrificing a chicken to try to get better. That's all. And I don't even know my father's name.' I gave myself the luxury of studying my own left thumbnail. 'My mother died when I was three. Red plague, I think. We lived in one of the river villages. I suppose the families were doing their best by me, passing me from house to house. At least I ate, most of the time. Then, when I was five, they apprenticed me to a tanner.'

'Tanner.' Anger boiled under the surface of her voice. 'The same tanner who gave you the brace?'

'Oh, aye.' I ran my hand down my shin, where the bone felt naked without its usual bolstering of copper and leather. *I* felt naked, all my broken pieces displayed, all the jagged edges there for her to cut me with if she chose. 'One afternoon the beatings escalated. I forget what I did to spark it, but it ended when I crawled under the woodshed and wouldn't come out. I didn't know any magic except a few chants my mother taught me. All I knew how to do was call for help.' I pinched at my kneecap. It didn't hurt, but it's hard to resist the ghost of old pain. 'Acarius heard me, and came. She must not have had the strength to call for him, at the end. He didn't even know she had died.'

She was still, but the line of her body was taut. 'How long were you under that woodshed?'

I shrugged. I couldn't remember; it had been at least three days. 'The important thing is that Acarius took me out of all that. Raised me. Gave me everything I have. Loved me, I guess.' I paused, and had to swallow. 'I *can't* leave him. Even if he wants me to. I can't.'

'You'll save him.' She almost seemed to be reassuring herself. 'You'll find a way.'

'I don't know why you're so confident,' I said.

'You'll find a way because you have to,' she said. 'Like me. I have to find my sister and free her. There isn't anything else for me.' Her hand found mine, fingers intertwining. 'I think you understand that, maybe better than anyone I've ever met.'

Her touch was, perhaps, meant to be soothing. Instead it sent a ripple of fire through my gut, disorientating, intoxicating. I scrabbled desperately for something sensible to say, some way to hide what I was feeling. She looked at me and, deliberately, moved her hand to my knee. Then to my thigh.

'Brix,' I said, unsteadily.

'Did I make a mistake?' she said. 'Do you not want this?' The firelight outlined her features, her face tipped up towards mine, lips parted just a little. She was made of gold, and I wanted her like a drowning man wants the surface.

'I do,' I whispered.

She put two fingers on my mouth. 'Then stop talking.'

I kissed her fingertips and then her lips, and for a long time there was only her – her heartbeat thudding against my chest, her fingers in my hair, her lips crushing mine against my teeth. When she pulled away, she was trembling like a person who's tripped and fallen. She reached for me. 'Come on.'

I let her take me by the wrist and lead me towards my bedroom. There wasn't anything else in the world, just the unhurried sway of her body under the robe, the way the firelight caught her hair, the way she looked back at me.

Brix turned and slipped my satchel off my shoulder, to the floor, then slid her hands up to the laces of my shirt. I was fumbling with the buttons on her robe when I realised she was still trembling. I stopped. 'We don't have to,' I said. 'If you're not sure. We can stop.'

'I'm sure,' Brix said. 'I wish I wasn't.' She stepped backwards. 'I'm sorry.'

It took me three heartbeats to make any sense of it, of the reeking alchemical paint, of the unshed tears in her eyes.

I looked down. I stood inside an inexpertly-scribed but very effective prison circle.

'What's going on?' I said. 'What's wrong?'

Her chin quivered for a split second before she clenched her jaw. 'I didn't want to do this, Corcoran,' she said, hoarsely. 'I didn't have a choice.' She picked up my satchel and moved to the door.

I didn't have to try the edges of the circle to know that it would hold me, at least for the next few hours. 'Brix.' I knew it sounded pathetic even when I said it, but I couldn't help myself. This couldn't be real. 'Please.'

She didn't look back. She did that much for me.

SEVENTEEN

I suppose you expect me to tell you my heart was broken, or that I was gutted, or some other trite poetical nonsense. The bards will have you believe that you can watch such moments go by, chronicle every thread of pain that stitches itself through you. The truth is, sometimes they hit you like hailstones. All you do is go down.

So I don't know how long I crouched inside the circle, trying to make sense of Brix's leaving, as though understanding her reasons would make it hurt less. Eventually I realised I was cold and sitting on the ground in my unlaced shirt. Exposed. Stupid. I had been so *stupid*.

The indications hadn't even been particularly hard to spot. There was the way the Guild kept appearing, no matter how discreet I was. Their divining hadn't got better; Brix had simply kept the tracker ring I'd taken off her in Fenwydd, the one I'd told her to throw away. Then there were her questions about whether I had all of the pieces of the doll, and her uncanny knack for tolerating me – I should have seen it. Keir Esras had known exactly which bait to use with me, and I had risen to it like a good little fish.

And gods, the things I'd thought about Lorican. The things I'd *said*. *Stupid. Stop this.*

But I couldn't stop. I sat there, blind as a stunned bird, remembering how to breathe. Finally, I made my mind count off the runes and start to analyse the prison circle.

The circle was scribed in blue paint, which made it more long-lasting than if she had used red. Maybe she didn't have any other colours. It was also a classic set of sigils, written as though it was copied from a model. Which it probably had been, come to think of it. I didn't see Brix as being a natural for spell-casting – but then, I didn't really know her, did I?

Stop it.

The only thing I had to do in that moment was get out of the damn circle. It didn't matter why she had done anything, didn't matter what I had been fool enough to hope for. There was a puzzle here, and I had to solve it.

It wasn't as harsh a spell as I had initially feared. And the circle had a time-dependent component; it would only be effective for six hours or so – which would be long enough for Brix's trail to go hopelessly cold. But I didn't have anything to scribe with, so I couldn't alter the spell. Which left two options: I could either erase part of the circle, or call someone else to erase it. I reached for the runes.

My hand stopped, as though bumping a glass wall, a half inch from the blue paint. I must have missed something. I scanned the runes again, willing my wits to engage. I couldn't afford to do this now, dammit.

There it was, my name in the upper half of the circle, surrounded by twisting sigils – the circle was locked, keyed to me like the wards on the tower had been, but in reverse: I was the only one who couldn't get out of this. I wouldn't be able to cross the paint, or touch it. Still, circles could only be keyed to one person at a time, which meant Jaern or Lorican could help me. Jaern was locked in Acarius' room. I cleared my throat and cupped my hands around my mouth to shout for Lorican.

Only I didn't shout. I couldn't make a sound. She'd silenced me, too. Of course she had.

You're missing things. Calm down, quit feeling sorry for yourself and think.

I put both hands on the back of my neck and closed my eyes. I had to quit feeling things, period. If I hadn't been so damn guilty. If I hadn't been so damn *lonely* —

My mind wouldn't allow me not to make the connections, wouldn't stop chasing back through my memories for proof. She'd tried, after all. She'd told me what all this was about, what she was playing for.

Anka, the sister. For whatever reason, Brix couldn't buy her freedom without selling me. It would have been an easy choice: her family over a skinny, sarcastic malcontent.

Think. Solve the puzzle.

'Well, Cricket.'

I opened my eyes.

Jaern stood in the doorway of my bedroom, observing the situation, the firelight from behind him throwing his shadow across the floor. 'Here we are,' he said. He sat on the floor, a few feet from me, and rested his chin in his hands. 'So, what are we going to do?'

I couldn't speak, but I could be creative with my gestures.

He didn't seem offended. 'Very high-spirited of you, but less than efficient. I assume you'd like me to get you out of that circle so you can go chasing after the little bitch, correct?'

My hand slammed into the invisible barrier around me before I had time to realise I was on my feet, trying to hit him.

Jaern didn't move. 'Still so sensitive?' He reached forwards and rubbed out part of the circle – just part of it, the silencing component.

'Bastard,' I said. I was still stuck. 'You were locked in.'

'My parents were married, as far as I know.' Jaern brushed the flakes of blue paint off his fingers. 'And a lock only works when the prisoner doesn't know how to make a key. Are you going to tell me what happened?'

I could make him let me out. I had his soul. All I had to do was concentrate and command him. I opened my mouth.

He held up a hand. 'Or force me to clear the circle, and let me read it from your insides myself. Your choice.'

He was trying to make me angry enough to be foolish. I took a breath. 'What?'

'I am being patient with you,' he said, 'because your necromantic education has been so shamefully neglected. Did you think there would be no consequences, when you use my soul to order me around like a servant? Did you think my soul wouldn't be *me*, poking around in your thoughts?' He stood, nose to nose with me. 'Every time you force me to do something, I learn more about you. I see a little deeper into your memories. I swim a little further into your desires.' He smiled. 'More intimate than I suspect you intended.'

'You're a liar,' I said.

'When I feel like it. But I still know about the time you saw Brix's tattoos across her chest, and you recognised the binding sigils, the communication spell. And I know what you said to Acarius, that last time you saw him here, when you had that nasty argument.' He clicked his tongue in mock disapproval.

Needles of ice jabbed into my chest. I hadn't told anyone about the argument. I didn't even like *thinking* about it.

'Does this conversation have a point?' I said.

'I'm just talking some sense to you.' He squatted and stared at the runes. 'You should take my help.'

I crossed my arms. 'You don't want to help me. You just want your soul back.'

'And you want to be rid of it.' He rubbed out one character and then let his hand hover over another, as though he was considering. 'Unluckily, to extract my soul we need that doll that you just let the bitch steal.'

My hand clenched into a fist. 'Don't call her that,' I said. The half-painful, hissing tug behind my breastbone confirmed that I had made it an order.

He glanced up. 'Willing to let me have another glimpse, just to protect her memory? Let's not be naïve, Cricket. People like her will always turn on you, sooner or later. You can't even blame them. It's in their nature to deceive and take advantage of their betters. You call *me* a liar?' He rubbed out half of my name. 'I'm honest about what I want. We're too much alike, you and I. You can tell when I'm trying to lie to you, which makes it somewhat unproductive. And I, of course, know everything about you.'

The magic around me flexed. There's no other way to describe what happened – it was like pushing on a rotting wooden door. The circle was almost broken.

'Then maybe you can explain to me why you're talking, instead of getting me where I can do some good,' I said.

'Because as soon as I erase the other half of your name, you'll go tearing after the – girl, and you won't listen to me.' Jaern wiped his hands across the letters, leaving one long blue smear. 'And I'm trying to convince you not to divine for her.'

'What? Why not?'

'Divine for the *doll*.' He straightened. 'What are the odds, after all, that she stole the thing for herself? Did she look like a necromancer to you?'

I pushed past him. I had only been in the circle for an hour or so. If I was quick enough, maybe I wouldn't need to divine. Maybe I wouldn't need to decide whether I was chasing Brix or the doll.

I halted on the cabin's porch. Even the dim firelight in the house was dazzling compared to the utter blackness of the night outside. There was no moon, and the cloud cover must have been heavy enough to blot out the stars. I could only see inches in front of me.

'Lorican,' I said. A startled snort from the darkness to my left. The idiot had slept through everything? I grabbed for a pencil to scribe an illumination spell.

Dammit.

Brix had taken my satchel. I would have to get a lamp, like a sap-skulled farmer. And it served me right.

'Wake up,' I said, in what I assumed was Lorican's direction. 'Brix is gone. We'll need the horses.'

I went back into the house to look for a thrice-damned lantern.

As it happened, I had to wait for daylight. Acarius had possessed exactly one lantern, a sorry, cheap affair that only half-worked. It had always hung on a peg by the fire, which was probably where Brix saw it and took it from. I fished a half-burned stick out of the fire and tried to use it to scribe, but that produced runes that were so soft-edged and smudged that the incantation was unstable. Even Acarius' inkwell, tucked into the corner of the bookshelf where he kept his journals, was dry.

There should have been enough reagents to make some alchemical paint in the upper floor of the tower, but with no lamp I wouldn't be able to see what I was doing well enough to keep from blowing myself up as I mixed the recipe. Jaern could have cast an illumination spell, but I knew he wouldn't do it unless I commanded him to, and I had no desire for him to have another look at my mind.

I sat on the hearth in front of the dying fire and answered Lorican's questions until the urge to stab someone became overwhelming, and then put my head down on my knees and pretended to sleep.

As soon as dawn broke, I went to the tower. This time I climbed the twisting staircase that lined the outer wall until I got to Acarius' laboratory.

Against one wall was a shelf full of clay jars and dusty, stained glass vials. There wasn't much left inside the jars. My grandfather never believed in over-stocking. Still, there were enough reagents to make a couple of vials of red and green paint. I mixed as quickly as I could, pocketed the vials, scrounged an old brush from the stained workbench and followed the stairs up to the roof.

The roof of the tower had once been the inside of the fifth storey. Now it was just a flat, round stretch of stone floor, scoured clean by centuries of wind and rain. I wrote a series of runes on either forearm, knelt, and began scribing a divination spiral.

It was foolish, if you like. Divination is toxic and can cause lingering hallucinations. I should have found a way to get Jaern or Lorican up there with me, so they could pull me out of the spiral if I started having a seizure. But I wasn't certain that Jaern would help me if I didn't force him, and I also didn't want him observing the divining. All he'd have to do is touch me during the spell, and he could pull the magic towards his own query.

And I couldn't face Lorican, not in the light of day, not until I knew exactly how much my mistakes had cost me.

When it came time to put a focus at the centre of the spiral, I took a deep breath and drew the piece of sigil-carved obsidian from my pocket.

Jaern was right. I couldn't divine for Brix, or even for Acarius' location. I didn't have any way to focus on Acarius – lacking a tracker, I'd have needed a lock of hair, a tooth, a fingernail – but I did have a significant piece of the doll. There was no way to save Acarius without the Empty One, so I had to find it. It was that simple, and that difficult.

I put the gem at the centre of the spiral, placed my hands carefully on the runes and pronounced the spell.

North-west.

My surroundings began to blur. I lost them less suddenly than I had when Acarius had contacted me – lost the beevine-scented wind, the trees whispering in the distance, the slick paint under my hands, one by one – leaving me with just the shifting pulse of the divinatory vision.

I smelled oxen, and the warmth of wood under the sun and . . . incense. That was unexpected enough that I leaned harder into the spell. Brix was taking the doll north-west, and the oxen argued for a caravan of some kind, but incense? What did that mean, a temple?

The magic surged through my veins, swirling with sensory impressions. Slick glass. Metal. Cold. Fear.

Cor Daddan.

It was the name of an ancient fort, a Daine ruin that had been the site of a bloody battle. I had only heard of it because it was on a trade route and sometimes caravans still used its wells. Why would Brix be taking the doll there? Why—

I brought it, like you said. Brix's voice echoed in my head, stark with horror. *I brought it, now you give me her flask. Let her out. You promised.*

Flask? That couldn't be right. Everything people had whispered about Tirnaal, the legends about djinn-blood and magic and people whose bodies could compress and expand . . .

The muscles in my forearms bunched. I struggled to control the spell. The *doll*. I needed to keep my concentration on it.

The flask is at the citadel. I'm not a fool.

Not Brix. She wasn't the one at Cor Daddan. I knew the voice, though, contemptuous, smug. I could almost see the look on Keir's face. He was communicating with someone over distance, maybe with some version of the incorporeal projection Acarius had used to speak to me. Nausea tickled the pit of my stomach and jets of bitter spit welled in my mouth. The toxicity from the divination spell was building up quickly. For a brief, infuriating moment I could catch the scent of what Keir was thinking, the purr of his greed.

Now it doesn't matter anymore whether the old man talks, or whether he dies.

A spike of agony drove itself into the base of my skull. The magic bubbled and changed around me, thick as honey, choking. I had to break the connection now, before it got any worse. I pulled my hands off the runes in careful sequence.

And then I was alone again, on my knees in the dawn light, alchemical paint still stinging against my clammy skin. I hitched myself away from the spiral and sat there shivering, waiting for the poison in my veins to fade.

The doll was going to Cor Daddan. Keir was already *at* Cor Daddan.

That meant in order to rescue Acarius, I'd have to get past wards, traps and a dozen wizards specifically trained to maim and kill with their magic. And that was without taking into consideration the plain swords and daggers that were likely there, the sheer distance between me and the ruined citadel, the price on my head, the improbability that I would catch up with Brix and the doll before they tortured Acarius to death. Any man of sense would have concluded the whole thing was suicide.

'Grandfather,' I whispered. 'What do I do? What am I supposed to do?'

I knew what he would say: *Wizards move on. Get up. Keep fighting. Don't let them see you weak, because they won't pity you.*

I swallowed again, several times, but it didn't help the nausea. It wasn't as though I didn't already know what I was going to do. It wasn't as though I could stop imagining Brix's face.

Get. Up.

I got up.

The tiny lake was the only thing nearby to wash in. I made my way there in the rose-pale light of the morning, scuffing through the tall grass, and squatted by the edge of the water to rub the paint off my arms. Then I dunked my head and face for good measure. I'd vomited into the bushes at the foot of the tower and I wanted the taste out of my mouth. I wanted the taste of the whole damn business gone.

I stood up, dripping and freezing. The cold was all right, actually. Staring into the green water, too numb to think about how much everything was going to hurt in a minute – that felt all right.

'What are you doing?' Lorican's voice, from behind me.

Gods, no. I couldn't talk to him, not when I had no idea what to do next. 'I'm either dancing a jig or washing, I'll leave it to your observational skills to determine which.' I swiped my sleeve across my face. 'Where's Jaern?'

Lorican grimaced. 'Sitting in the middle of the floor staring at the ceiling like a snake watching a mouse. I'll ask another way, then. What *were* you doing?'

'I was divining.' Why wouldn't he go away?

'And you know where to go?' he said. 'You know where Acarius is?'

'I'm a fool,' I said. The toxicity of the spell, the lack of sleep, the sick weight of my blunders – all of it crowded into my chest, and I couldn't get enough air. 'I knew someone was bringing the Guild down on my head. I knew Keir wanted the doll, and someone near me was trying to get it for him. I thought it was you, but it was Brix. All along, it was Brix. She's gone, with the doll, and I can't help Acarius without it, and it's my fault.' I breathed slow, through my nose. 'I was wrong. Stupid. There's no excuse, and I apologise.'

Silence crawled by, thick, uncomfortable. I licked a drop of water off my upper lip and forced myself to look at him.

'I'm sorry, lad,' Lorican said. 'I know she mattered to you.'

'Gods, *don't*.' The cold air bit at my wet hair. 'Don't do that. I know I'm a prick. I know I shouldn't have treated you the way I did. You should be angry with me. I can't – I don't–' I choked on the words, couldn't look at him. 'What in the hells did Acarius do for you that keeps you here?'

He didn't say anything for a long time. Eventually he bent and picked up a stone, and skipped it across the surface of the pond with one effortless flick of his wrist. 'Saved my life, as I told you.'

I started walking back towards the cabin, and Lorican fell into step beside me. 'Assume he hasn't told me anything. Saved your life how?'

'When I was sixteen I joined a work crew that was rolling out to Genereth,' he said. 'Orphan kid. There were a lot of us, all looking for work in the dye vats and fabric mills. I thought I might as well seek my fortune there as anywhere. Acarius was on the same cara-van. In the wastes south of the city we got hit by bandits. Everybody died, except your granddad.'

'And you,' I said.

'No.' Lorican halted. 'I died when I was sixteen, Gray.'

I froze, one foot on the porch step. 'What?'

'I took an arrow to the gut.' Lorican spoke with slow exactitude, like a man reciting a litany. He never took his eyes off me. 'Watched myself bleed out. Acarius had been over the hill when the bandits hit, taking a piss or something. By the time he got back, everyone else was dead and I was almost there. I must have been crying. He found me leaning against a wagon wheel, and kept saying it was going to be all right. And he had this . . . bottle, with red stuff in it.'

My throat went dry. 'You're aware, I suppose, how this sounds.'

Lorican gave a little shrug, his face taut. 'Goddess knows I don't remember much of it, lad. But when you close your eyes on that kind of hurt and then wake up in a different body, you believe. Somehow your granddad moved *me* – the part of me that thinks and feels – from my dying body into one that wasn't dying. I wasn't Erranter before. I'm not complaining, mind. They're my people now, and more kin than I had before.' He smiled. 'Besides, Erranter worship Linna. Makes sense for a man in my condition to pray to the Lady of Change, wouldn't you say?'

I swallowed, and tried to think of a logical question. 'And where did he get your current body?'

'Acarius found a dead Erranter kid among the orphans, somehow fixed the broken neck and put me into that . . . this body.' Lorican eyed me, like a wary dog. 'I know, it sounds—' He grimaced.

Plausible. It sounded *plausible*. I had never believed that Acarius was ignorant about necromancy; it wasn't like my grandfather to avoid an entire branch of study just because it was unsavoury. He had, at least, known enough to always teach me to keep away from it. Necromancy was vile, on a level with compounding poisons or selling back-alley curses. But what if it had been the only way to save a life?

And so – what? He had repaired a fractured spine? Built a 'hand-made body' like Jaern's, in the time between capturing Lorican's soul and implanting it? Had all this knowledge, but never seen fit to tell me about it? Was *this* why the Guild hunted him? Was this why Brix had stolen the damn doll for them?

Of course it is.

Because if Acarius could implant a soul and Keir Esras could force him to share that ability, overthrowing the Charter and revolting against the king would barely be a risk. The Guildlord could get himself a new body whenever he wanted. He could raise an army of marulaches whenever he felt like it, order any king in Varre around like a servant-boy. Hells, eternal life itself wouldn't be a problem.

Lorican could have been lying, of course, but what a strange and pointless thing to lie about. All at once, it wasn't so difficult to believe he cared about Acarius. Apparently there were whole chambers in my grandfather's life that I knew nothing about.

'I can understand why you'd feel obligated, after that,' I said.

'*Obligated?*' Lorican said, sounding incredulous.

I forced myself to move again, up on to the porch. There was no time. Every minute that passed, the doll was getting closer to Cor Daddan, and my chances of rescuing Acarius were getting slimmer. I had to get the horses saddled and collect Jaern before I left. Gods knew where I was going to get food; maybe I could wheedle some out of the villagers once I got out of the canyon. I chewed my lip, trying to think of how to put this in a way that wouldn't insult him. 'Look, I have to do something, and there's no reason to think it's going to turn out well for me. I don't want to get you killed.'

Lorican snorted. 'This crack-witted idea you're stuck on of doing everything by yourself – I don't understand it. Risk is everywhere. I might as well take this one. Why not let me?'

A dull throb of resentment welled up inside me. *Risk.* He wasn't the only one gambling. I'd lived my whole life on the theory that normal folk didn't help people like me, and I had been right, dammit. The last person I'd trusted was Brix, and now here I was, duped, humiliated. What had Jaern said? *Sooner or later, they'll all turn on you.* 'You don't owe *me* your life,' I said.

'It's the necromancer, isn't it?' Lorican looked upset, which I found vaguely reassuring. Upset people were more predictable. 'He's got some kind of hold over you, promised you something. That damn snake would cut your throat in a second, and you know it. He wouldn't even bother to clean his knife afterwards. You need to be rid of him.'

'I can't be rid of him, not without the doll.' Saying it was a relief. This would do it. This would make him go. 'Jaern's soul is bound to me, has been since we left Deeptown.' I watched him, waiting for the disgust to cross his features, waiting for him to realise that I wasn't worth helping.

'*Obligated*,' Lorican repeated. 'Why do you think Acarius sent you to me? Why do you think I went with him down to that deathtrap temple in the first place?' He paused. 'Gray, Acarius gave me my life back. He's the only one who even knows who I was before. He's the closest thing I have to a father or a brother, and I have to save him. How could I live with myself if I didn't try?'

I couldn't move for a second, couldn't put words and sentences together. What do you do when someone lays their loyalty in your hand?

'I'm going to Cor Daddan,' I said, finally. 'Acarius is there, and Keir Esras, and I think Brix is taking the doll to him. I'm going to try to catch up with her and get it back.' I took a breath; it was difficult to get the words past my teeth. 'If you want to, I could use help.'

Lorican nodded. 'Then I'll come with you, of course.'

EIGHTEEN

The road to Cor Daddan was a hard-packed ribbon of alkali-stained clay, not used by much of anyone besides military convoys or floating slaver camps. It ran north-west and climbed into high, cold prairie lands that seemed to stretch forever under a great, steely bowl of sky. Three days out from the cabin, we left the rock-paved caravan route. After that we didn't see any other travellers for a solid week. Eventually the land began to swell into low hills, and a purple smear of distant mountains appeared on the horizon to the west. The wind almost never stopped blowing, even when the rain crashed through and soaked the air with the glorious, spicy scent of sagebrush.

I'd managed to beg some food from the villagers, but all too soon it began to run thin. Jaern, who didn't need to eat, found the situation funny, I think. He rode perfectly, the way he did everything, and only deigned to notice me when he was bored. Lorican kept an even temper, but I caught him sneaking off a couple of times to do sunrise devotions to the Lady of Change, begging her and three travel saints I'd never heard of for luck. He mostly ignored Jaern, but he also never turned his back on the necromancer.

My scrying was consistent, though. Every night I found a stone and wrote a divination spiral with my carefully rationed paint, and every night the magic spat out *Cor Daddan*, *north-west* and *Keir*. It also wrapped me in a slick of claustrophobic fear and frustration that I took to mean *Brix*. We were close to the doll, and getting closer every day.

I came out of my spell on the tenth evening, panting, the stench of blood and incense and death vivid in my nostrils. I rubbed my hands against each other, stiff with cold, and glanced across the camp to where Lorican was moving in the brush, looking for firewood.

'He didn't hear you,' Jaern said, from beside me.

I startled. Jaern sat cross-legged just inches from where I had written my spiral. His face was lifted towards the sky, unblinking black eyes reflecting the sunset. Our camp was nothing more than a place off the road where Lorican had reckoned we could hide the campfire, which he had insisted on making no larger than a dinner plate. Miles of yellow grass and grey bushes whispered around us, moving in the wind.

'Hear me do what?' I said, hoping I didn't know.

Jaern didn't bother to look at me. 'Call her.'

I scuffed my hand across the flat rock I was kneeling over and wiped out the spiral, my heart hammering in my chest. 'I don't suppose there's any point wondering why you were sitting there and listening to me cast.'

'As it happens, infant, I had other business this evening. Your divinatory babblings, like your unfailing sarcasm, were merely a windfall.' He exhaled. 'So you're still thinking about her. You're persistent, Cricket, I'll give you that.'

'I don't like it when you call me that,' I said, 'and I don't believe you have any other business.'

'You're not the only one who can write a divining spiral.' He stopped, waiting for me to ask him what he'd been divining for. He wouldn't answer if I did; he'd make me order him, and take the opportunity to spy on my thoughts. The pattern had got tedious over the last few days. 'Well?' he said.

I knuckled grit out of my eyes. 'Well, how many hells can I be sent to for kicking a god in the balls?'

A snort of genuine, surprised laughter broke from him. 'If I'm the one sending you?' He tilted his head to one side, considering. 'Damn you to all of them, Gray. You're inconvenient. You're young, you practise a certain way. I know things that you don't.' He finally looked at me. 'Which I could teach you, you know.'

'At what cost?' I said.

'Ah. See?' he said, softly. 'There it is, suspicion. That's the reason you and I have difficulty.'

'What news from the magic?' Lorican strode up, dropped a scant armful of bleached, dry wood beside the fire and squatted on his heels. 'Are we close?'

'It's a caravan of some kind,' I said, mindful of the visions I'd had where I spent the whole time with the taste of trail dust. 'Wagons, a lot of people. And yes, we're close. Less than a mile. If we go tonight, we could have the doll by morning, but I can't just show up and demand it from them like a highwayman. In a camp that size, there will be guards.' I hesitated. 'I could try to use my licence sigil. Guild wizards have special legal privileges, and if the doll is still with this caravan, presumably the Guild hasn't shown up to take possession of it yet.'

'It's not a bad thought,' Lorican said, warily. 'If we travel the mile tonight, in the dark, then they're off-balance and unlikely to have an easy way to check your pedigree. You throw your weight around and demand to see the doll on behalf of the Guildlord. We can say I'm your servant. It could work, as long as we're quick, focused and you can keep a muzzle on *him*.' He nodded at Jaern.

'Muzzle?' Jaern stood. He had a manic look, like when a cat decides to hunt ghosts in the middle of the night. 'That's cute.'

'Stop it,' I said. 'Just, stop, and let me . . .' I flexed my hands and shoulders, still on my knees, still half-caught in the toxicity of my spell. Something dripped from my nose. I touched it. 'Let me think,' I said, staring down at my red-stained fingers.

'Is the woman still with this caravan?' Jaern said. 'It's just a thought, you understand, but it seems to me that she'd be able to point out that you're not a Guild wizard with relative quickness.'

I had sensed echoes of disappointment and frustration in every divining session, but that didn't mean Brix was there. It was a clero-mantic hallucination, an artefact of my own emotions interacting with the vision. Why would she stay, after all, when her bargain was concluded? That I *wanted* her to be there badly enough to skew the spell was disturbing, certainly, but at the moment that didn't matter. I couldn't let it matter.

I scrubbed my wrist under my nose and got to my feet. 'No. She isn't there. That won't be a problem.'

'You're not all right,' Lorican said, quietly. 'Gray, we don't have to decide tonight. There're still a few days of prairie land left to travel. We could do this in the morning, or tomorrow—'

'No,' I said. 'Anything could happen by tomorrow. The Guild could send a runner to get the doll. The caravan could move on.' The important thing was that I knew Keir was at Cor Daddan. This had to work. 'It has to be tonight.'

We rode, single file, and reached the caravan camp just as the last rays of sun had disappeared behind the horizon. The stench hit me in the face first, before I even saw the light of the campfires. Sweat mixed with animal pens, sewage and decay, ten times worse than the average village-stink. It reeked of suffering, years of anguish soaked into the canvas of the tents. This was no spice caravan – it was a floating slave camp.

My stomach churned. If we hadn't already ridden into the light from two massive braziers, I would have been tempted to turn around. I could pretend a lot of things, but acting like a Guild slave buyer?

'Halt!' A figure peeled away from the silhouette of the tents. 'State your business!'

There were actually several figures, and there was too much metal. The foot soldiers carried naked swords, chain mail gleaming on shoulders and at throats. The speaker – a man, judging by the voice – rode a massive piebald horse and stopped just short of running against my smaller roan. 'This is in the Makesh camp territory. Who gave you permission to be here?' His sword tip came around to hover near the level of my stomach.

'Get that away from me.' I slapped it sideways. It wasn't time for courtesy. 'I'm the Guild liaison and I will not be insulted.'

'Mages' Guild?' said the man.

'No,' I snapped. 'The Guild of Wandering Tent-Peg Makers. Do you know of another guild that has business with your house?' I pushed my sleeve up and held out my sigil-tattooed wrist, my heart banging against my eardrums. One of the others was holding a lance with its tip a few inches from Lorican's throat.

The man sat silent for a heartbeat or so, then sheathed his sword and nudged his horse forwards. The fellow was huge, as broad across the chest as a bear, with a scar from his lower lip to his chin. His black hair was cut short, almost, but not quite, like a soldier. A mercenary, then.

He seized my wrist in one beefy hand and pulled it towards the light from the braziers, squinting at the sigil. His other hand hovered near the hilt of his sword.

I tensed, but he released me.

'Apologies,' he said. 'We weren't expecting the Guild officer for another couple of days. Master Makesh will want to know why the plan has changed. My name is Gedion.' He glanced behind me at Jaern, who sat like an ivory statue against the night. 'Is that one your slave?'

'As is the other.' The words tasted bad, but I couldn't grimace. 'I suggest getting your weapons away from them and taking me to Master Makesh. Am I to be kept waiting all night?'

'No.' Gedion reined his horse sideways. 'Come with me, sir.'

Someone's wail sliced through the darkness – monotonous, disconsolate keening, a child screaming for its mother or a mother screaming for her child, I couldn't tell which. It caught me like a hook.

'Damn whiny bitch,' muttered the mercenary.

I forced my hand to unclench, but the injustice still rubbed at me, like a twist of wire against my skin. No wonder Brix had been willing to do anything to get her baby sister out of this world. I wanted to burn it down. Given the right reagents, I could.

Don't gag. Analyse. You can burn it down later, if you live through the night.

It seemed like an odd place for a slave camp, halfway to nowhere, and judging from the oxen I saw picketed, it wasn't a small private order being transported to some backwoods lord. I had got to twenty-seven tents, canopies and ramshackle-covered wagons when Gedion reached out and grabbed my horse's bridle.

'Master Makesh is in the blue pavilion, there.' Gedion pulled his horse and mine to a stop and gestured. 'I'll have your slaves taken to your quarters – just ask when you're done speaking to the Master and someone will show you your tent.'

Wonderful. Lorican had fallen into the role of my 'slave' pretty easily, but Jaern had ridden abreast of me, not bothering to hide his amusement. It didn't seem likely he'd go nicely. I gathered my resolve and looked at him.

'Wait for me there,' I said, and felt the tug as my will conquered his, as Jaern had another ramble through my mind.

Jaern fluttered his eyelashes at me. 'Of course.'

I got out of my saddle and handed my reins to Lorican. 'Take care,' I said.

'Yes, sir, I'll see to the horses, and have them ready for you.' Lorican met my eyes for a moment. 'I'll be watching for you, sir.'

Gedion dismounted and handed his reins to one of the other mer-cenaries. They all rode away as he led me towards the pavilion.

It smelled worse at ground level, disgusting odours swirling and mingling with a puff of spiced air that wafted from the open flap of the blue tent. The spices didn't help even a little. It was like someone had dropped a bottle of perfume down a latrine.

'Officer!'

I blinked. I don't know what I had been expecting, but it wasn't the garish figure in peacock-blue silk who came rushing out from the doorway. This couldn't be Makesh, could it? The man responsi-ble for all the pain around me?

'My apologies!' Makesh grabbed my hands with both of his and pressed them a trifle frantically, the gems on his rings digging into my flesh. 'Allow me to introduce myself – Tavas Makesh. We waited for you at the area Lord Esras specified for almost a week. I'm afraid we had quite despaired of your coming, and had decided to take the shipment on to Cor Daddan by ourselves. Lord Esras was so vehe-ment in his instructions.' He ran a practised eye over me. 'But I see you've had a rough journey. What am I doing, keeping you out here in the open? Come have a drink, some refreshments, before we talk business.' He gestured for me to precede him into his tent.

I went, fighting down rising panic. The interior of the tent exuded luxury, full of cushions and folding furniture. If it wasn't for the creeping stink, you could almost believe you were in a private room in a tavern somewhere. On one of the little tables stood a platter of apricots and roast ... something. Pigeons, maybe. My stomach cramped.

'Hungry?' Makesh gestured towards the platter of whatever-it-was.

I should have been, but the thought of eating anything made my mouth fill unpleasantly with saliva. I tried to remember I was sup-posed to be the one intimidating *him*. 'Tired, mostly, and trying to clarify things in my mind. You say you waited at the designated location?'

Makesh smiled. 'But somehow we must have missed your messenger. Terrible, I know. The investigation and punishment will be swift. Take your ease?'

There was nothing to do but sit on one of the ridiculous green pillows. It's impossible to look dignified while sitting on a pillow on the ground. I leaned one elbow on my knee, and rested my chin on my hand. 'It's not that I wish to assign blame,' I said. 'But, you understand, the Guild has to be certain of the people with whom it does business.'

'I can assure you, the Guild's faith in my clan is well-founded. After all, there are no other houses that deal in the merchandise the Guild needs. Tirnaal do involve specific risks.'

Tirnaal? Somehow I kept my features still. 'And we pay you well to assume those risks,' I said.

He smiled again. 'The pigeons aren't to your taste. Is there something else I can send for? Cheese, perhaps? Apples? Wine?'

How did diplomats stand this kind of fawning? I waved a hand in acquiescence. Eating would give me time to figure out the best way to demand access to the doll. I would just avoid the alcohol. In the best of circumstances, I get drunk quickly on an empty stomach.

Makesh picked up a tiny brass bell – the handle was a rather detailed depiction of a naked woman – and tinkled it delicately. 'I'll have them bring some wine and almonds. Now, tell me, Officer . . . what did you say your name was?'

I grabbed for the first collection of syllables that flew through my mind. 'Tellus.'

'Officer Tellus. What will it take for you to feel comfortable with the way my clan is handling this shipment? Officers we've dealt with in the past have, of course, inspected our manifest and the conditions in the tents. Others have preferred to deal more . . . directly with the merchandise.'

'Sample, you mean,' I said.

He gave a noncommittal shrug.

Don't gag.

'Well, I've just arrived.' I picked up an apricot. Maybe if I concentrated on the fruit, I wouldn't have to think about the trapped people, waiting somewhere in that maze of filthy tents to see if I wanted to 'sample' them. 'We could start with viewing the other merchandise.'

'*Other* merchandise?' He raised his eyebrows.

'Don't patronise me, Makesh,' I said. 'It would be in a very heavy box or bag, about this big.' I indicated the length of the doll with my hands. 'It's an alchemical tool and the Guildlord is intensely interested, and I'm supposed to ensure that his investment is intact.'

For a second his smooth cheer faltered. 'Are you accusing me of interfering with the Guildlord's property?'

I smiled. 'If you're not, then there's no reason I shouldn't be allowed to see it.'

'Of course. That's arranged simply enough. Tonight, or ... ?' I didn't like the way he was looking at me, speculative, calculating.

'Tonight,' I said, evenly. I had no idea how slave buyers performed inspections. But I needed to keep Makesh talking. The caravan heading to Cor Daddan meant the situation was worse than I thought. I had been hoping that even if Keir wanted to lead a revolt it would take a little time for him to get the necessary magical capital together; making an undead army would presumably cause enough toxicity to make the process a slow one. But if the Guild was buying whole caravans of Tirnaal slaves, the toxicity wouldn't be a problem.

'As you say.' Makesh glanced at the doorway. 'Ah, the wine.'

The tent flaps were stirring. They opened, allowing another billow of foul outside air to wash across the room. I stuck my thumbnail into the apricot and watched a drop of juice well up. I kept my head down as well as I could while the servant entered and offered a platter to Makesh. No sense in allowing extra people to see my face.

'Take some refreshment?' Makesh spoke around a mouthful of food. 'The roasted almonds are quite good.'

The servant stopped in front of me. So much for anonymity. I looked up.

'Wine, sir?' Brix whispered.

NINETEEN

Brix.

My mind winked out like a bad lamp. I took a pewter goblet of wine, swallowed a mouthful automatically and realised I was staring. I pulled my eyes downwards, but got stuck again looking at her feet.

Still bare, but not the same as the last time I saw them. She had new tattoos, lines of dainty blue runes scribed at the base of her toes like sandal straps, the skin still faintly red around the edges of the ink.

Binding sigils, incredibly strong ones. She might as well have been walking around in chains. Fear dug chilled hooks into my throat.

She's going to tell him who you are. She's going to—

After a moment I realised that Makesh was still talking and Brix was moving, serving cheese on a wooden plate now. She was wearing a thin black shirt and loose, calf-length black trousers, slave's garments. Why wasn't she saying anything?

'. . . think you'll find that we have some of the best conditions in the industry,' Makesh said. 'We've never had a run where we lost more than thirty per cent. Some houses might accuse us of pampering our merchandise, but' – he wagged a manicured hand, dismissive – 'I say we deliver a better quality. You'll never find a Makesh slave talking back to you, and you won't find prettier stock.'

Stock. He just sat there, smiling like a toad in front of the person he'd just compared to livestock. He didn't even look at her. Brix had

223

betrayed me, and in return she'd got . . . *this*? Sickness gurgled in my throat and I had to swallow it down. She wasn't tattling on me to Makesh, but that didn't mean that I owed her anything. I could just walk away. I could leave her there, let her see how it felt to trust someone and have them hurt you.

My eyes dropped again, against my will, to her fresh tattoos.

They're hurting her.

'I've already had some experience with your security,' I said. 'Quite thorough. You must have had trouble with rabble-rousers, people who want to *help* your slaves.'

It was the only signal I could think of, and it was useless. Brix gave no sign that she'd heard me, stepping silently around the tent. Makesh took a chunk of cheese and smiled blandly at me. When Brix stopped in front of me, I picked up a piece of the repulsive curd and her eyes met mine for a split second, carefully blank. Then she ducked back through the flaps of the tent and was gone.

'Plenty of idealistic idiots out there,' Makesh said, easily. 'But my boys more or less make hash of them. We've always prided ourselves on safety.'

'I think we're getting distracted.' I drained the wine. The empty cup would give me a reason to get out of there. I had to stay focused. Whatever Brix's reasons for not outing me immediately, I couldn't depend on them to continue. I got to my feet, less than gracefully. 'As I said, I need to inspect the merchandise, and I'm getting a little tired of this delay.'

'Of course.' He clapped. Quick as blinking, the tent flaps opened and Gedion appeared. 'Gedion will take you to your quarters and see that you have everything you need to freshen up, while I locate the shipment you're interested in. The Guildlord has an entire wagon of goods – it'll take a little time to find the correct box.' He smiled at Gedion. 'Gedion knows how to make our guests welcome in the meantime. Don't you, Gedion?'

The mercenary grunted in a fashion that was not particularly welcoming. He held the tent flap for me and then started off through the camp, striding at a rapid almost-trot. I did my best to memorise the maze of shacks and pavilions we passed. My best was awful. It took all of my attention just to keep up with Gedion.

I *couldn't* have gotten drunk that quickly, could I?

Eventually we arrived at a patched, nondescript tent. It was a decent size, though by no means as palatial as Makesh's. Gedion waited, staring pointedly at me – probably so I couldn't wander off. I had no idea what I was going to tell Jaern and Lorican, but I had no choice. I went inside.

I halted. The interior of the tent was pitch-black.

'You're very considerate,' Jaern said, 'but you can take a few steps without putting your foot on anybody's face.'

'Or the sarcastic son of a bitch in the room who's got spells scribed could make a light,' I said.

'Is that an order?'

I would have kicked him, if I knew where he was. I couldn't afford to let him in my head again, and he knew it. 'Screw you.'

A pause. Then, sweetly: 'Is *that* an order?'

I snorted. 'Where's Lorican?'

'Tending to the horses. Presumably sleeping near them. Hells, maybe they picketed him, who knows.' He pronounced a set of runes, easy, like sighing. Soft white light throbbed into being. It was the same spell he had used earlier, scribed around his wrist like a bracelet. He sat cross-legged about six feet from me, against one wall of the tent. An untouched plate of food and bottle of wine sat beside his knee. He gestured with the lit hand. 'The slavers seemed to think that someone from our party needed to stay with our things and he was beginning to bore me.'

My jaw tightened. 'We're enchanting random slavers, now?'

Jaern shrugged. 'I wanted to talk to you.'

'Well, get him back,' I snapped. I dug through my pocket for my last dregs of paint. 'I don't have time to talk. They're going to call me soon to "inspect" the doll and we need to be ready to act when they do. It's going to be more difficult to get out of the camp than we thought. I need to scribe, so you can keep your tongue between your teeth.'

'I suspect I'll be rather more effective at damaging slavers than you will, if you ask for my help,' Jaern said. 'But first we need to discuss what you're going to do about the woman.'

I managed to keep from freezing. My heart thumped in my ears. 'What? How did you—'

'I told you earlier. I did spells of my own while you were scrying for the doll.' He raised his eyebrows. 'You think I was going to let a child like you take charge of my destiny? You think I haven't done a little divining while you were carousing with the caravan master? I know she's here, I know you've seen her and I know you're distracted.' He tilted his head to one side. 'And so you've got to make a decision about her.'

'There is nothing to decide. She's nothing to me. I'm nothing to her.' Saying it out loud was like lancing some dark, ugly infection inside of me. 'She *left* me, do you not understand that? I trusted her, she left, I'm never going to see her again and this whole conversation is a waste of time.'

He sat there for a minute, his maddening half-smile fading into something I didn't recognise. If it had been anyone else, I would almost have said it was pity.

'It's worse, isn't it?' he said. 'Than a death. Realising when someone just doesn't want you anymore. Or maybe that they never wanted you at all. It's worse than losing them the other way.'

I couldn't keep myself from meeting his eyes. I hadn't heard pain in his voice before. The sound of it didn't make sense. I suppose the question must have been obvious in my expression, because he answered it.

'Oh yes,' he said. 'I lost someone. Nobody begins necromancy for any other reason.'

Abruptly I could almost see him, centuries back, before he looked like something sculpted, when he was still a normal half-ugly man. And then, what? Keening by a fresh grave? Listening to footsteps leaving? Something left a cut deep enough that nine hundred years hadn't dulled the sting. I wondered if his eyes had been black then.

'You can't get them back,' I said.

He shrugged again. 'Well, in a sense you can, even if they're not dead.' He paused, ran the tip of his tongue along his alabaster lower lip. 'But what you get back is never what you lost. I'll give you that.'

'You don't understand.' The words twisted their way out before I could close my mouth on them.

'On the contrary. I'm the only one who understands.' He had gone quiet, flat as an underground pool. 'How old were you, when you scribed your first incantation?'

'Twelve,' I whispered.

'And then you knew what you were born for. Then it suddenly made sense why none of *them* made sense, with their heads full of women and money and drink. People see the world and think it's made of wind and rock and water, when really it's made of spells and words. Our words.' He crossed his arms. 'So what are we going to do about the woman?'

Maybe it was something in the wine, or his soul squirming around inside my head. Maybe it was just that I was too tired to keep fencing with him.

'I don't know,' I said.

He studied me. 'How many of them can I have?'

I blinked, certain I had misunderstood. He had said it in the same flat tone. He hadn't even moved. 'What?' I said. 'How many of what?'

'The others, the traders and their hired muscle. You want to keep her – very well, as you will it. One can't argue with taste. But the others. I asked how many you'll allow me to have.'

'Have.' My mouth went dry as I said the word. Was he talking about taking slaves?

His teeth showed again, cold, a skull's grin in a statue's face. 'Keep.'

It clicked then. My mind seethed with the chatter of walking bones, with the lazy shuffle of the bodies he'd animated back in Ri Dana. He wasn't talking about taking slaves.

'You have to stop interfering.' He leaned forwards, sudden hunger blazing in his eyes. 'You have my soul, for the moment, so you can control me. I find that distasteful. As, I suspect, do you. We don't have to be at odds. It's very little I ask for. Just . . . let me go. I can get her back for you, and then we can get the doll together. I promise.'

He was lying. I knew he was lying. Even if he wasn't, I knew I couldn't allow what he was talking about. 'No.'

He grimaced. 'I thought you objected to slavery. How much is she worth, then? Why not let me have these misbegotten flesh-sellers?'

Because it wasn't just the deaths. There was no guarantee he would stop after he killed the slavers, and he had promised me *her*. Even your average love charm is a vile thing when it works, wiping out the personality and leaving empty space in a warm body. Odds were Jaern had something worse planned. This was wrong.

But what if it's not? What if it's all right? You've got a god, sitting here, asking to give you everything you want. Why not just let him?

I blinked again. 'No.'

'Careful.' A low, red current of anger wound through his voice. 'I'd rather do it this way, with your help. Don't force me to take steps that neither of us will enjoy.'

'I'm not talking about this anymore. We need to get to Lorican and then – what–' The room went fuzzy. I tried to step away from Jaern and staggered. 'What's wrong with me? What did you do?'

'If I was doing this, you'd be cold on the damn ground.' Jaern came to his feet so quickly that I didn't see him move. He caught my elbow, steadying me, almost anxious. 'A better question would be what *you* did. Did they give you anything to eat? Drink?'

I squeezed my eyes shut, then opened them again. It didn't do anything for my vision. 'Almonds. Wine.'

'And you obligingly drank it?' Jaern's face was close to mine, grim. 'Idiot. The caravan master must have known you weren't who you claimed to be.' He stepped away carefully, as though I might tip over the moment he took his hand off me. 'Stay on your feet.'

'Makesh *knew*?' My head was pounding now, but I forced myself to painstakingly follow the chain of logic. A wizard who can speak and scribe is dangerous, and I supposed an unlicensed wizard, unbound by things like the legality of bonewarp incantations, might seem particularly risky. So . . . what? Makesh had guessed that I wasn't who I said I was, but he didn't want to confront me directly? If he didn't want to risk me getting a spell off, he'd want to neutralise me somehow. Dumping something in my wine would work. Maybe that was why I was having such a difficult time thinking in a straight line, why I couldn't stop my emotions from bleeding everywhere.

'Of course Makesh *knew*,' Jaern spat. 'It's the only thing that makes sense. It's the only reason why he'd let the woman see you. He was presented with someone who was certainly not a Guild lackey, he knew Brix had been with a wizard and he was narrowing down your identity. Brix *handed* you to him.'

Fresh hurt sliced through me like a knife. I struggled to keep a grip on my focus. 'If they're waiting for me to go down, then we don't have much time,' I said. 'Anything could be happening to Lorican. We need to find him. You said he's with the horses? Are you sure?'

'Yes,' Jaern said, impatient. 'I told you, I saw to that, and we don't have time to waste on him, anyway. We can't leave without my doll.

Does my proposal still seem so wicked? Let me have Makesh and his people. Let me go.'

'No.' I held my ground, although I felt like retching. *She handed you to him.* I couldn't stop and feel the new layer of pain, or I'd never get moving again. 'I won't leave anyone behind. We're going to get the doll, we're going to get Lorican and you're still going to do as I say tonight. Nobody dies. We make no servants for the fake god.'

'Fake?' His face twitched. For a second I almost thought it *blurred*. 'You won't control me forever, Cricket.'

'Nobody dies,' I repeated.

He smiled. 'Have it your own way. What would you have me do?'

It was impossible not to wrinkle my nose a little. I steeled myself, and made it an order. 'I want you to divine for the doll and then take me to it. Then we go to Lorican and the horses and get the hells away.'

This time the buzz behind my breastbone rocked my whole body, thrumming in my teeth, vibrating in the hollows of my skull, Jaern's trapped soul seething and twisting its way through me. He was getting stronger, and I wasn't. I bent all my energy against him, with the abrupt concentration of panic.

It was enough. Barely.

He spat into his cupped palm and began scribing a spiral on the wall of the tent, muttering a fabulous variety of particularly filthy and creative profanity. When he had almost reached the centre of the spiral, he glanced up at me. 'I'll need a focus, you know.'

'Use its name,' I said. 'Empty One.'

'I want to be more bloody precise,' he snapped. 'When you use a name, infant, you get incorporeal visitation, not divining. Neyar's *teeth*, you're so ignorant. Give me my eye, the obsidian. It should have enough of the magic left on it to make the spell work. I'm damned if I'm going to do this twice.'

I didn't bother to ask him how he knew about that. Almost nothing in my head was hidden from the Lord of Secrets anymore. I pulled the rune-carved black stone out of my pocket and handed it to him.

He put it in the centre of the spiral, held it with one thumb and finished the last few runes. Then he pronounced it. His permanent translation spell must have faltered a bit as he concentrated on his divination, the incantation he spoke slurring back and forth between one I recognised and guttural, ancient syllables, humming with raw power. His runes came to life, searing purple fire against the canvas.

He put his long, delicate fingers on the runes like a man playing a lute. His eyes had dropped half shut, dreamy with pleasure, glazed with whatever vision he was seeing.

'Got you,' he murmured.

Then he inhaled the spell.

There's no other way to put it. He leaned forwards, nosing the air as if he was sniffing at the magic. The spell floated off the wall, into the air and up his nose, and I watched as his black eyes filled up with violet light.

'What—' I should have known by then that asking Jaern what he was doing was stupid, but I couldn't stop the word. I had never seen anything like this – had never even *heard* of anything like this.

'My divining is somewhat more potent than yours.' Jaern smiled again, and now the spell coated the inside of his mouth and nostrils, glowing, clinging to his tongue. 'I can feel where the doll is as long as I keep holding the focus – the stone.' He held up the obsidian, winking between his thumb and forefinger. 'Like a hound on a scent. I can't cast another spell without muddying this one, though. I hope you have a plan to get from here to there.'

I did. I didn't fancy it much, but I did. I had just enough paint left, and I supposed I could wash and swallow the runes off the canvas tent as easily as I could a piece of parchment. I pointed at the bottle of wine on the floor. 'Is that drugged?'

'Probably,' Jaern said. 'Why?'

I laughed. It hurt, echoing in my head. 'How,' I said, 'would you like to be invisible?'

Cold air gushed down the neck of my shirt as I stepped out of the tent, catching the tendrils of nervous sweat that had collected on my skin. Invisibility hurt more this time than it had before, maybe because I was still full of sedative. The magic throbbed like an old burn.

Jaern had exited just before me. He was mostly invisible too, just the faint violet glow of his own spell hanging in the air like a will-o'-the-wisp. Unfortunately, even a faint glow drew the eye at that time of night.

The first obstacle, therefore, was the man Makesh had undoubtedly placed to watch the tent. I shivered and stared into the darkness. I was betting Gedion or someone like him was close.

A spike of pain shot up my neck, twitching the muscles into a cramp. I squinted, concentrated on the air in my lungs. I had to push through the toxicity. The spell only needed to last a couple of hours, then I could get Jaern to break the ley and make it end.

Where was Gedion?

Only some of the tents had braziers, which seemed to indicate that they either belonged to important people or had expensive merchandise within. Our tent didn't qualify as important, apparently, but enough ambient light reached us to make it possible to see there *was* no guard.

'That doesn't make sense,' I muttered, then winced as the sound sent a jagged ache slicing through my head.

'So many things with you don't,' Jaern said. 'Are we going to stand here all night, peering?'

Maybe they had depended on the drug in the wine. If it was a slow-acting formulation, then perhaps they were waiting until I was down hard before attempting to tie me up or cut my throat. But there still should have been someone watching the tent. Maybe the guard had stepped away to take a piss?

'Come *on*.' Jaern coughed, a spume of violet light bursting against the sky. 'The spell won't last forever. Do you want to have time to pick up your Erranter pet after we get the Empty One, or not?'

I shoved the uneasiness down. If I could just find the doll and get us out of there, everything would be all right. 'Fine, lead the way.'

Jaern slipped through the dark in front of me, sticking to the deeper shadows behind structures. I kept my eyes on his will-o'-the-wisp, intent on not losing him. After all, it wasn't as though I needed to worry about being seen.

A heavy kind of silence lay over the camp, broken only by the distant mutter of voices and the occasional burst of raucous laughter from a knot of people around one of the braziers north of us. Jaern paused three times, once to let a pair of slavers walk by, arguing over whose turn it was to supervise the cook in the morning, and the other two times to avoid a bow-legged guard making a lumbering, circular patrol that kept crossing our route.

The second time Jaern's hand hit me in the breastbone, scrambled for my shoulder and then shoved me down behind a stack of food crates. I squatted in the mud, my eyes gritty with wine and exhaustion, vague dread twisting in me like a bellyful of eels.

'This feels wrong,' I whispered. 'Why aren't there more of them?'

'Shut up,' said Jaern. 'Unless you want me to kill them after all.'

Then he moved again, and I had to follow.

A tide of blood pounded in and out of my ears, louder with each step. We were getting closer to what I judged must be the centre of the camp, where the more expensive merchandise would be kept, less vulnerable to a sudden raid.

I halted, skin prickling.

You're missing something.

Jaern's fingers closed on my wrist and yanked me forwards. 'Don't stop, or they'll see me. We're almost there.'

I scanned the scene in front of us and tried to think. What was I overlooking? If I could just make the knives in my joints leave, I could remember. If I could just get rid of the nausea for a minute.

Ahead stood two structures. One was circular, like an overturned mixing bowl, the walls made of some kind of rough, hairy leather. The other was rectangular. No brazier, no slavers in sight.

'It's in the yurt.' Another puff of purple light, dragging me towards the door of the circular structure.

'Is it guarded?' I said.

I could hear the shrug in his voice, the malicious enjoyment. 'You didn't have me divine for that.'

The door was an arm's length from me. I worked to steady my breathing against the magic fire chewing at the base of my lungs, against the poison crawling in my belly. Where the tent flap met the ground, a thin line of yellow lamplight showed.

'You can still choose to do as I say,' Jaern murmured, in my ear, so close his breath hissed against my neck. It wasn't warm. The air left the dead god's lips impregnated with frost. 'Let me go. Don't be stupid, Cricket.'

My gorge rose. 'Don't touch me.'

Two hands planted themselves on my shoulder blades. Before I realised what he was doing, he had shoved me into the yurt.

A single oil lamp hung from the high ceiling of the yurt by a braided leather cord, throwing a guttering illumination over the interior. A clumsy wall of canvas stretched the diameter of the circular room, which held stacks of wooden boxes, bedrolls, bags of what looked like grain and, shackled to a spike and chain sunk deep into the earth – Brix.

When I burst through the door, tent flap billowing behind me, she jerked to sit upright. She had been lying on a ragged blanket, curled almost like a baby. The whites of her eyes showed in the dim light, her breath harsh and ragged. She didn't see me.

She had been weeping, I realised. She was still weeping.

I saw the moment when she found my shadow, quavering across the floor. She froze, and said nothing.

I halted, puzzled, suddenly certain I should remain silent.

She stared almost at me, drawing her legs up under her, the chain dragging along the floor. The sound rattled through my head, sunbursts firing across my vision. The spell's poison welled inside me, strong enough to taste, blinding. Was she mouthing something at me?

She got to her feet, hands outstretched, her lips still moving. My eyes still refused to focus. She hobbled towards me, shackles clanking as she moved.

Her fingertips brushed against my arm. I caught her hand in mine, and finally was close enough to see what she was mouthing.

It's a trap, she said.

Run.

'He's here,' said a female voice, behind the curtain.

'Run!' Brix shouted, pushing me away.

But the voice had already begun to chant the first syllables of a ley-breaker, fast. The invisibility spell crumbled, and the tent flap fluttered again.

'Jaern,' I said. 'Jaern, help!'

'Calling your pretty god-named slave?' Gedion stepped into the room as the scuffle of boots began behind me. He was smiling, a burlap sack in one hand. 'Who do you think told us to expect you, you dumb bastard?'

I had time to half-turn and see the slavers burst from behind the curtain before the first one grabbed me. I think I kicked one before the sack came down over my head. A cloying, nauseous fume poured into my nostrils, and from somewhere, far away, Brix screamed.

235

TWENTY

Water.

I'm drowning.

I gasped, straining for air around something crammed between my teeth, but I couldn't move my arms. Something held me, sitting upright.

'Again,' a man said. 'Get him all the way up.'

A bucket of cold water emptied on my head. This time I got my eyes open. Light stabbed at me, throbbed at the base of my skull. After a minute the man who had spoken came into focus.

Makesh. Leaning against the centre pole of . . . the yurt; I was still in the yurt. He held a thin *shan* cigar delicately between thumb and forefinger, watching me with the dispassionate interest of a cattle buyer.

'With us?' he enquired. 'Blackwit powder dissipating?'

Goat-sucker, is what I said. 'Gmnufuf' is what came out.

Makesh took a pull on the cigar and blew smoke out his nostrils. 'We'll have to ungag you eventually, but I've found with wizards – even cheap pretenders – it's better to establish a few things first. Impossible to be certain about where you might have spells scribed. I had one sent to kill me once with runes scratched on the inside of his lip.'

My skin crawled. I tried to turn my head and discovered I was sitting cross-legged on the ground with my hands tied behind me.

236

Judging by the pressure against my spine, I was tied to another tent pole. I could twist around enough to see we were in the area of the tent that had been curtained off before.

Brix was there, still in shackles, staring silently at me. Dammit. No Lorican, though, which was a small point in my favour. Maybe he'd slipped away, having caught wind of what was going on when Jaern packed him off to the stables – *if* Jaern had packed him off to the stables. I realised, abruptly, that I had no proof that Jaern hadn't simply killed him.

'I have a wizard.' Makesh flicked a bit of ash off his embroidered sleeve. 'She's nothing too fancy, you understand, but she's useful for sending messages to the Guildlord and for other mundane work. As you might imagine, it takes a few hours to communicate with a scrying stone. We're waiting for the Guildlord's reply, and, she tells me, for the ley-breaker she used to dissipate.'

Scrying stone – concentrated magic, and as poisonous as sucking a piece of sulphur. Another short road to a reeling brain and a rotted body. How in the hells did he convince a Guild wizard to risk herself like that for the sake of *messages*? What was wrong with pigeons?

'But your pretty slave was in contact with my wizard for several hours before you reached my camp.' Makesh clucked his tongue softly. 'You should have been more careful. He told us all about you – how to take you, which dodges you'd use to get into the camp. Even agreed to lure you here. So although I couldn't get the confirmation I wanted out of my own people, I think we can conclude without much doubt that you are *not* a Guild officer.' He drew on his cigar again, thoughtful. 'You know, if you were going to spend the money on a magic-trained slave, you really should have kept him in hand better. Not that I don't understand the temptation to be indulgent with that one.' He smiled, faintly. 'You *god-named* him, no less. "Jaern", indeed. What did you expect, spoiling him like that?' He paused, as if I could respond with the gag in my mouth, then went on. 'First question.' Makesh gestured to someone behind me. 'Just nod yes or no. Any spells scribed anywhere I can't see?'

Boots scuffed against the earth and two meaty hands grabbed me by the shirt and pulled me to my feet. Ah, Gedion was still here. I shook my head, not eager to have him searching around the inside of my mouth. A thick feeling rolled around in my skull as I did so, as though my wits were sloshing like noodles in a pot. They had given me blackwit powder, Makesh had said. A sedative in small doses, as I recalled. Poisonous if you took more than a couple of pinches. I wondered how it interacted with whatever had been in the wine.

'What's his real name?'

His. I blinked. He wasn't asking me the question. He was asking Brix.

'Grayson,' Brix said.

Pain exploded from one side of my head, a starburst of knives. When I could see I identified its source: Gedion had cuffed me across the ear. He came around to one side, so I could see him. 'Sure about that?'

'That's the name he gave me.' Her voice was carefully calm. 'If you damage him too much, you'll ruin his selling price. Wizards have to be able to see to make anything in the markets.'

'I don't care about his selling price,' Makesh snapped. 'His name. Don't make it complicated. I hate spending long nights and I'd rather know the basics before Numyra arrives to crack him.'

Another ball of pain burst over me, this time from the other side of my head. Both ears now rang. Gedion grinned at me, like a man enjoying a good bottle of wine.

'Stop doing that!' Brix got to her feet. 'You'll make him deaf!'

I didn't care so much about being deaf as about what Makesh had said. Pain was just pain, but the two words *crack him* sent something just shy of blind panic gushing through my body. They were going to try to break into my mind and steal my memories. They were going to take away every part of me that made me myself.

'Start answering.' Makesh met Brix's eyes. 'There must be talk, even among you written-on barbarians, rumours about what I do to people who cross me. *You* worked for Esras and you stole something. I don't think I was paid what I should have been for the use of you. Esras said you were stealing an alchemical tool, something the Guild forbade. I don't care about the king or the Charter or the rebellion or any of that tripe, but I care when my business partners don't pay me what my product is worth. It damages my *reputation*, you understand? I cannot permit myself to be cheated.' His gaze flickered my way, and then back to Brix. 'So I advise you, kitten, to think well about what you say next. I didn't pay anything for the wizard. I'm not losing any money on him, even if I ruin his hearing. Or break his mind, for that matter.'

'Don't,' Brix said, her voice not quite steady. 'His name is Corcoran Gray. Just . . . don't.'

'I'm glad we've come to an understanding,' Makesh murmured. 'Why is he trying to steal this doll?'

'Money; he knew what the Guildlord had paid you—'

Makesh moved like a snake, his manicured hand closing on my throat. 'I will cut off his nose,' he said, his voice still silky. 'And I will notch his ears like a pig and it won't cost me two pence. Esras is buying more Tirnaal than my house has ever sold to a single buyer and now we have a third party interested. The Examiner General is trying to start a magic war. I know it isn't the money; I'm not stupid.' His fingers tightened into my flesh. 'Now, before Gedion gets his knife out, what. was. he. stealing?'

'The doll.' There was no scenario in which this ended well. Brix clearly knew this, but couldn't think of anything else to do besides tell the truth. 'The necromancer's doll. To you it would've looked like a gold figurine and a collection of engraved gems, if you'd bothered to open the bag I put it in.'

The slaver's eyebrows twitched together.

He doesn't know what she's talking about.

'Necromancer,' Makesh said. 'Such men don't exist.'

'Fine, they don't exist.' She stood utterly still. Slowly I realised that, underneath the terror, something else was growing: Brix was *angry*. The tremble in her voice was *fury*. 'But that's what Gray wanted, and it isn't here, because I gave it to the Guildlord. You saw me hand it to him, for the gods' sake.'

No. My heart twisted in my chest. The doll was gone? How had my divining been so wrong? *No. No.*

Makesh studied her, a flicker of amusement playing around the corner of his mouth. 'I see,' he said. 'So it's just an alchemical curiosity, like Esras said? What does it *do*?'

'I don't know.' Brix spoke through her teeth. 'I'm telling you the truth.'

Cold air puffed into the room then, as the tent flap opened and a woman in filthy, unadorned robes strode in. She could have been any age between twenty and forty, mousy brown hair cropped short against her head and a set of rune-carved bone bracelets on either scrawny forearm. There was not, I noticed, a Guild sigil anywhere in evidence, but this must have been Numyra the wizard.

'The Guild says they didn't send him.' She halted awkwardly in front of me and met my gaze. Her eyes were odd, milky white with cataracts. 'Any luck?'

She couldn't have been less than half blind, a consequence of using unshielded magic that one normally only sees with certain priestesses using Temples incantations. It would have taken years of bad spells banging away at her vision to wreck it so thoroughly.

'I wouldn't still be here if I had had any luck,' snapped Makesh. 'Get to it.'

Numyra dug around in a voluminous, tatty pocket and pulled out a vial of paint and a spiky brush. She scribed a rune on my chin before pulling my gag down to hang, dank, around my throat.

'Don't do this.' I couldn't force out more than a whisper, felt the magical lock wrap itself around my tongue, twisting my speech, turning it mushy. 'Please. You don't have to do this.' Breath came hard, like drowning in a lake of ice, and I could hardly keep my eyes open.

'Hold him, now,' Numyra said. She studied my forehead with intense concentration. As I focused on her, she daubed me with a paintbrush. Freezing pain stamped itself against my skin.

'You won't be able to see to scribe at all, soon,' I said. 'How will the slavelord treat you then?'

Her gaze flickered away from her work for a split second, then back. 'Hold him,' she repeated. 'Not long now.'

Gedion's hands under my chin and on the back of my skull tightened. Even if I had been in a mood to joggle my headache by twisting my neck, it would have been impossible.

'Just ask me questions,' I croaked. 'Please.'

The corners of her mouth twitched down with concentration. 'Master Makesh wants to know that the answers we get are the truth.'

'Master Makesh wants to go to bed,' Makesh said, from behind her. 'Not stand around all night waiting for his lazy employees to do simple tasks. Come on, Numyra. He can't be all that special, why is this taking so long?'

'It's different than cracking a farmer,' she muttered. 'He'll have protections, likely. I had to set it so the fellow couldn't cast, couldn't use me own sigils while I'm –'

'I can help you with your eyes.' The words slurred on my tongue, soft, drunken. 'If you crack me, you'll have a drooling, mindblown lump on your hands and you'll go blind.'

She finished with a row of tiny runes down the bridge of my nose. 'Sorry, fellow. I've got me own work to do, haven't I?' The wizard glanced over her shoulder. 'Ready?'

'Gods, yes!' snapped Makesh. 'Long past! Open him up, already!'

'Stop,' I said. 'Wait.'

The wizard ignored me, pressed her thumbs beneath my eye sockets and pronounced the runes. The sigils came to life against my flesh, the weight of my ice-crown growing, crushing my head downwards. For a moment the sensation of being cracked open – stripped – *exposed* – was so overwhelming I couldn't even scream. Numyra's consciousness invaded mine like grubby fingers, poking through my wits, rifling all the private corners of me, grabbing, tearing, hurting, *hurting—*

I had always thought the mind was more or less like a library or a storehouse – shelves of memories, orderly stacks of experiences and beliefs. As it turned out, my mind looked like a big, dusty, wood-panelled corridor, with heaps of information drifted against the walls like scraps of parchment and doors opening on either side. My mind was incredibly untidy, in other words, a pack rat's nest of ideas.

CRACK.

I turned. Or my soul did. Or whatever part of me could stand, separated from my own memories, and play this damn magical game.

Behind me an ornately carved ebony door rattled on its hinges as someone twisted the handle, over and over, battering at it.

'Lock it.'

I startled, but of course Acarius was standing there, in my head. Or his memory was. Gods, I hated this.

'How?' I put both hands on the knob and tried to keep it from turning. 'I don't know how to lock up my mind.'

The Acarius-ghost adjusted its spectacles and folded its arms. 'Nonsense. Of course you do. You're not locking your mind, just specific memories. What do you do when you don't want a specific memory to bother you?'

I recited the ingredients and measurements for making alchemical paint, and rules for laying out runes on a grid or a spiral, and geometric theorems. I made myself do arithmetic problems, made myself remember obscure lore from dull-as-dust Temples texts. As I remembered and shoved all that information forwards, the parchment around me swirled and battened on the ebony door, a wall of minutiae the wizard would have to fight her way through.

'That won't keep her out forever, of course,' the Acarius-ghost said. 'But she'll have to look for a moment at all those memories to see if they're the one she wants.'

I'd have to go further in. I ran down the corridor, passing archways on either side that spewed forth clouds of useless information. They were the kinds of thoughts on the chattering top of my mind, stultifying idiocy about whether I was hungry and where I itched. There was another big ebony door in the corridor. The Acarius-ghost and I went through it and I slammed it shut and locked it – this time with all the annoying ditties that have ever snagged in my brain playing over and over into my mental ear.

'Passable, lad.' The Acarius-ghost was as stingy with praise as the real Acarius. 'But again, she won't stop there. She's looking for the reason you want the doll, and she won't find it in your memories about your dinners.'

'I can't let them find the doll.' More parchment. More meaningless memories. What else did I have that would slow her down? What about the rules for scrying? That came to hand as a thick book – bound nicely in blue, I'll note. My mind is apparently daintier in its aesthetics than I would have guessed.

'How to use the doll?' And now it wasn't the Acarius-ghost anymore, it was Brix's memory, crouching beside me, glowing like fire. 'That's all that you need to hide? Are you sure?'

THUD.

The door cracked, even bulwarked by all the trivia I could think of. Numyra was going to make it through.

'You've used up all the small memories, the ones that didn't mean anything,' the Brix-ghost whispered. 'You'll have to use bigger ones.'

I sprinted further down the corridor, to the next barricade. It was getting darker. I shut the ebony door, and then looked to either side of me to see what I could use to lock it with. There were two archways, gated with iron portcullises. From one came the scent of soaking cow hides, mud and blood, and a hideous shouting voice.

I flinched. 'I don't want to. Brix, I can't.'

Footsteps sped along the corridor on the other side of the door. Numyra was already through. Her shouts – narrating my lists, chanting my ditties as she came to them – were scarcely muffled.

'If it hurts you,' said the Brix-ghost, 'it will hurt her.'

I grasped the iron and shoved the portcullis open. A pool of oily black tar flowed out, voices echoing wherever it touched me.

Stupid little whelp. Why can't you do anything right?

Hide, then. Hide. Like a whipped puppy.

The stuff stuck to me, like smearing pitch. I gasped, dipped my hands in it and put it between me and Numyra.

The village dumps you here to eat my food, and you can't even remember to take a hide out of soak when I tell you. Are you even listening? Are you deaf as well as witless? You'll never amount to a pile of goat shit.

'It's a lie,' the Brix-ghost said. I nodded, and became aware I was sobbing.

But I had to grab another handful of the hateful stuff, had to cover every inch of the ebony door in that searing humiliation.

Worthless little son of a whore.

Don't you run away from me! Don't you dare run away from me!

Anguish cracked across my leg and I went down, terror rolling over me, a fiery tide. I pressed my dripping hands to the door.

From somewhere far away, I heard Numyra cry out in pain.

Then silence. Maybe she had given up.

'Brix,' I said. 'You think she's gone?'

THUD.

Not gone. I watched the pitch dissolve, bit by bit, as Numyra threshed her way through the memories, sorting, tearing, running. She was moving a hell of a lot faster than I could hide.

THUD.

'Brix.' I glanced sideways.

No Brix-ghost. Nothing. I had lost that, too. But when I looked down, I cradled the Empty One against my chest, gems in its sockets, sightless black eyes staring up at me.

I clutched it to me, turned to flee deeper and found myself facing a different sort of door.

This one wasn't made of ebony. It was made of steel, thicker than I'd seen in any prison. From the crack underneath it glowed a throbbing red light. Slowly I edged towards it, hand outstretched. Could I hide inside? What on earth did I have locked up in there? What piece of myself was so bad that my mind had decided memories of the tanner were better?

My fingertips brushed the metal at the same time that I heard the humming.

Not humming. Buzzing. Vibrating.

I backed away.

Nowhere left to go.

THUD.

The ebony door slammed open behind me, and Numyra's soul strode in to stand in front of the steel. I knew it was her soul because she was still somehow wearing her untidy robes, although she looked about nineteen, and spotty. It must have been how she thought of herself. After all, this wasn't my memory of her, it actually *was* her consciousness wandering around in my head.

For the first time it occurred to me to wonder how my soul appeared. Eight years old, maybe.

'Don't open it,' I said.

She kicked the door. 'This is where it is, isn't it? Whatever secret you've been fighting so hard to protect?'

'No.' I wrapped my arms around the doll. Whispers rose off the gold like steam. *Are you going to get me my soul?* Could Numyra not see what I was carrying? Wasn't information about the doll what they wanted? *Much simpler to extract a soul than it is to put it back.*

Numyra put a hand on the door. The buzz grew painful, a hurricane of wings. Could she not hear it? Couldn't she feel the roaring anger pounding on the metal?

No.

This was what I couldn't let them find. *This* was what Jaern had seen in my head, why he had given me to them. *You won't control me forever, Cricket.*

'Please don't open it,' I said. 'You'll die. It's not my memories in there. You have to believe me. Wake me up and I'll tell you whatever you want to know; I'll tell you about Acarius, about the doll, what I'm doing in your caravan, everything, just–'

She snorted, put her hands on the latch and pulled.

The bees spilled out and stung. They spun, a scarlet tide of claustrophobia, a hurricane of rage, pain, horror, pride – and a towering, unholy frustration.

A memory I didn't recognise reached out and whipped me across the face, a shouting, desperate voice: *I'm giving you eternal life. Just take it!*

The bees swarmed into a tighter group, coalescing and then coming apart again, pulsing like a heartbeat.

I won't forget about this. About you. I'll never forget and you won't escape me.

The group of bees almost made a human figure now.

'What *is* that?' shrieked Numyra.

People are always looking for something to worship. Might as well be me.

'End the spell and get out of my head,' I said. 'Break the contact, now! This one isn't a ghost!'

The remains of a slender young man stepped forwards. Or it might have been a girl; it was difficult to tell. Leathery brown skin, colourless hanks of hair clinging to a decaying scalp, upturned nose – or part of a nose – and a rough wool tunic over a body built of half-rotted bones.

But I knew the eyes.

'Oh, Gray,' Jaern's soul said. 'I've been a ghost for a long time, now.'

He took Numyra's soul by the throat. I saw the horrified realisation cross her face, saw the blood start as the tips of Jaern's fingerbones pressed into her skin. Her mouth opened. She drew breath to scream.

Then they were gone. Silence. Dark. Nothing.

Numyra was dead. Jaern was free. And the spell that locked me into my own head was still running. Without someone to erase the sigils, I was trapped.

I couldn't wake up.

TWENTY-ONE

But I did wake up.

I gasped, air filling my lungs with burning life. Pain squeezed me, but a good pain – the kind that went with a real body and real lungs, not the deepening pit of misery I had been swimming in. The blur around me cleared. The senseless buzzing in my skull retreated but didn't die.

That buzzing. Wasn't I supposed to do something about it?

And *that damn screaming*.

Was it . . . Makesh?

Somewhere, far outside myself, the spell changed.

Another voice chanted, at first so softly and rapidly that I couldn't understand it. And a deeper one, panicky, fumbling – Gedion, incanting a binding spell, and doing it poorly.

The pressure of Numyra's thumbs on my cheeks stopped. She shrieked and backed away from me, a ring of blood streaming down her throat like a macabre necklace, hands outstretched. The rune-carved bones on her bracelets burst into white light. By the time Gedion's hands let me go and I could turn my head, I had regained enough control to recognise who was casting.

Brix.

Brix, still shackled, stood in the corner of the tent, shouting the runes on Numyra's bracelet. A ball of blue fire pulsed above her head like a beating heart. I had just enough time to recognise the spell and drop to the ground, the tent pole shedding splinters into my arms, before the sheet lightning lanced through the yurt.

It hit Gedion first, a bubbling pillar of fire that nailed him to the earth. I shoved my face into my shoulder as deep as I could get it, eyes squeezed shut. The sickly-sweet smell of burned meat filled the tent. Heat flared against my back. Numyra's shrieks abruptly went silent.

Then it stopped, silent except for the gallop of my heart and the ragged, fast breath of the woman who had just saved me. I opened my eyes.

The sheet lightning spell had faded, but she hadn't moved. The runes tattooed on her left foot glowed a dull, angry red, pinning her in place more effectively than even the shackle. Her eyes were fixed on the smoking lump that had, until a few minutes ago, been Gedion.

And . . . I could see through her.

She still stood there, and most of her was opaque, albeit trembling. But the hand she held out, the one she had used to manipulate the spell, flickered in and out of transparency, like a schoolboy's idea of a spectre.

'Brix.' My words were still mush. I tried to scrape my chin against my own shoulder and wipe off the alchemical paint, but it wasn't very effective. It would have to be her, not me. 'You can reverse the spell on your foot by saying it backwards. I can't say it for you with this stuff on my face.' She didn't seem to have heard me. 'Brix,' I repeated.

She blinked, slowly. 'Corcoran?'

'I'm here,' I said. 'I'm fine.'

Brix pulled in her hand. 'I'm stuck. Makesh ran . . . he'll bring back guards . . .'

'It's the anchor spell on your foot.' I swallowed. 'It's going to be all right. Say the spell backwards, like you used Numyra's spell just now.'

She blinked. 'That's mad. Why should saying it backwards do anything?'

'Why should saying it *forwards* do anything, if you know so much about runic sub-types?' I said – or slurred. 'Anchors are weird, unique spells – if they were unbreakable, why would Makesh need shackles?'

She said the runes backwards, one at a time, and they went dark against her skin. She moved rapidly behind me to grab the knife sheathed on the remains of Gedion's belt. Then came a thud when she dropped it, before doubling the hem of her shirt over her hand and picking it up like a pan off the fire. 'I'll get you untied.'

'The knife was still hot.' My stomach flopped. 'Brix, you just . . .'

'I know what I did!' She squatted beside me, grabbing at my elbow with the transparent hand and yanking my bound wrists towards her. 'Why did you have to do it, Gray? Gods!' She sawed at the rope with frightening intensity. 'You can be so *stupid*! It's not even here. I don't even have the doll anymore. I had to give it to the Guildlord. You need to get out of here right now. You weren't supposed to come after me, you–'

'Why did you save me?' I said.

The rope parted under her knife. I brought my numb wrists around in front of me and rubbed my hands against my knees, trying to get feeling back into them. Brix stayed crouched beside me.

'I couldn't just let them . . .' The ferocity drained from her voice. 'You were supposed to hate me. I wasn't supposed to see you again.'

The circulation returned to my fingertips with painful crawling, as if ten thousand ants had taken angry residence there. I rubbed the goop off my face. 'Look, I understand that none of it was real for you. But all of it was real for me, Brix. And even if you don't . . .' I swallowed, as if I could get rid of the bitter taste of this truth. 'You should know what kind of person I am,' I said, hoarsely. 'You should have just asked me. You should have let me help.'

'Even if I don't *what*?' She stared at me.

'Nothing.' I began to think about standing up, if only to get further away from the choking, cloying stench of blood and burning. I wasn't sure I was sober enough for my legs to hold me.

'*What*, Corcoran?'

I scrambled to my feet, and only kept them for a second before I stumbled back to one knee.

She followed, shackle clanking as she did so. 'You think I wanted to hurt you? You think I had a choice?'

'Let's not get confused,' I said. 'I'm the one who's got the right to be pissed off, remember? I'm the one who got left in a damn prison circle, *alone*, to figure out the whole thing, *alone*. Don't start scolding me about *choices*.'

She licked her thumb and rubbed it against my chin, removing the smears of alchemical paint I had missed. For some reason this wasn't disgusting, and I knelt there and let her do it. 'If you had just stayed away from me, you would have been safe.'

'Safe,' I said. 'Like you kept your sister safe?'

She froze, her hand – the transparent one – still on my face. 'What do you know about my sister?'

'I'm not an idiot,' I said, 'or at least not about magic. I divined for the doll, and I got you, talking about her, a flask . . . I thought you'd go to her, if you could. That was the morning after you left, by the way; I hadn't hit the place yet where I thought you were maybe just selling me for money, like a normal mercenary.'

She flinched, and I paused, ashamed. I'd been trying to hurt her, and I had succeeded.

'She's alive,' I said. 'She's in Cor Daddan, the same place where they're holding Acarius – or at least she was.' I caught her hand and held it as she pulled me to my feet, looking through the spectral fingers. They felt warm and real enough, and gods, now I could smell her hair.

I cleared my throat. 'The flasks, I've only ever heard that was a myth. People whose bodies can expand and contract, be confined inside a bottle – this is really how it happens? This is why Tirnaal don't cast spells themselves?'

'It's a sin,' she said. 'Casting, I mean. The old people say it's a sin, that the reason we become unreal enough to be imprisoned is punishment for using magic, when the gods meant us to be vessels to enable the magic of others. Too much magic won't kill us, like it will you. It just makes us unreal – even the toxicity others dump into us will, eventually. They fill us up with all their bad feelings, all the poison, until we . . .' She looked down at her transparent fingers. 'Then they put us into a djinn's flask. We're awake the whole time we're in torpor, Gray. Trapped, unable to move, unable to breathe, to think. It's not like sleep. It *hurts*.' She licked her lips, her chest heaving with quick breath. 'Anka thought we could escape the Karrad temple where we worked, risk doing a few spells, get away before we went ghostly. But they trapped her, sold her vial to Makesh and . . . and Keir came to the temple and told me what I would have to do to get her back. Help capture an outlaw wizard, a necromancer who'd turned against the Guild. Simple. How was I supposed to know it would be you?'

'Me?' A short, bitter bark of laughter broke from me. 'Brix, I *worried* about you. I would have done anything I had to in order to get you that money, and you didn't even need it. How would it have mattered if you knew who I was?'

'Because,' she said. 'You weren't like other wizards – you didn't make any damn sense. You took my tracker off. The money *did* matter. Until you offered it to me, I thought my only chance to help Anka was to stay with you, draw the Guild to you. When you said you'd pay me, I thought maybe I could be rid of Keir, buy my own and Anka's freedom. Makesh isn't loyal to Keir, doesn't care who's paying him if they're paying enough. I thought forty pieces of silver –' '

'Did I not get it fast enough for you?' I said. 'Is that why you didn't trust me enough to ask me to help?'

'Stop it.' She had gone pale. 'Stop talking like I was on their side. They only used me in the first place because they thought a Tirnaal woman might make a good *shield* if you cast a spell. Keir was afraid of you, kept talking about how dangerous you were, how you'd broken his nose before. They thought you'd cast immediately if you saw him or Halling first. I was supposed to be a distraction. I thought you'd hurt me. I was *disposable*, do you not understand that?'

I didn't *want* to understand this. I didn't want to have it made plain how stupid I had been. 'You don't have to explain. I'm not–'

But she kept talking. 'After Deeptown I was going to tell you about Anka, but I had to do it without being overheard by Lorican, or gods forbid, Jaern. I couldn't get you alone. And then . . . I carry a speakfar spell, and binding sigils. They always mark us with spells that they can use to control us. You . . . you saw.' Her voice had gone dull. 'Keir used my ink to contact me, just before we got to the cabin. He told me Makesh didn't have the vial anymore, and showed it to me. I could *feel* it in his hands, Gray. I could feel *her*, hurting. No amount of money would have helped. All he wanted was the doll, and you said you needed it for Acarius. I knew I couldn't ask you to give it to me.' She stared at the ground. 'He was with the caravan himself when I met up with them, two days after I left the cabin. He was supposed to have Anka's flask with him, trade it for the doll. He *laughed*. Stood there, and told me I was a fool to think that he'd bargain with me, after I'd hit him in Fenwydd temple.'

'Why *did* you hit him in the temple?' I couldn't keep from blurting out the question. 'When did it start – the jail? The damn *barn*?'

'Yes,' she said, miserably. 'They knew you were in the barn, something about divining for the Temples book you stole. I had the tracker on. At first I was just supposed to make it easier to catch you, let Halling bring you to Keir to be questioned, but I couldn't stand there and let him hurt you. And then things just kept *happening*, you kept figuring out ways to get away–'

'I kept being a fucking idiot,' I said.

'Corcoran, I'm sorry.' A tremor passed over her lips, and her hand still gripped mine.

A dark, cool lake of ease spread in the middle of my chest, and I knew what she was doing. Slowly, I realised I had to be damn careful.

'Let go of me,' I said. 'I didn't ask you to take on any of my toxicity. I'm not Keir Esras, experimenting with magic I don't want to feel.'

'You've got to let me tell you that I'm sorry,' she said, fiercely.

She was sorry for tricking me. And she had tried to make it right. But she had nothing to say about whether the rest of it – the firelight, the one glory-filled kiss – had been real. A bright ribbon of pain seared its way through me, and I realised I had been hoping. *Again.*

'Fine. You're sorry.' I twisted away from her fingers. 'I'm not interested in forgiving you, so it's irrelevant. When we're out of this, we never have to see each other again.' I swallowed, but it didn't help. I was a liar, and a fool. Underneath the ache and the anger, I still wanted her. 'Let me see your shackle.'

'No. You should go.' She stepped backwards. 'Gray, there are dead bodies here. There was screaming. You have to go. Makesh will be back any second. I can't let you get killed because of me.'

The buzz behind my breastbone was growing stronger again, reminding me that I had a necromancer to find. 'I'll probably get killed because of *me*. Jaern's out there, and I've got to get control of him again. Numyra, the poor idiot, did . . . something. In my head. Whatever hold I had over Jaern is dissolved, at least for the moment.' I glanced at Numyra's remains, an idea growing in my head. She'd had paint, hadn't she?

'Gray, go now.' Alarm leaped into her voice. She grabbed my shoulders, perhaps with the intention of shoving me away. 'You have to –'

'I'm not going,' I said, through my teeth. 'I won't be in your debt and I don't want you on my conscience. We'll get the shackle off, find Lorican and figure out how we're going to get out of here without dying. Then we can part.' I found Numyra's brush and jar of paint, unburned where she had dropped them. I kneeled in front of Brix, thankful to be able to look at the ground. I should have been able to depend on my anger. I should have been able to leave her there. It was embarrassing to discover how much I still cared what happened to her. Still, just because my emotions wouldn't obey me didn't mean that I had to show her how stupid they were. I steadied my voice. 'Give me your foot. I'll see if, with your help, I can scribe a metal-breaker without passing out. And then we'll see what Jaern is doing.'

She rested her toes against my knee. The next moment the ground trembled, an explosion thudding through the night outside. I looked up at Brix. 'There he is,' I said.

Finding Jaern turned out to be the least difficult thing I had ever done. After I had scribed a spell on each forearm, we stepped out of the yurt to see a giant sphere of orange light spinning over the centre of the camp. Running *towards* it, on the other hand, had its challenges. Everyone we passed, slave and slave-trader alike, was running *away*.

Except Lorican. When I saw the Erranter he was running more or less sideways, looking in every tent he passed. He held a long, thick knife, the kind farmers use to hack down weeds – though I doubt that's the use the slavers had found for it.

He was alive. Relief washed over me. I cupped my hands around my mouth. 'Oi!'

Lorican's head came up. He jogged over to me. 'Thank the Moon-mother. I was starting to think you'd been snuffed. What's happened? The god's killing every guard he sees and then making them walk.'

'He tricked me. Tricked both of us. I lost my hold over him.' The buzz in my skull was getting stronger now, moving down my neck and towards my chest. Maybe Jaern's soul was still attached to me somehow. Maybe it was a matter of closing the door again. 'Is he killing slaves?'

'Aye. Near as I can tell he's not distinguishing much between owners and owned.' Lorican frowned at Brix. 'What's she doing here? Did you find the doll?'

'The doll's in Cor Daddan,' I said. 'I'm going to take care of Jaern. And Brix is—' It was a difficult question to answer. 'Leaving.'

'The hells I am.' The forced courage in Brix's voice didn't distract me from the nervous way she rubbed her hands against her trousers, as though she couldn't get them clean. 'They lied to me, and they've still got my sister. I'm going to help you get that doll.'

'No,' I said.

Stupid mincing cow.

I froze, with one foot lifted to take a step. That wasn't my thought. Not even my worst mental voice sounded like *that*. In fact, I only knew one person who sounded like that.

'Gray?' Brix's voice, worried now.

I had to get myself together. If the god really was speaking inside my head, I might not have many more minutes of sanity left. I turned to Lorican. 'Did they hurt you? Do you think you can find some horses?'

'Are you actually considering facing that necromancer by yourself?' Lorican scowled. 'You think you'd survive that?'

'I think I need to see him for any of us to have a chance.' I glanced at Brix. 'And you should go with Lorican, in case this goes bad.'

'Someone just gave me a speech about not leaving,' she hissed. 'No. You're going to try to do something magical and I can take the toxicity for you, accelerate your spells. I'm the only advantage you have over Jaern, so I'm coming with you. And Lorican has a knife so he's coming too.'

CRACK.

A wave of magic rolled outwards from the centre of the camp. The screams started again.

I ran towards the sound, already regretting the spells I'd chosen to put on my arms. How had I got to the point where I was *trying* to get a god tied to me again? All I had wanted to do was get Acarius out of jail.

Jaern stood on top of a wagon full of sacks of grain, symmetrical and graceful as always. It struck me as odd, remembering how he had looked in my head – how he saw himself. That body was nothing more than an ivory puppet for the rotting soul.

He seemed quite busy, alternately sending bolts of purple fire snaking after any running person that caught his attention – hitting accurately every time, I noted – and yelling orders at the small crowd of marulaches milling around the wagon wheels, glowing orange.

Two of the undead held a thrashing, screaming man. His torn linen clothes flapped as he babbled high-pitched nonsense to Jaern.

As we approached, his voice separated into words: '. . . I have some money hidden, lots of money. I'll give it to you. And my family has connections. What is it you want, a ship? Women? Shan? We can–'

Makesh. It was *Makesh*, with his blue silk robes stripped off, in what I recognised, abruptly, as his underthings.

'Hello, Cricket,' Jaern said, without taking his eyes off the slaver. 'Saved you one.'

I took a deep breath and coughed. The stench of death mingled with all the other various odours of that place. 'You . . . saved me one. After killing twenty or thirty people.'

Jaern shrugged. 'Peace offering. Hasn't this fool been annoying you?'

I advanced slowly, gathering myself. 'Get down before you do any more damage. *I'm* not a fool.'

And I'm a bloody god.

Jaern wheeled around to stare at me, nose wrinkled in disgust. *Attached to a cripple who's too cowardly to do what needs done. You hobble me and preach to me, and when I take control of our destiny, I do you a favour, you have the impudence to come prating to me about damage?*

I flinched. The words struck like gongs inside my skull, followed by a seething rush of images, injustices, deaths, vengeance, blood in rivulets splashing around the toes of someone's boots. Was *this* the cost of giving him orders, allowing him access to my mind?

Yes. And now I'm free and here we are.

'I asked you to divine for the doll. I asked you not to kill anyone.' I had to keep walking. In another six steps or so I would be close enough. 'The slaves didn't do anything wrong. Why them?'

'Well, they're not exactly dead.' Jaern extended one hand towards the marulaches. 'They're undead.'

And you should've been more specific. I did divine for the doll, and I'm taking you to it – just not in the way you expected. I'm not interested in pettifogging ideals. I care about results. Don't act like my marulaches aren't the lesser of two evils. Why do you think the Guild wanted my doll, if not to make their own army?

'It had occurred to me that they might also be after a kind of eternal life,' I said. 'If you're going to keep doing that, why speak out loud to me at all?'

Sometimes, Jaern said, *I rather enjoy having an audience – don't you? Do you think you're sneaking up on me, infant?*

I halted.

'Make him let me go!' Makesh shrieked. 'Wizard, make him let me go!'

'I'm here.' Brix had kept pace with me. She put her hand on my bare wrist. Healing flooded my veins, a sudden diminishing of pain and weariness so intense it was almost pleasure. 'I'll help you.'

'I'll help you,' Jaern mimicked, sing-song. Purple lightning still crackled around one hand, the sigils glowing through his shirt in a ring across his belly. 'So that's why you wanted to keep her. Your own private weighted dice, to make that pathetic silence spell you have on your arm worth something. I imagine there are other advantages as well.' His eyes swept her up and down, appraising. 'I can't say I understand. Mud and blondes were never to my taste.'

'This is all just fencing,' I said.

Aye, I'm finished. Jaern leaped lightly down from the wagon. The teardrop-shaped black vial that hung around his neck – the thing that had absorbed his toxicity and my crippled knee – flopped against his breastbone. Uneasily, I realised I shouldn't have forgotten about it. The flesh of his throat glinted blue and green for a moment, iridescent as a butterfly's scales.

No. Oh, no.

'What?' Brix said. 'What's wrong?'

I licked my lips, my mouth suddenly dry. 'Reflection. He has a reflection spell running. If I cast anything targeted at him, it would just bounce back at me, like an echo, or a mirror.'

'He can do that?' Brix glanced from the necromancer to me.

'He can do all sorts of lovely things.' Jaern whistled. The marulaches stopped milling, turned and started lumbering towards us.

'Let go, Brix,' I whispered. I backed up a step. 'Reflection is supposed to cause severe burns on the man who tries it. I've only ever seen it used on an iron *door.*'

'As has been noted, I'm not precisely a man.' Jaern smiled. 'Well, Cricket? Going to shut me up? Or maybe you'll use that considerable wit of yours for something besides plotting how to get under the girl's skirt and understand that I've just *helped* you. You're terrible at realising who your real friends are. The Guild thinks you or your grandfather know how to use that doll. They won't stop hunting you. Both political power and eternal life, as you pointed out, are potent motivators.'

The undead made a wall now, between me and him. I glanced over my shoulder, the sick panic thudding harder in my stomach when I saw that Lorican was surrounded by a ring of marulaches.

'I could have my marulaches tear his arms off, if you like,' Jaern offered. 'Or her arms off.'

'Let him go,' I said.

'Absolutely not.' Jaern's teeth glinted. 'He was one of your grandfather's accomplishments, wasn't he? I've seen into your head, remember, and I know that lovely little story he told you. Saints, I can't ignore that, can't go to Cor Daddan without him.' His eyes rested on Lorican for a moment. 'I think we'll break the accomplishment *there*,' he murmured, 'where it will make the correct point.'

'Screw you, spelldog,' Lorican spat. 'Screw—'

'Everyone seems to want to,' Jaern said. He lifted a hand, and the marulaches surged around Lorican. His voice cut off.

'Wait!' I cried. 'We don't have to do it this way.'

Jaern's attention came back around to me. 'Ah, but we entirely do. You won't come with me. I need to look after my own interests, see to my own vengeance. Marulaches are dull, and slow, but they're very difficult to defeat entirely.'

Why not just kill me? Jaern's mercy only made sense if his soul *was* still attached to me somehow, and he needed to keep me alive.

'Stop,' I repeated, and this time I put all my will behind it.

Please, let it be as simple as this. Please, let me be able to put Jaern's soul back in its cage.

Jaern leaned forwards, cupping his non-glowing hand to his mouth as though telling a secret. 'No,' he said, in an exaggerated whisper.

No. No, no, no.

I couldn't see Brix anymore, couldn't see Lorican. There was only Jaern, and the dead.

'You can't murder your way to the coast,' I said. 'You'll be alone, if you do. You don't want to be alone. And you need me. Somehow, you still need me.'

His smirk fell away. His hand went back to the pendant around his neck, caressing.

'I'm not going to murder my way to the coast, Corcoran.' His voice went soft, almost inaudible. 'I'm going to murder my way to Cor Daddan. When I get there, I'm going to murder *him*. For centuries, in that pit where he left me, I promised myself this, and I'm going to keep my promise. I'm going to find him, and I'm going to make him suffer, make him watch me take everything from him the way he took everything from me. When I've finished with that, you and I will neither of us ever be alone again.' A flash of pain rippled across his face, replaced in an instant with false cheer. 'You're going to help me.'

'You're not making any sense,' I said. 'You said your apprentice locked you in that temple. He must be long dead.'

'For a splendid mind, you persist in being a dull student. Who do you think I saw in your head?'

The air suddenly grew too thick. I couldn't breathe it. 'You're lying.'

It was the wrong thing to say. He flinched.

'*I'm* lying? So far, I've only asked questions.' Jaern stepped closer, until he was near enough that the faint, sweet tang of rot puffed around me. Magic throbbed around his wrists, lit runes skittering over his skin like insects. He leaned in until his face nearly touched mine, the pendant swinging in the space between us. '*I'm* not the one who needs to lie.'

I saw it then, floating across the searing loneliness in his eyes. I should have seen it long before, I know. I've knocked around everywhere, and I'm not naïve, but until that moment it didn't seem plausible that an undead god would be interested in a twenty-six-year-old failure with scars.

He didn't just want his soul. He wanted *me*.

'I'll go,' I said. 'If you promise to stop hurting people. I'll go with you.'

He laughed. 'No, you won't.'

Then he lifted his lips to touch my forehead. The vial around his neck hummed, and a black bolt of magic surged up his chest, out his mouth and into my skull. My knee buckled under me, but still I hung there, twisted, where the pain and the magic held me pinned to the empty air.

'Jaern, I'll come with you,' I said. 'You don't need to do this. Let me go.'

For a second I thought he would. He stared at me. Nine hundred years old, but in that moment he looked so young, like a hurt child.

Follow me. Gods, Cricket, stop me, if you can.

He turned on his heel, and was gone.

TWENTY-TWO

I didn't black out again.

Gritty earth bit into the palms of my hands as I hit the ground. I couldn't pay attention to any of the chaos around me – the screams, the dirt in my mouth, the shuffling rumble of marulaches as they followed him away – but I kept my hold on consciousness, dammit, and I got my face out of the mud.

I knew I should have been afraid. It seemed like a long time that I stayed there on my hands and knees, alone with the pain and stink, convincing my legs to stand up. My body, which had been poisoned, cracked, beaten and now magically injured, refused to humour my mind. Some part of me was vaguely worried about getting trampled. A lot of people seemed to be running past me, some alive, and some not so much. I couldn't find it in me to be particularly upset. It was a familiar loneliness, and a familiar pain.

Most of me, though, simply waited. It wasn't until I felt her hand under my chin that I realised I had known Brix would come for me.

'Gray.'

'I think I give up,' I said, slowly.

'Get on your feet.' She tugged at me. 'We have to go, now.'

'I can't.' But I let her shift me backwards, into a sitting position.

The light failed rapidly around us, decreasing to only the flickering uncertainties of the fires burning where braziers had been overturned. The darkness hummed with noise – screams, footsteps and the crackle of flames. She sat on her haunches in front of me. 'What did he do to you?'

'My knee. He . . . uh, put it back.' Even to *myself* that sounded insane.

Brix frowned for a second and then seemed to decide not to waste time on reasoning with me. 'We can't stay here. The Tirnaal slaves will be coming back as soon as it's light, and so will any of the slavers that managed to stay alive. Either group will have no reason not to kill you. We have to go.'

'I can't even stand up, Brix,' I said. 'I think Jaern took Lorican, if he's even still alive. I think Jaern's going to kill everyone at Cor Daddan. He'll get the doll . . .' I gritted my teeth. 'Go without me. It doesn't matter what happens to me.'

She deliberately drew her hand back and slapped me, once on each side of my face.

Hard.

'What–'

'Don't you ever say that again,' she said. 'You think your life only matters to *you*?' She stuck her hands under my armpits. 'Now *get on your feet*, you selfish little prick.'

With that, she yanked me upwards.

I think I screamed. I know that once I had my balance, I leaned heavily on her. Then a wave of pain hit me and I nearly vomited.

But I was on my feet.

'Not *little*,' I murmured.

'Why are you talking instead of moving?' Brix dragged me forwards.

'Not a selfish *little* prick,' I said, and was rewarded by her short, startled burst of laughter. 'Where are we going?'

'To find a horse, or a wagon, or at least a place to hide. Come on. Maybe we can find Lorican.'

But I was right – Jaern had taken Lorican. By the time we reached the darkness at the outer edge of the camp, Brix was half-carrying me. We managed to stumble blindly forwards for a little longer before my knee gave way irretrievably.

She let me down to the ground and then sat beside me. Her breath came rapidly, choking, hiccuping gasps. Suddenly she smacked me in the ribs. 'It's not fair!'

'Ow.'

'I tried so *hard*!' she shouted at me. 'I tried so *hard*, and I didn't save anybody. Not Anka, not you–'

I reached towards her, hesitant. 'Brix.'

'Don't make a joke.' The words came through clenched teeth. 'Don't you dare make a joke. They'll find us. It's only a matter of waiting for dawn, and they'll find us. They'll kill you, and I'll never see my sister again. I've lost everybody.'

My fingers brushed against her hair. She twisted against me, her body pressed into my chest, shuddering. Crying. And gods, what was I supposed to do about that?

I'm not interested in forgiving you, I had said. It should have been true. I should have been able to sink into the hurt and anger and extinguish the desire to fix this. I should have been able to strangle my feelings and make myself safe.

'I'm sorry.' The words came bubbling out of me and I knew I wasn't safe, wasn't going to be safe for a long time. 'Sorry for not being better at . . . at this. For being stubborn. I should have admitted there was no point a long time ago.'

She didn't pull away. 'No point?'

'I want – all I've wanted for the last seven months is to find him. Save him, get forgiveness, all of it. But . . .' I swallowed. 'As it turns out, I can't. Maybe I don't deserve it, who knows? Let's face it, Acarius is probably dead. Maybe he was dead even before I left the cabin, or maybe Jaern is going to kill him, but either way, there's no way for me to stop it or avenge it. I want to help you get your sister free, but I can't walk, Brix. I can't think of anything to cast. I don't even have the obsidian stone. I'm useless.' I slammed my fist against the thigh of my bad leg, welcoming the extra jolt of pain it sent through me. 'I'm hiding in the dark. I've *failed*. This is the moment when the idiot in a story would fall on his sword, except I don't even have a damn sword.'

Silence. If it was possible, I felt a little worse. Granted, it must have been difficult to think of an effective reply to that much spewing self-loathing, but anything would have been better than sitting there and thinking she agreed with me.

'Forgiveness for what?' she said.

It didn't matter now, anyway. My voice seemed like it belonged to someone else, full of gravel and curiously blank. 'He would never tell me anything. Anything. Even about magic, he would give me the barest foundation and then say, "Off you go, Cricket" and leave me to figure out the rest for myself. I nearly died learning the fire spells.'

'You fought over *magic*?'

'We fought over my mother.' The words were flooding out now, whether I wanted them to or not. 'I don't know anything about her. I don't know who I *am*, Brix, and he wouldn't tell me.' I shivered. 'I don't know what my mother was doing in that miserable little pit of a village, I don't know who my father was, I don't know why she died and I lived. And I couldn't find out, Brix. I spent last year looking, talking to people, and I couldn't find out. It was like I didn't really exist, and Acarius wouldn't help. That last time – I said things. He said things. I told him to go to the hells.'

'Gray.' Her hand found mine and held it. 'Everybody—'

'And I left,' I interrupted. 'Stayed away from the cabin for months, wouldn't talk to him, nothing. They came for him while I was gone, and he called for me – called for help, magically – and I didn't answer, until it was too late. When I got back there, the cabin was ransacked and blood smeared everywhere.'

Brix still didn't move. Maybe she hadn't understood what I was telling her.

'Acarius called for help,' I repeated. 'I didn't answer. I couldn't let that stand, not without at least telling him I was sorry. Now it's too late for that, too. Jaern will hurt the world because I couldn't swallow my pride and be good to my grandfather.'

'You really are an arrogant bastard,' she said, quietly.

I blinked. 'What?'

'You don't know everything about your parents, so you don't have an identity. You have one argument, and so the man who raised you will never forgive you. You make one mistake, and that's going to destroy the world?' She looked at me sideways. 'The *world*, Corcoran?'

'Are you saying that I'm overreacting?' Irritation began to penetrate the fog of despair around me. 'Jaern will get to the fort, and because they won't realise what he is quickly enough, he'll slaughter everyone inside and raise them as marulaches. A crew of undead that can cast spells. There's nothing that will be able to stop them.'

She sucked in her breath, then let it out in a low whistle. 'I hadn't thought of that.'

'I have,' I said.

'Well, clearly,' she said, dryly. 'If you could get there ahead of him, would it make any difference?'

'I don't know. Maybe.' I tried to picture a situation that wouldn't begin and end with an arrow in my guts. 'Say I told them about Jaern and they, for some reason, believed me. With the Guild on my side, someone could perhaps silence him before he pronounces whatever incantation he has in mind when he arrives. And then all of us working together might be able to figure out how to stop him. You have to give the Guild credit, they *are* good at hurting people.' I rubbed my eyes. 'I mean, they'd probably kill me directly after we stopped him, but ethically speaking that shouldn't matter, if I could prevent an undead plague ravaging the whole world. All of which is useless, unless I can somehow get my crippled leg over the thirty miles between here and there more rapidly than the non-injured necro-mancer with an unwearying army.'

'Oh, well, *ethically* speaking.' Brix rolled her eyes.

In spite of it all, I smiled. It was strangely comforting, that I could be sitting in the middle of my ruined life and Brix could still find my diction ridiculous.

She tilted her head to one side, thoughtful. 'The frustrating part is it's not even that far, as the crow flies. Thirty miles, you said. If we just had some horses, we could probably overtake him. It'll take Jaern a little longer than you'd think because he's got to cross a river with all of the undead, and they don't seem like terrific swimmers. Unless there's a magical way for him to cross a river without having to get in the water. Is there?'

Something niggled at my brain. I frowned. 'Say that again.'

'I was asking about crossing the river—'

'No.' I sat up straight, trying to think. Something. What was it? 'Just before that. What did you say?'

Brix sounded mystified, and a little annoyed. 'I said it wasn't that far, as the crow flies.'

Cricket, you idiot.

'I can get there,' I said. 'I can get there before him, crippled leg and all, if you help me. I can stop him.'

There wasn't any alchemical paint left in the camp, of course, but Brix knew which wagon held the ledgers, and I was betting that stored with them would be ink. I must not have been terribly coher-ent when I explained, because even after we managed to find me a sort of crutch – I think it was actually a piece of a tent pole – she kept interrupting me with questions.

'Flying.' She picked up a stone and smashed the lock off a small lap desk that we had unearthed inside the wagon. Inside the desk were three bottles of ink and a number of poorly-made quills. 'You *really* can fly? I thought you just said that to make those wizards angry.'

'Yes.' I gathered up the ink and quills and studied the canvas cover of the wagon, but it was still intact. If there had been a tear, I could have ripped off a piece of the fabric. As it was, I'd have to find a knife or come up with a different idea.

'Then why haven't we been flying this whole time?' Brix said, with the exaggerated patience that means someone is trying to be reasonable in the face of madness. 'Why waste time with horses? Why walk anywhere?'

'Because.' I hobbled closer to one of the dying braziers, dumped my loot into the dirt and began the very awkward process of sitting down. 'It's not something one does lightly. The last time I broke my shoulder and spent two weeks getting over the dry heaves from the toxicity.'

'I thought there were . . . shielding runes. Something. To protect against the poison.'

'Theoretically, there are. I just haven't figured out the ones for this yet.' I thudded to the ground and started peeling off my shirt. Nothing about this was ideal. And even in ideal conditions, this wouldn't have been particularly safe. I spread out my legs as far as I could and then laid the shirt flat on the ground between my knees. 'It's a . . . unique spell.' I glanced up and froze, arrested by the look on her face. 'What?'

'I thought we had got past the lying thing,' she said.

I paused, the quill between my fingers. 'It's dangerous, Brix,' I said. 'It's not a very stable incantation, and it's my own invention, which means it hasn't had generations of polish. It's dangerous and it hurts, even if nothing goes wrong.'

She raised an eyebrow. 'I suppose this is where you get noble and refuse to let me come with you to help?'

I started scribing on the shirt, as meticulously as I could in that dreadful light. She was right, of course. I had no intention of letting her get in the air. But I was beginning to know her well enough to know that saying so would do me exactly zero good. So I wrote my spell, and tried to plan how I could take off without her.

'I'm going, Corcoran,' she said.

'Sure,' I said. 'It's big enough for both of us.' But at least I didn't elaborate the lie.

I'd be alone again. But the other slaves would come back in the morning, she had said, and dawn was already starting to colour the horizon. She'd be with her own people. She'd be safe.

'Why the shirt?' she said. 'Why not scribe on yourself, like you did with the other spells?'

'I need to stand on top of the spiral to take off, and I'm not leaving the spell here on the dirt for anyone to ruin while I'm sixty feet in the air. I figure I can prop myself on one foot, with the stick, if you help me.' I dipped the quill again and took a deep breath, trying to settle myself. Magic in general is a sharp-edged plaything, a lover that is just as liable to slap you as kiss you. But this was a little different. If I got the flight rune wrong or sloppy, there wouldn't be enough left of me after the crash to even feel foolish.

Eventually I found the quiet room in my head, the place where the runes came one after the other, pouring out of my fingers and falling into their places. They spread across the linen like living jewels, blossoming outwards in a spiral.

I sensed Brix's uncertainty as she studied the runes. Flight looked nothing like your standard attack spells. She didn't speak as I finished and hoisted myself on to my good knee, helping me to my feet. She propped me in the middle of the rune spiral, and then stepped backwards, eyes fixed on me. Her toes stayed on the edge of my shirt's fabric, hands partly extended in front of her. As long as I kept my bad knee locked, I was fairly stable.

'I won't fall,' I said.

She glared at me. 'I know, because I'll catch you.'

I cleared my throat and pronounced the runes. Halfway through the spell, as the characters sparked with dangerous red light, I realised that Brix's lips were moving silently. When the wind started I lost track of her in the dust cloud that developed. I dropped to my good knee as I finished the spell, clenching the shirt in my fingers and bracing myself.

The wind would knock her back and away from me. It would have to.

This seemed stronger than usual, though, as the air picked up speed and circled back on itself. All other sound disappeared, drowned by what was now a proper whirlwind with me at its chaotic heart. The magic around me coalesced first into one dark, red-black wing, and then another.

There is always one moment where I can see the wings move towards me, but they haven't attached yet, and that precise split-second is the most difficult part of the spell. At that moment I have to choose. I could let go – let the magic drain away, drop my concentration and *not hurt*.

But pain isn't always something to fear. I held on.

The wings darted in like wasps. The magic sliced into the flesh of my back and shoulders, hot blood spraying down my sides. My bones changed alignment with a hideous crack. The whirlwind suddenly condensed itself beneath my feet and exploded.

No way out now. Fly, or fall.

The wide-open, terrifying sky roared around me, thick with silvery pain and pulsing, ecstatic speed. I laughed.

Fly.

TWENTY-THREE

No matter how brave you are, you wind up screaming during the first part of flight. Even if it didn't hurt so much to have your anatomy rearranged to be more bird-like, being flung upwards is bloody terrifying – every single time.

When I had used all the breath in my lungs and was hurriedly making sure I still had the spell-shirt clutched in one hand, I became vaguely aware of a noise like a whistling tea kettle. If I hadn't had to concentrate on getting my heels back and wings snapped open before the spell hardened, I would have recognised the noise before the whistling object came shooting past me, into the high clouds above.

As it was, I hung there on the wind for a moment against the new-born sunrise, craning my neck upwards and wondering what part of the camp I had managed to suck up with my ascent. A silvery speck appeared to be arcing back downwards. Maybe the whirlwind had picked up some metal implement? The whistle had changed, too. It was almost . . . words?

'GRAY!' shrieked Brix, as she plummeted past me, silver wings flapping around her body like a panicked swan, feet treading air.

Oh, shit. I closed my wings and dove.

'Heels back!' I shouted. 'Put your heels back!'

She was fighting the spell, instead of letting it stiffen around her. Understandable, but deadly. If she didn't get her feet pointing backwards, like a makeshift tail, she was going to fall. There would be nothing I could do to catch her. How in the hells had my spell encompassed two people, anyway? I gulped air and bellowed: 'HEELS!'

Her tumble arrested then as her body lengthened, feet together. She looked up at me, and I had a split second to open my wings before she passed me again, soaring upwards. Her toe clipped my shoulder and sent me twisting.

By the time I came out of the somersaults, I had run out of curses and was starting again at the beginning. The whirlwind beneath us had calmed, and the campsite looked like a colony of ants that someone had kicked apart. Brix's laugh startled me.

She was above me again, grinning like a kid at a fair. 'Why didn't you tell me it would be like this?'

And instead of panicking, which would have been an entirely logical reaction, I was proud of her. I grinned back, straightened my neck and shot forwards.

She figured it out a split second later and followed. The remains of the camp fell behind us in minutes as we moved through the pink clouds like dancers, swooping and circling past each other. Magic coursed over me like cold wine, heady, glorious. Most of my body had gone numb from the shaping magic wrapped around it, and my scruffy black raven's wings felt like a part of me. The agony – and maybe the seizure – would come later, after we landed. For now, I could lose myself in the joy, and in watching her face as she felt it, too.

Her wings were made of white, silvery light. Initially I had thought of them as swan's wings, but as I studied them from above and below I saw they were more like owl's or hawk's wings. Somehow it seemed surprising that they didn't look exactly like mine. It had been the same spell, hadn't it? So why the difference? Just the weight of a second caster's imagination, perhaps.

For Brix must have pronounced the runes and cast the spell at the same time I did. When I could risk a glance at the shirt that I still held with cramped fingers, I saw that the runes glowed with *two* colours, red and a silvery green, rippling over them like the iridescence on a starling's feathers. Which meant she and I were *sharing* control of the spell, pulling the magic together like two horses in harness. Any wizard would have told you such a thing was impossible. Magic is essentially competitive – you don't share a spell, you take it, or someone takes it from you.

But then again, any wizard would have told you flight was impossible.

The caravan track that I hoped led to Cor Daddan sped away beneath us, a brown ribbon on a dull, grey-green plain. My blood pounded and surged through me and I let myself climb higher into the sky, up into the wide, pale sunlight, as the wind scraped my hair back from my forehead. Brix always kept just a bit higher than me, though, her body rippling with silver light.

She caught my eye, then. 'How much further? What will it look like?'

A good thought, that. I turned my attention back to the ground, which still appeared to be mostly empty plains scudding past at an alarming rate. I had never achieved speed quite like this before, and I knew I needed to think about the consequences of it, which were almost certain to be unpleasant.

'It's a citadel,' I shouted back. Which wasn't very helpful, but I had an idea that we wouldn't find much else that looked like human habitation out here. I didn't know all that much about what, exactly, the old empire had built Cor Daddan to guard, but surely there couldn't be an entire town so far from everything. Was it . . . maybe to enforce taxes on wool? Could you herd sheep out here?

Then I saw the knot of orange light crawling across the prairie ahead of us, and my stomach gave a lurch.

Jaern. How had he come so far, so quickly? He must have been going nearly the speed we were.

Hang on to your concentration. If you're fast enough, maybe he won't—

A pulse of purple lightning ripped upwards, splitting the air.

—*notice you.*

For one heartbeat, Brix and I were stuck in that metallic, blistering anticipation. Then the thunderclap roared around us as the superheated air currents boiled and tangled on themselves, tossing us like dice in a box. My head filled with his voice, cursing in languages I didn't know, erupting with impotent rage.

And then he was gone.

We had passed him, and I couldn't even risk looking back. The unnatural speed propelling us had somehow increased, to the point that if I forgot to keep my head inside the capsule of the spell, the air passing me would tear my skin off. I glanced over at Brix, who wasn't smiling anymore, her face contracted in grim determination. The clouds streamed around her . . . but that wasn't quite right. I squinted, unwilling to believe what I saw. The clouds showed *through* her.

Idiot. Idiot. You should have known.

The spell was different because of Brix. She was pushing the magic, making the spell work faster than it ever had before, taking the toxicity. Normally the poison would have been crippling me and making me fly at the speed of a bird instead of, say, a pissed-off dragon.

And she was paying for it. Our time was up.

Even for birds and dragons, takeoffs and landings are the trickiest parts. I had solved the problem of getting airborne by building a whirlwind into the beginning of my spell. I had never, however, figured out how to land gently, since a reverse whirlwind would just suck you into the ground even faster than the normal rate of falling. Up until now I had ended my flights by either slowing the spell so I could spiral downwards, or losing control of it in gradual hiccups and trying to aim myself at deepish-looking water. Either approach was liable to end in bruises, if not broken bones. When it had just been me, a broken bone had seemed like an acceptable risk. But now I had to think about Brix whether I liked it or not.

Besides, if I tried to take control of the spell to land us, she might reflexively yank the magic away from me. Whatever part of it that she was running would unravel. We'd both fall – not spiral, just fall like stones.

So don't take it. Don't panic. Share it.

I felt myself relax in the shell of the magic, and looked at her one more time. Even under the stony concentration I saw the curve of her lips.

Trust her, at least for this.

I closed my eyes for a moment and forced my muscles to finish what they had started. I unspooled the tension in my neck and back, quieted the fear and tilted my wings, ever so gently. When I opened my eyes again I pushed the spell, delicately, into a huge downward spiral. It wasn't a grab, magically speaking. It was an invitation.

The spell flexed. For a second, it resisted.

Then she came with me, more like a dance partner than ever. We slowed, descending on a very wide curve. I watched our pattern, both charmed by its intricacy and afraid that I would snarl it up.

It wasn't until we were a mere hundred feet or so in the air that I saw the heap of yellow stone, about a mile from where I thought we would land. A few more moments revealed towers and walls, peopled with agitated dark specks – the ruins, in fact, of a very respectable imperial fort, an outpost at the edge of the world.

We had made it to Cor Daddan after all.

Alas, that was when the spiral flattened out. I shot forwards like a bolt from a crossbow, and when I tried to manipulate the spell the magic stayed rigid. We weren't slowing down anything like quickly enough. I could hardly see Brix, off to my right, but she had abandoned the spiral, too.

I took a breath to shout with, a difficult task with the wind hammering against me. 'We have to slow it down. Ease up on the spell.'

Her whole body gleamed, transparent, resting and loose inside the cocoon of magic propelling her through the air, wings still swept outwards. She didn't seem to have heard me. Terror burst back through my bloodstream as I realised what was wrong.

Brix was unconscious.

'Brix, wake up! Let go of it!' She didn't, though. How do you take something that's twined around another person's mind? I couldn't just let go of the magic, either. Someone had to control our fall, somehow. I tightened my attention on the spell, pouring myself into controlling her trajectory, reaching for her.

My fingers brushed hers. I grabbed her, and held on.

We descended in a straight line towards the ruins of the fort. We had slowed significantly – all that propelled us now was momentum and gravity – but we were too high. We darted over the tumbledown curtain wall, men-at-arms shouting beneath us.

Some madness possessed me to tilt my head to look at the wall of the tower as we hurtled towards it. I had a split-second to spot a broad window, covered in oiled parchment.

I flinched.

I deserve no credit for the flinch. I wasn't really thinking anything beyond *please, I'd rather not hit this wall*. But that instinct managed to twist my wings and wrench Brix and me sideways. Instead of cracking our skulls against the yellow stone, we went careering through the window and the parchment and into the cavernous room beyond.

My mind took in details with the useless precision of terror:
People in robes. Equipment. Shelves. Altar. Rune circle. Tapestries?

They *were* tapestries, hanging in loops from the ceiling, which I confirmed when we plunged into the middle of them. We tangled in them and then fell, inept flies in a giant, smothering, dusty spider's web.

A polished black floor rushed towards us as we tumbled downwards, on a diagonal that pulled yards of fabric after us. I hit what felt like six or seven people, ploughing through them and completely losing my bearings before thudding to a stop against a wooden pillar.

Something snapped in my shoulder. I slumped to the floor, howling like a jackal.

Shut up, the pain means you're alive. Try to move.

The first impact – tearing through the parchment window-cover – had ruined my concentration and ended the spell. I wasn't going as fast as I could have been when I hit. But . . .

'Brix!' I twisted my head sideways, trying to force my eyes to focus, ignoring the shouts around me and the thorns that seemed to be twisting inside my skull. I was in some sort of . . . big laboratory or library, walls arching away from me in a giant circle. The floor under me was slick black stone, obsidian, maybe, with red painted sigils in a curving line a few feet from my face.

And there were a lot of Guildies in here, occupied with picking themselves up and rushing towards me.

'Brix!' I turned the other way, looking for the window I'd crashed through.

She was slumped to the floor, limp, a ghost whose wings were just now flickering out.

The Guildies surrounded me then, approaching me cautiously. They were about my age, and just out of their apprentice robes by the look of them. I picked the one who seemed most senior, based on the wholly inadequate scruff of beard, and addressed him.

'You have perhaps an hour,' I croaked, from flat on my back. 'Maybe less. You're about to be attacked by a necromancer and a crew of undead. He intends to kill everyone in Cor Daddan. Get Keir Esras, and tell him to throw every weapon he has to the walls.' I sat up, and regretted it instantly. 'Oh gods, that hurt. That was stupid.'

The Guildies halted. I have no idea why; anybody should have seen I wasn't able to stand up.

'How are you still alive?' blurted the one with the pseudo-beard.

I fluttered my good hand in the air, fingers spread. 'Magic.' I tried to look past him, to see what was happening near Brix. 'Why is nobody going to find the Guildlord?'

The wizard glanced over his shoulder, and then stepped to one side. Apparently nobody needed to go find the Guildlord because Keir Esras was already standing there. He glared at me for a moment before enraged recognition burst over his face.

'*You?* How—' He stopped himself, and turned to the man with the pseudo-beard. 'Gwillam, secure the girl. Secure both of them. We're going to have to figure out a way to get the tapestries repaired before we go on with the experiments.'

Gwillam – if that was actually a name, which seemed improbable – moved towards Brix.

'Touch her and I'll burn you, *Gwillam*,' I snapped. 'Esras, did you not hear me? Send someone to the wall, you can probably see the marulaches by now.' I hadn't expected Keir to believe my words, but I had hoped he would at least *look*. Jaern's appearance should have been convincing, and perhaps terrifying, enough that the Guildies could arm themselves.

'Maybe—' began Gwillam, hesitantly.

Keir cut him short. 'You have been given an order, wizard. Execute it. There'll be time enough to figure out what this criminal's plan was later.'

'Plan?' I couldn't keep the disgust out of my voice. 'You think I came through *that* window at *that* speed and landed like *this* as part of a *plan*? Do you understand that I'm surrendering, here? Why would I do that if I wasn't telling the truth?'

'I think you managed to disrupt our experiment, and you're offering an extremely thin story in the hopes that we'll be distracted long enough for you to extract your grandfather.' He reached into his robe, and from somewhere in the voluminous black-and-grey folds he drew a tube of greenish-blue glass, capped at either end with what looked like a series of pewter rings. 'Now, *secure the girl.*' He handed the vial to Gwillam.

Gwillam approached Brix's motionless form with the vial held in front of him, like a talisman. In one sickening second I recognised what was going on.

'Stop,' I said. 'Wait. You have to listen. I'll tell you whatever you want to know, just don't do this.'

Keir eyed me as I tried to get on one knee. 'She's gone incorporeal. They're of no use outside of a flask once that occurs. Gwillam?'

With one quick motion, Gwillam stabbed the vial towards Brix. One rune-carved pewter endcap pressed into her belly. Her eyes flew open, and she gasped.

'Stop!' I lunged forwards, only to be met with Keir's boot in my chest. I sprawled on the stone floor.

Brix's body swirled, churning like steam or smoke. There was no scream, no blood. Just a low gurgling noise, like an emptying drain. For one moment her eyes found me. Then the smoke condensed into the glass, rapidly.

She was gone.

Gwillam pocketed the vial.

Then Keir grabbed me by the collar and dragged me backwards until I had to face him. Anguish exploded from my shoulder and my bad knee, my whole body mingling in one vibrant red note of pain.

'Now, on your feet,' Esras said.

I met his eyes, and he lost some of his smug triumph. For a moment he almost looked afraid, and he was right to.

'The necromancer *will* kill you, you stupid bastard,' I said. 'And if by some miracle he doesn't, I will.'

Then, into the silence that followed, came the incongruous and oddly didactic sound of someone clearing their throat.

'Don't swear,' Acarius said, from behind me.

TWENTY-FOUR

Acarius stood in the middle of a circle of red binding runes, looking more frightened than I had ever seen him – with a thin veneer of annoyed-as-hell-with-Gray. He watched as the Guildies picked me out of the pile of tangled fabric. 'Where's your shirt? Are you all right?'

'No,' I said. *'Don't swear?* I come smashing through a window and that's what you can think of to say?' Two Guildies grabbed me under the arms, and blinding, exquisite pain roared from my shoulder. 'Shit!'

'You're hurt.' Acarius stepped forwards, but he was already at the edge of the circle.

'How could you tell?' I knew perfectly well that I shouldn't have been angry with my grandfather in the first ten seconds of our reunion, but there we were. It was better than being terrified.

'Put him on the altar until we get the tapestries back in place,' Keir said.

They hauled me to a spot about twenty feet from Acarius, though not to the stone block that I had assumed was the altar. Here the black floor had carvings, which had apparently been inlaid with metal. Most of the design had tarnished. The place where I knelt, however, had been polished. Although the brightness of the pewter was marred with mottled brown stains, it was readable. A tight rune

spiral spun across the stone beneath me, antique, beautiful ...
familiar.

Nausea pitched into me, bright, insistent.

Except one thing made no sense.

'Why are we getting the tapestries back in place?' I said. 'Apart
from using them as busywork, so we can ignore Gray's warnings
that are meant to save our lives, because we've got our heads stuck
so far up–'

Keir struck me with the back of his hand, hard enough to snap
my head sideways.

'*Shut. Up.*' He strode past me, leaving his followers toiling with the
cloth. He moved to the stone block, where a roll of tools, several
small bottles of red fluid and a bundle of cloth sat. 'The tapestries
are a necessary component of a soul-catching ritual.' He unwrapped
the cloth.

'That's idiotic.' I ran my tongue across the oozing spot where my
teeth had cut into the inside of my cheek. 'They won't do
anything.'

'They're copies of the ones that hung in the original temple. We've
restored it to almost its former glory.' He smiled. 'I'll trust the
instructions your grandfather gave us. He had potent incentive at
the time not to lie.'

Temple. The room around me suddenly shifted into focus. This was
no library – it was the remains of a Jaern-temple, like the one under
Ri Dana. Of course, this one lacked the carpet of bones. But the other
one hadn't had tapestries. Why would Acarius have asked for them?

I glanced at my grandfather and took in the signs – the healing
cuts, the bruises, the way he was too skinny under his clothes. They
couldn't have cracked *his* wits, I knew that much; Acarius would
have puréed the mind of any wizard fool enough to try such a thing.
So they had tortured him, and he had been giving instructions,
delaying.

'Sir?' A man stuck his helmeted head through a crack in the big double doors. 'We heard a disturbance? Some of the men are saying they saw something flying—'

'It was nothing,' Keir said. 'Get out, and don't let anyone disturb me for the next hour.'

'Yes, sir.' The man-at-arms withdrew.

A rattle of panic had seeped into Acarius' voice. 'Keir. You can't attempt the ritual on him.'

'Maybe this time you'll give us some answers!' Keir shouted. 'Four slaves dead in the last week, simply because you wouldn't tell us the truth!'

Four slaves dead.

Acarius' face went still. 'Those deaths are on your hands. I begged you not to do it.'

'The ritual had to be tested. And when you refuse to tell us – well.' From the bundle of cloth on the stone block, Keir lifted the gold doll. The damn thing was intact now, jewels glittering in its eye and in sockets on its body. Each socket seemed to relate to a specific organ. I could see how it might be confusing matching the gems to their intended slots. Nothing intrinsic in a sapphire declares whether it should be a liver or a lung. He held the doll up so Acarius could see it. 'I'm going to start the ritual, and you're going to tell me where the gems belong. Accurately, this time.' He smiled, thinly. 'Or your grandson here will die like the others.'

Acarius' eyes shifted to me, questioning.

I tapped my bad knee with my good hand. I wasn't going to be much help, if he decided to start a fight.

Not that he could, as far as I could see. The prison circle had three layers of runes, he was wearing nothing but a pair of ragged trousers and a shirt and there was nothing he could do to scribe runes short of scratching on the stone with his fingernails. He couldn't get out, and he couldn't cast. Acarius couldn't save me. He couldn't save Brix.

All that was left was me.

'Experiments.' I tried to shift to get more comfortable, which was useless; there's no way to get twisted ligaments and broken bones to feel at ease. 'I take it that means you've been trying to run a necromantic ritual for immortality by trial and error? Isn't that expensive?'

'I paid nothing for *you*.' Keir was arranging the rest of the equipment from the bundle on the stone table. 'All I spent on you was time, chasing you across the province, letting your grandfather think he was contacting you unwatched. And after all that trouble, it was a near thing. The slave woman stopped talking to me just before I caught your scent in Ri Dana – had to be convinced to do as she was told.'

'Brix,' I said, through my teeth. 'Her name is Brix.'

'You've been a splinter in my foot for six months.' He glanced at me, oozing a sickening sort of glee. He selected a brush and a round box of red paint, squatted and began scribing a line of runes on the floor, working his way from the altar towards me. I watched him write my name. 'I rather think I would pay for the privilege of taking your heart out.'

'And pay more to get the rennen for the bottle, to catch the soul,' I said. 'Tedious, anyway, even if it's not expensive. Crushing beetle after beetle . . .'

He froze. 'How did you –'

'Jaern told me,' I said.

Keir snorted. 'Indeed. And have you been having visions of the Moonmother, too? Perhaps Farran's shown you how to win at dice?'

'He *spoke* to you?' Acarius said. 'He was *awake*?'

'A bit of an understatement, but yes, he spoke to me. At length. We were trapped, and I had to do the best I could. And now there is no time, Grandfather.' I paused. 'That prison circle you're in, the one keyed to soullessness. Why does it work on you?'

Acarius winced. He didn't answer me. But then, I already knew what he would have said.

'What next?' Keir said.

'Next you do what Acarius tells you to with the doll and, at the same time, take my heart out, I believe,' I said. 'Chuck a piece of it into the bottle, and try to curse me with immortality. And it won't work, because you're missing a piece. Why are you doing this, Keir?'

'The throne has ground wizards under its heel for long enough,' he said. 'Too many Guild wizards believe that the Charter is some kind of fence, protecting us. It's time for the power and potential of magic to be unrestrained. Surely you agree? I thought that freedom was the whole point of existence for illegal trash like you.' He held the doll in one hand and a pair of shears in the other, eyes fixed on me.

'And who's to rule instead of the king?' I said. 'Some undead version of you? The only "freedom" you care about is being able to kill without consequence. I'd rather be trash any day.'

Keir smiled and stepped forwards, holding the doll towards Acarius. 'Tell me if this is right.'

'Of course it isn't right,' Acarius snapped. 'It's missing an eye. Like I keep telling you, the doll is only good for putting souls in vials, phylacteries, containers. It acts as a temporary body, keeps the consciousness alive until it's transferred, and you need the *whole* doll for that. This won't help you raise an army.'

Raise an army. It made sense – this building had been a Daine outpost as well as a temple, and the scene of a battle. The fields around it were probably full of bones. Which meant that Jaern would have ample material to work with. The hair on my neck rose.

Keir put the points of the shears to the notch where my ribs came together. My bare skin rippled goosebumps out from the cold metal. 'Tell me now, Acarius. I won't wait longer.'

In a sense, it was fascinating being so close to such ruthlessness. With Jaern you could at least be fairly certain he was mad, and suffering. Keir was neither. He maimed and killed not for pleasure or revenge, but just because it was convenient.

'You fool!' Acarius was right at the edge of his prison. 'He'll die, just like the others, and you won't know *anything*! Let him go and I'll explain . . .' He hesitated, then closed his eyes. 'I'll explain how to catch a soul, when the subject is already dying. You can do that without the doll, just with the rennen and the appropriate spells. Please. See sense.'

'You're lying,' Keir muttered. 'You're still lying. I have your diaries. I *know* this doll has something to do with controlling the dead. If I have to kill him to make you raise him—' He took a step away from me, rearranging the gems in their sockets while still holding the shears, glancing upwards every few minutes to see if his followers had managed to re-hang his stupid tapestries yet. There was a set of scaffolding against one of the walls that they had had to climb. Most of them had finished and were now descending.

'It won't work to move his soul, won't work to raise the dead, no matter how you arrange the gems.' An increasing note of panic was creeping into Acarius' voice. 'It's not complete. Why won't you listen to me?'

'Tell me,' Keir said, 'or I'll just kill him now, and I'll do it slowly.'

The old man stared at me, then spoke, slowly. 'The obsidian are the eyes. Ruby is the heart. Emerald is the liver; the sapphire and diamond are the lungs. You have to scribe corresponding runes on the subject's body. Cricket, forgive me.'

'It's not your fault.' I cradled the elbow of my wounded arm in my good hand, which eased the pull on my shoulder a little. I had to think.

'Of course . . . of course! That would halt necrosis in each body system, wouldn't it?' Keir moved back to the altar, put the shears down and picked up his brush and paint. He came to squat in front of me and put the doll on the floor between his feet. Looking down after each character to confirm his pattern, he scribed a rune on my torso over each of my major organs. 'And the tapestries? When do we use them?'

'You don't,' Acarius said. 'I told you to hang them two months ago just to take up time, so you would stop hurting me. The tapestries don't do anything.'

You'd think being so close to dying would make it less satisfying to be right, but it didn't. I grinned.

The veins on Keir's neck stood out. 'Anything else you want to revise before I cut his chest open?'

'Just do as I tell you,' Acarius said. I didn't think he was talking to Keir. 'Remember, paralysis is useful.'

Keir fetched the shears and the roll of tools. He opened the roll, revealing a selection of curved forceps and slender knives.

Acarius wants you to do something. Think.

The doll was still on the floor near me. I could grab it, but I wasn't sure what good that would do. Hitting someone with a heavy weight wouldn't be all that easy, considering I had to fight from my knees.

Keir incanted under his breath. The runes he had scribed on the floor lit with a strange blue-black light, moving forwards from the altar. The hair on my arms rose in response to the sound they made, too low in pitch for me to experience as anything more than a steady hum of unease. Listening to it made me want to writhe, and not just because it hurt my ears.

The spell crawled along the line of runes towards the spiral where I kneeled. I watched it, and tasted bile in my mouth.

'Gwillam,' Keir said. 'Keep him still, and then fetch me one of the djinn flasks. I don't want to get sick in the middle of this.'

Do something.

I tensed. It would have to be quick.

Gwillam had just now wandered back over from the scaffolding. His nose wrinkled with dread and disgust, a man who would have made a perfectly competent village sorcerer pressed into awkward service moving souls.

The spiral beneath me lit, the hideous sound working its way up through my bones, pounding behind my eyes with splendid, multi-faceted pain.

'Don't, don't . . .' I dropped my elbow, hunching forwards, clutching at my ear. 'How can you stand it? How can you think with that noise?'

He stared at me, hesitant, and for a moment I couldn't make sense of it. The confusion on his face was too genuine.

He can't hear it.

'Don't,' I said.

'I have to,' Gwillam said.

I wasn't talking to him, but I couldn't make my voice obey me, couldn't think of anything except blotting out the sound. I tried to master myself enough to get my hand down. I would need it.

Come on, Gray.

Gwillam took brush and paint from the pocket of his robe and began scribing a paralysis spell on his arm.

Come on.

The hum had filled all of me, obscuring every other physical sensation, threatening to wipe out thought. Even the pain changed, sharpened, condensed to one glittering point in the middle of my skull.

'Be very precise with the incantation,' Acarius said. 'We don't want him awake during this.'

Get your mouth open, dammit, now!

Gwillam finished the final brushstroke, and I pronounced the paralysis spell.

The magic leaped from him towards me, a ball of purple light gathering in my palm. I had exactly one second to decide who I would aim it at.

'What—' Keir said, as it hit him. The bastard fell sideways, like a tree, surgical tools clattering around him. The line of runes from the altar went dark.

Gwillam was trying frantically to smear the spell on his arm when I dove for his ankles. He stumbled backwards, kicking. 'Get away from me!'

The other Guildies began running for us. Gwillam twisted to his knees, still tangled up with me, pawing for the dagger sheathed at his waist.

I grabbed for the brush and paint. If I could somehow get them to Acarius inside his circle, we might have a chance.

'Get off!' Gwillam grasped the knife, but I had the paint and brush. I slid them, skittering across the floor. Acarius squatted and caught them.

Boom.

Everyone froze and turned towards the big double doors at the foot of the room, which had just thudded on their hinges.

Boom.

The hive of bees came to life in my chest, buzzing in my teeth, filling my skull with stings. They mingled with the low vibrations still rising from the necromantic runes, until there was none of me left.

I arched backwards, every muscle in spasm. There was no place to hide, nowhere to get away from the noise. I couldn't breathe, think, move. The world bleached into emptiness.

'*Don't!*' I screamed.

Hello, love, Jaern said, inside my head.

TWENTY-FIVE

Jaern came into his sanctuary flanked by the dead.

The marulaches seemed to be mostly for dramatic effect, although the noise from outside indicated they were dealing with Keir's men-at-arms. When a Guildie ran towards him, yelling a hurried fire spell, Jaern merely stuck one arm out and caught him by the throat, cutting off the incantation.

'Stop that,' Jaern said, mildly.

Down, he said, in my head.

I shoved my face against the obsidian. 'Acarius! Down!'

The next instant a sheet of green fire pulsed over the room, hissing a mere twelve inches above me.

Tattletale.

When I could get my eyes open again, Jaern was wiping his hand on a hank of cloth. He dropped it on top of a heap of rags on the ground, and I recognised it as a piece of the Guildie's robe.

My mouth went sour. It wasn't a heap of rags. It was all that was left of a body. The green fire had cremated the flesh and left the fabric intact.

Across the room, the Guildies who had thrown themselves to the floor lifted their heads cautiously. Ashes hung in the air, and piles of clothes dotted the edges of the room. About eight of them hadn't dropped in time.

'*Stay down*,' Jaern snapped.

Nobody screamed. Nobody ran. Even Gwillam, who had been stretched prone just a few feet away from me, had frozen on his hands and knees. His eyes found me, wide with horror. He still had a knife in one hand. More to the point, he still had Brix's vial somewhere in his pockets.

'Help us,' he whispered. 'Help us.'

I dragged myself back up on to my knees. Maybe I could get Jaern's attention, give Acarius time to scribe something with the paint I'd thrown him.

'Jaern.' My voice wasn't obeying me. I had yelled it into oblivion, apparently; it came out as a rasping croak. 'Listen.'

The false god moved with an easy, lazy strut. He seemed to be paying no attention to the wizards around the room, but I was betting he knew exactly how many of them there were and where they crouched. The marulaches remained by the door, a wall of corpses, ready to bash in the brains of anyone foolish enough to try to leave.

'Don't waste your words.' Jaern drew closer, sigils burning around his neck and more crawling over his shoulder. 'Don't beg for mercy for these cretins. You won't get it.' He stood in front of Gwillam, contempt and amusement vying for mastery in his expression. Then he crouched like a cat. 'Shall we wake the Guildlord? Can you do that, boy? Or do I have to do it for you?'

Gwillam stared at him. 'I . . . yes, I . . .'

Jaern smiled. His long fingers rearranged the collar of Gwillam's robe, delicately. 'Say yes, *my lord*.'

'Y – y – yes–' Gwillam's voice rose with terror.

'Say it.' Jaern's grin acquired an edge. 'Say it, rabbit.'

'Jaern!' Acarius said.

A shimmer passed over Jaern's body. For a split second the icy façade cracked, and rage boiled through the fissures. He gritted his teeth. 'You don't exist until I say you exist, Acarius.'

My grandfather stood in the exact centre of his prison circle, brush wet between his fingers. It was simultaneously the safest and the most dangerous place in the room. Jaern couldn't physically approach him, but Acarius couldn't run. He was scrawling runes across his arms, legs, up and down his tattered clothes, so many that I couldn't sort them into individual spells. 'Your quarrel is with me,' he said. 'Why waste time with these others?'

'*Quarrel*. What a sweet term for it.' Jaern still hadn't turned to look at my grandfather, hadn't released Gwillam from that snake-stare. 'I'm waiting, rabbit.'

'Why wake Keir up?' I said.

That *did* get Jaern to favour me with a glance. 'So he can be afraid.'

'Don't kill this one.' Maybe I could keep Jaern's attention on me, preserve Gwillam and the precious vial he carried. 'You don't need to.'

Jaern studied me. 'Gods, you're quaint. Still trying to save the world?'

'No, you're the one who wants the world.' I swallowed. It was like forcing a ball of sawdust down my throat. 'I just want this one, not incinerated.'

Gwillam, the poor fool, chose that moment to try to crawl away. Jaern's hand closed on his arm. Sigils blazed on the back of Jaern's wrist and down each finger. The magic coiled around Gwillam's forearm like a gauntlet, flesh blackening under it. The char raced up his arm and reappeared at his throat, creeping up his face. I kept waiting for the wails to start, unable to look away, but Gwillam never made another sound.

Jaern watched him slump to the floor. 'Not incinerated, Cricket. Never say that I don't give you presents.'

My eyes stung. 'Bastard.'

Jaern wrinkled his nose. 'Prude.'

Keir burst into gasping life as the paralysis spell dissolved. He scrambled backwards first, and then to his feet, staring. To his credit, he took in Jaern's silver hair and elegant malice in only a few seconds. 'My lord! It's – I didn't think–' He seemed to recover his wits. 'I am your servant, the one who restored your temple.'

'Indeed.' Jaern rose gracefully. He glanced around the room, ignoring the death and fear. 'Tapestries,' he said, after a moment. 'My temples never had such things.' He touched the string of runes on the floor with one toe. 'And you've started a ritual without knowing anything about it.'

'I'm sorry.' Indeed, Keir looked as though he might be repenting of his entire career.

'You can't take Gray's soul out without a death.' Jaern grasped me by the collar and dragged me back to the spiral, where he planted me firmly. 'Not *his* death, you understand. That would defeat the purpose. Someone who doesn't matter much. A human sacrifice, in fact.'

'I can provide a slave,' Keir said.

'How clever of you.' Jaern whistled, and the marulaches by the door shifted.

Four of the walking dead marched into the room. By craning my neck, I could see they led two living men between them. One was Lorican, pale and bruised but seemingly intact. The other was – or had been – Makesh, the slavelord. The marulaches dragged him, terrified beyond madness, but he didn't make a sound. He couldn't, even though he was trying.

'What's wrong with his mouth?' Keir blurted, although anyone could see what was wrong with Makesh's mouth: he didn't have one. Where there should have been lips and teeth there was only a brown scar.

'He wouldn't shut up.' Jaern frowned at the spell on the floor. 'This is clumsy to the point of incompetence.' His eyes flicked to me. '*You* didn't have anything to do with it, I can tell. What, you were going to let him play merry havoc with both of our souls, just to see what would happen?'

'Both?' Acarius said.

For the first time the false god looked at my grandfather, and seemed transfixed. I had expected hate, or perhaps gloating. Instead his face twitched with raw, aching grief.

'It wasn't my idea,' Jaern said. 'It hasn't been pleasant for me, to be next to a mind so similar to yours.'

'*Pleasant.*' Low fury burned in Acarius' voice. He stalked slowly to the edge of his prison. 'You've killed what, forty or fifty people, just today? And tormented more? And you intend to hurt my grandson—'

'He's not your grandson,' Jaern interrupted. 'And do you think I'm so blind I don't know that you've been writing while my back was turned? Is that why you were stupid enough to think I wouldn't feel you taking the eyes out of my mosaic?'

'And are you stupid enough to expect me to feel *sorry* for you?'

'No,' Jaern spat. 'I expect nothing, which is all you ever gave me. I'm taking what I need. I know what makes him special, more than the hundreds of other descendants you probably have by now. Not your grandson, Acarius. Your great-great-and-on-to-ridiculousness-descendant. You didn't need to love him. But this is the one who looks like you. The one who has your talent. The one who needed you.' He grinned. 'So I'm taking him.'

'You can't have me,' I said. They both ignored me.

'None of this had to happen.' Jaern strode to Lorican. He grabbed the Erranter by the hair and yanked him away from the marulaches and around to face Acarius. 'This?' He shook Lorican like a terrier with a rat. '*This* was what you did with the knowledge I gave you? You've gone out of your way to save the lives of dogs. You've insulted my gift.'

'Let me go!' Lorican twisted, hands clawing towards Jaern's face. 'You bastard!'

'Oh, gods, be quiet.' Jaern put his free hand over Lorican's mouth. Runes blazed on the back of it. Lorican's eyes rolled back in his head and he went limp, hanging in the air the way I had when Jaern had wrecked my knee. Jaern stepped backwards, his hand stroking the black pendant that glittered against his chest. 'How shall I kill him, Acarius? Shall I use him to take out Cricket's soul, or shall I just let him burn?'

'*No!*' Acarius lunged to the edge of the circle.

'No,' Jaern repeated, sneering. 'I did everything for you, gave you eternal life. You shouldn't have locked me up, alone, buried alive in the dark. You don't get to tell me *no* after that. This is your fault. It's all going to be your fault.'

Acarius' words cracked like a whip, insulting, calculated. 'You think living this long has been a gift, you blind fool? You're pathetic.'

Jaern crossed the floor so quickly he blurred. In one motion he destroyed the edge of the circle, grasped Acarius by the elbow and yanked him out. They stood together for a moment, nose to nose, almost in the attitude of lovers ready to kiss.

'Come and kill me, then,' Jaern said, and it began.

Acarius got the first spell off, a stream of fire pouring from the centre of his chest towards Jaern. A patch on his ragged shirt glowed, where the runes he'd scribed were still wet.

Jaern spun like a dancer, caught the fire in one glittering hand and stretched it like silk between his fingers. In a second he had transformed it into a burning net, which he sent whizzing back towards Acarius.

My grandfather, whom I had always thought of as less than spry, leaped to avoid the net. He crouched and shot a swarm of glowing purple spiders at Jaern's feet.

Jaern laughed. He turned sideways, shocks of green lightning bursting from each palm. The spiders frizzled into nothing, while the lightning skittered across the floor and forced Acarius to leap again.

The speed picked up. They moved like fencers, chanting without stopping, spell after spell cracking through the air. The room went rank with the noxious fumes of magic and with the fear-soaked sweat of the living, who cowered against the walls.

I crawled painfully towards Gwillam's corpse and Brix's vial. Not that I knew how I was going to keep her safe once I had it, but at least she wouldn't wind up riding in the pocket of a marulach.

Ripples of pink crackled across the room and I pressed briefly into the ground as the magic pulse above me sucked the heat out of the air, my breath freezing in front of my lips. Next came a wave of silver that set most of the room vomiting, and Jaern to giggling.

'You've *practised* since I've been away,' he said, delighted.

I inched forwards. Gwillam's sightless, boiled-onion eyes watched me, ringed by eyelids that were mostly charcoal. I swallowed, astonished by how difficult it was to put my hand inside a dead man's clothes.

First I found a cheap dagger. I yanked the sheath off and put it into the hand on my broken arm, glad I could still – sort of – close my fingers. Gritting my teeth, I rifled around in Gwillam's pockets until I touched the cold pewter-and-glass of Brix's vial.

Now, if I could find more paint and a brush, I could at least distract Jaern long enough for Acarius to land a blow.

So loyal, Jaern said, inside my head. *Watch now.*

I rolled on my side, the vial clutched to me, eyes wide.

And Acarius lost.

Jaern parted his lips and exhaled a stream of silver light, curling through the air. It struck Acarius on the mouth. He gasped just before the shock wave burst from him. The entire room except me, Makesh and the marulaches froze, paralysed on their feet.

Makesh had slumped to the floor, fainted or dazed with fright, and the marulaches' lack of souls must have made them immune. But the rest – Lorican, Keir, the Guildies, all of them – fell into the spell together, turning to stone. I could watch nobody but Acarius.

His skin drained of colour, first to grey and then white and shiny. His clothes followed suit, hardening. At last my grandfather was nothing but a marble statue with living eyes, and the temple fell silent.

TWENTY-SIX

Jaern turned to me, eyes rimmed in red. One of his pupils had shrunk to a pinpoint; the other was widely dilated. He must have caught a spell, one that probably would have shattered the skull of anyone else. It gave his face a curious lopsided effect, contrasting with the otherwise rigid symmetry.

Makesh lay where he had dropped, curled into a foetal ball on the floor near the altar, rocking.

I tried, one more time, to sit up.

Jaern crossed the floor with that same rapid grace, reaching out to help me. I swung the dagger blindly, without thinking. It snagged across his chest, laying open a gash from hip to shoulder. He caught my wrist with one hand and held it away from him. The broken bones in my shoulder crunched.

I screamed until my breath ran out, and waited for the pain to recede. It didn't. I couldn't pull away from him. I couldn't fill my lungs again, dragging air into my throat in inadequate snatches.

This was my fault. I should have ended it long before we got to Cor Daddan. I should never have let him out of that prison circle.

'You're hyperventilating, infant.' He let me struggle for a few moments. 'Get it out of your system.'

He didn't bleed. His clothes stayed slashed, but the cut closed up, edges melting together like sand under waves. Runes blazed on the back of the hand that gripped mine. I could have wept with frustration.

The spell poured down my arm, the black pendant around his neck throbbing, buzzing. For the second time in my life he made the broken things in my body whole. My bones shifted under my skin. The ligaments in my broken shoulder and ruined knee jerked back into place. The god repaired my body, made it fit to inhabit for centuries.

'I don't care,' I said. 'I'll still kill you.'

'Try, if it makes you happy.' Jaern pulled me to my feet. 'Save the world. You'll have time. Now walk backwards.'

'No.'

'Stubborn.' He took me by the throat. 'This is not the time. Get back on the spiral so I can bleed Makesh and get on with it properly.'

'No.'

His hand squeezed, just enough to induce panic. 'Step backwards,' he said flatly, 'or I'll smash that vial you're holding into dust.'

'Leave her out of it.' My fingers tightened around Brix's vial. I had failed her, too. I had bent everything to keep her from being trapped, had done my best, and I had still failed.

'I'm not the one who keeps involving her, am I?' Jaern shoved. 'Go.'

I stepped backwards.

'Good.' He came with me, guiding me on to the spiral, pronouncing the spell as we moved.

One by one, the runes painted on my body lit. The magic hooked into the runes on the floor, holding me more efficiently than any chain. Taking a step would have done nothing but tear chunks of flesh off my bones.

My mouth filled with blood. I had to either swallow or spit if I was going to talk and I was damned if I was going to swallow. The red glob that landed on the floor was streaked through with vibrant blue-black. The necromantic spell was taking hold. I didn't have much time.

The hand on my throat released. Something I couldn't quite recognise flickered across his expression. It was almost . . . playful. 'Did you do that on purpose?'

'What?' I said. 'Spit blood?'

He grinned. 'Lick your lip.'

Slowly I understood that, in the middle of all that carnage, the god was *flirting* with me.

'Jaern,' I said.

For a moment he seemed to forget about the ritual, searching my expression. 'Going to turn me down, Cricket?' he said, softly. 'Without even thinking about it? If this body is a problem, I can always get a different one. Blond, if you prefer.'

I gritted my teeth. 'You think the *body* is the problem? After what you've just done – they didn't all deserve to die.'

'Everyone deserves to die,' he said, impatient. 'Even you, even me. Don't be irrelevant. I'm not asking for much and I'm not offering you nothing. You say you don't worship anything, but the name of your god is written in everything you do, everything you fear. You'd pray to it, if you thought it could hear you. You'd suffer to be worthy of it. You *are* suffering, in fact.' He leaned closer. 'Do you want to know what you worship? What you care the most about?'

'No,' I said.

'Love.' His deep voice rang the word like a bell. 'You want it like a child wants his mother.'

I turned my face away, not that it made any difference. I could still feel his eyes on me.

'You're attached to the girl,' he murmured. 'Fine, there's no accounting for tastes. After the ritual you can have her. I'll help you get her out of the bottle – it makes them whole, the djinn-folk, being more or less in torpor under glass. I'll even teach you to put her back in, if you like. There's no point throwing tantrums when you could just ask nicely.'

'I'm not stupid,' I said. 'You can't stand her. Why would you help her? What would you be getting?'

'I'm not helping *her*.' He rolled his eyes. 'I'm getting the same thing I'm giving you. Eternity, in the company of someone who understands me. I expect we both will have our occasional . . . diversions. But thirty or forty years isn't so long, when you've got centuries ahead of you.'

I pulled on my wrist again.

His hand moved not at all. 'I can afford to wait.'

'Let go of me,' I said.

'I'd rather not,' Jaern said, 'until I have some assurance that you won't make this process tiresome. You still think that if you kill me and give the girl back her sister-brat that she'll be grateful. She won't. She'll take her family, she'll put up with a few caresses from you and then she'll leave again. Even if I'm wrong and you get your lifetime with her, she'll die. You'll be alone, the way I am. You don't understand what that's like, the way the loneliness eats you.'

I snorted. 'Lonely? You?'

'He died.'

I stiffened. The naked pain in the two words was too large to be spent for an apprentice. The agony, the ache – I recognised it. The hateful *vulnerability*. I had felt that when Brix left me.

I spoke as carefully as I could. 'You mean . . . ?'

'Acarius, yes.'

'. . . died?'

Jaern watched me through half-lidded eyes. 'Temporarily.'

Why hadn't Acarius *told* me? I should have known him better, put it together sooner. 'You loved him.'

'Everybody,' Jaern said softly, 'worships something, Cricket. I had a little while. A few dozen years. A blink. And then he was dying.

Wouldn't let me stop it. Wouldn't let me keep his soul safe, in a new body. He said it was a sin.' Jaern's fingers dug into my skin. 'A *sin*. To take a body from some fool who didn't appreciate it and use it to preserve a soul like his. What was I supposed to do?' He paused, as though he half expected me to give him an answer.

But I had no answers. I couldn't even sort out my own objections. How did someone so afraid of death wind up drinking it?

'It's not a large leap from playing with dolls made of bone to making bodies like a tailor makes a suit,' he said. 'It's not my fault that I'm a good tailor. And you look like he used to. I thought I was hallucinating when I saw you the first time, seeing what I most wanted, mad in the dark. Gods, you look like him.'

'I'm not him,' I said.

'I know,' Jaern said, but he didn't, not really.

'Here I hoped it was my scintillating personality that did it for you.'

It broke the trance. He blinked, then smirked. 'Well, I'll admit that without the mouth you'd be less interesting.'

'Are you going to let me go?'

He raised his eyebrows. 'Are you going to play nice?'

'No,' I said.

The smirk turned back to a grin, full of teeth, sharp. 'I suppose I can't actually complain.'

'How did you manage with Acarius, anyway? Was he unconscious, or drunk, or what?'

Jaern shrugged. 'He did his best to make it impossible. It's hard to move a soul that doesn't want to be moved. But I did it anyway. I may have . . . been a little angry with him.'

'Tricked him,' I said.

'Thought he'd forgive me. He didn't.' He looked at the dagger. 'What do you want the knife for? You can't hurt me with it.'

'Nothing. I want my damn *hand*.'

'Suicide won't do you any good, either.' His eyes narrowed. 'I won't let you die for good. The ritual is all but complete. I'll catch your soul and move it.'

'I don't want to die.' I meant it. I was twenty-six, and I wanted the rest of my years. That much of his fear I shared. After all, I had spent my whole life working to arrange things to prevent the unexpected. Death was nothing if not unpredictable. Annihilation would be bad enough, but what if dying didn't mean silence? What if the priests were right and it was nothing but the kind of darkness that breeds ghosts?

He released my wrist. 'You wouldn't be the first genius to find martyrdom alluring.'

There was no way out, not this time. He was going to make me watch my life end and my unlife begin. Worse, he was going to make me watch him cut through the world like a scythe, making more orphans, breaking more hearts.

'I'm not a genius.' I toyed with the dagger, remembering the first argument I'd had with Jaern – a lifetime ago, in the dark of a different temple. What had I said? 'I believed you when you said Keir took out Acarius' soul.'

He considered this, then conceded. 'It wasn't even a very good lie. I took Acarius' soul, of course, before he imprisoned me. Keir is nothing. I pulled the name out of that entertaining mind of yours the first time I touched you.'

Something flickered in the back of my head.

You can't separate a soul from a body. That's what I had said, arrogant prick that I was. Why had I believed that? *You can't separate a soul from a body.* What had he retorted?

'You can't do that,' I said, mechanically.

He laughed. 'Of course you can, infant.'

My memory suddenly snapped into place. *Of course you can, infant. What do you think a dagger to the throat does?*

'Now, we understand each other.' Jaern stretched his fingers with precision, like a musician. 'We should begin.'

There *was* a way out. One.

'Your soul comes out first during the ritual?' I said, falling back on questions until I knew my own mind. Gods, I didn't want to do this. Fear flooded my veins, so complete that I almost felt calm. It wasn't fair, having to choose.

'Obviously. It's oldest.' He studied Keir's line of runes. 'I'll have to repair this inept business first.'

'And when does the human sacrifice come in?'

'It will activate the runes on the altar, in a few minutes. Make it so the soul will go into the vial, instead of straight to the afterworld. It's a matter of having enough blood to fill all the channels.' He glanced at Makesh. 'Hardly a *human* sacrifice, though, is it? I had wanted to use Lorican, but that's not possible now. Happily, we don't need him. Is this consent, Gray?'

Lorican. Another person who had tried to be kind to me, another statue, standing there with frozen terror on his face. Another person I'd failed.

I gritted my teeth. 'You don't care about my consent.' Still, what if I did let Jaern finish the ritual? I could always kill him later, when I had time to think and study. It was even possible that I could restrain him for a while, wasn't it? I could get him to teach me about the spell binding Acarius and Lorican and all the poor half-witted Guildies – even Keir. Perhaps I could figure out how to reverse it.

What if I didn't have to gamble? What if I didn't have to suffer?

I forced myself to ask another question. 'After that you take out my heart?'

'While Acarius and Lorican watch, yes.' He waved a hand. 'A nice touch, don't you think?'

So my grandfather *was* alive and aware inside his stone skin. My chest contracted, but I didn't have time for that fresh slice of horror.

Unless I changed my mind, soon I would know whether my guess was good or bad. If I was right, Acarius and Lorican and everyone else would be free. If I was wrong—

Theory. That was what it came down to, again. Just bare, crazy *theory.*

'You're a bastard,' I said.

'*You're* repeating yourself.' Jaern picked up the doll and fitted the obsidian into its empty eye socket, then cradled it absently in the crook of his arm. He took Keir's fallen paint and brush, squatted and started touching up the edges of the sigils. They were still dark, which meant I had just a few moments left to make my move. 'You should sit down, by the way, or you'll fall.'

I didn't have to do it. I could stop fighting. I could have a little peace to read and learn and do some good with my wits. Maybe I could even have Brix – have a life. Maybe I could protect the world from Jaern, keep him distracted.

I don't have to do it.

Brix.

I looked down at the vial I held, warm under my fingertips. I could get her out, but then, sooner or later, I would have to explain. Even if I was able to lie, eventually she'd pull the truth out of me and I would have to stand there and meet her eyes.

What an idiot I was, after all, thinking I had ever had a choice.

'Gray.' Jaern spoke gently. 'Sit down.'

Slowly, I went back down to my knees. I put Brix's vial on the floor beside me, where it would be easy to reach afterwards.

'You're wrong, you know.' Jaern paused, brush between his fingers. 'I do care. I wish you were willing. If you are, it won't hurt. I can give you that – it won't hurt.'

I knew he was trying to be kind to me. Perhaps that was why, even then, I couldn't quite hate him. Magic was Jaern's addiction, too.

'It *does* hurt.' I tightened my grip on the haft of the dagger. 'I'm scared as hell.'

'Don't be.' He straightened. 'It's going to be all right.'

'No, it isn't.' I took the knife with both hands, put the point beneath the notch of my sternum and pushed it in.

'*Stop!*' He lunged at me.

Warm liquid poured over my hands. The pain was narrow, though, a lancet through the centre of me, mixed up in the heat and the metallic stink and the fear. I ignored it, focusing on Jaern.

Fall. Fall.

For all his speed, Jaern only had time to take two steps towards me before he stumbled. He stared at me, at the scarlet puddle collecting beneath my body, then at his own treasonous feet.

Fall, damn you.

I drew a hitching gasp as something pulled away from inside me, thread by thread, unravelled.

'Gray, how–' He stretched out his hands in front of him. 'Gray. My soul. I don't have it – I don't – I'm–'

Afraid. He was afraid.

Breathe. It took so much thought to keep my lungs moving, to keep from coughing my guts out, to keep myself conscious. I had to stay alive just until the last trace of his soul left me, and I had to figure out how to speak at least once more. I wasn't going to let my last words cause suffering, even *his* suffering.

Breathe.

'Not . . . alone,' I said.

Jaern smiled, tender, lost.

And he died.

I slumped backwards seconds after Jaern fell, my head thudding against the stone. It took longer to bleed out than I had expected, but he was right. Mostly, it didn't hurt.

I was cold, though. Colder than I had known anyone could be, lying on that glassy black floor.

Sound spilled around me.

Some part of me knew it when the necromancer's spells crumbled. The marulaches dropped, empty corpses once more, and pattered like leaf-fall in an autumn forest. People frozen into statues regained their humanity, groaning and crying. Someone – probably Makesh, with a newly restored mouth – started to shriek.

And I was cold.

Hands fumbled with the dagger, and then stopped. 'I can't take it out. You'll just bleed faster. What were you thinking? What–'

Acarius. So I *had* managed it. I had saved him. After a bit of effort, I achieved what I hoped was a reassuring smile, although my overriding emotion was a vague sense of being pissed off about dying. I wasn't *finished*. It wasn't *fair*.

'Cricket, what have you done?' Acarius said.

I reached for Brix's vial with slippery fingers. Acarius took it from me.

'Her . . .' I whispered. 'Out . . .'

'I'll stop this.' Acarius was sobbing. 'I'll keep you alive. Cricket–'

It's all right. Get her out.

I wanted to say it, even concentrated hard. But the weight on my chest was too heavy.

Acarius did as I asked, though, fiddling with the vial. It took him a few seconds to arrange the pewter rings in the right combination. I fought to keep my eyes open.

Someone gasped. Then Brix was there beside me, warm, whole, her hands on my face. 'Gray.'

It's all right.

I couldn't tell her. There was too much blood in my mouth. I choked. She stroked my cheeks, gentle, the way you would comfort a baby.

'Help me,' Acarius said. 'I need another pair of hands. Lorican, help me! Drag that over here!'

'Gray, I'm sorry,' Brix said.

Finally, I got enough air. Finally, I got my tongue around the words. 'Love . . .'

I coughed. Something tore in my chest. Warmth flooded my gut.

'Here! Now!' Acarius shouted. Something cold and metallic touched my lips, but I couldn't see what. He started chanting.

I needed to take one more breath. The last. I knew it was the last. 'Brix, I love—'

TWENTY-SEVEN

'—you,' Jaern's voice said.

I stopped, startled.

Nothing hurt. That didn't make any sense.

Acarius, Lorican and Brix stared at me, a few feet away. They had all been bent over a body on the floor. Acarius held the gold doll, and an empty glass bottle. Keir Esras himself stood a short distance from him, goggling open-mouthed at whoever it was they were working on.

Acarius recovered first, rising to his feet, cautious. 'Cricket?'

'What?' But there was still something wrong with how I sounded. And I was sitting up, somehow. I didn't remember sitting up. 'How did I get over here?'

Acarius took a step forwards. On the floor behind him, with the knife still protruding from its chest, lay my corpse.

I was dead.

'Now, it's not as bad as it could be,' Lorican said, straightening and coming to stand beside Acarius. 'Don't panic.'

I looked down at myself and – despite Lorican's advice – instantly panicked, feeling at my arms, legs, chest – all new, all familiar, all perfect, riddled with spells that lay dormant under the alabaster skin. I scrambled to my feet, testing the ground under me. It was all sickeningly real. '*Shit!*'

'It was the only intact body we had to hand,' Acarius said. 'We had no choice. *Don't panic*. And dammit, stop swearing.'

'I'm *dead*!' I snapped. 'This is an *excellent* moment to swear!'

Brix stood. 'You're talking; I think that means you're alive.' She walked towards me. 'We just have to figure this out.'

'Why are you so calm? You find *this* acceptable?' I waved my hand – or Jaern's hand, actually, with a smudge of alchemical paint still on the fingers. She caught it and held it. Her touch brought me back to my senses, made me realise that there were consequences for someone other than me. 'Brix?'

'*We will figure it out*,' she said.

'I'm a selfish prick,' I said, hoarsely. 'You were transparent. Are you all right?'

Suddenly, she smiled. 'Still not *little*, though, I take it.'

Probably for the first time in eight hundred years, my body blushed. 'Shut up.'

She intertwined her fingers with mine. 'Good to know it really *is* you.'

My forehead wrinkled. 'I don't see how that follows.'

'I don't know anyone else who would say *shit* instead of *thank you* after being resurrected,' she said. 'And nobody else gets embarrassed quite as quickly as you do. I'm all right, if you are.'

I couldn't even categorise everything I was feeling, let alone explain it. I kept stumbling over the big central fact that I loved Brix. I needed her like I needed my breath and blood. I had been, before my death, fairly certain that she loved me back. At the moment she was joshing me. Granted, it was probably only to keep me from hitting the gibbering phase of madness – still, it seemed hopeful. But once we were safe again, it was entirely possible that the over-whelming weirdness of our situation would strike her, and she'd be gone.

So no, I wasn't exactly all right. I was trying to decide how to tell her this when something moved at the edge of my vision. It was Keir Esras, slinking towards the door.

'Keir,' I said. 'What do you think you're doing?'

He halted, for all the world like a man caught stealing apples. 'I was just—'

'Don't go running off.' Even with Jaern's voice I didn't sound like Jaern, which was both reassuring and annoying. I needed the tone of haughty command, at least until I decided what to do with the Guildlord.

And not only him. Lorican was hovering near Acarius. Six or seven Guildies remained alive scattered around the sanctuary, all in various stages of shock. Makesh was still curled up beside the altar, rocking and moaning. Add in any possible survivors outside, and it came to a significant problem. Victory, if that's what you called it, was somewhat fraught.

'What do you want?' Keir seemed to be trying to pull his dignity together, without much success. I'm not sure whether he wasn't entirely recovered from the paralysis, or whether he mistrusted the evidence of his own eyes and thought I was Jaern. His attitude split evenly between bargaining and grovelling.

'Djinns' flasks,' I said. 'You've got quite a collection of them somewhere, I'm guessing. Fuel for the army-raising and your immortal rebellion.' I grimaced. 'Gods, it sounds even crueller and stupider when you say it out loud. At any rate, I want you to take me to them.'

Brix drew in her breath. Her grip on my hand tightened.

Keir hesitated. I suppose he had some justification, given that I was asking for items worth several years' pay. Then again, those 'items' were actually *people*.

'Right.' I turned to Lorican. 'How are you? Are you all right?'

Lorican stared at me. 'How do you think I am?'

'Okay.' I gestured with one arm, impatient, and nearly knocked Brix over. 'Fine, stupid question. Several of you were statues, I died, it's been a strange day. Are you functional, or do you need to sit down, or what?'

'I'm on my feet,' Lorican said, 'which I reckon will have to do. What do you need?'

I motioned to Keir. 'Could you just—'

'Aye.' Lorican moved behind Keir and caught him, one hand on the Guildlord's collar. 'I thought the almighty Examiner General would be more . . .' His nose wrinkled.

'Just hold him,' I said. 'He's going to do as we say.' It's difficult knowing what you're doing with your face when you've only had it for a couple of minutes, but I must have managed a reasonable facsimile of a menacing stare. 'I still have all of Jaern's spells. Hells, there's even a few here he didn't get around to using.'

'Very well.' Keir went pale. 'Anything you want. They're in the scriptorium. I'll show you.'

'Lovely.' I grabbed for Brix's shoulder as she was about to step away. She halted. 'What is it?'

'Just stay next to me, please,' I said, under my breath. 'Please. This body is a different size than mine was. I can't quite tell where my feet are and I need your help to not trip.'

She gave me a quick sideways look. 'Oh gods, I hadn't thought of that.'

'Quit talking about it. We're trying to keep me from panicking, remember?' I said, through a fixed smile. 'Acarius? What about these others?'

My grandfather stood with folded arms, frowning at the room in general. 'It's . . . a bit of a conundrum. There's really only three possibilities. Containment will be awkward, since this place only has two very small cells.' He glanced at Keir. 'As I have reason to know.'

Keir swallowed visibly.

'Next option is killing everyone,' Acarius said, without taking his eyes off the Guildlord. 'Which has the advantage of simplicity.'

... *although not of morality,* he had said, when I was eleven years old, *since morality is never simple.* I could have recited this lesson from memory. I didn't, however. Keir looked frightened enough to pass out. Someone who had murdered people simply to test a spell deserved to feel afraid.

'Or you could let them go.' Acarius shrugged. 'I leave it to you.'

That was complicated, too, not least because eventually the Guildies would realise they had us outnumbered. Luckily, everyone in the room – except possibly my grandfather – was as dazed as me.

'I think the Guildies should make themselves useful,' I said. 'Drag the corpses to one place, cover them, sort out which of the survivors need care.' I paused. 'We should probably tie Makesh up before he does himself a harm.'

'All the corpses?' Lorican said. 'Including yours?'

He pointed, and I looked at what he was pointing at and saw my old body's dead face. The vacant eyes were still open. For some reason, *that* was what did it.

I would have gone down if Brix hadn't caught me. She shoved my head between my wobbling knees and kept her hand on the back of my neck.

'Don't faint *now*,' she said.

'Ha,' I said, and fainted anyway.

After that things happened quickly. Brix brought me around by the simple expedient of sticking her thumb and forefinger in my armpit and pinching. When I was done being appalled, Keir led us to the cramped, dusty scriptorium, where some hundred-odd djinns' flasks lay arranged like scrolls on the shelves. Luckily only about half of them were occupied, since there was no way of knowing which one held Anka.

Even if the vials had been clearly marked, one look at Brix's face told me that we couldn't leave anyone imprisoned. After a solid twenty minutes spent opening flasks, Keir and his remaining friends no longer had us outnumbered. Granted, the Tirnaal men and women who came out of the flasks were largely disorientated, nauseated and hysterical, but they *were* on our side.

A blonde girl of about fifteen was in the thirty-seventh flask. I was the one to open it, which is why I was the one she puked on as soon as she took form.

She wiped her chin with the back of one trembling, tattooed hand. 'Who in the hells are you?'

'Corcoran Gray.' I stepped back from the puddle. 'You're welcome. And I've had a worse day than you have, so be civil.'

Like the others she was reeling on her feet, but she still managed to glare at me. 'What—'

'Anka!' Brix shoved past me, reaching for her sister.

Shocked recognition burst over Anka's face. I watched as they hugged each other. I watched them weep and laugh and keep touching each other's faces, as though to be certain they weren't dreaming.

It was good, knowing that they were real. It was good knowing I had done what I promised, even if I wasn't sure *I* was real anymore.

Acarius' hand rested on my shoulder.

'We're not finished, Cricket,' he said, quietly.

And so my grandfather and I turned back to the shelves of vials, and went back to work.

It took hours to sort it all out. We finished freeing the remaining Tirnaal. The wizards I had left under Lorican's eye were nothing more than flunkies, most of them numb with shock. They were grateful enough to leave with waterskins and a loaf of bread apiece from the fort's storeroom. I made them take the catatonic Makesh with them, with instructions to take him to Ri Dana and, presumably, his slave-trading relatives. His mind had utterly given way, and I couldn't even look in his direction without making him shriek in terror. Even Brix, to whom I gave the decision, seemed unwilling to torment him further.

Keir Esras presented a different problem. It wasn't as though I could disarm him and turn him loose, since his weapons were in his head. An intelligent man would have simply killed him, but Jaern had been right about me: I couldn't stomach the act of taking a life. We left him inside a prison circle with a supply of bread and water. That, and the knowledge that I was going to stop at the next city and let the rest of the wizard's Guild know they had been harbouring a necromancer who couldn't even raise dead properly.

After all, the Guild's criminal records did not feature a description of my current face.

But I wasn't all right.

We spent several days at Cor Daddan, dividing the food stores and the horses left in the stables, dismantling the necromantic tools in the temple, cremating the dead. As long as we had work to do and not much time to sleep, eat, or think, I could keep myself from remembering what had happened to me.

Brix had her hands full working with her shattered people. Lorican, who had already dealt with the concept of being in a new body, seemed slightly bored by the whole thing. The Tirnaal survivors all stared at my damn pale skin and silver hair when they thought I wasn't looking. Anka stared even when she knew I *was* looking.

Always in the background was the shroud-wrapped bundle that I hadn't quite been able to put on the pyre with the rest of the bodies. Acarius had agreed with uncharacteristic gentleness when I stammered out what I wanted.

When everything else was done, we dug the grave by ourselves. He and I sweated until we had a decent hole, and then buried my old self in the hard dirt and yellow grass outside the wall.

We stood there for a while, awkward. It's not fitting to weep at your own interment. It seemed foolish to have a funeral, considering I was only sort of dead.

'I didn't want this,' I said, after a moment. 'Eternal life. I didn't want it.' I touched my shirt, over the teardrop-shaped black pendant that still hung around my neck. At least the wicked little thing had gone quiet and dark. I had considered burying it with my bones, but that seemed irresponsible, like tossing poison into a river. Jaern had said it had an *entity* inside, after all, and he'd been able to heal and harm using it. Between the pendant and the spells that crawled under my new skin, my resurrection was full of difficulties.

'Is that what's worrying you?' Acarius sighed. 'Cricket, you haven't got eternal life.'

I glanced at him. If he was trying to make me puzzle something out, I wasn't sure I could avoid throwing a punch. 'What?'

'I didn't catch your soul in a vial. I put it directly into that body. Bodies with souls in them age and feel pain and are in all other ways entirely mortal. Bodies without souls are – well, you saw.' He tapped his own chest, a trifle rueful. 'You *see*, I should say. My soul isn't *in* this body. I've had to spend centuries betwixt and between, outliving everyone I love. I wouldn't do that to you.'

'How many people *have* you done this to?' I said. 'Me, Lorican . . .'

'Not many,' he said. 'It's very rare, my being there at the exact moment someone is dying and having a suitable body at hand to place the soul in. You understand that Jaern created dead bodies when he wanted them. I don't. I never have.'

'And he took out your soul,' I said. 'Where has *that* been, all these years?'

'The cabin.' He studied me. 'A vial, hidden in a cache that even you never found. How did you capture Jaern's soul, by the way?'

I sighed. 'I drank it.'

He frowned. 'You what?'

'Drank it,' I repeated, dully. 'And don't start shouting at me about how stupid it was, because I *know*.'

'*Drank* it,' he muttered. 'I never thought of *drinking* the damn thing. And that worked?'

'Yes.' I stretched my neck, first to one side and then the other. 'While we're asking questions, how did the Guild manage to capture you?'

He twitched his shoulders irritably. 'I was a damn fool, if you like, but you were gone and I was . . . restless. Ready to take any job to keep busy. They had been watching the cabin for weeks, learned exactly how I came and went. When I was down in the village buying cheese one day, two of them slipped into the cabin and wrote a prison circle on my bedroom floor. I'd left the wards off because—well, I thought you might come home. Then they came to me and said there was a necromancer stalking their village graveyard, and would I help?' He snorted. 'I stepped into the bedroom to get a cloak and they had me. Keir took all my diaries, too, my papers.' He paused. 'I made a mistake, there. After the first few months of Keir trying to break into my mind, he hinted that he'd figured out the location of the doll. I panicked, thought the only way to keep it out of his hands was for you to get it. And like a simpleton, I started trying to contact you while he trotted off to trap you. I should have known it was a trick.'

'About the doll,' I said. 'I'd like to get clear on how, exactly, I exist.'

'You exist for the same reason as everyone does.' He leaned on his shovel, a dangerous twinkle in his eyes. 'Your father and mother loved each other very much, and—'

'Oh, shut up.' I pinched the bridge of my nose, exasperated with how difficult it was to put into words. 'Why didn't you tell me?'

'Tell you what?' he said, with elaborate patience.

'Anything. You didn't *know* anything about my parents, did you? My mother was just one of your many descendants.' I closed my eyes briefly. It still hurt, even though I thought I understood. 'All that time, I thought you were hiding something from me, some terrible truth about who I really was, about why she died.' I tried to laugh; it came out more as a hiccupping gasp. 'And you didn't even know her.'

'I didn't,' he said softly. 'I tried to make up for it, teach you what I knew, but you wanted to know about her so desperately. I didn't – I just didn't know *how*, Cricket. I'm sorry.'

If he kept being gentle with me, I wasn't going to be able to get through the rest of this conversation. 'I've had enough of that nickname to last me the rest of my unnaturally lengthened life,' I said. 'Stop it.'

He snorted. 'Here I was hoping we'd make it at least an entire week before we had an argument where you behave like you're fifteen.'

'Then quit treating me like I'm ten,' I retorted. 'Look, why did you come for me? I mean, Jaern was right. Out of all your descendants – how do you *have* descendants, in passing?'

His lips twitched mischievously. 'I have descendants because I had *a* wife, and I loved her very much and–'

'Gods, stop,' I said. 'I don't care how many hundreds of years ago it was.'

His good humour faded. 'You don't quite understand. There's no reason why you should, I suppose. I did love my wife. She died having our second child. I was busy raising them. I didn't meet Jaern until they were both established with families of their own. I wasn't planning on falling in love again, but there it was.' He shifted his weight. 'And there's no need to act shocked because I happened to fall in love with a man.'

'It's not that,' I said. 'Have as many husbands or paramours or whatever as you please. But *Jaern*?'

Acarius swallowed. 'He wasn't always the Lord of Secrets, you know. When I met him, he was–' He stopped.

317

I waited, listening to the wind in the grass and the beat of my stolen heart. If there was one thing the last few months had taught me to recognise, it was the sound of grief.

'I couldn't kill him,' he said, eventually. 'I knew he had to be stopped, but I couldn't – I was too weak. Instead I spilled blood to lock him into torpor, shut him into the coffin. And it worked, until last year. That's when I heard that someone was hunting necromancers, asking about old Jaernic texts referring to the Ri Dana temple, trying to put together the spells to create marulaches and move souls. It was all at risk, and you and I were already at odds and–' He rubbed at the back of his neck. 'I asked Lorican to help me get the obsidian stones from the mosaic. I thought it would be enough, making it so nobody would be able to complete the Empty One. I know I should have got the doll myself, I . . .' He paused. 'Lorican was hurt, and I couldn't bring myself to go back down into the room where Jaern was. Not even for the doll, not even for the privilege of dying. It took so much suffering to trap him in the first place, and I wasn't sure what would wake him.'

'He woke up when you took the obsidian,' I said. '*Felt* you, I guess.'

'You have to believe me, lad.' His voice was hoarse. 'I swear the spells were still strong when I saw them. He was still asleep. I never would have sent you down there if I had known he was awake. You don't know what it took, once I realised how dangerous he'd become. You don't know what I sacrificed.'

'Dammit, I don't know *because you never told me*.' I kept my eyes on my shoes, biting down on the frustration welling inside me. 'I mean, I can see how it would be difficult. Tell your grandson you're involved with a necromancer and, what, eight or nine hundred years old? Difficult to bring up without explaining the decades of lying and hypocrisy.'

'You still consider yourself my grandson?'

It brought me up short. To have children – and grandchildren, and great-grandchildren – would have meant to watch them age and die. And not just once, but hundreds of times. And yet he had found me, raised me.

'We always do this,' I muttered. 'It's like a law. Of course I'm your grandson, Acarius, otherwise you couldn't make me this angry. Can we just . . . stop?'

'Aye.' He smiled. 'I will if you will. In our defence, we neither of us are very good at not arguing.'

'We make up for it with our luck and charisma.' I dragged my wrist across my lower lip and chin, where sweat had collected.

'I am sorry,' he said. 'That I didn't tell you.'

'I know,' I said.

'And, in answer to the question you can't quite get out, no, never with the body you're in. And never with the body I'm in. Jaern put me in an old man's body as a punishment for daring to consider aging and dying, after I had ended it with him. He made his master-piece, that body' – Acarius nodded towards me – 'ten years after that. So no need to feel . . . awkward, shall we say.'

I shuddered. 'Well, thank the gods, otherwise this scenario would get even more horrific.'

'Horrific.' Acarius spoke almost inaudibly, sudden, sharp pain in his voice. 'Was I supposed to let you die?'

My eyes blurred with hot tears. I couldn't look at him. 'I'm sorry, Grandfather. For all of it. I tried to do what you wanted. I promise I tried. I'm sorry. I'm so sorry . . .'

'None of that.' His voice went gruff. 'Ancient history, and besides, considering I wasn't there to help you . . . you've done well, boy. You've done everything, more than anyone could have asked.'

'Not everything.' I took a deep breath. 'We have the doll. Do you want me to–' The words were slippery. I had to concentrate on them, as though they were a spell. 'Your soul. I'll help you put it back. If you want me to.'

'Gods and little saints,' he said, quietly. 'You realise what you're offering?'

'Yes, and I don't *like* offering it,' I said. 'The privilege of dying, I think you called it. But it's . . . I don't want you to suffer, Acarius.'

'Corcoran, I–' He swallowed. 'When the time comes, there is no one I want beside me more.' He cleared his throat. 'Now, are you going to tell me what else is bothering you?'

But I couldn't, not for several minutes. Finally, he put his hand on my head, like he had when I was a little boy, and ruffled my hair.

'I came for you because you needed me,' he said. 'I kept you with me because I needed you. I had been alone for too long, avoiding connecting with anyone. It had been too painful, losing them over and over. But then there you were, talented, courage to the backbone, stubborn.' He spoke carefully. 'You love her. That much is obvious, Cricket.'

'I don't know–' My words dried up.

Acarius' hand dropped to my shoulder and squeezed. He didn't tell me it would work out, that of course Brix would stay with me, that if she minded the new body it meant that I was better off alone. Instead, he told me the truth.

'Nobody ever knows,' he said, softly. 'Come on. We should be going.'

TWENTY-EIGHT

A week after I died, the remnants of Makesh's slave caravan arrived at Cor Daddan.

It was a very different group of people than the one that Jaern had decimated. The Tirnaal slaves had taken control of the supplies, horses and wagons, and had arrived at the walls of the fort ready to do battle to free their imprisoned people. When they understood that they were already freed and we weren't enemies, the problem shifted abruptly from 'where should all the Tirnaal go' to 'how will we convince them to leave us a few horses'.

Apparently the slavers made a habit of capturing entire families when they could, and people searched the crowd we'd liberated for mothers, cousins, children. I spent a surreal half-day witnessing all the reunions. I wanted to talk to Brix about it. I caught her brilliant smile across the courtyard, and knew she wanted the same thing.

So, I hid.

Now that the Tirnaal were more or less sorted, there was no reason to remain at Cor Daddan. Brix would leave with her people.

Or maybe she'll come with you . . . or let you go with her.

It was a terrifying thought. I found myself inventing reasons to help Lorican with the horses that day, or ranging far afield looking for wood for the cooking fires. Anything to be in a place where Brix couldn't talk to me alone.

I knew the reprieve wasn't going to last. She would catch me, make me have the conversation with her, make me listen to her explain whatever decision she was going to make. I managed to avoid her until evening, and even then I kept busy enough trying to coordinate the supper meal that she couldn't do more than stand beside me and look irritated. My cowardice and intelligence took me all the way to night, and the problem of housing everyone.

Cleanliness was the issue. Half the courtyard was a charnel, full of smoke and the sickening stench of the funeral pyre. For other reasons, we all avoided the temple – Keir was imprisoned there, for one thing. For another, there was still ash on the walls.

But Cor Daddan had housed a significant number of people during its heyday. We ended up putting most of the Tirnaal refugees in the old infirmary, which was at least big and bare even if the cots had rotted long ago. The rest slept in the wagons outside the walls. Brix, Anka, Lorican, my grandfather and I retained our residence in the fort's smoky, low-ceilinged kitchen.

After everyone else had fallen asleep, I lay on the flagstone floor and hoped I'd be tired enough to pass out. I wasn't.

I listened to Brix breathe. I watched the fire flicker. For a long time I rehearsed speeches in my head.

I'm going home to the cabin. I want you to come with me.

No matter how many versions I imagined, the most probable answer was always the same.

I can't. Not now that you're like this.

I let out my breath in a long hiss.

'It's me, isn't it?' Anka said.

I got up on one elbow and turned towards her. I couldn't find her for a moment in the dim light. She normally slept not far from her sister, but she wasn't beside Brix's shadowy form anymore.

In fact, she was sitting cross-legged, a foot from me, presumably scowling. The kid had a permanent scowl on her face, and hadn't stopped staring me down since we'd met. I had never known anyone before who was such an unlikely combination of intimidating and annoying.

'What's you?' I said, because there didn't seem to be anything else to say.

'The reason you're avoiding my sister.' She shifted the position of her feet. 'It's me, isn't it? You don't want to be with her if she's saddled with me.'

Reluctantly, I sat up. 'To be honest, it hadn't occurred to me that you were a factor.'

Her voice sounded faintly shocked. 'That's rude.'

'I am rude,' I said. 'It's part of my charm.'

'You're an arse,' she said.

'You puked on me when I was just trying to help,' I retorted. 'We're even.'

But, for some reason, she seemed less upset with me than she had been. Perhaps she was stymied. Her gaze bored a hole in the side of my head.

'She's done everything for me,' she said. 'I can barely remember our parents. Brix's like my mother, father, everything. We're all each other have got. I have to look after her, you know?'

For not being able to actually sleep, I still felt too groggy to do justice to a late-night heart-to-heart with a tattooed kid. My grandfather would have come up with something wise or kind to say. I, on the other hand, blurted: 'Listen, is this the conversation where you tell me that you'll kill me if I break her heart?'

I could almost hear Anka turning red. 'Yes.'

'Fair enough,' I said. 'I'd kill me, too.'

Silence. I began to hope I was making a good impression.

'So what have you been doing, then?' Anka said, after a while. 'Other than getting too damn much firewood and never sitting down, like a ninny?'

'Don't swear,' I said, automatically.

She sniffed.

'You're fifteen,' I said. 'I'm allowed to tell you not to swear for at least another five years.' I hesitated. 'I love Brix. I want to spend the rest of my life with her. But I would rather be alone than hurt her, and I'd rather be alone than force her. I don't know how to ask her without making her feel obligated to say yes. And I've changed bodies since we met, and she could be forgiven for not liking this one. Does that explain it?'

'Oh.' Anka's voice altered. 'You're *scared*.'

'Shitless,' I agreed.

'Are you actually asking *my baby sister* whether you're allowed to marry me?' Brix said, from the dark.

My mouth opened, but nothing came out.

' "I'd kill me, too"?' Acarius said.

I put my burning face in both hands. 'Dammit, somebody wake Lorican, we might as well make sure everybody can hear me failing.'

'Don't swear,' Anka said, primly.

Muffled snickering drifted from the direction of Lorican's bedroll.

Soft footsteps, and then Brix's fingers grasped my wrists and pulled them down. 'Gray. Hey, it's all right.'

'It is *not*,' I said.

'Go back to bed, Anka.' Brix pulled me to my feet. 'And everyone,' she added, sharply. 'Come on, Corcoran.'

I felt for her hand and held it. In the dark it was easier to forget about what I looked like, and touching her again settled some of the shadows rattling around in my head. Still, I couldn't imagine how I could have bungled the moment any more thoroughly. 'What a mess.'

She didn't answer, leading me out into the hallway. The fort was confusing enough even in the daytime; I have no idea how she had managed to memorise it well enough to know where she was going. After several moments of manoeuvring through passageways, she pushed open a door, led me inside and closed it behind us.

We stood in a room without a ceiling, open to the stars and the white wash of moonlight. It had evidently been used as storage at some point long past. Ancient, half-open bundles of what looked like wool sprawled against one wall.

'How did you know this was here?' I let her lead me to the bundles. She was more beautiful tonight than ever.

'We've been pulling wool to make bandages for the last two days. Which you would have noticed if you'd had any rest in the last week.' She plopped herself down on the wool. 'Sit. Why haven't you been sleeping?'

'If I veered so drastically in conversation you'd say I was avoidant,' I said, but I obeyed. I had to. She hadn't let go of me.

She brought my hand upwards and dropped a kiss on my palm. A sharp, sweet mixture of desire and relief burned through my veins. She pushed me gently down on to my side, and then stretched out next to me, her back to my chest. She pulled my arm around her and cuddled down as though I was a blanket. 'So?'

'So I haven't been sleeping because everything in my life is ruined,' I said.

'Could you sleep like this?' She snugged her hips up against mine.

My heart quickened. 'Not *sleep*, no. This is . . .' I blinked. 'You – you don't want to be close to me. Not like I am now.'

'Don't tell me what I want.' She rolled to face me. 'What if something happens to me? Like I'm in an accident?'

'Uh–' I scrabbled to think about anything beyond the softness pressed up to me. The boundaries of my skin seemed blurred, blending into her warmth. 'What?'

'An accident. Say my hand was cut off.' She put her hand against my belly. My entire body came to singing, vivid life. *Uncomfortable* life, considering. I couldn't smother a soft moan, but she didn't move away. 'Would you still love me if I only had one hand?'

'Of course.'

'What if I got . . . a plague or something? Got pockmarks?'

I shook my head. 'This isn't—'

'Developed a twisted back?' she interrupted. 'Some women do, when they get old. I might get a hump.' Her hand was still on me, and gods, now it slipped under my shirt, tracing the edge of my ribs, and then back down to the arch of my back. Shivers of bliss followed her touch.

'Yes, fine, I can't think of a scenario where what you look like would change how I feel about you. But it's . . .' I swallowed, overwhelmed by the sweetness of the caress. 'It's not the same thing. Asking you to overlook the fact that I look like Jaern. It's not the same.'

'Why not?' She tilted her face up towards mine, her lips brushing my chin. 'We have to deal with this, Gray. It's not fair to shut me away like this. I miss the way you used to be, but you don't get to decide for me how I feel about this body. I've been watching you. You don't even move the way Jaern did. It's *you* in there, and I'm lonely for you.'

I wasn't going to hide from her anymore. I drew a breath. 'Do you love me?'

She went still. 'I thought you knew.'

'I can't lose you again,' I said. 'I can't wonder whether you're just sorry for me or guilty. Maybe I shouldn't need you to say it, but I do. I need you to tell me the truth, whatever it is. I need to know whether what we had was true for you.'

'You mean, was I trying to take you to bed at the cabin only because I had to?' Her voice was steady, but it still made me wince. 'Am I here with you *now* only because I have to be?'

'It's just—'

'I know.' She paused. 'I'm not a slave anymore. Not here, and not with you. I'm not doing anything with you because I have to.'

I kissed her forehead. I think I was trying to be reassuring. I'm not sure it worked, since I kept kissing her, working my way down to her ear, and then her throat. I couldn't help it.

She kept speaking, still so quietly I could barely hear her. 'I knew I was going to break your heart, and I couldn't see a way out. I tried not to fall in love with you. You might be romantic. I'm not. You're worried that I'm awarding myself to you like a medal for saving lives?'

'I think my word was "obligated",' I muttered.

'I want to be with you because you make me happy.' As she spoke, her breath tickled my skin. 'I've known since the alley behind Lorican's pub. You saved my life, and you didn't have to. You're a good man. I just couldn't see how you'd have anything to do with me if I told you the truth. The kiss, even that night at the cabin . . . I meant it. But I knew what you would think of me when I left.'

'The leaving,' I said, 'that wasn't *you*. That was Keir and the slave markets and everything that tried to crush the both of us.'

'So what *is* me?' She pulled away, just enough to get a view of my face. 'You don't know what I've been. You don't really know anything about me.'

'Don't tell me what I know.' I pushed a lock of hair out of her eyes. '*You* make me laugh. *You* don't let me get away with any of my bullshit. And you make me better. You make everything about me better. I don't care who you were, I care who you are. I *like* who you are. So stay with me, Brix. Please. Just stay. Or hells, move on, and I'll stay with you.'

Her hand moved again until it rested against the crest of my hip. 'Well.' She smiled, impish. '*I* think *you're* pretty.'

I shifted, a red mantle of shame blooming over my body. 'Don't make fun of me.'

'I'm not.' The teasing dropped out of her voice. 'Will you believe me? We can figure it out, all of it. I want *you*, forever. The body you're in just doesn't matter.'

Everything important in the world was in my arms, tight against me. What was I so afraid of?

'Brix, I don't know how to *do* forever,' I whispered. 'I don't know how to do any of this. There's never been anybody but you, and I don't—'

Then she was kissing me, full and warm, her scent and her taste breaking over me like waves of fire. Her hand slipped downwards until it came to rest on the ache between my legs. It took me a moment to realise what was happening, to get past the roar of the blood in my veins. I made one desperate attempt to regain the sense I'd had just seconds earlier. 'Tell me,' I insisted. 'Then gods, yes, I will do whatever you want. Even though I was hoping for a roof, honestly.'

She laughed, with the starlight caught in her hair.

'All right, Corcoran Gray, I love you. *You*. The inside of you, your soul. I loved you when you were a skinny, sneezy wizard and I love you like this, and I love you when you're so smart you're stupid and I'll love you when you're old.' She kissed the tender place beneath my jaw, and then the exquisitely sensitive place above my pulse. 'And *now*, will you stop talking?'

I bent my head. My mouth found hers again.

And I don't know what I said after that, or if I said anything at all.

ACKNOWLEDGEMENTS

I'd like to thank Molly Powell, who did an amazing job editing this book. Her suggestions made the story so much better, and were delivered in such a painless fashion that I actually enjoyed taking my book to pieces and putting it back together again. I must also thank Jo Fletcher for taking a chance on me while I was in the slush pile. My wonderful agent, Kurestin Armada, is one of the hardest-working people that I've ever met. I'm so happy to have her in my corner. Thanks, Kurestin, for believing in me and the book.

Laura, Ben, Lori, Kate, Tania and Bill – you guys were the nicest writing crucible I've ever seen or heard of, and I'm so proud that all of us have emerged, shiny and in print. Becky and Emily, do you know what a luxury it was that you let me talk about this stuff, and actually acted interested?

To Fadzlishah Johanabas, the best friend I've never met – for all the countless drafts, the highs and the lows and the decade of companionship. Thank you, my dear friend, for always being there, even though you're halfway across the world.

I owe thanks and probably ice cream to my three lovely kids, who have been very patient about living with a mother who regularly spends hours with imaginary people. I love you guys so much. My husband Phillip has been unstintingly supportive through a lot of moves and a lot of long walks, and he has talked me out of many a tangle – thank you for telling me to chase my stories, babe. I love you, and I will even go camping with you again.

Thanks Mom and Dad, for the typewriter when I was eight and for the books I inhaled every waking moment. Thanks to my brother Mark for liking some old stories when I needed the win, and to my sister Kindra for the phone calls and Jaern's Playlist.

And finally, dear reader, thanks for coming with me on this ride. I'll see you around.